Bevis Longstreth has  known ancient treasu... textile, which was lit... world of lovingly drawn characters whose unfolding story captures the imagination and heart of the reader. We are encouraged to see the Pazyryk with new eyes — not simply as a work of art in a sterile, ice-filled tomb, but as a gift of love and a celebration of humanity.

*Jennifer Wearden, Former Curator of Textiles, Victoria & Albert Museum*

What will we make out of the world around us? This is the question at the heart of Bevis Longstreth's extraordinarily textured *Spindle and Bow*. Longstreth takes us back to the most unfamiliar times and cultures in order to examine the essential questions of what it means to be human in the world. Along the way, we learn about gypsy caravans and Satraps' palaces, the purification of gold and the mysteries of one of the greatest carpets ever made. This richly woven novel reminds us of the importance and possibilities of Art. Longstreth reminds us that what we make out of the world around us is a moral issue of the utmost relevance.

*Karen Shepard, Author of* An Empire of Women *and* The Bad Boy's Wife

Bevis Longstreth was inspired by a rug, and what a rug! The Pazyryk, the oldest and one of the most interesting and beautiful rugs every found. It led him to undertake an almost fanatical research effort from the great Hermitage Museum to the Altai Mountains. *Spindle and Bow* is the result — a profound and exciting love story set in a time and place as unfamiliar as it is exotic. The lovers, Rachel and Targitus, are compelling and unforgettable.

*Jeremy Grantham, Chairman, Grantham, Mayo Van Otterloo & Co. LLC*

This is a love story, an imaginary history of the controversial origins of the Pazyryk carpet, a lesson in how a rug is created from the preparation of the wool to the last knot, and a lesson in Central Asian geography, all woven together into an exciting, spell-binding story that I found hard to put down until the very end.

*Gail Martin, New York City antique textile dealer*

Hali Publications Limited
(A member of the Centaur Holdings PLC Group)
St Giles House, 50 Poland Street, London W1F 7AX, United Kingdom
Tel: +44 (0) 20 7970 4600
Fax: +44 (0) 20 7578 7221
www.hali@centaur.co.uk

Published by Hali Publications Ltd., 2005
© Bevis Longstreth 2005
Bevis Longstreth asserts the moral right to be identified as the author of this work.

A catalogue record for this book is available from the British Library
ISBN (hardback): 1 898113 60 2
ISBN (paperback): 1 898113 55 6

Colour origination by PH Media, Roche, Cornwall
Printed and bound in Great Britain by CPI Group, Chatham, Kent
Set in Aries 9.5/13.5

All rights reserved. No part of this publication may be reproduced, stored in a retrieval system, or transmitted, in any form, or by any means, electronic, mechanical, photocopying, recording or otherwise, without the prior written permission of the publishers.
This book is sold subject to the condition that it shall not, by way of trade or otherwise, be lent, re-sold, hired out or otherwise circulated without the publishers' consent, in any form of binding or cover other than that in which it is published and without a similar condition including this condition being imposed on the subsequent purchaser.

# Spindle and Bow

Bevis Longstreth

HALI PUBLICATIONS

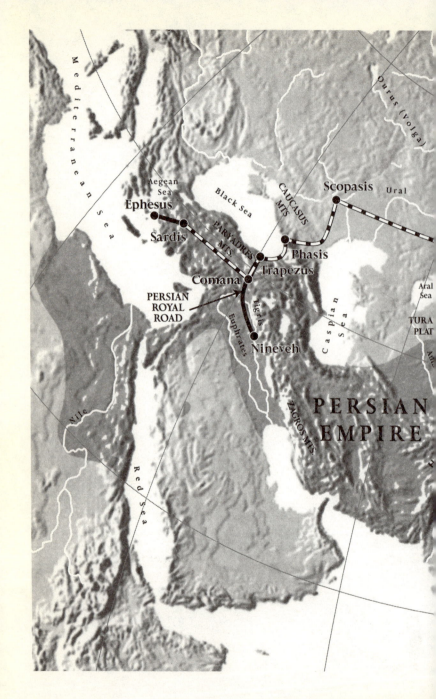

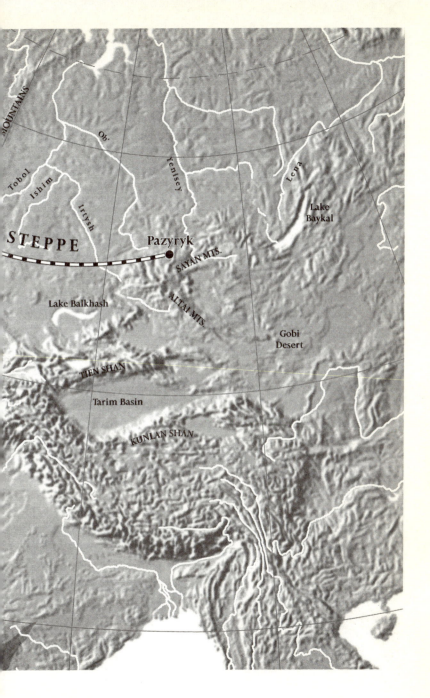

BEVIS LONGSTRETH

Bevis Longstreth is a graduate of Princeton University and the Harvard Law School. From 1981-1984 he served as a Commissioner of the Securities and Exchange Commission. In 1993, he retired from the practice of law as a senior partner in the New York City law firm of Debevoise & Plimpton to teach at Columbia Law School and pursue other interests, among which was writing. Over his professional career he has often spoken in public and written many articles and two books on finance, corporate behavior and the law. Mr. Longstreth has a long-standing interest in textiles. He is a trustee of The Textile Museum in Washington, D.C. and has lectured on the Pazyryk carpet at the Hajji Baba Club of New York City, where he is a member, and at the Oriental Rug and Textile Society of Great Britain. *Spindle and Bow* is his first work of fiction.

## ACKNOWLEDGMENTS

This novel, my first effort at extended work with the imagination, would not have reached the printer without inordinate levels of enthusiastic criticism, encouragement and support from a number of volunteers who took pains to read and comment upon the manuscript. They include Judy Amory, Marit Kulleseid, Mary Mallia, Gail Martin, Molly Rauch, Franny Taliaferro, Jennifer Wearden, Amy White and Marie Winn. I am enormously grateful to them, one and all.

Family members probably don't count as volunteers, for their interest in reading the manuscript might just be an instinct to avert reputational loss for the family. If so, they never let on. Their contributions were many and rendered with exquisite sensitivity.

I am grateful to literary agents Esther Newberg and Jud Laghi of ICM for taking me on as a client and undertaking with zeal to place the manuscript with a reluctant audience of big US publishers. Their enthusiasm for the novel came at an important point of inflection.

I owe a large debt to Karen Shepard, Lecturer in English at Williams College and an accomplished novelist, who immediately upon hearing of my project offered to help and, after critiquing my first chapter, gave such valuable insight, in such restrained and sometimes oracular ways, that I couldn't refuse her offer to continue reading the chapters as they came off the computer. Her wise critiques became a central part of my education and training as a writer of fiction.

It was HALI magazine that got me started on this quest. On the 50th anniversary of the discovery of the world's most famous pile rug, the Pazyryk, HALI published an article by Ludmila Barkova, the curator responsible for the Pazyryk where it resides in St. Petersburg's State Hermitage Museum. It hooked me. I am most grateful, too, for the time and attention Ms. Barkova and Dr. Elena Tsareva of the Russian Ethnographic Museum gave me when I visited St. Petersburg in 2000 to examine the Pazyryk up close.

The wonderful sketches of the many motifs in the Pazyryk were rendered by Ben Potter, a young, inventively compelling artist who lives and works in Wisconsin. I am grateful to him for his interest and professional help.

Finally, I wish to record my thanks to my wife, Clara, my son, Tom and his wife Julie, for joining me on a trek to the Altai Mountains to spend several days camping close by the great ice tomb where the Pazyryk had rested for twenty-three centuries. Without their company, there would have been no trek, and without the trek, no novel.

B.L.

# PROLOGUE

As the crow flies, the Great Ulagan Plateau lies 285 miles southeast of Novosibirsk, a city of one and a half million straddling the Ob River. By air, a flight from London brings one to this Russian city in ten hours, having covered some five thousand miles and passed over Amsterdam, Berlin, Warsaw and Moscow before reaching the halfway point.

Beyond Moscow one passes the Dneister, Bug, Dnieper and Don, grand rivers all, flowing south into the Black Sea. One passes the fabled Volga and the smaller Ural, each flowing south into the Caspian Sea. To the east, rivers flow north to empty into inland seas or wind through marshes leading to the Arctic Ocean. At the edge of the vast Eurasian Steppe, in sight of the Altai Mountains, one arrives at Novosibirsk. It takes another three days' travel by jeep to reach the plateau, which is just north of the Russian frontiers with Mongolia, China and Kazakhstan.

The Great Ulagan and its approaches project an immense alpine landscape punctuated by high cliffs, deep gorges and moraines crowded with bare rock and scree. Towering above the plateau is

# SPINDLE AND BOW

Mount Belukha, at 14,783 feet the highest peak in the Altai, an inaccessible wall of ice and snow.

Nine miles up the Great Ulagan is a flat, dry valley known as Pazyryk. There, in the summer of 1949, a Russian anthropologist was excavating the last of five cairn-covered "princely kurgans" of the Pazyryk Valley, a mile above sea level. They belonged to the Massagetae, a branch of the Scythian tribes who had inhabited much of the steppe stretching from north of the Black Sea to the Altai Mountains during the middle of the last millennium B.C. They were semi-nomadic herdsmen who spoke an Indo-European language similar to Persian.

Robbers had violated the burial shafts of the royal kurgans soon after they were sealed. Water had then filled the underground spaces and frozen. The insulating effects of the mighty cairns of stone half a football field in diameter that rose high above the shafts had maintained this condition, turning the kurgans into freezers for more than twenty-three centuries. The first four kurgans had yielded a trove of artifacts, all preserved in exceptional condition. The fifth had been saved for last, because it was grander and seemed to dominate the others. It was encircled by twenty-one stone plinths, evenly spaced and set vertically to tower as much as twenty-three feet above the ground.

Chopping and melting the smudgy yellow ice and lifting the huge boulders that blocked access to the lower reaches of the burial shaft made excavation excruciatingly slow. As hopes soared, impatience threatened to overwhelm the team's training and discipline. When, finally, they pulled away the double ceiling of a vast funerary chamber, the team felt tipsy with excitement as twentieth century light shone upon grave goods placed there some two thousand three hundred years before.

The ceiling, floor and walls were lined with black felt pegged to the smoothed log surfaces. Along the south wall was the sarcophagus, a hollowed-out tree trunk fifteen feet in length. There, with head pointing east, was the naked, embalmed corpse of a man resting on his back. His left hand lay across his chest; the right hand covered his pubis. The man's right index finger had been neatly attached to

# PROLOGUE

pubic skin with deer gut stitching. Tall with a thin face, he had a prominent, slightly hooked nose, high cheek bones, long upper lip and protruding chin. His well-preserved hair was chestnut. He was of mixed Indo-European and Mongol stock.

Close by the man lay a woman. She was in the same condition as he, except that her right hand lay across her breasts while the left covered her pubis. She, too, was tall and strongly built, but her hands and feet were delicate and beautifully shaped. Her facial features were not well preserved. Her head had been shaved. Beside her were long plaited tresses of black hair adorning an elegant headdress. She was Caucasian.

Along the east wall were wooden hassocks carved in hour-glass shape from single blocks of wood. Next to them were three wooden tables with turned legs. They were set with quantities of goat cheese and grains as well as spoons, knives and cups.

Along the west wall was a hexapod from which hung a finely tooled bronze censer filled with small stones. Beside a felt covering were two small leather pouches inlaid with gold leaf. They contained fistfuls of seed: one of hemp, the other coriander.

Along the north wall were bundles of gold leaf, piles of sheepskin and goatskin, stacks of lumber and thin strips of leather plaited together and covered with gold leaf.

Outside the funerary chamber, in the undisturbed northern third of the shaft, were the frozen bodies of nine horses felled in the prime of life. Four were bulky draught animals without caparison. Five were lean mounts typical of the best strains of the Turkmenistan and Fergana breeds. Each was richly caparisoned with complete harness and full leather head masks. Leather and wooden images of both natural and fantastic animals in striking poses embellished the riding outfits.

In a heap among the horses, compacted into a frozen ball that was easy to mistake for detritus, was a woolen weaving. Upon thawing, it proved to be a perfectly preserved pile carpet measuring about six feet square. The exquisite quality of this textile was obvious in the density of the symmetrically tied knots, the soft and springy feel of the wool, the blends of dye color, its striking motifs, the overall design and the precision of execution. On view in the

Hermitage Museum in St. Petersburg, it remains, today, the world's oldest pile carpet. Its discovery astonished textile scholars, who generally believed that pile weaving had developed more than one thousand years later in the great urban centers devoted to carpet production. In both technical and artistic respects, it was a towering achievement, a challenge to any textile that would come after.

The carpet was woven in the Iron Age, about four hundred years before the birth of Christ, when the power of the Achaemenid Dynasty and the Persian Empire which it ruled were cresting. Men had been riding horses for over 3,000 years. Women had been weaving cloth for more than twice as long. And by then the artistic capabilities of humans were as developed as they would ever become. Sixty-four years later, Alexander the Great would defeat Darius, King of Persia, in the great battle of Issus. Two hundred years later, the Chinese would construct the Great Wall.

Many mysteries emerged from the fifth kurgan. Chief among them was the human drama behind the contents of this icy Siberian tomb. Who was this man? This woman? How were they related? What strands of life did they share? What had brought them together in death? And what was their connection to the magnificent carpet? These questions have resisted intense scrutiny for more than half a century. The archaeological method was found wanting. This triangular tale could only emerge from the fabric of myth.

# CHAPTER 1

Sardis – 407 B.C.

Her rebellion began by accident. A single weaving error. So perfect had her work in the palace workshop been that the mistake might have seemed an act of God. In the large spread she was weaving, white in the center field with three blue borders of equal width, she missed three warp threads in shooting the shuttle through, only noticing the mistake several wefts later. The idea struck as Rachel started to unravel the work. She imagined a series of identical "mistakes" spaced enough apart and positioned so that, at a distance, one might barely discern a deliberate design in the shape of an "R", sized just to fill the center field. White on white, subtle enough to be all but invisible.

To disobey was one thing, but to disobey and deceive, and use her skill to make the deception hold, filled her with excitement.

Looking furtively at the master, who was seated on a dais in the center of the room, she recalled her first meeting with him, just one year ago. Her skills as a weaver had become widely known in Sardis, extending even to the palace. She expected to be warmly embraced by those in charge of the workshop.

"Why do you want to work here? You're only sixteen. Your father can support you."

Rachel's face flushed, as if struck by the master's hand. She came to have her work examined, not her state of mind. Was he questioning her motives?

"The best weavers in Sardis are here; I want to be among them."

She knew that line by heart, having used it more than once in eroding her parents' resistance. Watching his reaction, she feared the full argument would have to be repeated, to be judged anew by the master. Her parents had preferred marriage and motherhood among their people to commerce among palace weavers, who fit every kind of background and description. Dissuading them from blocking her path took time and many painful skirmishes. Wincing as she recalled the worst of it, Rachel brightened when the master asked for samples of her work. He examined them in silence. Then, giving nothing away, he set her the task of preparing a loom to weave a piece of wool cloth, observing the time it took. He watched as she began. She knew he was looking for errors, timing the shuttle sequences, examining the play of her fingers across the warp and weft. A steady heartbeat surprised her, as did the realization that she was actually enjoying his attentions. "You're too good to pass up on account of age," the master had concluded. "We work during daylight hours, six days a week. In your case, Monday through Friday and Sunday. You can leave early enough to get home for Shabbat. Workers are paid monthly. Do you accept?"

Rachel nodded, whispering "Thank you," as she tried, without success, to conceal her joy. Once outside, she kept breaking into favorite nonsense songs and a sequence of hops, skips and jumps during the long walk from the palace to her home near the Pactolus River.

After several months of work, the excitement of being the youngest weaver ever hired by the elite workshop was gone. She hadn't known that, in the Satrap's weaving rooms, the work was handed down by a small coterie of designers to what seemed an army of weavers, who were expected to follow the designs precisely and work the looms quickly to fashion cloth for royal needs. As the master put it in his oft-repeated mantra, "Perfection AND

## 1: SARDIS − 407 B.C.

Production." What rewards there were for exceptional performance came only for accuracy and speed.

The master and his assistants commanded two huge adjoining rooms with many windows, where eighty women toiled over as many looms from morning to night. Breaks were few. Constant co-ordination of eye with hand strained both mind and body. Beyond numbness, cramps and normal human functions, only the occasional visitor gave excuse to pause.

The master was a brooding presence, whether overseeing the room from his central perch or circulating systematically past every loom. The air was a blend of not unpleasant smells, ointments, perfumes, animal fats and dyes, fixed in place by the ever-present mordant of human sweat. Rachel quickly realized the master could reckon at a distance the pace of work in the adjoining rooms simply by listening to the murmur of shuttles passing back and forth through warps to knock against loom frames, wood on wood.

Disillusionment came only in part from the repetitive routine of weaving for hire. Rachel's main plaint grew from a sense of unrealized promise. I am here because I want to be an artist, she kept telling herself, not just a weaver. Indeed, that ambition had been the key to parental acceptance.

Rachel had been ordered to produce not one but six of the large spreads for the Satrap's personal quarters. Each spread was to be identical. When she finished the first, she carried it to the master for inspection. Facing him, she waited. Clutching her hands first in front and then in back, she studied his eyes as they moved swiftly up and down from border to border. Fear gripped her. What folly I've committed.

Now his hands moved across the weave, top and bottom, fingers registering thickness, uniformity and possibly much more.

"Enough," he declared abruptly. "The work is flawless. What we've come to expect. But to finish in three weeks. Remarkable." Folding up the spread and tucking it under his arm, the master said "Back to your loom." and walked away.

Although her heart stopped pounding, excitement grew as she warped the loom for the second spread. She began to weave, tingling all over, out of control and transfixed by the shuttle, shot from left to right and back again as if by external force. The rational side of her mind watched helplessly across the divide as her spontaneous side proceeded with an irresistible plan. She would place the remaining letters of her name in the five spreads yet to be woven.

With the completion of each spread, her confidence grew. So, too, did the thrill of living in a secret world of her own devising.

Months after completion and acceptance of the sixth spread, Rachel was summoned to the master's office. His fury hit Rachel the instant she entered a room too small to contain his words. Her feet were leaden, anchoring her in place. Rachel was charged with having disgraced the workshop, of failing those around her, of abusing trust. Punishment was certain. When the tirade was over, the master asked, "What could possibly have motivated you?"

Rachel was scared, confidence shattered. She was unprepared to parry the master's charges. Softly, she spoke the truth. "I don't know."

"That won't do! You must have had a reason. Tell me. If you don't, we will have to assume the worst, that you set out to embarrass us, and the Satrap."

Rachel started to cry.

The tirade resumed.

Rachel was sent home, with a warning that she would be summoned to trial and judgment by the Satrap's counsel of advisers the following day. Approaching her family's house, she decided not to tell her parents. She hoped, as irrationally as she had believed that she could deceive and somehow get away with it, that some escape from her plight would materialize, allowing her to keep the matter private. What never occurred to her until much later was the possibility that at some level she had expected to be caught, that getting caught had been her purpose.

She had trouble participating in the family dinner conversation. She ate less than normal and even failed to comment on the olive bread, a favorite of hers, baked that day by her mother. Aware that her distracted behavior might cause inquiry, she felt helpless to avoid it. Like a drunken rider steeled to make it home without losing his

## 1: SARDIS – 407 B.C.

way or the horse beneath him, Rachel contained her distress; her parents failed to notice and the night passed.

At daylight, Rachel rose and returned to the workshop. She had worried throughout the walk that everyone would know exactly what she had done. They will be looking at me, she thought. Entering the room, heat spread from her neck to the tips of her ears. She followed the familiar route to her station like one stepping across a floor covered with eggs.

Sitting at her loom, too nervous to weave, Rachel awaited the summons. She stared at the warp and weft of her work, glancing neither right nor left.

"Rachel, are you all right?" Vashti's words were slow to register. When they did, Rachel turned to look at her friend, sitting four rows distant, across a sea of flashing movement. Except for Vashti, no one seemed aware of Rachel's condition.

Vashti was one of two concubines who had befriended Rachel shortly after she had started working in the palace. Vashti and Milto had served Tissaphernes, predecessor to Cyrus the Younger, now the Satrap of Lydia, who had passed them over as too old for the harem. They were still attractive women who, when at leisure together, found it irresistible, despite strict rules, to share experiences. Having an audience for their exchanges produced a kind of competition to recall the most intriguing and even shocking aspects of their concubinary lives. No doubt when the audience was a seventeen-year-old virgin whose father was an elder of the Jewish community well known in Sardis for rectitude, the shock value of their tales fired more than their memories, leading to embellishment. Naturally, Rachel's parents had taught her nothing about the ways of pleasing men.

In Sardis, young Jewish girls enjoyed surprising freedom. At thirteen, a girl could marry without her father's consent. Unfortunately, Jewish parents, like their Persian counterparts, failed to teach their offspring what they needed to know to use their freedom wisely.

Vashti and Milto overcame Rachel's deficit, allowing her vicariously to experience the art and craft of being a courtesan. Like a large sponge lifted fresh from the Aegean, she soaked up all they offered.

Before Rachel could respond to Vashti, a chamberlain to the

Satrap appeared in the work room, his deep voice echoing from walls and ceiling as he pronounced her name. Rachel arose. The chamberlain took her firmly by the arm and together they disappeared beyond the doors of the workshop, in the direction of the palace. Her removal happened so swiftly that all she could remember was the anxious and surprised look on Vashti's face.

The connecting halls were many, some long, others short, confusing as to direction with right angle turns too numerous to remember. The glazed tiles that lined the floor, walls and ceiling were so rich in color and dramatic in design that Rachel almost forgot where she was headed. She caught sight of diamonds and fleches, stars and scrolls, palmettes and rosettes, griffins facing lions, and raptors swooping down on rabbits. The chamberlain whispered "Here we are," returning Rachel to reality. He had deposited her in front of the Satrap's most senior advisors, who functioned as a tribunal when need arose, as it frequently did in the Satrap's principal palace. She recognized only one of these men. She knew what the Satrap looked like, but he was nowhere to be seen. The young prince was normally much in evidence throughout the palace and adjoining buildings and grounds. Rachel's father had often spoken of the many changes, most of them positive, that Cyrus had made since having been appointed by his father, Darius II, the previous year, to replace Tissaphernes as general commander of the maritime regions. Though he had barely come of age, Cyrus quickly took root as a stern, trustworthy and generous leader. Among Sardians, the number of his admirers was growing like barley in summer.

Looking at Cyrus' three advisors, who faced her across a large table covered with linen she recognized as a recent product of the workshop, Rachel thought of the man they served. Everyone who worked in the palace knew that the Satrap had been named Cyrus for his royal ancestor, Cyrus the Great, founder of the Persian Empire. In the year or so that he had been in Sardis, much had changed. The petty bribery and palace thefts that were so prevalent under Tissaphernes were gone. Through carefully orchestrated arrests, public trials and even more public punishments, Cyrus had made his point: corruption among his servants would be discovered and severely punished.

## 1: SARDIS – 407 B.C.

Loss of feet, hands and ears, even eyes, was not uncommon.

In that first year the Satrap's tribunal had been busy. Sardis was the capital of the western part of the Persian Empire, covering a vast area of land stretching from the east coast of the Aegean inland to the Taurus Mountains and beyond to the Euphrates. Cyrus sought to raise standards to reflect the city's importance.

A throbbing pain began in Rachel's head as she realized that her behavior could be considered the equivalent of palace bribery or theft.

Stretched to exhaustion by a parade of wrongdoers tossed up for trial by Cyrus' investigative forces, the trio before her looked both exhausted and short on patience.

That Rachel had woven the letters of her name in six blue and white spreads was beyond dispute. Nor was there any question of intent. The skill at play in these spreads was no accident. The tribunal's sole focus was causation. In Cyrus' court punishment was in proportion to wickedness. Sanctions were intended both as retribution against the wrongdoer and deterrence for others. Motive was a measure of wrong-doing.

"Why did you do it?" the panel's chief asked.

Rachel stood mute. She was dressed in a dark cotton smock of ankle length. Its girth could accommodate two Rachels and still droop. It had short sleeves and a rectangular opening cut too big for Rachel's delicate neck and shoulders. Oddly, what surely was someone else's apparel proved an effective foil for Rachel's pale ivory skin.

It was hot. Beads of sweat had formed on Rachel's brow just below the wisps of black hair that had escaped the band she used when weaving. Her wide set cheekbones glistened from descending droplets. One could see the pores of her soft skin, open from neck to shoulders, even to the point where a youthful cleavage began. There was tension in her bright eyes.

"This was no casual impulse. Your weaving reveals extraordinary care and craft, sustained over weeks of making not one but six separate spreads of large loom width. Premeditation. You are a Semite. Your father is known to us. A wise and respected elder in the Jewish community. Those who know you in the workrooms believe you are devout. They say you know the Scriptures and many of your people's proverbs, that you can recite them from memory. So, then, you will know this:

> 'Righteousness exalteth a nation:
> But sin is a reproach to any people.'

Why have you sinned?"

Rachel shifted uneasily, but remained silent, recalling one of the many proverbs she had learned as a girl:

> "He that keepeth his mouth keepeth his life:
> But he that openeth wide his lips shall have destruction."

The chief tried another proverb.

> "Foolishness is bound in the heart of a child;
> But the rod of correction shall drive it far from him."

Rachel cried out, "Masters, I have not denied my actions. I have no lying tongue or proud look. What I did I can't explain. But it's said:

> 'He that covereth his sins shall not prosper:
> But whoso confesseth and forsaketh them shall have mercy.'"

Moisture had now soaked the top of Rachel's smock, deepening its color at the edges. Her mind was a jumble: fear of the coming punishment, anger at being depicted a child and frustration over her unwillingness even to explain her own behavior, much less defend it. Recognizing her act now, before the tribunal, as they would see it, a sustained declaration of pride, even a prideful search for attention, however misguided, was her undoing. Shame returned her to silence.

In frustration, the chief began a third proverb:

> "The king's wrath is as the roaring of a lion..."

Appearing from a side portal, a young man added a second line:

> "But his favor is as dew upon the grass."

The Satrap's intervention produced astonishment on both sides of the table. It also brought the proceedings to an end. "In the silent corners of this girl's mouth I hear an anguished cry of guilt. She has already suffered for this wickedness. It's enough. Let us now show mercy."

It was obvious he had stood at the portal during the entire interrogation. Rachel's amazement, equaled by that of the tribunal, only intensified as the Satrap summoned Rachel for tea, thanking his advisers and dismissing them.

## 1: SARDIS – 407 B.C.

"I'll lead the way." Cyrus moved quietly from hall to hall until he entered the inner rooms of the palace to which he and his personal servants alone had access. Here the walls and floor were adorned with glazed tile, luminous in blue and white, brown and black, yellow and green, of ionic and floral patterns. Interspersed were friezes of glazed brick depicting men on horseback, with oval shaped faces, moustaches and long beards, pronounced nose and pointed caps. Across the way more friezes contained drawings of women riding on horseback, hair long, flowing over capes.

Rachel was emerging from the dream-like sequence of events that had brought her to this tactile paradise. Now, alone with the Satrap, her mind jumped ahead. She was horrified to realize that she might need a trick the concubines had never mentioned: how to deflect a man's ardor without being harmed. She tried to believe the royal prince's interest was solely one of woven design and her skill at the loom. But the thought of what Vashti and Milto would say to that idea plunged her into renewed confusion.

They had arrived in a sitting room, richly adorned with tile work on the walls. A wool kilim of red, white, black and midnight blue in intricate geometric design covered the floor. Two upholstered settees of spare design faced each other across the carpet, which echoed in two dimensions the bolder geometry of the room, a perfect cube whose proportions Rachel sensed quite unconsciously as her thoughts searched for some line of defense, a path of escape.

Rachel was far beyond experience or the power of logic. With preternatural clarity she studied the scene unfolding before her. She had no plan of retreat. Surrendering to the senses, she rationalized that the search for one could be postponed.

Following behind, she took a seat opposite the Satrap and, without discomfort, responded to his intense gaze with one of her own. He was a prince, to be sure, accustomed to command. His eyes were large and dark. More oval than round, with a neatly trimmed beard of nut brown hue, his face was interesting, she thought, despite its iconic perfection. She saw a sensitivity just beneath the Satrap's brusque exterior, perhaps even a vulnerability in those wide open eyes and the facial lines that faintly framed them.

All was still until a young, beautiful man appeared, bearing a tray with tea and service.

This must be Artapathes, she surmised, the Satrap's closest scepter-bearer, whose faithfulness to Cyrus was known throughout Sardis. He wasn't a eunuch like the others, she had heard. *I don't know what they look like, anyway*, she thought, a faint smile forming at the corners of her mouth. He wore bracelets and a necklace worthy of the noblest Persians. At his waist hung a dagger of gold.

There were many delights: the sweet smelling nectar favored by Cyrus, a blend of wine, honey and flowers, and the famous Lydian "blood figs." From the tea, the strong scent of rosemary imposed itself, interfering, as the proportions of the room had done, with her flimsy effort to devise a plan. Artapathes served Cyrus first, then Rachel. Departing, he left them alone to sip tea across the flat weave.

"Do you want to explain yourself?" Cyrus asked, offering her a fig.

Accepting his offer, she replied, "No, Your Majesty."

"Don't you wish to tell me what you were trying to say?"

Rachel feared he already knew the answer to that question, perhaps even better than she did. In silence she moved her head slightly, side to side. A fly lighted on the nectar. Rachel longed for another fig, but thought it better not to help herself.

"How old are you?"

"Seventeen, Your Majesty."

"Call me 'Cyrus' in these rooms." He gave her a long, quizzical look. She dropped her gaze.

"Are you a virgin?"

Assaulted by a question she had never imagined being asked, Rachel struggled to respond. She surrendered to instinct.

"Of course. Until I marry. This is the law of my religion. Of the Torah. Is it not true for your religion as well?"

Cyrus took another long look. "I did not bring you here to compare religious beliefs," he said.

Rachel stared at the kilim, shifting uncomfortably. There was a lump in her throat.

"Down that hall, to the left, there is a bath. You'll find towels, robes and a variety of soaps, lotions and perfumes. Go, wash and

# 1: SARDIS – 407 B.C.

relax, dress in a robe that becomes you and return."

Rachel had steeled herself to resist an attempted embrace. She hadn't anticipated so measured an approach. Unprepared, she couldn't have parried this inviting offer had she wished to. Rising, she stood up straight, took a deep breath and looked him in the eye for an instant; then turning, she crossed the room and made her way down the hall.

The bath had obviously been drawn recently with her in mind, for it was filled with very warm, pellucid water. Rachel recognized the shimmering marble from which the bath had been carved. On many walks she had visited the quarry where this smooth stone, unmistakable in its soft whiteness, had been cut. It was located high up a ravine in the Tmolos mountain range south of Sardis, where a tributary to the Pactolus River cascaded over marble cliffs and smooth white pools.

Beside the bath, on a matching marble table, Rachel found several lydions, each filled with a different perfume or ointment. By smell she recognized saffron, a delight to the senses, and baccharis, a softener for the skin.

Despite her attempts to stay wary, the bath's seductive appointments pushed against Rachel's fears. She rationalized the pleasures she was experiencing. Trying to understand, even defend herself, she turned to the story of Hadassah, which she had heard several times in weekly Jewish assembly over the past two years. It had first been told in Sardis by the senior member of the group from Jerusalem who came to collect the Temple tax paid annually by the Jewish community of Sardis.

Set in the Persian palace at Susa, in the time of Ahasuerus, the King of all Persia and Media, the story started with the King's wife rejecting his summons to a major feast for the leaders of his kingdom. Angered by this public show of independence and worried about how her behavior might affect other married women, the King banished his wife and opened a competition within the kingdom among the fair, young and virginal to become his new Queen. Hadassah, or Esther as she was also known, met the qualifications and was put forth in the competition by Mordecai, her father's nephew, who had raised her after the death of her parents. Kept with the King's concubines for twelve months of preparation, the contestants went, one each evening, to the King. In time it was Esther's turn. As it was her training and skill to do, Rachel could recall the exact words of the story.

"So Esther was taken unto King Ahasuerus into his house royal. And the King loved Esther above all the women, and she obtained grace and favor in his sight more than all the virgins; so that he set the royal crown upon her head, and made her queen."

For the raconteur, the main points of the story were the boldness of Esther and the bravery of her people. Rachel tried to imagine the skills Esther used, as a virgin, to capture the King's love.

Immersed to her neck in warm water, Rachel played with the idea of doing what Esther had done. Of course, Rachel heard Esther described as being very beautiful, something she believed she was not. But there were other common strands. Wasn't she being invited to bed with the Satrap of Lydia? Wasn't he unmarried, like King Ahasuerus? Might he not see her as a prospective bride?

Her effort to emulate Esther was burdened by the facts. Instead of concealing her religion, she had asserted it as a possible shield. Instead of calling on skills vicariously taught to her by palace concubines, she lamented not having learned how to freeze a suitor's ardor. Instead of taking pure delight in her situation, with a part of her mind she renewed the search for an escape. Brashness had gotten her as far as the bath. With just a small step from there to bed, she longed for the path home.

The glint of afternoon sun, beaming through a small window above the bath, brought these ruminations to an end.

"You do look rested," Cyrus said upon seeing Rachel emerge from the hall. Her black hair was brushed back, glistening with dampness. "That bath took you well over an hour. I suppose I encouraged you. But you've put that ill-fitting smock back on. I thought I told you to pick one of the robes!" Cyrus' expectant look at seeing Rachel emerge from the bath turned sour.

"I must cease all activities outside the home before sunset on Fridays. The sun is but one hour from setting; only by leaving now

## 1: SARDIS – 407 B.C.

can I be home in time. I am sorry to end our visit. Please understand my need. And, thank you for this hospitality."

"That problem has nothing to do with me. You can't be thinking you can take the pleasures of my bath and then leave."

Rachel had expected this verbal assault. She feared that a physical one loomed just behind. Falling to her knees before him, she spoke, seemingly to his feet.

"Your namesake, Cyrus the Great, freed our people, exiled in Babylon. Thus did he honor our God and the Torah. And he committed Persian gold to rebuild our Temple. I beg you to honor him by respecting our laws."

With head still bowed and eyes downcast, she backed away and got to her feet. For a moment she felt suspended, hanging by a thread. Then, looking furtively at his face, she could see both anger and ardor melt away. Cyrus was above all a decent man and fair, one well aware of the great edict and prepared to do it honor, at least when confronted with so stark a choice, honor or dishonor, with any chance of wavering removed by Rachel's sharp eloquence.

"We'll resume our visit some other day, some day other than Friday," Cyrus said, his frown turning slowly into a tiny smile of surrender.

# CHAPTER 2

Altai – 407 B.C.

Targitus rose before dawn. He left the family yurt quietly, catching the large felt drape he had gently pushed away before it could flap against the sides of the opening. Left sleeping were his father, Matyes, king of the Altaians, his mother, Sparetra, and his older brother, Ishkapai. The family's dog, Taiga, who acknowledged but one master, slipped out before the drape fell back in place. The moonless sky was still dark, stars bright. He whistled softly. A gentle whinny directed him toward Belukcha, his piebald gelding. A few long strides and he was beside his horse, running one hand gently up the horse's forehead as the other flattened against his muzzle to offer a mound of crystallized honey. The heat of Belukcha's breath on his skin was a welcome contrast to the chilled night air. It's seriously cold, he thought, reluctantly admitting that for his Altaian village the corner of the year had been turned.

Bridling the horse and unhobbling him, Targitus leapt upon his back without adding blanket and girth. When anxiety displaced the normal rhythms of his sleep, his habit was to ride bareback to rendezvous with the rising sun atop the high spur that separated the

## 2: ALTAI – 407 B.C.

Balyktyul River from the Great Ulagan River in the U-shaped valley known by the same name. The spur commanded the land stretching out to the south, beyond which Targitus could see the great snow-capped peaks of the Kurai Range running east-west. The mightiest of them all, Kis-Kishtu-Aik, was positioned precisely on a line from the spur to the Great Ulagan village in which Targitus lived at the end of the valley where the Great Ulagan River flowed into the mighty Bashkaus, king of waters. Great Ulagan was the principal village among many that together comprised the Massagetae branch of the Scythian people, located in the Altai Mountains some 3,200 miles east of Sardis.

Riding north up the valley, he judged the time remaining before sunrise and nudged Belukcha into a canter. Taiga varied her position, sometimes ahead, sometimes behind, never far away. Targitus knew he would have to hurry, and the time for swiftness was during the few miles of gentle incline before the steep climb to the top of the spur began. Given his head, Belukcha would always retrace the same path up to the summit, but it was Targitus' practice always to find a different route. Being superstitious, he feared the experiences of past visits to the spur could affect the next one.

Light from the East pushed against darkness. He could make out clumps of larch in the narrow hollows that transected the hillside rising steeply in front of him. He liked the sense of privacy afforded by these trees, which if followed along the inclines would mask his approach to the summit until he was three-quarters' of the way up. He knew no one would be watching for a lone rider at this hour; nonetheless, being hidden from view felt good.

Reaching the summit, he sat his horse for some minutes, gazing south to the purple-dark Kurai Range, its white peaks brightening by the second. Targitus was tall and lean. He had a high forehead and a long, sharply profiled face with distinct chin. Narrow and strongly projecting with a slight hook, his nose was an exquisitely sensitive barometer of changes in the weather. Having turned a sanguineous color during the ride, it now signaled cold.

In the chilled fall air he could see through the whiteness of his own breath a blanket of fog hovering over the village. How many others, he wondered, had come to this place of solitude over centuries past? The petroglyphs nearby, horse and deer-like figures drawn millennia before on greenish slate, a drawing tablet upended by force of nature to thrust out of the earth's shell, confirmed ancient human presence. Who they were didn't matter. Just the evidence of their presence was comforting. Targitus knew they had come, as he did, for solitude and space.

He wondered whether they had gods. The subject matter of these ancient drawings conformed to his own notion of divinity. He suspected that the animals depicted on the green slate were no less important to these early artists than they were to his present-day Massagetae. If there were gods who looked after us, he had reasoned, they must be responsible for providing the animals essential for human-kind to survive. One by one the animals were born and died. Collectively, rebirth was a constant, continuing forever. Surely these animals were touched by the gods, perhaps even earthly manifestations of them, worthy of worship and thanksgiving.

There must have been a divine spark in the making of Belukcha. This horse's acceptance of his master and willingness to do his bidding were the mark of a superior creature. Experience had taught Targitus that loyalty among humans varied with time, place and circumstance. Yet within Belukcha's kingdom loyalty was as constant as the moon's cycle. And he knew that Taiga, exemplar of the canine world, was easily the equal of Belukcha in loyalty to his master, although in service of lesser rank. Such qualities had to be God-given. For a people divinely favored.

The peak of Kis-Kishtu-Aik ignited as the first rays of the new sun met pure white snow. The blaze of warm light grew as the sun's beam chased the penumbra of darkness down the mountainside. Minutes later the sun peeked its orange-red face over the hills defining the Great Ulagan's eastern boundary. The moment Targitus had come to see was over. He was refreshed. Dismounting, he hobbled Belukcha and sat down beside clumps of edelweiss, veronica and thyme. Taiga joined him, warm tongue licking cold hands.

Looking down at his village, hidden from all save his horse and dog, Targitus felt safe, as if enclosed in a cocoon, and strangely

## 2: ALTAI – 407 B.C.

removed from the problems he'd come to the spur to disentangle.

The Altaians were governed by a king, to be sure, but not by him alone. Matyes had been chosen king of all the Altaian villages by a council of elders, who gave weight not only to the fact that Matyes' father had been king before him, but, of more importance, to the skills Matyes displayed in both fighting and leading the community. The council by tradition had the power to choose. While the blood line of a king was an important factor, it was not the only factor, and within the memory of some of the elders, it had not been enough in the case of at least one appointment made some three generations earlier.

The whole village was alive to what had occurred at yesterday's council meeting, called to arrange for a delegation to undertake the long and arduous expedition to Sardis. Matyes had been asked which of his two sons he intended to place in charge. It was obvious that a son of the King was the appropriate ranking personage to undertake this important mission. It was equally clear that, since the King had only two sons and no daughters, one should remain with the King in the Altai. The elders believed the purpose of this expedition had an important bearing on which son was chosen, but they'd been unwilling to express themselves on such a personal and delicate subject. Age was not a factor. Both were adults: Ishkapai twenty-five, Targitus twenty-two. There were other issues, however, that the council hoped the king would weigh carefully in making his selection.

Matyes had promised a decision by noon the next day. Targitus knew his father was struggling: first, because knowledge of the planned expedition had become widespread throughout the community since the idea was first advanced in early summer; and second, because of Ishkapai's persistent efforts to get himself chosen.

Rehearsing the events of the past several months, Targitus tried to sort out the problems. Did he want to go? Of course. Was it possible that his father might pick him? Again, an easy yes. In fact, that was the issue that had brought him to this summit. He had not sought the assignment; yet he knew the elders wanted him, and for good reason. The purpose of this mission was to discover the process by which gold was separated from silver and other base metals. By all reports it was a secret practiced only in Sardis. To gain access to the process would require cleverness and luck. To master and then retain the details of this process would require a special talent for memorization. To stand a chance of success the leader would need a gift for language. Targitus knew the elders believed he excelled in these skills to a degree well beyond his brother. Deep in thought, Targitus plucked a tiny bouquet of edelweiss and thyme, then deeply inhaled its fragrance. "You know, they're right," he declared, speaking in the direction of the reclining Tiaga.

The Altaians had plenty of gold. It had supported them in trade with people from the south and the west. And they had learned a few decades ago how to rid the ore, which often contained as much silver as gold, of all base metals. But the process of separating silver from gold, so that each metal could be reliably purified for use as currency, had escaped them. The purification process had been practiced in Sardis since the days of Croesus. Knowledge of its existence had spread eastward as purified gold and silver coins found their way into the trading markets, but knowledge of the process had spread not at all. Having plentiful quantities of gold ore, the Altaians realized how important for trade, and the wealth of their community, the ability to mint coins of pure gold and silver could be.

So, Targitus reasoned, his father might pick him, despite his brother's being the first-born, the more dominant physically, the more creative mentally and eager to be named. Were this to happen, the question would become, should he accept? The considerations were many; a jumble hard to sort out. He knew his brother. There would be great anger.

Physically, Targitus was quick, strong and athletic, but in every way his brother was the better. Not by much. Just enough, as they grew up, to punish Targitus physically whenever they came to blows, as frequently they did. Ishkapai always won. At twelve Targitus had gone to Matyes to complain, only to be turned away as a coward and told that fighting with his brother was their business alone. Never again had he complained. Nor did he explain the source of frequent cuts, swellings and bruises.

The fact that Targitus was gifted with an unusual intelligence didn't help matters. Growing up, Targitus would often, with parental encouragement, perform feats of memory. He could recite poems after one hearing. With practice and maturity, his skill grew more remarkable. He became a showcase for parental pride, mastering longer poems and even repeating long strings of random numbers fed to him by Ishkapai and others eager to see him fail.

If Targitus was the self-conscious worker bee of the family, Ishkapai was the unconscious hare, darting, sometimes brilliantly, always unpredictably, this way and that. He had a superior capacity for imagination and ingenuity. He was impressive at puns and other forms of word play. His redesign of the Altaian bridle achieved greater simplicity and strength. His experiments with arrows led to the use of different shapes for different purposes. And, yet, for the elders these skills were overshadowed by Targitus' memory and a rather stolid dependability. He became a favorite not just within the family but throughout the community.

As the brothers matured, the community made more demands on them. The cool and reckless verve that during childhood had made Ishkapai more exciting to be around than his brother depreciated in value against Targitus' steadfast character. His probity and caution were unusual in one so young. The community's growing respect for Targitus was matched by a reciprocal decline in its admiration for Ishkapai's seeming indifference to the opinions of others. This, in turn, led to an increase in the pattern of pain that Ishkapai inflicted on his younger brother, physical prowess being one area where the first-born could prove himself distinctly superior, again and again.

Suppose, if selected, he were to decline, or better yet, inform his father before a decision was made that, if chosen, he would not accept. Might this not be the best thing to do, since his brother was so eager? Might it not be good for the community not to enrage his brother unnecessarily? He found reasons why Ishkapai should lead. Yes, he was more gifted in relating to people and far more in his mental capacity for memorization. But Ishkapai was no simpleton. His insights regarding human behavior were at least the equal of Targitus' and among the group he led would be others with adequate memories to supplement his. By sharing knowledge throughout the group, there should be no risk. In the end, it wouldn't really matter which of them led.

Having resolved this much, Targitus came easily to the next decision. He would await his father's judgment rather than pre-empt it by declaring he would not go even if selected. Here he allowed modesty to cloud his customary foresight. He reasoned that there was at least an equal chance that Ishkapai would be chosen, and it seemed in some way unfair to his brother to diminish that choice by withdrawing from the field before the decision was made.

The sun was bright in the sky when Targitus returned to the village. By the time he had watered Belukcha, rubbed him down with a horn brush and left him to graze, the council of elders had received Matyes' selection. Targitus learned of his father's decision through the hateful glare of his older brother, who was the first of the family to see him as he returned to the village center. Ishkapai passed his brother without breaking stride.

Targitus ran to the central yurt where council meetings were held. Inside he found his father seated with most of the council drawn up in a semi-circle around him. The air was moist with the scent of mint tea. The tenor of the assemblage was relaxed and happy. Matyes was quick to greet his son and convey his decision. Before Targitus could speak, the others rose as one and, gathering round, embraced Targitus in turn while extending compliments to one another on their decision. Such was the din that Targitus was not heard to exclaim "I will not go." Repeating these words, he finally made himself understood. There was silence in the yurt.

Matyes spoke. "What do you mean? You have been chosen. You will go."

"In either of our hands the mission will succeed. It's right for Ishkapai to go. As the eldest." Targitus never doubted the logic of his early morning cogitations or his ability to change his father's mind.

Matyes and the council tightly surrounded him. Pointing out that this mission was no ordinary trip one takes to the steppes to trade with Scythians, they said there was no margin for error. It was his duty, as son of the king and a future leader of the Altaians, to head the expedition to Sardis.

## 2: ALTAI – 407 B.C.

Targitus responded with uncommon passion. "My brother wants desperately to go. I want, almost as desperately, to keep peace in the family. Ishkapai will succeed. Let him be the one."

His argument provoked a rising tide of criticism, much of it unfair, rooted in Ishkapai's flamboyance and youthful rejection of authority. Maytes stood to the side as the debate raged. Finally, raising his arms above his head and turning to his father, Targitus said, "Your silence is a command. I will go."


It was September. In the Great Ulagan, frosts began in mid-August. It was too late to launch the expedition before the onset of winter. Moreover, given the rivers that would have to be crossed to reach the steppes, it would be better to commence the trip in March, when ice would allow easy passage. Targitus had plenty of time to prepare.

The Altaians knew Sardis was an immense distance west of their own mountains. They knew that Scythian tribes occupied the steppes west from the foothills of the Altai, where lands of the Massagetae ended, all the way to the European outposts north of the Black Sea. Among these tribes they would be welcome, as Scythians felt strong kinship across the full sweep of the steppes and had always responded to appeals for help on those rare occasions when a tribe was threatened from the south. And travelers had told them Sardis was still farther west, somewhere south of the Black and Caspian Seas, on the other side of a great mountain range. Beyond that, Targitus realized, they didn't know much.

In the weeks that followed his father's announcement, Targitus made many decisions regarding the trip. He would take six companions, each with two carefully selected geldings, to assure that supplies could be carried and tired horses given enough rest to improve their chances of survival. His mentor and friend, Tymnes, would be his chief aide. Tymnes was twice Targitus' age and more. He was the best horse handler in the village. He had taught Targitus how to play and fight in the saddle. Targitus felt an unbreakable bond with this man, a bond established in childhood and strengthened year by year as Targitus came of age.

Before selecting the other companions, Targitus planned to pick from the village herd the top equine candidates to make the journey.

One afternoon he mounted Belukcha and set off to a remote part of the Bashkaus River, upstream from the village, in search of a number of the wilder harems, which liked to keep their distance from the village. The day was clear and unusually hot for September. Cloud formations at different heights in the sky foretold a weather change approaching from the north. Speaking to Belukcha and Taiga, he cautioned them to prepare for rain and the cold front that would follow around dusk. And having issued this warning, Targitus chuckled. Indeed, he thought, if these animals could speak his language, it would have been they, much earlier, who cautioned him. The Altai's ineffable vastness, which confronted a rider at the top of almost any peak or saddle, was equaled by the sudden changes in weather that passed across its uneven surfaces as rapidly as the waters of the Bashkaus rippled across the rocks and pebbles of its great river bed. From the heat of day to the cold of night, from the still of a sunrise to the blow of wind announcing change, from the immense whiteness of billowing clouds whose size was confirmed by the dark banking shapes of kites crisscrossing the sky and, far above them, the dots of circling eagles, weather's presence across the spacious Altai was palpable.

Riding up the valley into a waxing wind, which was an anodyne to the heat of the afternoon, Targitus returned to the vivid dream of the night before, which had awakened him just before dawn. He had been looking up in the sky. There he'd seen an object, whitish, shaped like a rabbit, pierced through its length by an arrow that protruded front and back about six inches each way. The object was gently circling and losing altitude as it did so. Its steady, silent movement commanded attention. A spiritual feeling possessed him. Realizing the object was going to land in nearby woods, he tried to calibrate the spot and went off to retrieve it. He thought of it as a source of food. It was shot by a hunter, who would be searching too. He must be a very good bowman. Targitus must try to find it first. And then, the scene ended, incomplete. Again, he had looked up, and again he had seen the same object in the air, circling with an arrow through its length, exactly as before. He had set out to search. The dream ended.

## 2: ALTAI – 407 B.C.

Finding the horses quietly grazing on a large meadow near the Bashkaus, just below a narrow where the river grew turbulent and noisy, Targitus dismounted. He saw a possible advantage to leaving Belukcha unhobbled, free to mingle with the harems. With plenty of crystallized honey for bait, he started to examine the horses under the charge of four stallions. It would be slow work, because Targitus had learned from sad experience that only through close examination could the qualities of a horse be discovered. There was one easily visible feature, however, that would eliminate a horse immediately. As all Scythians knew, a white blaze on the forehead was a sure sign of soft feet.

Gaining a semi-wild horse's confidence took more than a handful of honey. Targitus spoke gently to each horse he approached. He would talk it into accepting the halter he carried, sliding the crownpiece gently over the ears as the last morsel of honey was swallowed. With his undivided attention on a particularly attractive black gelding, it was not surprising that he missed the signs among nearby horses of some disturbance. Nor, given his choral-like murmurings to the large black horse and the overtones from the roaring Bashkaus nearby, that he failed to notice the whinny of Belukcha. Taiga had picked just this moment to go upwind of Targitus for a long drink.

Four men with faces partially concealed with cloth and the rest garishly colored reddish-orange with cinnabar surrounded him. They were tall men, powerfully built. They spoke not a word, seeming to be awaiting orders from beyond their circle. Targitus saw there was no way to break out. A voice from some yards away issued an order. Instantly, the men laid rough hands on him and with sinews tied his arms behind his back and bound his feet together. Then, lifting him up like a larch pole, they carried him to a pleasant glade beside the river and dropped him there, where he was quickly joined by Taiga.

Targitus couldn't imagine who was directing the group, none of whom he could recognize. He thought immediately of his brother, but never had Ishkapai needed others to inflict pain. Whether because he saw it as unfair, or because he enjoyed meting out the punishment himself, it hadn't happened.

Taiga was barking furiously at the men, having positioned himself between them and his master. Above the din, Targitus shouted, demanding to be untied, to know the purpose of this outrage, to know who these men were. No one answered. The voice of command, much closer now, spoke again. "Remember, below the head." And then, almost as an afterthought, "Get rid of that dog." At once the four men, who were standing a few yards from Targitus, advanced on Taiga. He could see that they had wooden clubs in their hands, a foot and a half in length. Taiga was a fighter, and loyal, but not to the point of self-destruction. After a glancing blow landed on his flank, he made an escape, vanishing among the horses that now stood curiously facing the group at the river's edge. Returning to their victim, the men began a vigorous kicking. It lasted for some time. Targitus could roll. But, except for assuming the fetal position, he could do little to escape the attack, which came from all sides at once.

Finally, the voice cried, "Enough. The clubs. Below the head." With singular care, each man in succession took a shot at Targitus, keeping up a rhythm as they methodically brought their clubs down on every part of his body until nothing remained untouched. Long before they had finished, Targitus was wishing they had used an early blow to the head to render him unconscious. The pain was excruciating. Shock and a growing fear of the unfolding design made it worse. There was method to the beating. In the hands of even one of these attackers, the club could have been lethal.

At a command from close by, the clubs were stilled. Through dust and sweat-drenched eyes, Targitus saw the covered figure of the fifth man. Targitus had trouble getting his eyes to focus. The salt's sting was sharp, a contrast to the growing numbness of his beaten body. Through the streaks of cinnabar that concealed the natural contours of the fifth man's face, Targitus was finally able to make out a pair of unmistakable blue eyes, "cornflower eyes" his mother had called them for the plain intensity of their color.

Targitus could not speak. He knew he was close to unconsciousness. And he knew his brother wasn't finished. He heard Ishkapai's next command, but could not make out its meaning. Roughly he was seized by the four men, turned over, propped up on his hands and knees and given the necessary support to keep him in place. His leggings were torn off. Dust filled the air around him. His eyes closed to

## 2: ALTAI – 407 B.C.

lessen the salt's pain. A thought muscled its way into his clouded mind. He was on the verge of trying to say "no" when thought gave way to the deed itself.

It was quickly over. Had Targitus been able to see, he would have observed Ishkapai in his ultimate act of mastery over, and humiliation of, his younger brother before a picked audience of four men and the uninvited harems of horses that stood silently observing the bestiality. Before departing, Ishkapai ordered the men to remove the sinews from hands and feet.

It was some time after Ishkapai and his men left before Targitus could muster the voice to summon Belukcha. The horse came to his side, reins hanging to the ground. Targitus had been left on his stomach. Turning to his back was a slow, painful process, requiring him to concentrate on each step.

Two things occupied his mind: overwhelming thirst and the cold air causing him to shiver. He thought he might be capable of holding onto the reins. If Belukcha could grasp his whispered instructions enough to move to the edge of the Bashkaus, perhaps he could relieve his need for water. He tried repeatedly. Belukcha seemed to understand. A pattern developed. He would call her to stand over him until he could seize the two reins in both hands. Attempts using one rein or one hand failed quickly. A single hand lacked the strength necessary to move his body. Watching his still numb hands entwine the reins, he imagined they must belong to someone else, someone who had come to help. He would feel his body move a few inches at a time, and then notice his hands slipping from the reins. And so it went, again and again, progress measured in inches until a splashing about signaled Belukcha's entry into the water.

Reversing the process that had enabled him to reach the river's edge, he succeeded in turning over. Worried that by turning away from the water he might not be able to drink, he turned toward the swift-flowing current, only to find his nose and mouth under the icy flow. After seconds of drinking, the fear of drowning in these few inches of water possessed him. He could not raise his neck to gain air. Face down, he tried to twist his body to the side. He lacked the strength. He then realized his hands were still clutching the reins, his arms outstretched in front of him. With what strength he had left, he jerked twice on the reins. Belukcha responded by lifting his head, and with it came the arms and head of his master. She stepped out of the river, dragging an exhausted Targitus the short distance needed to avoid drowning. His hands slipped away from the reins and he remained prone beside the river.

Chills seized his body from head to toe. Cold weather had moved in without the predicted rain to announce its arrival. A north wind intensified the cold. Combined with the icy waters which edged against his body, it bespoke mortal danger. Aware of his plight, Targitus could do nothing. With the swiftness of the onset of a winter's darkness, he lost consciousness.

At first he saw only the fire. Then he realized someone was kneeling astride him, engaged in massage. What he took to be the fire's warmth was, in fact, supplied by Sparetra's energetic rubbing. So welcome. And yet, so painful. The renewed flow of blood brought aching pain wherever the loving hands of his mother were engaged.

Targitus asked his mother how she had found him. She replied, between the deep breaths of one working hard, "Taiga. I'll tell you more later."

The next evening, upon awakening from a long sleep, he pressed her.

"I was directing the preparation of dinner when she appeared. She looked beat. I thought her tongue might fall out. She seemed to be concentrating on me. Catching gasps of air, she whined again and again. I got the message something was wrong. I checked with those around the village who might have known where you were. One saw you depart early in the afternoon and showed me the direction you had taken. Another seemed sure you had not returned.

"I organized a body of men. Taiga led us to you."

Sparetra nursed her son back to health. Bones were broken. The mending required splints and bandages to hold the bones in place. Even the bruises took weeks to heal. Targitus was under severe pres-

## 2: ALTAI – 407 B.C.

sure from both parents to explain what had happened. He would only describe an attack by four men, faces obscured with cinnabar. He attached no motive to their behavior. Nor did he provide a clue to their identity. His lies were those of omission.

Ishkapai knew his brother. Targitus closed himself off from friends as his broken bones and bruised muscles and joints healed. Often he feigned weakness of body to avoid exposure when it was really weakness of spirit that he sought to conceal. At times he believed the whole community knew of Ishkapai's degrading dominance. He couldn't shake the thought that as they looked at him, expressing sympathy and good wishes for a speedy recovery, they were imagining the event in all its detail. That behind their empathy lay laughter and ridicule, even contempt. Mortification was complete, overpowering common sense. Why wouldn't he expose his brother's villainy? He wasn't sure himself.

There were few taboos among the Massagetae. Sexual mores were relaxed. There were no bars against sodomy or incest. Rape, however, was condemned. Perpetrators were put to death.

Word of such a heinous crime could not rest quietly in the Great Ulagan valley, especially when it was known to four men in addition to their leader. Four male tongues gave abundant scope to the chance that at least one would wag in incriminating conversation with a woman. Sparetra commanded immense respect on the distaff side of the village. When her request for help in identifying the villains went forth, many women hoped to be the one to respond. It was only a matter of time. Before Targitus' collar bone had knit solid, Sparetra had been told the disgusting story. From her it passed to Matyes, whose anger he made no effort to hide. Yet, both parents sought to prevent the full account from becoming known, a fruitless endeavor given the fast expanding circle of villagers who had heard the story. There was a difference, however, between knowledge derived from whispers and a public acknowledgement by the family. What Ishkapai had done to his brother, on becoming officially public, would grow to a major humiliation for the entire family. This must not be. Instead, they decided on a non-public execution of the four and banishment of the fifth, their son, to Kara-Ozok, an Altaian village far below the Great Ulagan, on the Chya River to the south.

Neither Matyes nor Sparetra did more with Ishkapai than ask why. And his only response was a proudly unabashed silence. The banishment was designed to bring Ishkapai to his senses. It would last until Targitus returned from his mission to Sardis, and thereafter for so long as Targitus demanded.

The four men were taken away from the village by the King's guard. Word circulated that they had been flayed alive, strangled slowly, then cut into pieces to be devoured by wolves and kites. Their bones were never found.

Targitus hadn't been consulted by his parents. Indeed, he didn't discover that they knew what Ishkapai had done to him until after the four had been killed. The first gleaning of his parents' discovery came from Ishkapai, who burst into his brother's recovery room late on the afternoon of his last day in the Great Ulagan. "With you gone, this banishment won't last. I'll be back in the valley before you're back from Sardis. And then things will be different. Don't expect a hero's welcome."

Targitus guessed the truth. Turning away, he said, "I have nothing to say to you. Leave me alone."

Ishkapai was on the verge of responding when Sparetra entered the room with supper. Sparetra looked from one son to the other. Targitus caught the surprise in her face and then, as she recovered her composure, watched her put down a large wooden serving plate and, seizing her older son's arm, turn him firmly around and usher him from the room.

Ishkapai's visit had opened the wound that just days before had seemed to mend. As Targitus would discover, it was a wound too deep for superficial repair. Successful healing had to begin deep inside. "How did you find out?" he demanded.

"I've brought you lamb for supper. A fresh one. It grows cold. Do begin." Unlike her face, which revealed nothing, the voice betrayed tension.

Targitus was not deterred. Facing her, he seized a piece of lamb between thumb and index finger, as if to check its temperature; then, putting it back on the plate, he wiped the grease across his shirt and

## 2: ALTAI – 407 B.C.

said: "Mother, don't play with me. Where is Matyes? I must know. Ishkapai has been banished. How wide has the story spread?" Still hoping there was some way to deny what had happened, he said, "We need a plan."

Sparetra leapt at the opening. "I'll find your father and return. You're not yet well; eat your supper. I'll be as quick as I can."

With winter coming on, the healing powers of time were at hand. To Targitus, his mother seemed relentless in her ministrations. Indeed, he thought her the happiest when feeding, bathing or massaging him, as if again he were her baby. When breaks and bruises had fully mended, Targitus sensed a change in Sparetra. A sadness seemed to engulf her, as if she couldn't accept her own success in nursing her son back to health. As if to lift his pains she had to take on some of her own.

At last, all physical evidence of the deed was gone. Plans for Sardis consumed much of Targitus' time, when he was not doing the normal winter chores of a leading member of this herding society. The village was strenuous in its avoidance of the entire subject. Gradually, the mental anguish of knowing that the village knew lessened. By midwinter, so often had the events of that afternoon along the banks of the Bashkaus been retraced in his head, that what had been daily torment became distant memory. There proved to be a limit, however, to time's curative powers. Subdued but not vanquished, memory's pain remained in the deep recesses of his mind.

In March, Targitus and his band of six departed for Sardis. They would cross the Bashkaus just below the village, where it widened enough to remain frozen well into spring. Targitus had prepared himself for this, his first contact with the river since the degrading incident last fall.

The day they rode out of the valley was cold and overcast. Snow flurries filled the air, biting at exposed skin. The only promise of spring was the loud, trumpeting shrill of the first wave of cranes returning to the Great Ulagan to mate. Heard before they were seen. Looking up, the stalwart band of travelers watched as the cranes passed in V-formation, necks and legs outstretched, their flight straight as an arrow, their wing beats deep and even, all rigorously tidy except for their voices, whose rollicking discordance belied the cadre's tight discipline. "An omen," Targitus cried out, "a propitious omen for certain." With gentle head shakes, the band's fourteen horses broke the spell. A loud hurrah and shouts of good luck burst forth from the villagers. They were away at last, spurred on by Taiga's heart-stopping cries as Matyes restrained her from following her master.

# CHAPTER 3

Sardis – 406 B.C.

The daily trip from the palace to her home near the Pactolus took Rachel about an hour. She could have walked the route in her sleep, or on the blackest night. Eying the sun, which hung three fingers' width above the distant horizon, in the direction she must go, Rachel reckoned the minutes before the softening orange orb would touch the bright line between earth and sky. There was time enough, she thought, but the pace must be brisk.

The palace, with its workshops, storage areas, cisterns and a newly designed garden still under construction, was housed within the massive walls of a citadel crowning the mountain spur that towered some six hundred feet above the developed area of Sardis, mainly to the northwest, in the Hermus River valley. The road to the palace was steep and heavily fortified by triple walls of great thickness and height, which joined those of the citadel atop the spur. On her walks past these protective curtains, Rachel would imagine the siege that gave the city to Cyrus the Great, some 140 years earlier, commencing the Persian reign. The hand-to hand combat that occurred on the path she trod brought on goose-bumps. As the story was told by Sardians outside official Persian circles, Croesus held out against the Persian army for fourteen days, only then to succumb through the treachery of a disaffected Lydian soldier, who disclosed to Cyrus that the source of the citadel's water supply was not on the spur's height, but in subterranean springs far below. Access to the springs was afforded by an underground tunnel over four hundred feet long, hewed out of rock to connect the fortress above to the life-supporting waters beneath. Noting that the walls were ancient yet unscathed, Rachel found this story believable. In a fair fight, the fortress seemed impregnable.

As she began to descend the palace road, her eye was drawn to the northern slopes of the Tmolus Range, now draped in the creamy white of chestnut in flower. The blooms were by day a sparkling foil for the sun as it inched its way across the bright Anatolian sky and at night a soft shadowy glow of ghostly white. Unthreatened and unthreatening, she mused.

The walk would give Rachel time to think. Rather quickly, she resolved not to tell her parents. Having not disclosed her creative adventure with the spreads, she saw little choice now. To relate her encounter with the Satrap would require a number of other disclosures. Her parents wouldn't understand. Recriminations would follow. But, she admitted, there was more to it than that. What about her treatment of Cyrus? What would her parents think? She was no Esther. Would her father want her to move in Esther's direction? Might he view this encounter, and Cyrus' apparent interest in Rachel, as a potential blessing for the family, an opportunity worth exploiting, as Mordecai had developed the opportunity created by Esther. Indeed, thought Rachel, with a new insight about her father, might Benjamin not see this encounter as a sign from Yahweh, leaving the family no choice in the matter? How often she had heard him ascribe to his God a clear signal in regard to some important decision he faced, thereby eliminating doubt, the serpent coiled about human choice. Rachel wondered whether maturity would open for her the channels of communication her father enjoyed.

Knowing the likely answer, she felt alone.

## 3: SARDIS – 406 B.C.

Entering the workshop as usual on Sunday morning, Rachel heard a buzz. She knew news of the inquest would reach her colleagues. There was excitement in the room. She could feel it and guessed they knew just enough to believe there was much more to discover. Many an arched eyebrow and knowing smile confronted her. Squirming with embarrassment, she prepared to proclaim her innocence. Would they believe her? Did it matter, as long as she challenged their salacious assumptions? Locked in debate, she missed Vashti's approach.

"May I give you some advice?" Vashti whispered, leaning close to Rachel's ear. Rachel could feel the sweat beading across her face and watch it streaking down her gown. Worse, she could smell it, a pungent odor not unpleasant to her but one she imagined Vashti would find revolting. Embarrassment led to more sweat, which stung her eyes. She had nothing to wipe her face.

Rachel thrust her bench back from the loom, causing a loud scraping noise. Rising quickly, she moved away from Vashti, half-circling her loom to place it between them. Lifting her arms in turn, she pulled the sleeve of her smock to soak up the sweat in her eyes. Only then did she notice Vashti's arm outstretched across the loom, offering a handkerchief. She felt confused. Even more embarrassed.

The looms had stilled, the buzz around the room had ceased and all eyes and ears had focused on the couple. She looked deeply into Vashti's eyes, searching. She saw a face well used, bearing lines of age and experience to be sure, but perhaps of wisdom too. Her eyes were dark, deep set and edged with sadness, like those of an old dog. But the story was in the lines. They told of gentleness and understanding.

Through the warp and weft of her loom, Rachel replied softly, "Why, yes."

Vashti advanced toward Rachel and took her hand, saying, "Come, let's take a breath of air, where, if we are lucky," her voice rising to reach the corners of the room, "we can enjoy a little privacy."

Bathed in hot sun and blinded upon emerging from the workshop into the large central patio of the palace, they made their way to the shade of an immense chestnut tree, one of a row transplanted with foresight at least two generations earlier from the chestnut forests that graced the Tmolus Range.

Vashti came right to the point. "You looked so uncomfortable in there. Tell me about it."

"When I am nervous, feeling young and stupid, the sweat keeps coming. I'll take that handkerchief now."

"You're self-conscious. I'd be the same."

"I want to defend myself, but don't know how or even from what. Or whether to try. It might make matters worse."

"I'll guess you have nothing to be defensive about."

"I am afraid you're right," her tone expressing ambivalence. Rachel shrugged, relieved at having someone to confess to.

Earnestly, she told her story. When she'd finished, Vashti said, "You're at once younger and older than I thought. Naïve, bold, unpredictable. I wish I could have seen his face." Vashti took Rachel's hand. "We're out of time. My advice is this: Give them nothing. Don't explain, don't excuse and don't try to defend yourself. It's hopeless, because some will not believe you, and those who do will think you a failure. Let them indulge their fantasies. It will make them happier, and you more mysterious and powerful. The less they know the more they will project onto you their exciting inventions. And it will happen without deception. But try the truth and it will destroy you."

Rachel struggled to understand. The concepts were outside her experience. But she had no one else to turn to. "I'll follow your advice, even though, and you must believe me, I seek only to be left alone."

Detecting in Vashti's face a look of skepticism, Rachel said, "You don't think I am seeking power, do you?"

With a smile and warm hug, Vashti demurred. They returned to the workroom. For the remainder of the day Rachel kept silent in the face of knowing nods, friendly, ingratiating winks, even hints of respect from her colleagues. In the days to come she would gradually grow to enjoy the web of mystery and excited admiration that the workers wove about her. Keeping secrets had long been a source of pleasure to Rachel. Here the secrets of her time with the Satrap exuded a pleasure that doubled with the mischief of allowing her colleagues to be deceived by her silence. For the second time in her young life, Rachel found deceit exhilarating.

# CHAPTER 4

Sardis – 406 B.C.

With the speed of summer swallows word traveled from the Eastern Gate of Sardis to its populace. As the long afternoon sun of a late June day hung above the city, a Sardian rider galloped through the Gate shouting "Scythian Barbarians." A circle of anxious citizens gathered around his lathered horse. Some had heard of Scythia and of Scythians, but knew nothing more than the possibility that such a place and people might exist somewhere far to the Northeast. None knew of the Altai or the Massagetae who lived there. The rider poured forth his limited store of knowledge, embellished without restraint.

"Barbarians are approaching. From Scythia. Uncouth, wild and warlike. They set their elderly parents out to be eaten by dogs. When their loved ones die, they chop them up and eat them with the flesh of cattle. They scalp their enemies to ornament their horses. Look to your children; they will soon be at our gates."

By the time this account had reached the center of Sardis, it had grown into an hysterical tale of imminent, hideous peril. Those in the path of this hurricane were led to believe that living children would be hacked to pieces and fed to dogs. Fortunately, word of the approaching band of strangers reached the palace in time for Cyrus to place a reinforced guard at the Eastern Gate with instructions to determine who these riders were, what their business was and, unless good cause was found for keeping them out, to welcome them to this famously open, cosmopolitan city.

There were seven in the band of Altaians who approached the gate, and twice as many horses. With a wind from the east, the collective aroma of these equestrians and their mounts, ripened over weeks of hard travel, assaulted a city famed for sweeter perfumes. Pulling up in front of the unit of smartly dressed guards, the band appeared more beaten than barbaric, more suppliant than threat. They were, to be sure, very different in appearance from anything Sardians were accustomed to. They rode horses of about fourteen hands, slightly smaller than those used in Lydia. Each rider led another horse on which was tied baggage suggestive of a long journey. The manes were hogged, not the fashion then current in Sardis. And most unusual, all were geldings.

The Altaians wore conical leather helmets rising to a point with a graceful bow-shaped curve in the back descending to cover the neck. The leather was tooled in a band around the forehead and down to the neck with bits of blue and red stone sewn in artful curves within the band. Long tunics of leather or felt descended nearly to their knees. They were cinched tight with belts from which hung decorated scabbards housing akinakes and gorytos containing composite bows and arrows of varying lengths. Dust accumulated from many weeks of travel dulled the bright decorations of their tunics and belts. Slim trousers and leather boots completed the dress.

Targitus, first to enter the city, was the only stranger to wear a torque, fashioned of gold in the shape of a round rod wrapped thrice around his neck and terminating at each end in griffin-head finials finely worked both inside and out. The ribbed back of this fantastic creature was formed of gold alternating with inset stones of turquoise. The heads displayed long hooked beaks and large round eyes.

Deeply tanned, all but one rider wore ungoverned beards of considerable length. Some were dusty blond, others reddish or brown, unusual colors to the eyes of Lydians, Persians and Semites.

## 4: SARDIS – 406 B.C.

Targitus knew about the Satrap and his palace atop the Acropolis, which he could see to the south, rising to a giddy height above the city. His plan was to proceed immediately to the palace and there pay his respects to the Satrap, explain the nature of his mission and at the right moment seek co-operation. He would speak in Persian, an Indo-European language similar to his native tongue. During the course of travel, Targitus had taken every opportunity to speak with those along the way who knew Persian. He had also paid well-spoken men he encountered to travel with the band for as many days as they were willing in order to tutor him. He hoped to have acquired enough Persian to steer his band through the early encounters with Cyrus and his servants.

Whether he had mastered Persian well enough to be persuasive in advancing his mission was another matter altogether. It was his chief source of anxiety. An accomplished speaker in his own tongue, he was acutely aware of his limitations in the use of Persian.

Dismounting, the band of seven approached the guards with an openness that bespoke a peaceful mission. Identifying themselves as Altaians from the great Eurasian Steppe, some 3,200 miles to the northeast, above the Caspian Sea, Targitus asked to see the Satrap.

The leader of this specially assigned guard detachment was Artapathes, Cyrus' closest scepter-bearer. He looked at the band in wonder on hearing the distance they had traveled from a place unknown to him.

"Tell me," he said, "how long have you been on this journey?"

Targitus replied "Today is our 101st. We had good fortune along the way. No bandits. No fighting. We planned for a trip of up to four months. With luck, it took just a bit more than three."

"Your torque marks you as a chieftain, Targitus."

"I am a prince of our people in the Altai, a son of our King."

"And what is your business in Sardis? I know the Satrap will want you to stay this evening in the palace and meet with him over dinner to explore your purpose in detail. But come, give me some idea."

Targitus was feeling the heat as he swayed slightly forward and back, as if still moving on his horse. "We come in peace. We are tired and the sun is hot. Might we proceed to the Satrap's palace?"

Targitus thought he caught the slightest sign of embarrassment crossing the face of Artapathes as he said, pointing up to the palace now gleaming softly in the late afternoon sun, "Please mount for the ride to the palace, where we will get you and your group to a room with a bath. Then the Satrap will meet you."

Before leaving the gate, Artapathes instructed half of his guard to disperse through the city and advise its citizens they had nothing to fear from the Altaians. "It's hard to reverse a fear once instilled," he said, "but at least we can start."


Targitus led his freshly scrubbed band of Altaians to a receiving room, where they found Cyrus awaiting them. Targitus saw a man exuding the brio of youth and station. He was standing in front of a throne of gold. He wore a necklace of curiously wrought gold encasing perfectly matched stones of turquoise. Exquisite bracelets of lapis lazuli and carnelian embellished each of his wrists. The subdued colors of his robe were a foil for the bright elegance of his jewelry.

Cyrus stood at the head of a massive wool pile medallion carpet containing an eight-petalled flower. Targitus had never seen its like before. Dominated by hues of dark blue, ivory and madder, the medallion was surrounded by a broad border edged on each side by a neat guilloche pattern, its central area depicting cloud scrolls. The carpet covered all but a foot or two of the taupe tile floor.

The complex patterns of the carpet were echoed in the geometric motifs and colors of the tiles covering the four walls. Though flat, the ceiling had been designed to appear as a dome. It was painted twilight blue with the North Star at its center, exaggerated in size as befitted this symbolic entrance to the afterlife, from which streamed out the light of the Gods. Other stars traced circular paths around the North Star, just as they did when one lay down on a clear Anatolian night to face the sky. Glancing from the Satrap to the decorations of the room and back again, he thought the energetic grandeur of the surroundings a perfect match for the distinguished leader. He guessed Cyrus was about his own age.

Here stood two princes, both limited by being second-born; but

## 4: SARDIS – 406 B.C.

each from vastly different social and economic circumstances: Cyrus, Satrap of a flourishing urban center in the Persian Empire; Targitus, emissary from a semi-nomadic pastoral people somewhere beyond the edge of the known world.

Targitus studied Cyrus' necklace, so refined compared to the torque he wore, yet made of the same materials. And then the beard. He knew it had been trimmed for display, probably earlier that day, unmarred by even one errant hair. The contrast with the overgrown thicket he displayed made Targitus feel awkward, even out of place. Looking at his followers, he could see they felt the same. I mustn't show it, he reminded himself.

Targitus introduced himself and his colleagues. Wine was served on silver trays passed by well-dressed servants. Targitus saw that Cyrus seemed to be waiting for something. With an inner smile, he realized the man could count. Since only six of his seven guests had entered the room, Cyrus was delaying the ceremony of formal greeting until the arrival of the remaining Altaian. A second round of wine was passed. Drawing close to his host, Targitus whispered that he should not delay on account of the absent guest.

Raising his glass, the Satrap said "Targitus, you and your companions have traveled farther than anyone I have ever had the privilege to greet in this palace. Artapathes tells me you have shed layers of dust collected in over 3,000 miles of riding. We were happy to extend the pleasures of our bath. The smiles on your faces permit me to hope you have enjoyed yourselves. Whatever your purpose, I thank you for coming in peace. That you have, I have no reason to doubt. Never, since the beginning of our Empire, have your people attacked us south of the Black or Caspian. It was my namesake and Darius two generations later who made war on your people. In our Empire those events have been forgotten by all but a handful, who know better than to bring the subject up. I raise my glass to each of you, to the long lives I wish for you, to friendship, and some day, Targitus, to each of us being in position to commit our peoples to enduring peace."

Targitus responded. "Speaking for my band, and my people, whose wish it was that we journey here, I thank you for the warmth of your bath and your wine, for the kindness of your palace staff and for your own trust and friendship. We are excited to be in Sardis, and hopeful that our mission, which we commit to your care, will prove successful. And now, we have gifts."

"Splendid. But, before gifts, your mission."

"Of course." Embarrassed, Targitus knew exactly the cause of this oversight. The tautness of his mind and body through the long journey had, like a bow pulled to its limit, suddenly been released upon journey's end and the soft pleasures that followed. Just in time he recalled his father's rule: "Never explain or excuse a lapse."

"We have come all this distance because we wish to learn what you in Sardis discovered long ago, the process by which gold is purified. You may have heard that, in the Altai, we have much gold, but it's found with silver and other metals, especially copper. Given the Altai's distance from your city, we thought that sharing your secret wouldn't cause any loss of wealth or other harm to Sardis. We have heard of your generosity and fairness. We bring hopes that you will not send us back. That through the knowledge we gain here, and the friendship we build with you, a permanent bond of peace will be forged between our people and yours."

"I see. Ambitious quest. And novel. We have long guarded the secret of purification. The results have been rewarding, as you see in the wealth of our city. I can promise you nothing except a fair hearing. We will give it careful thought."

His voice, which had been stern in delivering this message, suddenly turned soft and appealing. "And now, you spoke of gifts?"

From under a cloak put aside as he came into the room, Targitus took a package, carefully wrapped in felt. Handing it to Cyrus, he declared, "The duties of Satrap for the Western frontier of the Persian Empire are immense, his burdens heavy. Here's an anodyne to your stresses."

Opening the package, Cyrus found a gloriously designed and gilded silver rhyton, the body covered with horizontal fluting, the protome in the form of a recumbent ram, beautifully rendered with hammered circles and dots depicting fleece. Holes in the ram's nostrils would permit wine to flow. Targitus watched Cyrus examine the

## 4: SARDIS – 406 B.C.

gift. He liked the Satrap's attention to detail. The Altaians were rewarded by his enthusiastic cry. "Here's a vessel of the highest art and workmanship."

While Cyrus stood admiring the gift, Targitus moved to the entrance of the room to take the hand of the seventh Altaian. He led the young woman forward to stand directly before the Satrap.

"And here, Cyrus, is our second gift to you: Argali, whose riding skills and ability with the bow rival any man's. She made the trek with us concealed as a man, but came prepared to dress as you see her now. She's yours. She has known no other. In parting with Argali, the Altaians incur a loss, for we love her deeply. But if you love her well, that loss will be one we gladly accept."

Targitus could see that Cyrus was astonished. To such a degree that his lambent facility with language abandoned him for a time. In front of the Satrap, offering her hand, stood a tall, surpassingly beautiful young woman. What she wore had been the subject of intense thought by Targitus, whose attention to detail had, against the odds, been nourished instead of distracted by Argali's sensuality. She appeared in a long loose robe of midnight blue, cinched at the waist with a thin gold belt. The robe was ornamented with large rosettes fashioned in gold and sewn neatly in two vertical rows of four each. She wore a conical cap with a drape extending just below the neck. Dyed a brilliant red with madder, it too was decorated with gold plaques of four hemispherical bosses arranged like petals around another central boss. On her feet were tidy shoes of madder-dyed fabric, with gold plaque ornamentation identical to that of the headdress.

So ample was the robe that, despite the cinched waist, Argali's athletic figure was left mainly to the Satrap's imagination.

One could easily imagine the beauty of her face a true reflection of all that remained unseen. Her blond hair was pulled back and neatly tucked beneath the drape. Soft golden wisps teased her forehead, just below the cap. Her nose was straight with a slight upward turn at the end, like a button. She had high cheekbones and a fair complexion darkened by the summer's sun. Her mouth was generous with the hint of a smile. Her eyes were of colors all her own.

Targitus watched Cyrus search for something appropriate to say.

Awkward moments passed. Then, without a word, Cyrus took Argali's hand and led the group into the dining room. It was evident that the second gift had delighted the Satrap. Was it enough to assure success for their quest? Though the celebration continued far into the evening, they were offered no clue and knew better than to ask.

The Satrap had planned a verbal contest for the pleasure of his guests. Careful in many ways, he had overlooked the fact that, other than Targitus, the Altaians knew hardly a word of Persian. In the midst of dinner, three pages appeared before the gathering, prepared to debate the question, what is the most potent force in the world: wine, woman or a king? The Altaians feigned appreciation for the performances, comprehending nothing. Targitus knew enough Persian to grasp and at times be amused by the argument.

When the pages were finished, Cyrus picked as the winner Pesacas, who happened to have argued the case for woman.

"As customary in these contests, my judgment rests on eloquence alone," Cyrus explained to Targitus. "Pesacas was surprisingly good tonight."

"Ah, might not his eloquence have its source in Argali's presence at table?"

Glancing at his new companion, Cyrus said, "I think you have it."

More than once during the evening Cyrus had expressed privately to Targitus his surprise at the discipline displayed by the Altaians in bringing Argali to him a virgin. "Where did she sleep?" he asked when they were standing away from the rest after the meal had been served.

It was a topic Targitus was happy to discuss. "I shared my yurt with her. As leader, I had to bring her to you untouched. Now, don't think I am immune, particularly from the sight of such beauty, but neither were the others. The yurt could shelter two with space between. I knew I could keep my distance. Of the others, I was less sure."

Targitus could see his story had appealed to Cyrus, perhaps because the Satrap would have found it hard to exercise similar restraint. There was more to tell, but in mid-sentence Cyrus broke off their separate conversation and motioned Targitus to rejoin the group as after-dinner wine, sweetened with honey, was being served.

## 4: SARDIS – 406 B.C.

As he answered the Satrap's question, his mind filled with satisfying images of his nights with Argali in the yurt. The avoidance of contact. The averting of eyes. A surfeit of polite talk. The rewards of discipline. But, then, the uninvited image of Ishkapai pushed Argali aside, re-enacting the scene that had haunted Targitus across the steppes, doggedly following him to Sardis.

Targitus emerged from memory's pain to see Altaian heads beginning to nod. Cyrus had noted them too, a signal that it was time to end the visitors' first night in Sardis. Targitus made a last attempt to get Cyrus to explain what he meant by "a fair hearing."

"I've heard your message. In the days to come I will deal with the request fairly. That's all. Come now, your men are exhausted. To quarters. And a good night's sleep."

Rising, Targitus and his men took their leave of Cyrus and Argali, whose composure, Targitus imagined, concealed a torrent of conflicting thoughts.

In the morning Targitus and his five male companions were moved to quarters near the royal goldworks, an area to the northwest of the Acropolis, just east of the Pactolus River as it flows out of the Tmolus Range toward the Hermus. It was to be their home for the next month. Despite the spirit of that first evening, it was uncertain whether the Satrap would share the city's secrets.

# CHAPTER 5

Sardis – 406 B.C.

Recalling the Satrap's last comment when they parted just a month earlier, Rachel was quick to suspect something unusual when the manager directed her to interrupt a routine project and undertake a purple robe for the Satrap.

The trades people of Sardis claimed many inventions. In the days of Croesus, Sardis had minted the world's first coins. And it had been Sardis, before that, to develop the first dyes for use on white wool yarn. While no one seemed to know exactly how or when this achievement occurred, Sardians had no doubt their city had been first. Yet they had never claimed to have been the first to discover or use purple dye.

Purple was no ordinary color. In the teachings of Moses, it was reserved for the vestments of priests. In the empire, only royalty could afford it. It came from a purple-bearing sea snail. But not in abundance. Each animal yielded only one drop of dye, and then only if collected by smashing its shell right after the catch. Hundreds of these snails were required to tint a single piece of cloth.

From the first time she had heard this story, Rachel had been

## 5: SARDIS – 406 B.C.

curious about the process of extraction and especially the ancients' discovery of the dye, which was no small feat since the color of the drop of dye when taken from the mollusk was not purple but yellowish-white. It took oxidation to turn the royal color.

She had never handled wool dyed purple. Now, with hanks of purple yarn hanging from her loom, she ran the soft wool through her fingers, admiring the shimmering color. Was the discoverer a weaver? Rachel imagined the scene. One evening an Aegean fisherman put a heaping pile of fresh snails on his dining table, where they were cracked open and eaten with lemon juice, an oxidizing agent, by his large family and guests. At each person's place was a spotless white woolen napkin, woven by his wife for special occasions. By the end of this feast some of the napkins had soaked up the juices running freely about the table. To everyone's astonishment, those napkins had turned radiant shades of deep purple. The fisherman's wife deduced the source of that extraordinary color, changing forever the role played by those little mollusks in the cycle of mankind. Their value as a source of food was but a tiny fraction of their value as a dye.

Rachel paired the purple dye mystery with a similar one she had imagined for sheep: the first time a weaver restrained the killing hand of her husband, bent on putting food on the table. Hers would not have been the bleating lamb lover's plea, although Rachel, who had often grown attached to particular sheep in the course of plucking, combing and shearing, knew that argument must often have been made. Rather, this woman would have convinced her husband that the sheep's one-time value as food was overwhelmed by its multi-year value as a source of wool and milk.

She had never seen a sea snail. The need to extract the dye immediately meant that the shells were crushed at collection points along the coasts of the Aegean and the Mediterranean, the dye harvested and then transported to centers of weaving such as Sardis. So valuable was this dye that it served as a favored tithe, "the tithe of purple" exacted by the empire through its satrapies, to honor the gods and perform works of mercy. As far as the average Sardian was concerned, the sea snail's treasure was confined to dying wool yarn to be woven into textiles for the backs of royalty and carpets for the floors and walls of their royal houses.

She was not immune to the feeling of pride, but her suspicion that Cyrus ordered her selection gave her qualms. Wasn't there a select group that Rachel hardly knew who wove all the clothing for the Satrap?

What she hadn't anticipated was the reaction of the weavers to the assignment. Their curiosity upon Rachel's return from the inquest now turned nasty. Whatever uncertainties Rachel might have had, there were no doubts elsewhere in the room concerning the Satrap's involvement or his motives.

One woman's envy could be easily dismissed. But the knowing hum of multitudes? This collective of weavers turned an envious eye toward Rachel, as she sat miserably at her loom. She felt her young, still soft shell punctured by their malice, which was palpable. Defiance and shame washed over her. She wanted desperately to get out of that poisonous place. Pride and Vashti's message held her back. Eyes lowered, she focused on the loom before her and began to warp.

"Vashti, I need to speak with you." Rachel had been waiting for her friend at the bottom of the acropolis. It was early morning. They had half an hour before work began.

"I see you have a lot on your mind," Vashti began, as side by side they commenced the climb.

"I feel like I am sliding down a slick stream with no way to stop."

"Time's on your side. You're young, half the age of most of them. Here's the first thing to understand. They won't hurt you. With your skills you're going to meet envy all the time. You'll become inured to it; pass through it as wind through the tamarisks. Why do you think you were chosen?"

Rachel sighed. "Because I am good. Perhaps the best for the job. Because the Satrap knows I am." Rachel looked for Vashti's support but couldn't read her expression. "Because ... You think he's got

## 5: SARDIS – 406 B.C.

other motives? I know. There are other, more senior, weavers good enough for this. But ..." Her voice grew faint, pleading. "I am trapped."

Vashti didn't respond for some time. Finally, she said, "You have no need now for escape. Much honor awaits you in weaving the purple."


Time eased without erasing the tensions of the workshop. Gradually, Rachel became consumed with the details of the robe, putting aside the smirks and whispers of the women around her. And their envy gradually dissipated, like hot embers at the edge of a fire that cool for lack of stoking.

As she was beginning to weave the purple robe, the master appeared at the door, visitor in tow. He enjoyed showing off the workshop to the Satrap's guests, who were curious to see the source of Sardis' reputation for fine textiles. Normally these visits caused not a ripple in the smooth operation of Rachel's loom. At the sound of the door opening, Rachel took her normal fleeting glance to confirm the presence of a guest.

At the door stood a strangely dressed man with abundant beard and intense eyes that, Rachel noticed, were searching the room, as if to catalog its contents for future use. His deeply tanned face and neck were darker than the sun-bleached hues of his beard and served as pleasing contrast to the shining gold torque around his neck and the bright colored stones sewn into his tunic. He was tall. His easy stance suggested one accustomed to lead.

It took Rachel a moment to realize that this stranger had ceased scanning the room. His eyes had settled on her and there they remained. She returned the gaze and saw in his face an awareness that she had done so deliberately. Like being caught by her mother rummaging through her parents' things. A shiver started at the nape of her neck and descended her spine. It was not unpleasant. And then, after what seemed to Rachel so long an interval that the whole room must have become aware, her silent connection to the stranger ended, as the master ushered his guest out of the room, shutting the door with a gentle click of the latch behind him.

Returning to his sleeping quarters one night just before dusk, Targitus saw a young woman coming towards him, with the determined stride of a horse heading for the stable after a long day's ride. As she approached, he studied her face and eyes, attracted not by their beauty, for he could see there more promise than reality, but by an intensity augmented by her black hair, ivory complexion and resolute gait. He saw too that she noticed him studying her, that it didn't seem to embarrass her, that her expression as she passed was one of textured curiosity. Something twitched in his mind after she had gone, and the image of her approaching him stuck in his head as he cast about for the answer.

Rachel had recognized Targitus immediately. The intensity of his eyes in watching her approach had again summoned pleasant sensations. She quickened her pace as they passed. Had she been willing to look back, as she hurried towards her home, she might have noticed that the stranger was following behind.

On her return home the next evening, Rachel realized she was searching for this man as she approached the goldworks and was disappointed not to find him there. It was with a shocked blush that she discovered in her parents' sitting room the very same man, engaged in animated dialogue with Benjamin over a pot of strong herbal tea. Sarah sat beside her husband, listening. Rachel's younger brother, Jacob, was just outside the circle of conversation, playing on the floor.

Introductions followed. Targitus acknowledged having seen Rachel in the palace workroom; Rachel admitted having noticed him at the door. Benjamin explained to Rachel the purpose of the Altaian's mission, which he had just learned about from their guest. On finishing the story, Benjamin said, "The mission's success remains uncertain. Cyrus has still not given approval."

Rachel looked inquiringly at Targitus.

"That's right. So far he's been non-committal, even though we've been here, beside the goldworks, for more than two weeks."

Conversation veered away from the Satrap to the Massagetae, the stranger's distant lands in the Altai Mountains and some of what lay between their home and Sardis. Finishing his tea, Targitus excused himself, saying he had to rejoin his followers for supper. They rose,

## 5: SARDIS – 406 B.C.

walking Targitus to the door. Benjamin summoned Sarah to say goodbye. He took one of their hands in both of his and bowed, an Altaian custom, thanking them for being so gracious and friendly.

"You must visit us again; come whenever you have time," Sarah said.

"I will do that," he said, holding Rachel's hand longer than the others, long enough to make her self-conscious. His parting look expressed a curiosity unsatisfied. She worried that her parents had noticed.

After he had gone, Benjamin expressed doubt that the Satrap would share the City's secrets with the Altaians. "Why should he?"

Sarah reminded her husband of the valuable gifts the Altaian had given to Cyrus.

"Didn't say what they were, did he. Doesn't matter. The Satrap receives gifts every day. Bribes, actually. They don't work. I can't imagine any gift these Altaians could provide that would be valuable enough to move him."

"How did he happen to be having tea with you today?" Rachel asked.

"It was quite peculiar," Benjamin replied. "He came up to me as I was leaving the house this morning. Described himself and his mission. I saw immediately that he was a prince. That's what made it peculiar when he called himself a temporary 'neighbor' who wanted to get to know the neighborhood. I invited him to take some tea with me later in the day. It seemed the right thing to do. I felt he wanted to be invited."

Listening intently, Rachel kept her thoughts private.


The next week Targitus returned to find only Sarah at home.

"I shouldn't see you without Benjamin. But …" She hesitated. Targitus saw her confusion and turned to go, saying, "I'll come again."

"No. You're from another land. And we are welcoming people. Come in. I'll brew some tea. Benjamin took Jacob on a trip up north. They won't be back for hours, but Rachel will be home soon."

"I am curious to learn something about how your family came to be in Sardis. Some family history. When was Rachel born? And

Jacob? How long have you lived here?"

They were sitting across a low table on which their cups of tea were placed. A soft breeze cooled the room. As Sarah began, Targitus divided his attention, one half devoted to Sarah's story, the other to recalling his first impressions of Rachel, recorded as she had sat across from him the week before, just where Sarah was seated now. Listening to Sarah, he saw Rachel. At seventeen, a work in progress. He credited himself with the discerning eye necessary to imagine her at twenty-one.

"We met in Babylon. We were part of a close-knit Jewish community. All of us were descendents of Judeans taken to Babylon after Nebuchadnezzar destroyed Jerusalem. We married in Babylon eighteen years ago and came here. Sardis had a big reputation for gold refining. Benjamin, you know, is a goldsmith. He was attracted to this city."

"Was Rachel born here?" Targitus asked, trying to sound matter-of-fact.

"Yes, a year after we settled. Then, after a nine-year gap, Jacob was born. We were blessed."

Targitus had finished his tea. Sarah was filling his cup when he asked, "Has Rachel always loved weaving?"

Just then Rachel entered the room. Surprise crossed her face as she recognized the visitor, who had gotten to his feet.

"Oh, my, yes," Sarah responded before addressing her daughter. "Our friend's returned. He's interested in family history," Sarah said. "I've told him why we settled here. But I am afraid that's going to be all for this afternoon, because it's gotten late; you and I must prepare dinner."

Targitus looked slightly disappointed. "Of course. And I must be going. Again, my thanks for putting up with my questions."

Rachel felt a strange sadness. Her mother's parting invitation to visit the family again did little to erase the empty feeling.

The pain began a few days later. It began as an ache in one of his molars, too dull to pick out the exact tooth. Through the day the pain gradually sharpened. Targitus' idea of leadership was never to com-

## 5: SARDIS – 406 B.C.

plain. Forced to admit to a toothache worse than any he had experienced, he told himself it would pass with the night. And he willed it so.

Sleeplessly, he waited. At dawn the constant ache was coupled with pounding throbs. In his Altaian village, long before sunrise, a shaman would have addressed the pain. I am quite helpless here, Targitus thought, mentally checking off those, like Cyrus, Artapathes, Mitradates and his Altaian band, to whom pride sealed off access. Rachel's family stood out on his very short list of those to whom he would allow himself to go for help. He resolved to arrive at their house just before Rachel would have left for the palace workshop.

Rachel was about to open the door when a loud knock announced an early visitor. Before she could respond, the visitor spoke: "It's Targitus, your Altaian friend."

Rachel stood still, invested with swirls of excitement. Recovering, she threw open the door, which struck Targitus a glancing blow to the head.

"Oh! I am sorry," Rachel cried. Targitus doubled over, hands to his forehead. "Look, I've hurt you!" Redness marked the point of contact, which had begun to swell.

"Perhaps I should have let it hit me harder," Targitus replied, laughing. "I've come with an unbearable toothache. Your door could only lessen the pain. I hoped you might know someone who could treat me."

"Don't you mean 'someone else?' I am so sorry!"

Rachel was joined at the door by Benjamin and Sarah.

"I can see you're in pain, and exhausted too," said Sarah. "Of course, we know just the man, Ezekiel. He's an apothecary. He's helped us before. I'll lead you to him."

"Mother, I'll come with you. It's on my route."

As they walked together in the gathering warmth of morning, Sarah and Rachel told Targitus of their own experience with Ezekiel.

"It was the day I turned thirteen. The pain grew unbearable, like yours. Dull at first, then sharpening. It radiated out from a single tooth, which began to throb. Recognize the condition?"

"Fits like a glove. Your story distracts me. Go on, please."

"Father was the first to offer relief. Toothaches, he claimed, were linked to Yahweh, who could bring them on as well as take them away. He had a friend who knew an ancient incantation. It was specially designed to bring relief through an appeal to God. Supposedly the incantation never failed when used by one of faith. Father said he had tried it himself once and it had worked. He insisted I use it, and nothing else, three times daily until the ache disappeared.

"I mouthed the incantation, afraid my faith would be inadequate. The ache in my tooth worsened. I moved through thresholds of increasing pain. I was amazed each time the outer limit of what I thought I could endure enlarged. A second time I recited the words. The pain continued."

Sarah picked up the story. "With Rachel in tow, I left the house in search of the apothecary I had heard of from friends. They said he knew something about the treatment of pain, particularly the commonplace types that accompany childbirth and toothache. We found him and in no time he had cured her. As he will you. Here we are."

Knocking on the closed door, Sarah looked relieved when it opened to reveal a white-bearded man, of craggy face and bowed figure.

"Sarah, and Rachel. How good to see you. You've brought a friend. Please, all of you, come in."

"No, we can't. I must return home. Bread's in the oven. And Rachel's on her way to the palace." Introducing Targitus, Sarah explained his problem and asked for Ezekiel's help.

"Of course. I understand. Now off with you before the bread burns."

With a wave to the men and a kiss to Rachel, Sarah hurried away.

Bidding Rachel a good day in the workshop, Ezekiel ushered Targitus into his house and shut the door. Rachel looked up at the acropolis, hesitated for a time and then, with a reassuring glance in the direction her mother had gone, opened the door and ducked back in.

Targitus had noted the man's sly expression, thinking it not unfriendly. The complex smells that assaulted him upon entering Ezekiel's abode would have taken a large catalog to describe. Unmis-

## 5: SARDIS − 406 B.C.

takable was the musty smell of stale air infused with fennel, frankincense and thyme. They stood, looking beyond Ezekiel into a large room filled with all manner of beakers, vessels and vials set on tables, chairs, shelves and even the floor. Suspended on twine stretched the length of the room, just above head level, were countless cuttings of herbs and other flora. A furnace filled one corner of the room, bags of powders and other supplies occupied the other three corners. Several oil lamps augmented the meager supply of natural light from a small north-facing window. There seemed no chance of movement in this disorderly space without causing breakage. And yet, Ezekiel said, "Please come further in," and turning, fished out of the debris a three-legged stool for Targitus, which he was reluctant to use until the apothecary's gesturing with both hands, in repeated sweeps from door to stool, grew too insistent to refuse.

Targitus rose as Rachel appeared, momentarily back lighted when the door opened to admit her.

"I have some time to spare." Neither man showed surprise.

The smells continued to assert themselves. In addition to the herbal odors, Targitus now detected floral and chemical scents, burning acacia in the furnace and burning flax and sesame oils in the lamps, all seasoned with the bodily smells of an apothecary too distracted to bathe.

"Young man, did you fall in your haste to find me? That lump on your forehead grows by the minute."

"Not at all. Just a backfire, to quell the major blaze."

"I see. I like that. Now, you're seeking my help. But first, I must ask you, a stranger to Sardis, can you trust me?"

"If Rachel does, I do too. I understand you eased the pain in her tooth after incantations to Yahweh had failed. Yet, you are a devout Jew, Rachel tells me. Weren't you afraid of crossing God's will?"

Ezekiel's face brightened with a broad smile. He rubbed his hands together, then moved closer to Targitus, so that hardly a hand's width separated them.

"People like me are experimenters. We work with our hands, our eyes, our ears, our nose. And our brains. Things we can touch, see, hear and smell, these we can think about and come to understand. Toothaches are common, like colds. They come to people of all faiths. I can't prevent them, but I can treat the ache. I use an herbal medicine, the clove, which around here a clever few, like Sarah, also use in cooking."

Reaching a small ceramic vessel on a shelf near the window, Ezekiel poured forth a number of cloves, handed them to Targitus and advised him to place them, one at a time, directly over the aching tooth, keeping it in place with his tongue until the clove's oil was exhausted.

"How will I know?"

"When the pain resumes, of course," Rachel interjected, laughing.

Taking the remedy in hand, Targitus said, "But what about Yahweh?"

"He has his realm; I have mine. There need be no conflict. What we apothecaries can not understand belongs to Yahweh. What we comprehend belongs to us, and I believe Yahweh must agree; otherwise, why would we be allowed our discoveries? If a clove works on the ache in a tooth, use it. You don't offend our God by being practical. As for your gods, I know nothing. Go on, now, try the clove."

Targitus slipped the first clove under his tongue, pressing it against the offending tooth. The first hint of relief was swift.

"We know nothing of cloves in the Altai. Where do they come from?"

"The myrtle tree that grows far to the south. Dried flower buds. They travel the Royal Road, as do many other wondrous things. Rachel knows. I am sure she would be happy to supply you with cloves to take home. You must, for your climate is too severe to grow the tree."

"What other wondrous things, Ezekiel?" Rachel asked. "Show our visitor something else."

Turning toward a dark corner, Ezekiel rummaged around until his hand closed on a small vial. Removing the stopper, he invited Rachel and Targitus to smell the oil within. Heads together, they caught a sweet powerful odor at the same instant.

"It's strong and pleasing," Targitus pronounced. "And entirely new to my nose. Do you know it?"

"Oh, yes. It's terebinth, a cooking oil squeezed from pistachio nuts. Mother often uses it to flavor bread."

Ezekiel declared the vial a gift, insisting that Targitus take it home with him.

"What do I owe you, Ezekiel, for what my tooth tells me will soon be a cure?"

The apothecary took two steps back, so that he might speak directly to them both. "Consider this Sardian service to a stranger. An act of 'hesed' to use the Hebrew. You may pay me nothing. Nothing, except kindness to Rachel, who I see even in this dim light brightens at the sight of you, recovering."

Rachel hoped the shadows of Ezekiel's room hid her blush, which had passed by the time they reached the street.

"I must go now, quickly. They don't like lateness. Remember to change cloves."

He took her hand and bowed. Their eyes met for only an instant. Enough for Rachel to imagine a tight embrace. Turning to face the formidable height on which her workplace citadel stood, she set off.

She didn't look back. Rehearsing her parting reminder made her blush again, this time over the inanity of her words.

# CHAPTER 6

Sardis – 406 B.C.

Completion was sweet. Rachel folded the purple robe with care and delivered it to the master. She was pleased with her work. Exuberant. For an instant she toyed with the idea of assuring the master that it contained not a single letter from her name. Experience erased the instinct for play. The master had no weakness for humor.

Later that day the master appeared before Rachel's loom, where she sat still as a stone, resting from her exertions. Returning the robe, still carefully folded, he said: "You are to deliver it in person. The guard at the door will accompany you." Before his knowing smile could form itself, she lowered her eyes, embraced the robe and walked toward the waiting guard, who followed closely behind as she exited the room.

Recalling virtually every step of the way, she needed no guard to lead, and indeed, this guard chose to follow, presumably the better to keep her in sight and within reach. The abruptness of her departure had left no time to deliberate or confer with Vashti.

Entering the Satrap's greeting room, she knew, once again, she was on her own.

## 6: SARDIS – 406 B.C.

"You've come at last. Let me see!"

Gently he took the robe from her, and as gently laid it across the table where they had sipped tea and eaten Lydian blood figs together just three months before. Rachel watched him inspect the robe, his eyes and hands functioning smoothly together to evaluate the work. Bringing his eyes within a couple of inches of the cloth, she knew he was reckoning the wefts per inch of warp. He gauged the fineness of the wool. Pointing, he noted Rachel's placement of the varying shades of purple yarn that inevitably result from multiple dye lots. These subtle variations of color, or abrash as the effect was known, were always a challenge to the weaver, affording scope for artistic expression in deciding whether and how to impose choice.

The purple color seemed to enthrall Cyrus. To say the robe was purple was like describing the forest as green. At points it shone, returning light to the observer's eye in a blaze of purple, like the audacious purple in pansies, straight and fresh against the pastels of a spring morning. At other angles, the purple seemed to capture light, absorbing it to add depth and intensity to the color, like the fall-blooming aconitum. Or, seen from another position, the robe conjured in the mind's eye clumps of bright flag iris, thin and tall, irrepressible in a summer zephyr. Rachel beamed as Cyrus examined her craft.

Cyrus was a man given to detail. Very little escaped his glance. He had a reputation for noticing the little things about the manners and dress of those about him. He was known to give similar attention to his own dress. This robe was the first all purple garment the Satrap had ever commissioned. Cyrus bent low over the inspecting table and, lifting the robe high, swung it in counterpoint to his body to fall with a swish about his shoulders.

Rachel uttered a tiny sigh as the robe worked its magic, imprinting on the Satrap the signature of royalty. "Oh, Your Majesty, how well it becomes you!"

Cyrus extended his arms to Rachel. Drawn in with no time for reflection or fear, Rachel accepted the embrace, which lasted a moment longer than could be justified by enthusiasm alone. Long enough for Rachel to feel his body along the full length of hers. Like rebirth as an adult. Breaking away, she felt a blush pass across her face and gather in force at the tips of her ears. Fearing Cyrus might notice, she turned away, a move that only served to expose further her tingling ears. Searching for something to say or do, she shifted her weight from one leg to the other, her back to the Satrap.

Finally, Cyrus said, "Come, its past mid-day; you must be hungry! Have something to eat with me." Summoning Artapathes with a small gold bell, he directed that a meal for two be served.

It was August. The harvest of fruits and vegetables was at its peak. Before them on the table, again covered with an exquisite weaving from the palace workshop, Artapathes laid out fresh bread infused with rosemary, sheep's cheese and chestnut blossom honey, olives marinated in oil flavored with onions, oregano and marjoram, bunches of fresh grapes, peaches and apples, quince and pears, raisins and almonds, and a couple of small melons, neatly sliced in eighths to show off their deep orange ripeness and ease their consumption hand to mouth.

The wine came last. Artapathes set before them a neck amphora, beautifully shaped in harmonious curves from the flanged lip to the opposing handles, from the body of the vessel to the taper descending to the pedestal on which it securely rested. The odor of red wine escaped from the amphora to mingle with those of herb, fruit and spice. Gracing the face of the amphora was an imaginative painting of satyrs treading grapes in a portable winepress under vines heavily laden with grapes.

Two gold cups, with upward curving arms for sipping, came next. Placing them neatly beside the amphora, Artapathes then turned to the north wall, where a silver rhyton in the shape of a lion-headed horse rested. Before he could bring it to the table, Cyrus waved him off.

Rachel caught the exchange between the men. She knew something about rhytons, although until that moment she had never seen one. She knew they were hallmarks of the upper class and strongly associated with banquets. The concubines had described these all-male drinking parties to Rachel. She knew they included only women whose profession it was to entertain the male guests with their various talents: rhapsodist and harp-singers, flautists and

## 6: SARDIS – 406 B.C.

dancers, performing, reciting, engaging in intellectual conversation and, not least, making love.

Rachel wished to examine the vessel on the wall, but thought it better not to ask, given that Cyrus might misconstrue her artist's interest for something else. She could see it was shaped like a curved horn, with the entire forepart of the fantastic horse at its base. Barely visible was the small perforation between the animal's front legs that allowed wine to flow in a thin stream.

Cyrus said, "It's my favorite. This rhyton's been passed down in my family for generations." Rising, he motioned Rachel to where it hung for a closer look.

"It was made by a great craftsman." Looking down at his robe, his fingers caressing its softness, Cyrus added, "One like you. Your skill at the loom is beyond talent. An exquisite gift that you use to full advantage."

Blushing with pleasure, Rachel fidgeted, eyes safely focused on the Satrap's sandals.

Returning to their seats, Rachel filled her plate while Cyrus poured the wine. To reassure her, he mentioned it had been diluted in the customary ratio of three parts water to one part wine. "There's the pitcher if you want more." Rachel felt a flush. Lifting her cup, she tasted the wine, rolling it around her mouth, brow knitted, as she had seen her father do a thousand times. "Perfect," she announced. As they ate, she sought some way to distract him from a quest that now was becoming plain. By directing the conversation, she might erect a shield. Targitus? His mission had touched her deeply. Hadn't this Altaian traveled for almost four months to discover a secret with no certain prospect that its possessor would be willing to share? His plight tugged at her heart. Here was a chance to plead his case while, at the same time, diverting Cyrus' attention. Or would the subject annoy? Unsure and afraid, she decided to defer.

She tried a question about Darius, Cyrus' father, the Persian King who had appointed him Satrap. He answered at some length. She then asked him to tell her about his mother, Parysatis, whose mysterious power within the family was at the root of many rumors circulating in Sardis. Again, Cyrus spoke at length and with great warmth.

She then asked about his older brother, Artaxerxes, having heard it said among the gossip mongers in the workshop that this man's sole advantage over Cyrus was age. The Satrap shied away, giving only a perfunctory description of his brother. Rachel thought she detected some competitiveness, hardly surprising given the education he would have experienced with his brother and the sons of noble Persians at the King's court, where comparative measurements were taken daily in all manner of human endeavor from the bow and javelin to the horse, from history and language to matters of discretion and self-control.

Having covered the subject of family without difficulty, Rachel grew bolder. "Your Majesty, tell me what you most enjoyed growing up?" Much to her surprise, she noticed that her wine cup was empty.

"I was consumed by hunting. We would go off on horses, for days at a time, in search of prey. The possibility of danger was new, and to me, thrilling. I never returned from the hunt without hoping, even plotting, to go out again as soon as possible."

Rachel thought this connection was promising. She had heard palace gossip about the Satrap's love for tales about hunting, particularly his own. "Was it ever really dangerous?" she asked, as Cyrus poured dark red wine into their cups.

"Once, we had ridden far into the bush, with dogs, following what seemed a stale scent. The dogs were moving slowly, often separating from one another to sniff out different routes, a good sign the scent was old or uncertain.

Suddenly, the dogs picked up speed, dashing up a long draw that rose toward foothills. I spurred my horse ahead of the others, trying to stay close to the dogs, now in full pursuit of something. I wanted to be first. The draw narrowed, making it hard for my horse to keep up. Rounding a turn I saw the dogs and a large bear. Barking wildly, the dogs had formed an arc in front of the animal. Behind the bear, a cliff made escape difficult.

I approached the bear. It held its ground as I raised my javelin for an easy kill. Just as I released the shaft, one of the dogs lunged at the bear, which moved to bat the dog away with its paw. Instead of a clean hit, the javelin grazed the bear's flank, causing shock and pain.

## 6: SARDIS – 406 B.C.

He charged, hitting my horse before it could turn or brace itself. Down we went. The bear mauled the horse and then turned on me. I had just enough time to draw my sword. As we engaged, I was able to get the sword in front of me. The weight of the bear's attack caused the sword to pass through its body as it knocked me down. In the throes of death, the bear thrashed and its claws ripped my left arm before it came entirely to rest on top of me. I could barely breathe, not only because of the dead animal's weight, but because my sword's hilt was bearing into my chest even as I noticed the glint of the blade emerging from his back. Lucky for me, a companion had arrived on the scene. Dismounting, he began to bully the bear off. It was not easy going, but finally, with the help of my squirming, he succeeded in separating the killer from the killed."

Looking at his left arm, which was partly covered, Rachel could make out some nasty looking scars. Cyrus pulled up his shirt sleeve, revealing the full extent of this old injury. Rachel had seen knife and sword wounds before. In a crowded city, arguments were often settled at the point of a well-sharpened bronze or iron blade, and the resulting wounds were commonplace. Properly dressed, they would heal neatly. The wound from a bear claw was different. More gouge than cut, the V-shaped wound could not be closed by stitch or bandage. It had to heal more slowly from the bottom up, prolonging the obvious risks of infection. This difficult path to recovery was written all over Cyrus' left arm, where scar tissue, still pink to dark red, had awkwardly filled the gaps in flesh.

"Oh," she exclaimed.

"They still look bad, don't they. But fully healed, with no effects except some loss of feeling. Here, rub your finger along this big one, and see if I can feel it." He took up his wine cup and deftly moved around the table separating their couches, seating himself close beside her so that she could touch his arm without a stretch. As her fingers moved along the spine of his wound, they traced in her mind the path of his blood and pain.

For Rachel, whether or not he could feel the touch of her fingers was not the point. Starting at her finger tips, warmth radiated through her body. She couldn't have restrained it, and had no wish to do so. Removing her fingers from the arm did not remove the warmth that now embraced her from the inside out. "Could you feel that?" she finally asked.

"Yes, but barely, with a tingle that's slightly unpleasant."

Cyrus rang the bell, summoning Artapathes to remove the food, for they had finished the meal. "Leave the wine."

Cyrus looked content. The food was gone, the door was closed behind Artapathes and there was no apparent need to call on him again. Pouring more wine into Rachel's cup and his own, Cyrus said, "Have you seen my garden? You pass it on your way to the workshop."

"Every morning. I'd like to talk about that, but let me ask something else first. Your visitors from the Altai are staying near our home. My parents and I served tea to their leader. We helped him treat a bad toothache. I'd never met a Massagetae before. He's interesting."

"Did he tell you what he's doing here?"

"He said you had not yet decided to share the secret. I hope you will. Altaian gold, even purified, is no threat to us. It would be cruel to send him back empty-handed. I am sure you're not that sort of man."

Rachel had never asked the Satrap for anything. Until now, with this impulsive outburst. Seeing consternation in Cyrus' face, she realized he might be unhappy about her interest in Targitus and the Altaian mission, so much so that her entreaties might make him less, rather than more, willing. It was too late to back off from what she now realized might appear to Cyrus a sudden obsession.

Silence ensued. Rachel felt awkward, then alarmed as she watched the nervous movement of his eyes, the biting of his lower lip. Rising, Cyrus turned his back to Rachel and moved a step or two away. He seemed to be staring at the rhyton, lost in thought. Finally, turning again, his face was composed. He spoke as a smile slowly formed.

"You're a puzzle. I've heard you. But I want something in return. To begin with, a promise. Don't speak about those Altaians again."

Rachel felt relieved. She promised, raising her right hand, palm open, for emphasis. Quickly he extended his own, grasping hers firmly and holding it as he asked, "What were you saying about my garden?" as if the subject of Targitus had never come up.

# 6: SARDIS — 406 B.C.

She described her daily visits with his plantsmen. Her knowledge of the plant world was not equal to his, but her questions displayed an inquisitive and practical mind well versed in the details of his design.

"Your plantings require a lot of water. Isn't that a problem on the top of this mountain?" Rachel inquired.

"It's just a matter of labor. You know, I brought up huge amounts of top soil from the rich fields below and piles of humus collected under the chestnut forests. And, if you dug down in the soil that I placed in the garden, you would discover masses of worms that we collected to enhance the soil. The worms are still there, and multiplying. I daresay there wasn't a single worm on this site until I brought them for the garden."

Rachel hoped Cyrus' obvious pride in his garden would distract him from what she now knew for certain was his original purpose in summoning her. As long as she kept asking him questions about the garden, his pleasure in answering would delay the moment for altering their relationship. After all, she reasoned, if he sent her back to the bath, he'd have no one to talk gardening with. Their one-sided conversation had kept him fenced in. But, sitting beside him, she could sense eagerness, a search for the right moment to engage with her on a different plane. She imagined him functioning simultaneously on two very different levels, one intellectual, the other, sensual. Or was that her own state of ambivalence and confusion?

Cyrus had risen from the seat, taking Rachel's hand to bring her to a standing position beside him. "Look at me," he said.

As she turned to face him, Cyrus took her face firmly in his hands. Gently he drew her towards him. They embraced, mouth to mouth, nose to nose, tongue to tongue, for longer than Rachel had imagined a kiss could last. Her arms sought his body, enclosing it at the waist and holding on until he dropped his hands from her face. Contact with this prince, the taste and smell of him, left her speechless.

Cyrus said, "The bath awaits you."

Rachel saw the dilemma. The bath, with risks and rewards to follow. Or escape. With muddled feelings, she relied, again, on instinct.

As Cyrus sought her lips a second time, Rachel spoke quickly.

"About your garden. I wanted to mention the herbs. You know, in the triangular beds. I recognized many of them: marjoram, oregano, rosemary, basil. They're doing well. Did I miss any? And the low cut lavender, edging around the herbs. Lovely."

Pausing but a second for breath, she continued. "This morning the plantsmen were putting tulip bulbs in the ground. Tulips are rare. I've never even held one in my hand. You have so many. I was surprised by the way they were placing them in the holes, pointed end down. I would have guessed that end would be aimed at the sky."

Agitated, Cyrus extended his arm and index finger, accusingly, at Rachel. "Are you sure? Were you close enough to really see?"

She assured him she had been only inches away from the bulbs.

With an abrupt turn, Cyrus took leave of Rachel, shouting as he left that he would try to return quickly, then adding "You needn't wait." In an instant, he had rushed out of the room and was gone. Alone, Rachel felt relief and disappointment. They couldn't be disentangled. Like the white and yoke of an egg after beating. She knew precisely the prospect that had prompted these feelings, something as dangerous as it was imprecise, something that would not happen right now, having been ambushed by tulip bulbs.

She rose to leave. Her gold cup still held wine. Walking quickly to the north wall, she took down the silver rhyton, returned to the table and poured the cup's contents into the open horn of the curved vessel. She then raised the rhyton with both hands above her head. Tipping the vessel, she directed the thin stream of wine into her mouth.

# CHAPTER 7

Sardis – 406 B.C.

Targitus had been summoned by the Satrap. A palace guard seemed to be expecting him. He led Targitus into a small anteroom near the front of the palace and indicated he was to sit on one of the marble benches drawn up on opposite sides of a matching marble table. Expecting the Satrap's imminent arrival, at first Targitus paid his surroundings scant attention. Long minutes passed. Finally, to escape impatience, he began to survey the room.

The plainness of its furniture stood in contrast to the four walls, ceiling and floor, which were covered in tiles of different painted designs, geometric, floral and figural, motifs of intricacy and balance. One wall depicted three figural scenes separated by blank squares in white. One showed a god fighting a minotaur, his sword plunged into the minotaur's stomach, his left hand grasping the animal's horn. Another depicted a goddess wearing a bright red dress. She had black wig-like hair, wings joined at the shoulders and in each hand the tail of a white panther with red spots. The third was of a striding archer, bearded, with pointed cap and short kilt, a quiver on his back, all in reds and blacks.

The opposite wall contained birds and animals, hen and chick compositions, pegasoi confronting one another, griffins in the same configuration and a powerful chariot scene. There was a harnessed horse with fringed mane and a white dog with black spots running alongside the swift moving chariot.

Targitus didn't notice Cyrus' presence until he spoke. The Satrap wore a white tunic partially shrouded by a robe of royal purple.

"A pleasant meeting room, don't you agree?" Cyrus said, as he seated himself across the table from Targitus. A servant placed a pitcher of red wine, two ceramic cups and a bowl of olives on the table.

"You might not recognize its shape."

Targitus caught a condescending tone.

"It's the golden mean." Eyes fixed on Targitus, the Satrap paused a few moments. "I see you're perplexed. The golden mean is a divine proportion derived from the curve of the chambered nautilus. It expresses nature's perfection. May I pour you some wine?"

Targitus nodded, wondering what the Satrap meant. Taking the offered cup, he lifted it to his lips and tasted the dark red liquid, which emitted the smell of crushed peaches.

"This room is ..."

Cyrus cut him off. "Let me come directly to the point."

Targitus couldn't read the Satrap.

"I am told you've been paying attention to one of my weavers."

Targitus was nonplussed. What could Rachel possibly mean to this prince. Responding in a matter-of-fact voice, he said, "You must mean Rachel. She lives close to our quarters. Her parents have twice invited me to their house. We talked chiefly of Sardis. They speak most favorably of your rule. They've been friendly and gracious."

Targitus took another sip of wine and reached for an olive. There was no place for the pit. Palming it, he said, "I hoped you had summoned me to discuss our petition."

Cyrus continued to stare. Finally, he said, "I am prepared to grant your request, on one condition." Cyrus hadn't touched his wine.

"Don't see Rachel again. If you do, your mission is over."

Cyrus held his cup over the table, arm outstretched, challenging Targitus to do the same. Targitus didn't know whether he cared. Their

## 7: SARDIS – 406 B.C.

cups touched and they drank before he could decipher his feelings.

"I promise," Targitus said. The Satrap's urgency seemed to be generating a sense of loss that wasn't there just minutes earlier.

Cyrus rose.

"You may enter the goldworks tomorrow." Turning abruptly, he left the room.


It took but a few minutes with Mitradates, head of the operation, and his fellow workers for the Altaians to realize that, despite the lofty process of purification carried on in this place, the all-male enclave was a den of bawdy chatter from morning till dusk. Like it or not, the Altaians would receive a continuous education in Sardian-style debauchery. To digest it, however, they needed the help of the translator assigned to them by the Satrap, for the language of this class of Sardian was hard even for Targitus to understand.

Targitus knew that, by inventing the gold purification process, Sardians had become rich. It took him a while to appreciate that, with wealth came leisure and the pastimes it supports, eating, drinking and carnal delights, all of which had grown to excess under Persian rule. Of course, the goldworkers had no time for leisurely indulgence. They took pleasure in vicarious pursuit of Sardian hedonism. Compared to the Altai, he thought, Sardis was a more layered society but not necessarily better for its complexity. Altaian pleasures were simpler and enjoyed directly or not at all.

Seated on a large overturned ceramic vase, the immensity of Mitradates' partially covered body stood out. Layers of fat covered well-exercised muscles. Deep rivulets of sweat, a natural condition for this hirsute captain of the goldworks, sprayed out from the mop-like surface of his gigantic head whenever he moved. Mitradates spoke as much with his hands and torso as with his voice. Turning to face Targitus, Mitradates asked "Why purify gold? It's easier to part a lioness from her virginity than to part gold from silver."

Targitus stood in the hot sun a few feet from this parked leviathan, guessing the vase must serve as a kind of throne for him and wondering at the mechanics by which he had turned his head some ninety degrees with no visible help from a neck.

"I must take your word for that, my friend," replied Targitus, laughing, "for I've no experience with either. Our purpose is precisely the same as those Lydians who broke the code long ago: to make coins."

"I take it you already know the cupellation process," Mitradates said.

Targitus nodded. "We learned our process from westerners. We melt lead with impure gold. The lead forms a mass with the base metals. The noble ones are left behind. Is that the way you do it?"

"About the same," replied Mitradates. "We heat the mixture till its very hot, using a blast of air blown into the furnace through a long clay pipe. Sometimes we put a goat's bladder on the end as a bellows. You must know how poisonous the lead fumes are. Without good ventilation, a real killer.

"I told Artapathes, more than once I told him, let young Cyrus know we have the means, here, to put someone away without a trace, no marks on the body."

"Does the Satrap have a need?" Targitus said.

"He's got no wife and too many concubines. Took over the glutted harem of Tissaphernes, a man of grand desires and limited tastes. The Satrap's a plantsman. Knows the value of pruning." Mitradates looked pleased with himself.

"Has he taken you up on the offer?" Targitus asked, as he connected this idle banter with Argali, now ensconced among the Satrap's concubines. By all reports, she had become an immediate favorite. That made sense, Targitus thought, given the Satrap's grant of access. Should he question Mitradates about Argali? It was tempting to try, but unlikely to be helpful, and possibly dangerous. And, anyway, this chatter was nothing more than the carefree associations of a buffoon, a knowledgeable one whose expertise Targitus had traveled far to get, but a buffoon, nonetheless.

Mitradates continued the lecture. "Now, let's talk about cementation. That's what you came here for. And, I am going to teach you. I heard from Artapathes that none of your band can write. Neither can I, but that's not the point because I've spent my life here. How

## 7: SARDIS – 406 B.C.

will you retain all I teach you? This is not like remembering someone's name. Or remembering how to relieve yourself, front or back, or satisfy that ache in your groin. It's complicated."

"You make a good point. But don't worry. All we need is to be shown how."

In the weeks that followed, the Altaians were taught the ways of parting gold from silver. The lessons were practical, hands on, never abstract or theoretical. They learned what worked and what didn't. Underlying principles were of no interest to Mitradates and his crew. In their hands, as in the hands of the gold refiners who had preceded them in pioneering the process, cementation was more art than science.

What did Targitus and his band learn? That the parting process demanded high levels of human skill and patience applied for prolonged periods of time under trying physical conditions. The furnace of iron-rich clays, in which parting vessels were placed, had to be maintained within a tight, moderately hot, temperature range for up to five days and nights. If allowed to become too hot, the mixture of reactants would vitrify, slowing the reaction down and preventing extraction of the gold. If not hot enough, the silver wouldn't part from the gold. The correct temperature was well below the melting point of gold and just below the melting point of common salt. With these two yardsticks, and an eye trained to detect the particular reddish hue of the parting vessels when the temperature was right, a furnace tender could hold that temperature as long as the wood supply lasted.

With a wave of his vast arm, Mitradates summoned one of his minions to turn before Targitus and show his back. There were dark red lines crisscrossing from shoulders to waist, the unmistakable remnant of the lash.

"Fell asleep on the job. Only once though. Cementation is a complicated process, demanding on my boys. The way I get results couldn't be simpler."

Targitus was far away, at the edge of the Bashkaus River. Staring at the man's back, Targitus winced, realizing as he did so that Mitradates was watching.

Cementation required quantities of slow-burning wood. This meant hardwood, some deciduous variety readily at hand. Acacia was the wood of choice. The Altaians would have to use something different. Perhaps birch.

The work of separating silver from gold was done in a parting vessel, just an ordinary rounded coarseware cooking pot with wide flanged opening and lid for sealing. The material to be refined was placed in layers in this pot. It might be grains of gold, electrum coins, gold foil or recycled jewelry. The impure gold was surrounded by two thoroughly mixed ingredients known as the cement: the reactant, common salt, and an inert carrier, brick dust. The greater the exposure of the impure gold to the reactant, the more effective the parting.

As the days passed, Targitus and his band began to comprehend the process. It was hard going. As with many forms of expression, much can be learned by watching the artist at work. And except when the translator was present, that was all they could do.

As Mitradates described it, the concept for cementation was relatively simple: to deliver to the reactant a continuous flow of hot air laden with moisture and to take from the gold the silver chloride resulting from the combination of chloride from the salt and silver from the gold. The porosity of a clay cooking pot made it an ideal vessel for this exchange. The volatile silver chloride would vaporize to be absorbed by the brick dust and the walls of the parting vessel. The gold was typically recovered by washing the vessel's altered contents in water. The purified silver was released later by first smelting the brick dust and parting vessel shards with lead to absorb the silver salts, and then oxidizing the lead and other impurities through a continuous blast of hot air.

Mitradates was curious to see the gold of the Altai in its natural state. He wanted to check its color and other qualities against gold from the Pactolus. Targitus had brought a small sample and one day, after their second week together, the men made a comparison.

"Different color," said Mitradates, stating the obvious. "Our gold comes with a lot of silver. We don't know why silver grows with the gold. Looks like your gold has less silver. It's darker."

Targitus was puzzled. "Are you sure metals grow in the ground?

## 7: SARDIS – 406 B.C.

Your idea is new to me. But it makes sense. I've seen rocks push their way up and out of the ground. Do you think they're growing? I wonder if there's something we can add to the ground to make them grow more rapidly? But rock in the mountains, what we call bedrock, never moves or seems to get larger."

"I don't mean rocks, I mean metal in rocks. It's the metal that grows in rocks just the way barley grows in ground. And as for what makes them grow, it's Gods like Cybele who cause these things to happen. That's what my wife says. That's what the priests at Cybele's altar tell her. It takes more than logic, because barley comes from seeds we plant in the ground, and I've never seen a seed grow iron, copper or gold. But my wife says that's the point. There's no earthly seed for metal, so it must grow by God's hand."

Targitus pondered these notions but came to no conclusion. This didn't bother him. He had lived long enough to believe that little about the world could be understood.

The Altaians needed more than close observation to understand why two of the workers, who seemed senior in both age and status, would go from furnace to furnace at intervals throughout the day and night with stones roughly four inches by two, on which they scraped a gold sample from the parting vessel. It was obvious they were testing the gold, and that there was great skill and experience involved, but more they could not glean. Not until Mitradates took Targitus to the Pactolus River, responding to his desire to see where gold and silver grew in Sardian rock, did the mystery become clear.

They had first climbed the foothills of the Tmolos to bathe under the falls of sparkling cold water. Targitus took note of the soft white stone around him. "I think this must be the marble quarry I heard about," he said. When having tea with Rachel and her parents, she had given him an ecstatic description of cascading waters and pellucid pools. A place, she claimed, where white marble was water-honed to unnatural smoothness. He could see the sparkle in her eyes as she urged him to visit the spot. Now that he was here it was easy to picture Rachel under the falls.

"This quarry's our sole source of marble. Happily for us, it's enough, as you know from looking around."

Deep in thought, Targitus was barely aware of his companion. Damn Cyrus. He must be infatuated to make such a demand. But it seems so unlikely. Suppose I asked her to bring me here. What's wrong with that? And, anyway, how would he know? For me she's forbidden fruit. Perhaps for him too.

"Does the Satrap use spies?"

"Don't they all? Without doubt there are network reports on you and your Altaians. Count on it."

Refreshed from their bath, Mitradates and Targitus descended to the broader stretches of the Pactolus, where it was possible to find nuggets of gold ore by hand panning. Reaching down through the swift flowing river, Mitradates seized something, almost losing his balance in the process. Raising his hand in triumph, he careened about on one foot, the other dancing wildly in the air in search of a new spot to land. His balance restored but gasping for breath, he handed a dark stone to Targitus. "Here is the Heraclian stone. At the goldworks, we call it a touchstone. I must tell you what it does." And so he did, on the shore of the gently flowing Pactolus, which in earlier times was widely believed to be the world's only source of touchstones.

During the cementation process, the gold had to be tested to assure that the end product reached the level of purity desired. The time required varied considerably, so frequent testing was necessary. The touchstone enabled the gold from the parting vessel to be assayed for purity. The gold was rubbed down one side of the touchstone and compared with a sample of gold of the desired purity, which had been rubbed down the other side. When the two were the same color, the process was complete. Mitradates didn't know what special characteristics made the Heraclian stone work so well. He promised to outfit the Altaians with a large supply, against the possibility, which Mitradates took to be a certainty, that the rivers of the Altai would not yield a stone equal to those found in the Pactolus.

# CHAPTER 8

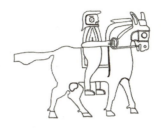

Sardis – 406 B.C.

Rachel didn't see or hear from the Satrap for over a month. She was surprised. Kept busy in the workshop, she dwelt on the subject during walks to and from the palace. Mainly she felt relief at not being pursued. But furtively, in that corner of her mind where the irrational, inconsistent, droll and strange thoughts gather, there was a sense of disappointment. Outside the palace workshop, beyond the loom's dominating influence, no amount of trying could resolve these conflicting thoughts.

Arriving home one evening in early November, Rachel found both her mother and father at the door to greet her. They were agitated. "Rachel," Benjamin exclaimed, "at last."

Closing the door with exaggerated caution, as if any sound would set off alarms, Benjamin handed Rachel a plainly wrapped package bearing only the word "Rachel." Sarah explained that a palace guard had delivered it.

Rachel took the package in her hands, catching the pleasant odor that came from within. Opening it, she found another, wrapped in red fabric and tied with white wool thread. Sewn to the package, in an oriole's nest, were two tulip bulbs. Nearby was the seal, imprinted in beeswax.

With understanding came greater alarm. How could she avoid having to explain?

Benjamin's face grew red. "What's the meaning of this? Speak child."

Rachel was hot. Her hands tightly gripped the package.

"Why don't you untie it?" Sarah said, eyeing her daughter with an expression of wonder Rachel had never seen before.

She saw no way out. She carefully pulled away the yarn holding the fabric in place. Inside were two boxes of chestnut, each with a top hinged with tiny leather straps and held in place by a bronze latch. They were long and slender, but slightly different in size. She unlatched the larger box and slowly lifted the top. She and her parents bumped heads in their eagerness. In the box they saw the warm glow of polished gold. Gold worked into the form of a drop spindle. Rachel and Sarah had never seen such a thing, although legends familiar to Persian women told of queens who went to their graves with their favorite golden spindles beside them.

Benjamin cried out, "That spindle; I made it for the Satrap, a special assignment, a secret one, and now, here it comes, for my daughter!"

Rachel's face was covered with sweat. She felt numb except for a pounding in her head. With a desperate desire to put this scene behind her, she eased the latch on the smaller box. It contained two tiny gold earrings, each in the shape of a resting ewe, with a golden wire extending above in the shape of a hook. She caught her breath.

At just that moment, her young brother arrived.

"Jacob," Rachel said. "You're just in time to help us with dinner. We need some herbs cut from the garden. Come along, I'll show you." With that, Rachel rushed out the door, dragging her brother behind.


That night, after Jacob fell asleep, Rachel was summoned into her parents' room. She brought the Satrap's presents, as requested. Her time away from the house had been put to good use.

Benjamin began: "Rachel, why has the Satrap given you these things?"

## 8: SARDIS – 406 B.C.

"Father, that's what I've been trying to figure out. I think I know. The clue was those tulip bulbs." Rachel recounted how she had woven the purple robe. And been asked to deliver it in person.

"It turned out I was right in thinking his bulbs had been planted upside down. Given the Satrap's passion for his garden, and the expense of those varieties, my warning was important. His behavior proved it. I haven't seen him since. These gifts are his way of thanking me."

"Wouldn't the tulip bulbs have been enough?" her father asked, his voice rising, incredulous.

"He's the Satrap. Commissioning these things would not seem much." She felt in control. They could be convinced.

"I made them; I charged for them, Rachel, and the price was high, too high for even a Satrap to use merely as a 'thank-you.'"

Benjamin's voice rose an octave as he made these points with a tone of triumph. The day had been unusually hot, making the room warm from the outset. The trio were perspiring freely. A growing tension blanketed the space, emitting its own odors, which were trapped in the stifling air.

"What have you done for the Satrap?"

For some minutes, Rachel had feared her father would reach this point. "No, father, nothing like that," she said bravely, aware that her sense of control was slipping, dragged down by rising guilt.

Benjamin's voice grew louder. "Oh, Rachel, come now. These gifts are exceptional. Tell us the truth. Since the Satrap can command female companionship, he could have done so with you. But having commanded, he would have no need to reward. These gifts suggest something different." Putting a hand to his head, as if searching for something there, he paused, then raising his hand higher with index finger pointing to the sky, he said, "Like Esther. Your favorite!"

Sarah, who had stood silently behind her husband, broke into the inquisition. "You don't speak for me. I don't understand yet, and I don't know whether she's given us the whole story, but one thing I do know: we have not raised a seductress."

Rachel listened in amazement as her parents talked about her. Benjamin's attitude was shaped by his role as a goldsmith, aware of the value of his work, rather than as a protecting parent, defending the virtue of his only daughter. He repeated the charge again and again, increasingly confident that his was the only possible explanation.

Sarah waited to respond until he had finished. Then, with conviction tinged with sadness, she said, "Even were I to grant you superior insight into the mind of a Satrap, there are two actors in this play, and one of them, our daughter, I repeat, is no seductress. We must find another answer. We should give ourselves time. There are serious, even dangerous, issues to sort out. Now, let's go to bed." Putting her arm around Rachel's shoulders, she added, "Think carefully whether you have told us all there is to tell."

Rachel retreated swiftly, grateful for the reprieve. She marveled at her mother's intuition, her skill at emotional map-reading, the sure sense of when to take charge.

As for herself, she realized how well she had mastered the art of telling half-truths, the ease with which she could muscle aside the instinct to confess. She thought of Targitus and her success in convincing Cyrus to help the Altaians. A complicating strand to the story. Disclosure would feed her father's fantasies. She tried to sleep; the night was long.

The next morning, Rachel left for the palace workshop as usual. But the jumble of thoughts crowding her mind during the long walk was anything but usual. How to deal with the Satrap? With her parents? Knowing there was much left untold, worrying about her mother's reference to danger, afraid there was little chance to convince her father of the truth, and that the more she told him the slimmer the chance, Rachel felt overwhelmed. Again she would turn to Vashti for advice. After all, at Vashti's urging, Rachel had disclosed most of the purple robe episode, making Vashti the only person with enough of the story to give counsel. And, anyway, hadn't her past suggestions turned out well?

During the mid-day break, Vashti and Rachel went to their customary spot beneath the large chestnut tree. Sitting down, Rachel described the events of the day before. Vashti listened intently, quiet until she was sure Rachel had finished.

## 8: SARDIS – 406 B.C.

"Your father's right. They're extraordinary. Are you sure you told me all there is to tell about the purple robe?"

"Did I mention the Targitus part?" Answering her own question, Rachel proceeded to tell that part of the story.

"This has gotten dangerous. The Satrap's smitten by you. Infatuated! And now jealous as well. The gold pieces are one side of a two party covenant. Accept and you must yield yourself to him."

"That's what I suspected. But I don't have to accept them. Where's the danger?" Rachel asked.

"In believing you have an option. The 'gifts' are in the nature of a summons, to be ignored at great risk. You bargained with him for Targitus. And won. Now comes the accounting. The Satrap could have commanded. That he did not is a measure of his respect. He's a fair man who rewards love with love, loyalty with loyalty. But he's also severe, known to give more than he got, whether in reward or punishment." She paused, deep in thought.

"I don't know what he would do if you reject the gifts. But it won't be playful."

The midday sun turned the air hot, even under the ample branches of the chestnut. In raised beds nearby, thistle, bergamot, zinnia, lantana and monarda were concentrated, some gardener's gift to the lepidopterists of Sardis. Rachel gazed at the swallowtails and fritillaries dancing wildly about the flowers, pausing at each just long enough for a sip or two of nectar, as if each flower were a different person on a very long reception line with time to greet them all running short.

"Vashti, you may not understand, but I don't want to be bought or forced into relations with Cyrus. I suppose you'll think me a child in wanting to give up my virginity to love. Surrender is possible only once, and I want it to be a willing—no—an eager act of giving. Not a bargain and sale."

Vashti said quietly, "I wasn't born a concubine."

Rachel flinched, turning red. She was trying to apologize when Vashti said, "I interrupted. Finish your thought. Please."

"I remember things you've told me. That love of the sort I am talking about doesn't last, that love-making is more skill than emotion when done well to give pleasure to men, but granting all you say, it's no way to start. I want to begin womanhood with a man I choose to love. You don't know the "Song of Songs." It's about a maiden who loves a shepherd and a king who loves the maiden. The king is so smitten that, despite having "threescore queens and fourscore concubines," he composes erotic poetry to woo her. But, then, he sets her free to love the shepherd after hearing her steadfast response:

'I am my beloved's ...'

"Why can't I talk to Cyrus as the maiden talks to the king? I could even recite it to him. I could bring Cyrus to the same place the maiden brings the king."

"What a romantic you are," Vashti replied. "And inventive. Using that poem's a nice idea, particularly if it worked. I've underestimated you before. Taking a bath in the Satrap's private rooms and then escaping, untouched. Extracting his promise in favor of the Altaians. Audacious. But here the facts are different. In the story, the maiden had her beloved. You don't. Pleading this case could recall Targitus to an already jealous mind. Not a good plan. And look, the Song of Songs is a poetic story, beautiful but not necessarily true to life. No, I think the risk's too great. Your appeal could infuriate him, endangering you and possibly Targitus as well."

Rachel looked like a puppy whose hopes for an outing had been suddenly dashed.

"The Satrap must have all the women he wants. Why me?"

"His favorite concubine is a woman named Aspasia. They say it's her natural manner and reserve, her unstudied beauty, that attract him. I imagine he thinks you're cut from the same cloth. Add the mysteries of your talent and the thrill of the chase."

Rachel's face formed a helpless grimace.

"I see two choices. You can submit. In that case you'll want to make the best of it, perform your side of the bargain as well as you can and keep your wits about you as things develop. A chance to redefine the relationship might come along. And until it does, you'll be eating the salt of the palace. Or you can leave the satrapy. He's unlikely to pursue you."

Rachel couldn't place herself on either path. She could not con-

## 8: SARDIS – 406 B.C.

template becoming a concubine; even less could she visualize explaining the decision to her parents. Yet, leaving the satrapy had vast implications. Where would she go? The satrapy was large; getting beyond its borders meant traveling well beyond the lands she knew. Wouldn't she need to know someone, a source of help in a strange land? And what about her parents and Jacob?

"Isn't there another …?" Rachel asked, her voice barely audible. Vashti cut her off. "No. That way leads nowhere."

That evening, on the walk home, Rachel struggled unsuccessfully against Vashti's analysis. Slowly she came to see that asking Cyrus to leave her alone was dangerous, that his reaction was unpredictable, that it might cut off her freedom to relocate or something worse. She also realized that simply refusing the gifts without relocating was, in Vashti's opinion, to invite a sentence of death. With pain, she saw that leaving Sardis was the better option, even though it raised many questions. How to present this to her parents? Recalling the previous night's arguments, she wondered anew how to convince her father she was still a virgin. Did he really think she had seduced the Satrap? Or that the Satrap had seduced her? Entering the house, she knew it would be a long evening.

Sarah greeted her just inside the door. "Here you are. Your father and I have some questions. Jacob's at a friend's house until bedtime. Come, help me put dinner on the table. You look tired. You know your father and I often disagree. But on one thing we are together. We don't think you've told us the whole story."

Benjamin joined them in the kitchen and piled on. "We want the whole story."

Selective disclosure or candor? Feeling more vulnerable than the night before, she chose candor. She described her visits with the Satrap. And included the Targitus incident.

Benjamin thought Rachel's behavior seductive. Shaking her head slowly, Sarah said she wasn't so sure. "I hope she was just doing the Satrap's bidding, without giving cause."

Rachel was non-committal. She then recounted Vashti's advice, her determination not to submit and the decision to relocate beyond the satrapy's borders.

Benjamin didn't interrupt. Both parents remained perfectly silent after she finished. Then her father said, "Your Vashti friend is right; he's smitten. And I am right too; it's your doing. In your own way, you've led him on. But your friend Vashti is wrong if she thinks you can just return the gold and relocate. We won't let that happen. I've given this much thought. Your part was unconsciously played. Even invoking his jealousy by flirting with Targitus. So Sarah, you see I agree with you. But here's the important point: Rachel has been chosen. Not compelled. Selected for a special relationship with the Satrap. This is important. For you. For us too, your family. Here's the truth. The gifts are a sign from Yahweh. They can't be returned. We are blessed by these events. Didn't the Satrap come to me, among all the jewelers in Sardis, to make the gold pieces? When the order came, my first from the Satrap, I thought it might be a sign, Yahweh's response to our reverence. A blessing on my work. And now I discover the pieces were for my own daughter. Can this be a coincidence? Of course not. Yahweh's consent. No, beyond consent. Relocation? Impossible. Surely, you see that."

Preparing the meal, Sarah was silent. Bruised by this blunt assault, Rachel felt her mother's silence as a sharp knife twisted inside. Abandoned and alone. They stared nervously at her, then at each other and back again to her, watching the tears, welling up in her eyes, streaking down pale cheeks.

Pain overwhelmed what was left of Rachel's long-observed duty to honor her parents. Whispering, she broke the silence. "I didn't seduce the Satrap. I didn't invite his affections. How have I flirted with Targitus? What have I done to deserve this? It's hard to argue with you, Father, for Yahweh's always on your side. He proves you right by sending signs."

She was almost as shocked as her father was by this counterattack, which left her emotions in a jumble. Contributing to her disarray was a sense of not having been completely honest with herself or her parents.

Sarah found her voice. "Benjamin, we are in trouble with Rachel.

## 8: SARDIS — 406 B.C.

We haven't handled things well. I am afraid we're losing her."

Benjamin replied: "I don't understand. What might be wanton behavior is, by the grace of Yahweh, a blessing for our family. With Rachel's relationship, and my own, our future is assured. Doesn't she understand?"

"Don't speak of understanding. The way you talk makes me think you care more about your relationship with the Satrap than with your daughter. Where does it get the family or Rachel if she ends up in the Satrap's harem, on the bottom rung of the ladder? How much do you love Rachel?"

"What do you think? My only daughter. And because I love her, I am trying to save her. But she doesn't realize that. Neither do you."

Rachel had been a willing participant in the fiction that she wasn't hearing the argument. She could remain silent no longer. "The choice is Yahweh or me."

Sarah sighed. Moving to Rachel's side, she put her arm around her daughter and whispered: "She's right. But that 'choice' is your invention. And you're forcing it upon us."

Benjamin looked hurt and defiant. He opened his mouth to speak as Sarah continued. "You call yourself Yahweh's servant. And became so of your own free will. Now, without her consent, you're trying to make your daughter his servant too. Is that his way or yours?"

Rachel swiftly left the room, eyes downcast.


"I hoped you'd come early," Vashti said from the bench beneath the chestnut as Rachel appeared at the entrance to the courtyard. "I have news."

"Me too." Hot from the climb, she sat down beside Vashti. Cool night air lingered under the mantle of this vast-limbed tree.

After recounting the evening's events, Rachel confessed the muddled state of her mind.

Vashti said, "What I have to report may help. Last night, at a celebration given by the goldworkers, I heard a rumor about Cyrus. That he'd become infatuated with you. The story came from Mitradates, head of the goldworks. Apparently, when Cyrus finally allowed the

Altaians to study our refining techniques, it was on condition that Targitus never see you again. Mitradates thought it strange, a demand that only made sense by one obsessed."

Rachel now understood why, despite the family's encouragement, Targitus had never visited again.

Tears filled her eyes as she asked, "What am I going to do?"

Vashti demurred. "I can't decide for you. But, I've done some thinking about where you might go, if you choose that option."

Rachel looked up, eyes met. "There's a weaving center in Trapezus, a fishing port on the Black Sea, many days travel to the northeast. I used to know a few of the weavers. It would be a good place for you.

"I've heard Greeks can be hard on Jews."

Vashti replied: "Greeks trade there. And some live there as well. But Trapezus is in Colchis. You've probably heard the saga about Jason's quest for a golden-fleeced ram. He was searching in Colchis. Most of its inhabitants are Colchian. But I hear there's a small Semite community there too."

"How would I get there? No horse and not enough money to buy one." Rachel had stopped crying.

"I checked on caravans You're in luck. There's a big one bound for Babylon that stopped here yesterday. Reprovisioning. Leaves at dawn tomorrow."

"All I would need is some extra clothing and sandals. I'd take my spindle, some yarn and the money I've saved."

"I could add something. It might be enough."

"If I left with the caravan, I'd avoid confrontations at home and in the palace," Rachel said.

"Yes. But remember your choices: acceptance, which will delight the two men in your life, or escape, which will anger them but preserve your freedom."

"Father would add Yahweh to that group." They exchanged wry glances.

"It's still hard to believe I have only those choices," Rachel said. "They seem so irrevocable."

"At your age, nothing's permanent."

# CHAPTER 9

En Route to Trapezus – 406. B.C.

The caravan emitted the putrid smells of sweat, dung and decay, a foil for the grunts, shrieks and songs that are the rhapsodic music of the Royal Road. Traveling about thirty miles a day, the caravan looked like a single elongated organism, self-contained and self-sufficient. So regular was the placement of its parts, and so familiar the daily routine, that a participant could be excused for believing at times that the caravan was stationary with the landscape on either side passing slowly by.

One evening at dusk, exhausted travelers could be seen readying camp for the night, each group vying to be the first to complete their chores, settle down for dinner and then turn to the opium-smoking sessions that followed. For the third time in as many nights, Rachel was urged to join in this custom, which was as embedded in the life of the caravan as the abuses of language used by camel pullers in addressing their charges.

On previous occasions, she had successfully resisted. From the outset, she had been aware of the potential dangers a young woman would face traveling alone in a vast caravan, particularly one, as she imagined it, over-laden with treasure. Showing uncharacteristic caution, she had kept to herself as much as possible. Gradually, as the days passed, Rachel had lowered her guard, sharing with a small but growing circle of companions the work of preparing the main meal of the day, as well as the conversation and gaiety that accompanied it. While not concealing her sex, she kept her body well covered.

Again, she said no, but the man, a boisterous type accustomed to banter, feigned insult, finally persuading her. In truth, Rachel relented as much from curiosity as concern for the man's feelings.

When her turn came, Rachel received the communal pipe in her hands and began to inhale the sweet, cloying smoke, dispersing its mind-altering properties throughout her lungs and stomach and then expelling the residue gently through her nostrils. The goal, she was told, was to maintain a steady flow of as much opium smoke as her body could ingest without disturbing her stomach or impairing her breathing. No one told her how to spot that point. Feelings of intoxication gripped her almost immediately. Frightful pleasures embraced her mind as she inhaled a second time. By the third inhalation, her grip on reality had begun to slip. Fear and a slight twinge of nausea brought her first encounter with opium to a close.

The attention of those around her turned to the next in line, to whom she passed the pipe. The mind-loosening effects of the drug remained. She had been so alert to caravan dangers that her life-changing choice had lain heavy and undigested at the back of her mind. Now unafraid, she began to relive her decision to leave home. She wanted to believe there had been no real choice between freedom away from Sardis and captivity at home. However gilded captivity might be, and she supposed it could be very pleasant, even exciting, and good for the family, she tried not to re-examine those possibilities. The attitude of her father had made leaving easier. "When he finds me gone, he'll realize I am not the little girl he imagined."

She wasn't so consumed by the pleasures of opium that all sense of loss was gone. In her relaxed state, she began for the first time since leaving home to experience the pain of separation. She missed her family. Anticipating a future without them increased the pain. In ways still a child, but forced to behave like the adult she was becom-

## 9: EN ROUTE TO TRAPEZUS – 406. B.C.

ing, Rachel edged away from acting the grown-up as memories of her family flooded her mind, mingling with hateful thoughts of the Satrap. She began to imagine a day when she could return without danger. Cyrus would be gone. She would send word to her family, explaining her situation. They would contact her and, when all was safe, summon her home. The certainty of this scenario restored mellowness to her mood.

It was late August. The summer had been dry. Clouds of dust and the smell of animals had lingered in the air above the Royal Road from early morning. The intensity of camel dung grew as this, Rachel's sixth day with the caravan, unfolded. In a dip, she caught sight of dusty green tree tops, suggestive of a water hole.

She loved making camp, a scene of organized chaos. Yurts went up. Supplies were taken down from pack animals. Camel pullers, bare to the waist, skin thick with dust, tugged at lines, pulled at tent poles, pushed donkeys, hauled water, put aside bales and cordage, corralled ponies, beat camels and cursed the vast army of dogs that trailed the caravan despite every effort – short of poison – to discourage them.

Into this beehive of activity, Rachel had plunged to do her part. Hair pulled back in a shawl, she was helping to put up a yurt. Concentrating on that task, she hadn't seen her father's approach before she recognized his voice speaking her name from twenty yards away.

Rachel felt her heart quicken with excitement and fear. Turning in the direction of his voice, she saw Benjamin standing still, two horses in tow. He wore a look of astonishment as he studied his daughter working next to swarthy camel pullers, sweat covering her deeply browned face.

Pushing aside her alarm, Rachel began walking towards him with bounce in her gait. She felt proud to belong to this caravan and was now happy to have her father see her as a working part of it. Her next thoughts were of concern for him. He seemed smaller than she remembered. "You're covered with dust. You look tired, and hungry. It's so good to see you!"

Instinctively, Rachel threw her arms around his neck, giving her father a long, hot hug.

Mumbling, Benjamin said, "We met with Artapathes and Vashti."

Rachel ended the hug. Looking beyond her father at the horses, Rachel said, "I am not going back."

Seeking privacy, they moved to the edge of the campground. Before sitting down with his daughter, Benjamin tended to the needs of his horses. Rachel helped. Neither spoke as they watered and fed the horses, then hobbled them with hemp. At last Benjamin turned to his daughter and said: "Now, let me try to answer your questions."

He sought to alleviate her suspicions. Just describing the visit with Artapathes didn't do it. Rachel knew her safety in Sardis could only be assured if she submitted to Cyrus. And, she remembered, that outcome had been her father's wish, claiming Yahweh's blessings. When her father handed her the golden spindle, fear returned.

"You took the presents to the palace and gave them to Artapathes. Yet you still have the spindle?"

"Your mother told him you were disturbed by the gifts. But pleased by them too. It was the implication that was upsetting. She said that you saw the presents as a cage, easier to enter than exit. She told him we didn't know you'd leave home. And that we had no idea where you'd gone."

"But the spindle?" Rachel asked.

"Yes. Here's what happened. Artapathes gave us a warning. He said if you had not left Sardis, you should do so immediately. He explained that the Satrap had been, as he put it, 'impressed' with you. By your skills as a weaver. He had enjoyed your company. He had responded to your entreaties. He had been moved to order these gifts. Your disappearance and their return would be seen as ungrateful, unfriendly behavior. Artapathes foresaw danger if you remained in Sardis or even within the borders of the satrapy.

Vashti's judgment confirmed, Rachel thought. "The spindle?"

"Artapathes placed it back in my hands, directing me to give it to you when I could. He said the Satrap had no use for it. Afterwards, your mother said she thought Artapathes was taking a chance to be generous, that Cyrus wouldn't approve and might even turn

## 9: EN ROUTE TO TRAPEZUS – 406. B.C.

nasty if he found out."

Rachel remained suspicious. She knew there was more to tell and chose to be provocative. Leaving home had strengthened her independence, to be sure, but it was six days' exposure to the brash caravan style of life that made her feisty.

"And you've traveled this far just to give me the spindle?"

"I came to escort you to Trapezus. I know you told Vashti you didn't need an escort after the caravan leaves you at Comana. It's going to be rough travel from there. Local tribes can be dangerous. I want to see you safe in your new home on the Black Sea."

Rachel looked quizzically at her father. His tone seemed bittersweet. Recalling his arguments to Sarah, she was amazed by what appeared a complete change of attitude. Against her will, his solicitude was softening her trail-hardened exterior. But she still wasn't convinced. Then he did something he'd never done before. He apologized. Each word had been memorized. Later she would imagine how carefully he must have rehearsed the scene.


In twelve days, they reached Comana. With many farewells from the close band of travelers who had befriended Rachel and Benjamin, father and daughter sat their horses to wave goodbye as the caravan turned south toward Melitene and the Euphrates. Then, before the dust could settle, they moved East at a trot along a less-traveled route toward the Lycus River, from the other side of which they would ascend the Paryadres Mountains, a range running east-west some twenty-five miles south of the Black Sea. They hoped to make Trapezus within six days.

Fatigued, they came to the summit of Theches, a mountain in the Paryadres range, by late afternoon of the fifth day. The temperature had plummeted the night before, and all through the day, an early snow fall had wet the warmer ground, turning quickly to water. As they climbed Theches, the ground grew firm and the snow held. By the time they reached the peak, the trail they had followed, which led over the top and down the other side of Theches to Zigana and thence a short distance to Trapezus, hosted an inch or more of snow.

They had expected to reach Zigana by nightfall. The steepness of the climb slowed them, as did the snow. Slippery conditions on the north side made descent in the remaining hours of fading light impossible. They would have to make camp at the summit.

Despite the blanket of snow, they could see easily enough a well-used campsite. The snow was now intermittent, small flakes sparsely scattered across the sky. Benjamin said, "The snow's going to stop soon. It will be cold tonight."

Dismounting, they tended the horses, feeding them with what remained of their provisions. They set up camp quickly. A small tent was erected, the snow swept away and felt rugs put down, affording some insulation from the cold dampness of the ground. With flint Benjamin ignited some of the tinder kept dry in a pouch carried at his waist. Gently feeding the flame with bits of bark taken from a dead but still standing conifer, Benjamin nursed the fire to a crackling and popping state of health.

They foraged for firewood in opposite directions, hoping to gather enough to keep the fire alive through their meal and into the night. Benjamin had better luck in the search, returning first with a load of wood so large it blocked his sight. He staggered and nearly fell several times before feeling his way back to the campsite, helped by the smell and sound of the fire.

Rachel watched her father's difficult return, then drifted farther and farther away as her search yielded few results. She was sure that others had looked in this direction, picking clean the deadfalls in the sparse, weather-beaten forest that grew at the summit.

Frustrated, she paused to gaze to the west, where the sky was clearing to open the way for a setting sun which, though below the ridge line, could be imagined by dint of the soft pink-orange rays that infused the forest in front of her. Snow hugged the base of the forest, white on black, light below dark, as the sun's luminous presence created long slender shadows of the trees, standing tall and dark above the carpet of snow. The sun turned the forest from an opaque dark mass to an open network of pathways that glistened with light, linear rooms alive with contrasts.

Twenty minutes from the campsite, she began to find dead

## 9: EN ROUTE TO TRAPEZUS – 406. B.C.

wood. Quickly gathering as much as she could carry, she started back. As the light ebbed, she, too, had trouble finding her way, although her sight wasn't blocked completely because she couldn't carry that much wood. And so, through the sparse forest, without being seen herself, she could see the four men standing over her father next to the fire.

Armed with sword and bow, they appeared unfriendly. Instinct took command. Rachel threw down her load, broke into a run and shouted her father's name. Still in the forest, she was some distance from the group. Just at that moment, a loud crack came from the fire, the result of a sap-filled log exploding. No one had heard her.

Instinct gave way to calculation. Hiding behind a tree, she cocked an ear and began to think.

The wind had picked up. Loud whispers from the conifers made it hard for Rachel to hear, but she could tell they wanted the horses. She could understand her father better than the others. He was trying to convince them he was alone. Rachel reasoned that, if they believed him, they might feel kindly enough to take only one horse. If she appeared, they would take both. And they would know her father was lying. And, anyway, she thought, what would she accomplish by bursting into the campsite? She had no weapon. Indeed, she lacked the experience of using a weapon, even if one were available. If they wanted to hurt her father, she realized, they would be as likely to do it in front of her as they would be if she were not around. The more she thought, the more frightened she became and the more reasons she found for staying hidden.

The leader of the bandits pushed past Benjamin, seized the bridles and, slipping them on the horses, gestured to one of his companions, who proceeded to untie the hemp hobbles. Rachel watched the other two men pick up baggage and tent, roll it all into packs and make them fast to the backs of the horses, using the hobbles as ties. She tried to make out what they were saying. All she heard was the leader's dismissive words, "Forget him." They were going to leave Benjamin alone, a thought that now filled her with relief even as she watched their horses and belongings being taken.

The thieves mounted their horses and began to move away from the campsite. The youngest, called "boy" by the others, was the last to depart.

He had mounted his horse but, instead of moving away, sat perfectly still for a moment. Then he strung his bow, nocked an arrow and took aim at the man beside the fire. The arrow's flight was true. Turning his horse, the young archer trotted off after his colleagues. By the time Rachel had run to her father's side, he was dead.

Rachel was utterly alone, at the summit of Theches, with nothing except a fire and half a night's supply of wood to comfort her. Her father was nearby, an intense, religious man, a fine craftsman in the working of gold. But his presence held no comfort now. It was the source of guilt and recrimination.

Unable to face the horror of what had happened, she left him where he fell, with the arrow of the youngest bandit motionless in his heart. Only later in that worst of nights, when the cold penetrated her body to cause unbearable pain, did Rachel approach her father's body, and then only for the purpose of using the clothes he was wearing to help with the cold, praying as she pulled the arrow through and stripped him almost naked that he and her mother would understand.

Trying to sleep, Rachel lay down where the felts and tent had been. The fire cast its warmth and glow in a circle that contained the spot where she lay. But sleep proved impossible. An expression of her father's came to her: "He was gathered to his people." Rising, she moved to her father's body, now bathed in the light of a full moon. Falling to her knees beside his head, she found comfort in speaking these words. His composed face was ashen, the color of leaves at rest in a stream-bed. In the morning, she would try to bury him.

Returning to her place, she rummaged through memories of her father collected since he had found her in the caravan. Many things, large and small. The carefully rehearsed apology. She could recall every word. "I've been wrong. Yahweh is your God just as he is mine, and the God of all our people. I was wrong to believe he spoke to you through me. It is you, not me, to whom Yahweh will disclose his

## 9: EN ROUTE TO TRAPEZUS – 406. B.C.

plans. Will you accept this apology?" She could see him dropping to his knees, a beseeching look on his face. After they left the caravan, he became increasingly affectionate. She recalled how often he squeezed her hand, at meal times and before going to sleep, looking in her eyes with a love she'd not seen before. How with great tenderness and care he had picked out burrs caught in her hair and then combed out the separated strands for her to braid. Was it necessary, she had wondered during these moments together, for him to lose his daughter physically in order to hold her spiritually? She berated herself for not telling him she recognized these changes and how she had come to love him, combining forgiveness with acceptance. The more she recalled, the deeper her grief became.

She replayed the sequence of events again and again. If only she had followed the instinct that caused her to cry out and run. What might have happened? Perhaps the bandits wouldn't have hurt them. The arrow appeared to be an act apart from the group's strategy. The archer looked to be no older than she was. Someone she could have stood up to. This was a chance event. Surely one that wouldn't have happened had she made herself known.

Wanting to sleep, Rachel could not escape the cauldron bubbling over in her head. Each rehearsal of the afternoon led back to the missed opportunity. The white glint of her father's naked body stoked her insomnia. Finally, within a hour of dawn, Rachel's bludgeoned mind gave up, allowing sleep to overcome sadness and remorse.


Although dawn was breaking, the sky was still dark. Opening her eyes, Rachel saw above her, within arm's length, the outline of a man's bearded face, shrouded in a peaked hood. The smell of horse was overwhelming. Terrified, she seized the spindle, broke the thong from which it hung around her neck and thrust its long golden point at the chest of this unknown assailant. His hand took the attack. He cried out in pain as the spindle's point pierced through until the whorl, like the hilt of a sword, stopped further passage. And there it remained while the man used his other hand to disengage Rachel's grasp and pin her to the ground.

## SPINDLE AND BOW

Targitus was quick to recognize Rachel as the young weaver he had gotten to know in Sardis, the one who took him to Ezekiel, the apothecary, the one he had come to miss from the moment Cyrus ordered him to stay away from her. Following that directive, he had observed her once or twice around her house, but only at a distance. To make sure it was she, he had bent over her sleeping form to get a close look. It must have been her nose that sounded the alarm.

It took Rachel a second longer to realize that the man whose hand she had impaled was Targitus. Staring up at him, unable to move against the pressure of his left hand holding her in place, Rachel slowly digested the fact that she knew this long-haired man.

Looking at his right hand, from which the steady drip of warm blood could be seen, falling beside the nearly frozen form he held tightly in place, Targitus said, "I meant no harm. If you're willing to take back your spindle and hold it in peace, I am willing to return it. And then be glad to hold your hand and hear your story."

The man's traveling companions had joined in a semi-circle around Rachel. Amazement showed in their faces, illuminated by the approaching sunrise, as they glanced first at the man stretched out on the ground, red on white, with an arrow beside him, then at their leader's hand, raised up, palm open with a golden spindle pierced through, and finally at Rachel, a disheveled waif in clothing too big for her frame, pinned to the ground by their leader.

"We had stopped for the night. My father was surrounded by them. They took our horses and supplies. Then killed my father. I didn't try to stop them."

"They were four?"

Rachel nodded, now beginning to sob for the first time, the safety vouchsafed to her by the Altaians having warmed her spirit enough to let sorrow and grieving begin again.

Targitus released his hold. With a touch of the dramatic, he grasped the spindle by its whorl, drew it swiftly out of his right hand and wiped clean the shaft on the edge of his tunic. He then returned it to her, whorl end first, as one might surrender one's sword to a champion in battle.

Taking the spindle, Rachel rose from the ground to stand

## 9: EN ROUTE TO TRAPEZUS – 406. B.C.

amongst the men. Her sobbing continued. The men began to fidget, shifting needlessly from one leg to the other. Sayles, the best linguist next to their leader, broke the silence. "We rode through the night. To take advantage of the moon."

Targitus had read the tracks in the snow, enabling him to grasp much of what had happened the night before. He picked the youngest Altaian, Marsyas, the one with the softest heart, to guard Rachel. Ordering him to provide Rachel with warm clothes and food, he set off with the others, a band of five, in pursuit of the bandits. "Have a care," he cautioned Marsyas. "Don't play with the spindle, it's dangerous."

Targitus knew the bandits wouldn't have gotten far before camping for the night. After all, they had nothing to fear. The tracks left the night before were still visible and easy to follow. Hurrying away, Targitus warned his companions that with sunrise the temperature would rise above freezing, melting away the hoof prints of their quarry like lost wax in a bronze casting.

The Altaians tracked the bandits for an hour over rough terrain. The men began to grumble. Low murmurs warned Targitus of a problem. He stopped the column and turned his horse to face them.

"I know what's on your minds. Why are we wasting time in pursuit of a bunch of bandits who did us no harm? The girl can ride one of our spare horses. It's less than a day's travel to Trapezus."

Targitus, nursing his right hand, would use his head but not his bow. That left four companions to apply their weapons to the task at hand.

The men had moved from single file to face their leader, four abreast.

"Four and one-half against four is not risk free," Scyles observed. In addition to his skill with language, Scyles was appreciated for his humor.

"True. All true. But listen and I'll explain. I got to know the girl and her family in Sardis. They were kind to me. We became friends. The father's death must be avenged. You'll all agree to that. By chance we're the only ones who can do it."

The sun was high in the sky when the Altaians came near the bandits, resting beside a rushing stream on the northern slope of the

Paryadres Range, on a little-used bridle path to Zigana. The gurgling rush of the mountain waters masked their approach.

Dismounting, the Altaians moved swiftly through the forest to encircle the bandits. On a signal from Targitus, mimicking the golden eagle, the four rose up as one, advanced quickly from the forest cover, took aim and let fly their arrows. The bandits, caught unawares, had but an instant to contemplate their end, delivered swiftly by the arrows' bronze trilobite heads. Four shafts, each wrought of soft wood with feathered ends, carried true to their targets.

Altaians were well accustomed to fighting with bow and arrow. The task of hitting a man at thirty yards from a dismounted position wasn't much of a challenge. There was a bit of finishing work to do with two of the victims, when the Altaians bent over their targets to retrieve arrows and check for personal belongings worth taking. Drawing knives, the archers quickly freed four scalps from the bandits' skulls and tied them in place on the reins of their horses.

Altaians were superstitious about their arrows. Those which had found their mark were recovered whenever possible, to be treated thereafter with the kind of respect one might lavish on the staff of a shaman. These arrows possessed a mysterious quality. The owner believed such an arrow, having found its intended mark once, had the power to do so again and again. It was not unusual to find in an Altaian warrior's case an arrow that had taken many lives.

With arrows and scalps in place, the Altaians rounded up the stolen horses and those of the bandits besides, gathered up the loose supplies, tied them to the horses, and set off in the direction they had come, up the mountain range to rejoin Marsyas, guarding Rachel at the summit.

When the Altaians reached Rachel's campsite, the sun was out of sight below the mountains extending southwest. In its place was the chill dusk of a fall evening. Marsyas had built a fire, which now roared a welcome to the returning band. Targitus reined his horse to a standstill in front of Rachel. He was leading her father's horses. Their entrance, from exactly the place where she had last seen her

## 9: EN ROUTE TO TRAPEZUS – 406. B.C.

father's assailant, revived the grim events. Seeing bloody scalps on the reins of the Altaians' horses made her light-headed, then faint. She quickly sat down beside the fire, staring at nothing until the men returned from tending the horses.

The Altaians told their story around the fire, where chamomile tea sweetened with late summer honey was passed in horn-shaped gourds. Dinner was served. Afterwards, the men drifted away. With time on their hands, Targitus and Rachel sat awkwardly looking at each other across the fire. At last, Targitus broke the silence by asking Rachel how the day went.

Rachel replied, "It was difficult. Marsyas was a great help. Tried hard to make me laugh. I failed him most of the time."

Soon after the band of five had departed, Rachel asked Marsyas to dig a grave for her father on the only level spot of ground that could be found away from the main path through the pass. On the mountain's shoulder, the grave was dug along a north-south axis. Rachel then helped place her father gently in the mountain vault. She found comfort in pointing his head south towards Jerusalem, the sacred city of light that had illuminated his spirit. Behind closed lids, she imagined, his eyes were open wide, searching the sky for Yahweh.

As Marsyas shoveled loose soil and rock over Benjamin's body, Rachel wished for some token to place with him, but nothing had been left behind. Nothing except the arrow that had slain him. Remembering her father's unfaltering ability to find Yahweh's hand everywhere and, through ingenuity worthy of a mystic, to find blessing in every misfortune, Rachel tried to think as her father would on this occasion, had their positions been reversed. Might not the arrow have been more than an instrument of death? A messenger of God, perhaps, at once rending the flesh and infusing the spirit with a new beginning. If so, shouldn't the arrow be placed in Benjamin's hands, pointing to the sky, the direction of her father's new flight path?

In a moment, the arrow was in place, steadied by Rachel's hand until enough dirt had been shoveled to support it. Upon completion, the grave mounded slightly, the arrow's head just breaking the surface, noticeable only to someone who knew it was there. "Father, now you belong to the eternal," she whispered.

Targitus knew nothing of Jews or Jewish faith. Patiently, he listened as Rachel described the burial. Then came the questions. "Is there just one God? Only for Jews? Has He taken your father to another place?"

"Their God. Yes, most Jews believe that. They also believe He presides over all peoples. But we say that Jews are His 'chosen' among all."

Targitus looked puzzled. "It's hard to see how He could be everyone's God if he prefers some over others. Where's the proof?" Targitus asked, turning didactic.

"My grasp of these matters has always fallen short. I wish my father could respond." She started to cry.

Targitus saw sadness in Rachel's face, but embarrassment as well. He guessed the problem was less her grasp of Jewish faith and more her doubt.

It was after dark, the fire's embers subdued but not their smell. Getting to his feet, Targitus apologized for being a bully. "My questions were thoughtless. I am sure you're exhausted. And we haven't even spoken of tomorrow. We'll go to Trapezus, where I'll help you get settled with the weavers."

"I must get word to my mother. We'll need a scribe and someone to carry a message. Is it possible?" Her voice turned plaintive.

Targitus nodded. "Of course. That too. I'll make the arrangements. Perhaps we can stay over a day to make sure things will go well for you there."

Rachel knew she was to sleep in Targitus' yurt. This plan had been set in place that morning, before Targitus rode off. There had been little discussion. Targitus would sleep with the others in a somewhat larger yurt, crowded by his presence. Since they would have but one night with Rachel, this seemed the obvious solution.

Targitus offered Rachel his hand, which she accepted, feeling vulnerable as he helped her to her feet. He led as they walked the short distance to his yurt, now made visible by the rising moon.

In Sardis, Rachel had responded to this strange-looking man. She liked what seemed to be his ingenuous nature. And tonight, while overbearing, his interest in her father's religion had been genuine. Now, as he led her to his yurt, she realized that, left there

## 9: EN ROUTE TO TRAPEZUS – 406. B.C.

alone, she would have no shield to deflect her thoughts through a second long night. Either with him or alone, she was going to feel insecure and exposed. Glancing back toward the fire as she bent to enter the yurt, she watched his silhouette pass through flickering moonlight to vanish into the large yurt.

# CHAPTER 10

Trapezus – 406 B.C.

It took them the better part of a day to descend to Trapezus. Winter was coming, but the warm afternoons of a lingering fall deceived the populace of this bustling port into believing they had plenty of time. At sea level, the air was moist and much warmer. Targitus and Rachel followed directions to the weaving center, about a mile west of the central square. The owner of the building was on site. He told them they were late by a few months. "Those weavers were a peculiar lot," he said. "Never satisfied. The market for their products was strong; yet they constantly complained. First, it was the building. Bad lighting. Too hot. Then, the rent. Too high. And always the cost and quality of the wool. Of course, it was imported; how could it be otherwise in a crowded port surrounded by steep mountains?"

Noticing his dark skin and curly hair, Rachel thought him odd-looking. For some reason, he brought to mind the exotic Egyptians she had once seen in Sardis. Later, as she got a better look at the people of Trapezus, she discovered that this man's looks were commonplace.

Nothing about the yawning space of his building or the protruding excess of his stomach explained this puffed-up self-impor-

## 10: TRAPEZUS – 406 B.C.

tance. "They were the only weaving group in town?" Targitus asked.

Nodding, the man rocked forward and back, from heel to toe.

"There's a Jewish community here, isn't there?" Rachel said.

Still rocking, the man shook his head. "Not for a long time."

Rachel felt sick. She wanted to scream. Instead, she inquired gently, "Might you know where the weavers went?"

"Don't expect any guarantees, but they said they were going to Scopasis, somewhere above the Caspian on the Oarus River. Said it would be a good source of supply." The man stretched his long arm to indicate the way out, sweeping them into the early evening's luminous light.

To Rachel, the place names meant nothing. For Targitus, it was a different story. As they rode back to the central square, he described the journey. "Scopasis is a Scythian village near the Oarus, some 275 miles upstream from the Caspian Sea. We passed there on our way to Sardis."

"Is it difficult?"

We cross the Caucasus Range. Between Mount Elbruz in the west and Mount Kazbegi in the east, there are many established passes. And countless goat paths. We'll use the Sharivtsek Pass again. It was not hard on the trip west. You'll come with us to Scopasis?"

"How long's the journey?"

"If we leave tomorrow, we should reach your weavers within twenty-five days. Your option is to stay here, looking for employment among these sharp traders and boatsmen. They're known to prey on people like you. Or you can wait for a caravan bound for Sardis. It would be unusual for one to pass this way, even in summer, since it's far from the main caravan routes coming from the northeast. But especially so at this time of year."

"Aren't you tilting the options?"

Without embarrassment, Targitus broke into a wide grin. "Maybe, but the choice seems clear. And I want you with us. Why? We had a woman in our band on the trip west. It went well. I'd like a woman for the trip back, or at least as much of it as possible.

"My luck ended in the palace workshop. How could I help you?"

"Fair question. In the Altai, we believe a person need not have good fortune herself to assure good fortune to others."

Rachel nodded at this new idea.

"And I need you to teach me your people's ways. Twenty-five days should be enough, even for this Altaian."

Standing squarely before her, Targitus loomed large, now more a source of comfort and support than of insecurity. And of mystery besides. He was hirsute, with skin reddish-brown in the filtered sunlight of late afternoon, dark brown eyes open wide and a prominent aquiline nose below, projecting an expression of earnestness. Growing up in the Great Ulagan, he had made friends and swayed minds by an openness tinged with naiveté. What at first was his natural behavior had become calculated technique with the reinforcement of success. Guile parading as charming ingenuousness.

Looking straight into her eyes with a soft smile, Targitus winked, as if to say he knew there was but one choice, that the outcome was not hers to select but his to dictate, that this was just a game in which each of them played an assigned part.

Rachel returned the smile and laughed until the implication of his point about caravans registered. "Without a caravan how will I get a message to my mother?"

"We'll attend to that right now. The lack of caravans doesn't mean there's no commerce between Colchis and Lydia. We'll find an obliging merchant. But first, a scribe. Come."

Directing the Altaians to set up camp on the outskirts of Trapezus, Targitus dismounted, beckoning Rachel to do the same. Handing their bridles to Tymnes, Targitus whirled around to face the central square and, grasping Rachel's hand, set off swiftly.

The Altaians replenished their food supplies the following morning. They packed a quantity of millet, the dominant grain in Colchis. As a special indulgence, which Targitus justified by Rachel's presence, they obtained ten freshly slain pheasants, which were to Colchis as gold was to Sardis. By noon, they had departed along the coastal route, Rachel with them.

It would not be easy to get over the shock of finding the weavers gone. But there was nothing in Trapezus to keep her. The pain of los-

## 10: TRAPEZUS – 406 B.C.

ing her father wouldn't be lessened one way or the other. In place of the uncertainties of being alone in Trapezus, she chose the certain risks of a difficult journey across the Caucasus Range. The key was Targitus. She trusted him, just as she came to trust her father. She wore her dependence with growing comfort. While she could vividly recall how she felt outside the apothecary's shop, she was sure that feeling played no role at all in reaching her decision.

Rachel was struggling with the ebb and flow of her fortune. Could life be a balance; with each setback an offsetting advance? Wishful thinking. No fortune could be good enough to compensate for the death of her father. But, perhaps. Hadn't she been spared? One life for another? Rachel's faith in Yahweh was fragile. But, she wondered, could her fate be His design? His purposeful intervention in response to a father's prayer? Or the product of any deity's design? She would not rule out these possibilities.

Why couldn't Targitus have arrived a day earlier? That would have been good fortune indeed. But she couldn't shake the bittersweet notion of life that had long dogged her thoughts, this idea of balance. One had a run of tragedy and then, with a turn of the wheel, something good happened. What Rachel didn't know was whether the balance she saw in her own short life was there only because God was turning the wheel. She lacked the faith to believe. But, if not God, then who? Sometimes, we seem to be masters of our fate. At other times, not. She saw a chance to save her father but didn't try. Where did that fit in?

Benjamin had taught Rachel the epic poetry of Job. Much she had committed to memory. Yet, knowing the words and loving the evocative beauty of its imagery had failed to illuminate the underlying message. Rachel found difficult the idea that God would inflict suffering on one who had not sinned for no reason other than to show that His purposes were beyond man's ken. Benjamin could not explain this puzzle in ways she could accept. His argument, that suffering must be accepted through a trusting and absolute faith in God, was disturbing. Rachel was especially troubled by Satan's successful provocation of God, causing him to inflict terrible suffering on Job. "Could God, if really God, have to prove himself to Satan? And who was this Satan, that he could goad God so?" Recalling her debates with Benjamin, Rachel could see her father's grimace as he grappled with her questions, never emerging with a convincing explanation.

And what of justice? Rachel wondered why Targitus had delivered swift vengeance to the bandits. Was he an instrument of divine justice? Or acting on his own, perhaps, because of her? She liked that idea. If Targitus hadn't acted, would God have found another way? In Rachel's brief experience, rewards and punishments often fell short of what justice, fairly weighed, would demand. Was God just? In this world? In the one that followed?

Targitus interrupted her musings, riding up from his customary position at the back of the column. He had endured the jibes of his fellow Altaians, who accused him of behaving like a stallion leading his harem from behind.

Rachel rode just ahead of him, leading an extra horse. They were moving through meadowland. The immense sound of crickets filled the air, as did the insects themselves, leaping in random motions side to side across the trail to escape the crashing hooves of the sixteen horses that made up the Altaian caravan. The air was still warm. The smell of grasses crushed by the horses ahead blended with the constant smell of horse, the occasional whiff of dung.

"You must be wondering what to expect. Our plan is to follow the coast, which curves north. When we reach Phasis, some four days' travel, we will turn northeast and follow the river. We will pass a lowland plain. It will turn into foothills. Continuing north, eventually we will reach the pass. This may be more than you want, but the Phasis is not just a river. It's spiritual. Colchians believe they are descended from this river."

"Do you believe that?"

"I don't look at beliefs too critically. Rivers sustain life. I can see how an idea starts."

"When do we pass over the range? That's the dangerous part, isn't it, given the time of year?"

"The Phasis ravine is our route over the Caucasus. It's well traveled. You'll be safe."

Rachel wanted a sense of how high the pass was. Targitus

## 10: TRAPEZUS – 406 B.C.

claimed, with only a bit of exaggeration, that it wasn't much higher than the mountain pass where they had met. "The northern slopes of these mountains are gentler than the southern, as we discovered on the trip to Sardis. So the hard part will be getting up to the pass. We won't be alone. On the northern descent, we'll find herds of sheep and goats, escorted by ferocious dogs and lonely shepherds. All this activity should gladden your heart. And you're right about the weather. We will keep you well covered. At this late date, we must expect snow; it will slow us down. In truth, I foresee some cold, damp and generally unpleasant conditions, but no serious danger."

Rachel had been filled with fears piled one on another before they left Trapezus. About the distance, the mountains, the weather and the destination. About her father and her family, about the weavers and the Altaians. And about the many dangers she could imagine and the many more she couldn't. And so, with amazement, she noticed how comforting she found the voice of this man, so evidently in charge, so thoroughly informed, so thoughtfully solicitous of her state of mind. The timbre of voice and quickness of response threatened to become more important than the message, so accustomed had she grown to allowing him to do all the thinking. As she did when he took charge of getting a message to her mother. With a wrench, she concentrated again on his words, which had continued, steadily, to lap at her ears.

The first night that Targitus joined Rachel in his yurt for after-supper tea came as a heavy, cold rain descended on the travelers in the midst of their evening food preparations, a week's travel from Trapezus. An ample fire warmed those close to the flames. Damp clothes radiated steam as they ate a gruel consisting of wheat, barley and chickpeas, seasoned with olives. The supply of olives, taken from Sardis, had dwindled. They would embellish only a few more meals.

Evening was a happy time. The ache of muscles that had endured a long day's ride receded against the warmth of hot food and drink in the stomach and the fire's heat as it passed across weathered faces. A collective sense of well-being set in, regardless of weather.

Man-talk was restrained not at all by the presence of a woman. They simply spoke in their native tongue. Rachel didn't like it, at first wondering whether they were talking about her. She knew it would be fruitless to object. In time, she relaxed, having discovered the delicacy of their choice of language.

Rachel finished her plate and was handed a cup of tea by one of the Altaians. She turned toward the yurt to escape the downpour. After a stride or two, touched by a sliver of guilt, she looked back to find Targitus watching her go. In the bright flickers of firelight she could see the sheets of rain raking his face, his beard like a saturated sponge shedding below what it absorbed above. He resembled nothing so much as a long-haired, long-eared dog wistfully obeying his departing master's injunction to "Stay." With a peremptory shout, she invited him to get some tea and join her inside. As he rose to follow, murmurs from his circle of companions rose above the splatter of rain.

It was in the privacy of his yurt that dreadful evening that Rachel and Targitus commenced in earnest to explore each other's lives. The vulnerability Rachel had felt when they were alone that first night on top of the Paryadres Mountains was gone. Joining Rachel in the yurt, Targitus said, "That's the first order you've given me. I liked it."

They began. Perhaps it was the distance from home, or the forced maturity that her father's death brought about during her days on the road, or the fact that Targitus was a stranger who would pass from her life upon reaching Scopasis, as suddenly as he had appeared above Trapezus. Whatever the explanation, Rachel was almost reckless in her desire to tell this man about the Satrap.

Targitus was a good listener. A patient one, too, for her story was long.

"And so, I really had no choice."

The same intensity that had struck him that day in the palace workshop, when he saw a young woman's eyes connect with his, returning his gaze with a curiosity at once artless and piercing, struck him now.

Artless? he wondered. Could Cyrus have been so jealous of a woman whom, as Rachel claimed, he had never even kissed? Wasn't she his to command?

"Do you have any idea why Cyrus cared so much?"

"I gave him no cause to care. He took a momentary fancy to me. That's all. Satraps are accountable to no one save the King."

Her response sounded defensive to Targitus. "'Fancy' may not do justice to the Satrap's obsession with you. In granting us access to the goldworks, he invoked one condition: that I stop seeing you. The man was unbalanced by jealousy."

Rachel looked shocked. "I can hardly believe it. What could have driven him to feel that way?"

"Only you can answer that," Targitus replied, getting to his feet. "It's time for sleep."

Leaving to join his Altaian companions, he suggested they pick up the conversation the following evening. And so the pattern was set.


The next day, they stopped for the noon meal deep in the Phasis ravine. It was unseasonably hot. Dappled sun in a cloudless sky splashed away the shadows as a strong wind shook the leaf cover above. While food was being prepared, Rachel set off, alone, to explore an outcropping of rocks that she had noticed above the trail a short distance downstream. After scrambling up the steep side of the ravine, she discovered the rocks framed a huge cave, the mouth of which was high enough for her to stand. With bright sun streaming through an opening in the trees, she thought the darkness that gathered just beyond the cave's entrance more allure than threat, a mystery to be probed. Entering, Rachel detected the civilizing signs of others: heat-burnished stones set in a circle, animal bones off to the side and a drawing etched in a smooth surface of the otherwise craggy wall. The smells of moisture and decay brushed cool against her flushed face as she moved forward into what quickly became total darkness.

With arm outstretched, she advanced until her hand felt the ceiling. Forced onto her hands and knees, she continued, coming soon into a cavity where again she could stand. Immediately, a cacophony of high-pitched squeaks and squeals assaulted her ears.

Terrified, she froze. The flapping of a vast multitude of wings began, an overtone to the squeaks and squeals. Rachel had disturbed the slumber of an army of bats, now frightened and angry at the intruder. The bats' attack came in waves, wings touching, brushing, even slapping against her face, arms, chest and legs as they flew past to safety outside the cave. At the first touch, she screamed. And a second time before realizing no one would hear. While in flight, the bats were defecating, whether from fright or revenge. Rachel knew something was pelting her, but not until the bats were gone did she discover, by touch and smell, what they had left behind.

She was laden down with bat dung, head to foot. It clung to her in mounds, making movement difficult. It's odor would have been unbearable to anyone with a choice, but Rachel was trapped. She moved back slowly along the route she had come until, reaching the cave's entrance, she lost consciousness, victim of fright, exhaustion and the overpowering stench.

When she failed to reply to his shouts, Targitus set off to find her, telling the others to begin the afternoon's journey. He followed her trail downstream and then up to the overhanging rocks, where he found her outstretched at the mouth of the cave. Bending over, Targitus realized he was re-enacting their encounter on the top of the Paryadres. As he lifted her, she awoke with a cry.

"Don't talk now. Let me get you down."

The dung clung to her, wet and slippery. Perversely, the fresh air seemed to release more of the smell, magnifying its effects. With Rachel in his arms, Targitus picked his way down the steep side of the ravine, risking a fall to reach the sacred river Phasis before the stench overcame him.

"You'll have to wash off this dung. It's going to be cold."

Targitus wasn't sure whether to stay or leave. With so much dung on her clothes, could she get them off by herself?

"I'll get you some dry clothes and be right back," he said.

"No. Don't leave me. Here, help me remove this." Her shirt was so layered with dung that alone she couldn't muscle it off.

They were in a glade, and the hot beams of the sun, now directly overhead, were there, too, unimpeded by tree cover. Targitus helped

## 10: TRAPEZUS – 406 B.C.

her out of her clothes. He then led her by the hand to a bright pool of nearly still water at the edge of the rushing river.

"Here's the place to wash. I'll get fresh clothes and be right back. Be brave," he said with a smile, pointing to the pool.

By the time he returned, having washed himself and changed clothes, Rachel was lying on her stomach, stretched out in the sun.

"From here you look good, except for a little bit of dung, clinging to your back. If you'll allow me."

Handing her the clothes, he turned his back while she slipped on undergarments and pants. She walked to the pool's edge and invited him to proceed. Cupping his hands, he took water and applied it gently to her back. He used the soiled shirt, now rinsed, to stop the water from wetting her clothes. He enjoyed touching the pale whiteness of her back, feeling the curves of her muscles, the bumps along her spine. When she turned to get the clean shirt, left on a nearby bush, he averted his eyes, but not before catching sight of her breasts. He thought of sheep's milk, apricots and olives, none of which he had enjoyed for a long time.

Rachel was too tired to care much about what Targitus saw or didn't see. He was, today, more than ever, an object of need. Only later, on revisiting the bat cave incident, would she blush at her nudity and linger over missed opportunity.

That evening Rachel cancelled their post-dinner visit, pleading exhaustion. When they sat down the next evening to enjoy tea in her yurt, Rachel said, "Tonight, I issue my second order. We will talk only about you and your mission."

It didn't take long for Rachel to get him to acknowledge his powers of retention. She almost blurted out something about her own gifts, but the habit of keeping secrets overcame the urge. Getting others to disclose without giving in return was an early skill she practiced with odd delight. She would wait.

Rachel was dumbfounded by the story of Argali, a woman she had never heard mentioned in the palace. Not because of Cyrus' gleeful acceptance of the gift or Targitus' belief that, in return, Cyrus had shared Sardian secrets, but by the fact that the Altaians had carefully planned such a gift and delivered it without blemish, as Targitus claimed with pride, to secure the secrets. Staring at the Altaian opposite her, she wondered at his claim to have traveled so far in the same yurt with such a beauty without exercising what Persians claimed were loose Scythian customs.

Beyond surprise, Rachel was amused by Targitus' assumption that his gift had been the key to unlock the Sardian secrets. She wanted to remind him that, in the hunt, the prey has more power at large than when caught, to tell him that at a vulnerable moment in her relationship with the Satrap, he had exchanged an explicit promise for the implicit one she had allowed him to believe. Instead, in an unreadable voice, she asked, "Am I Argali's replacement for the trip home?" Laughter was his only response.

Just as she had surprised herself by revealing the cause of her departure from home, tonight she found herself, without foresight, risking an attack on her protector's attitudes, as if she and Targitus were two gods engaging in dry discourse on the peculiar habits of their flock. "Is it customary for Altaians to trade their women for influence?" Rachel could see from the look on her companion's face that her question was as confusing as it was unexpected. She tried to look indignant. And, as she challenged Targitus, she was also rummaging around in her head for some analog to Argali's situation. Esther, perhaps. Might Argali prove so compelling to Cyrus that she became his queen? Might Argali have become her rival had she stayed, her replacement when she left? She beat back a flicker of envy. And, then, it struck her. She was the closest analogy to Argali, and her father to Targitus.

Stung by her question, Targitus was too busy marshalling his response to notice that, in an instant, Rachel's haughty scowl was gone. No matter. His sally could not be stopped.

"Massagetae are not as limited as you think," Targitus said. "We knew some things about Cyrus. Enough to believe that he would welcome Argali. She came freely, to serve the tribe. Our women are strong. They have ridden into battle. And been chiefs of their tribes. I'll tell you about one, Tomyris. A legend. Have you heard of Cyrus the Great?"

"The Satrap's ancestor. But let me tell..."

## 10: TRAPEZUS – 406 B.C.

Raising both hands, palms out, Targitus cut her off. "Didn't you order me to do the talking tonight?"

Quiet had settled over the campsite. The purr of a turtledove had given way to the whistle of a scops-owl. Excited by her brashness and the exchange, she would not let an owl turn her mood melancholy. Sitting cross-legged facing the Altaian, she felt the freshness of a cold breeze through the yurt's central opening. For the first time since her father's death she felt happy.

Targitus resumed his story. "She was queen and ruler of the Massagetae. Cyrus decided to move his army against her. But first, he offered his hand in marriage. Tomyris refused, recognizing the offer as a ploy to gain her lands. She warned him not to come into her territory and assured him that she would stay away from his as well. The Araxes River separated their dominions. Tomyris told Cyrus that, if he preferred to fight, either to withdraw his army three days' march from the Araxes, and she would cross to do battle, or she would withdraw the same distance on her side and he could cross to engage her. On advice of Croesus, the former king of Lydia, Cyrus crossed the Araxes. Again on advice of Croesus, he tried a ruse. The idea was to leave a small detachment of feeble soldiers about a day's march from the river, equipping them with banquet tables filled with good food and ample wine, and then take his main army back to the river's edge to await an attack on this detachment by the Massagetae. Croesus believed that the Massagetae, after overwhelming the Persians, would enjoy the food and drink to excess, making them easy prey for Cyrus' main army."

Rachel sat shivering but enthralled. Pausing in his tale, Targitus rose to start the fire that he wished he had kindled before they got settled. His men had made the task easy by stacking dry wood inside the yurt. He placed tinder at the center of the shelter and interlaced the logs above. Then, striking stone against iron, he directed sparks at the tinder until it caught. Blazing up, fire brightened the enclosure and smoke mingled with fresh night air. Sight and smell tricked the mind into feeling instantly the warmth that was yet to come.

Rachel watched Targitus with something more than pleasure. Whether in speech or motion, this man was practiced. He exuded a brio of accomplishment. He knew it too, Rachel thought. She felt safe beside him, enfolded by his competence and concern. She imagined cutting his hair, which had grown shaggy and long. Her skin tingled.

"Please continue," Rachel said, her eyes searching for his through the flames that separated them.

"Tomyris sent a third of her army forward. They wiped out the Persian detachment and applied themselves to the banquet tables, whose offerings had the intended effect. Falling upon the engorged enemy, the Persians killed many and took the rest as prisoners. Spargapises, son of Tomyris and general of the army, was among the captured.

"When the Queen learned of these sad events, she sent a message to Cyrus, saying: 'Give back my son and get out of my country with your forces intact, and be content with your triumph. If you refuse, I swear by the sun our master to give you more blood than you can drink, for all your gluttony.'

"Cyrus ignored the offer.

"Meanwhile, Spargapises begged to be freed of his chains. He assured the King he would not attempt escape. Cyrus obliged, whereupon Spargapises seized a weapon and killed himself. Tomyris moved her army forward. There followed a great battle, won by the Massagetae. Cyrus was killed and his body brought to the Queen. She pushed his head into a large skin filled with human blood, declaring as this was done, 'Though I have conquered you and live, yet you have ruined me by taking my son. See now — I fulfill my threat: you have your fill of blood.'"

Rachel remained silent. Where the owl failed, Targitus' account of this legendary clash succeeded. Rachel sat before the fire, subdued and sad. Here, she realized, was another link between her people and his. Cyrus the Great. Great in his magnanimity towards the Jews; great as enemy of the Massagetae. It was now late in the evening. Targitus wore a tentative expression, like an actor after the curtain falls. Rachel had felt how proud he was of his people and their leader, of the earnest attempts at statecraft by Queen Tomyris and finally of the killing of Cyrus. She knew he had tried to answer her challenge. She worked to order her thoughts, made more difficult by the tears in her eyes. She hoped they were hidden from the firelight. Because,

## 10: TRAPEZUS – 406 B.C.

were he to ask her why, she wouldn't have known what to say.

"Your story's surprising. I see how proud it makes you as a descendent of these warriors. Fair and fierce, you've made them. But it troubles me too."

He added wood to the now ebbing flames. "That should lessen the smoke: I see it's making your eyes water."

"Cyrus the Great, trickster to the Massagetae, was a hero to the Jews. Liberator of the Jews, he was slain by the Massagetae." Rachel explained how Cyrus had conquered Babylon and granted permission for the exiled Jews to return to Jerusalem. "You remember my telling you about Yahweh, our people's God. Well, one of our greatest poets has Yahweh refer to Cyrus thus:

> 'That saith of Cyrus, He is my shepherd,
> And shall perform all my pleasure:
> Even saying to Jerusalem, Thou shalt be built;
> And to the temple, Thy foundation shall be laid.'

I am not a fervent believer. My father grieved over my lack of conviction. But I can accept Cyrus the Great as our savior.

"There's something poignant about this," she continued. "Tonight, in the foothills of the Caucasus, we uncovered opposing views of this man."

Targitus sat mute and motionless close to the circle of fire. Only the owl interrupted the quiet. Inching his way around towards Rachel, he gently took her hand in his and looked into her eyes, etched by reflections of the flames. She returned his gaze until its intimacy became unbearable. With a tiny gasp, she averted her eyes, turning to stare at the fire. She asked if he would like to hear a few more lines from the same poet. He nodded.

> "So shall my word be that goeth forth out of my mouth:
> It shall not return unto me void,
> But it shall accomplish that which I please,
> And it shall prosper in the thing whereto I sent it.
> For ye shall go out with joy,
> And be led forth with peace:
> The mountains and the hills shall break forth before you into singing,

And all the trees of the field shall clap their hands.
Instead of the thorn shall come up the fir tree:
And instead of the briar shall come up the myrtle tree:
And it shall be to the Lord for a name,
For an everlasting sign that shall not be cut off."

When she had finished, Targitus rose, still holding her hand so that she followed naturally, rising beside him. A few inches taller, he looked at her smiling and said, "I liked that. I liked it very much." Releasing her hand, he turned to disappear into the darkness.

Left alone, Rachel's mind danced about like butterflies over a patch of purple monarda. She had always delighted in the power of beautiful words drawn from her mind and shaped by her voice to appeal to an audience. Tonight's recital had expressed as much subtlety of inflection as she could command. She knew he had been moved. Yet her pleasure at his response, indeed, her growing attraction to him, was marred by ambivalence. Wasn't he altogether too foreign to be able to understand her, or she him? Didn't the undisclosed matter with Cyrus, so fraught with difficulty in its power to diminish them both in the eyes of each other, make any closer relationship risky? Wouldn't it be wise to match her physical distance from the man with emotional reserve?

The scops-owl had been joined by his mate. Their muted whistles made it seem they were circling the yurt.

# CHAPTER 11

En Route to Scopasis – 406 B.C.

Targitus groped his way back to the shelter where his men slept. Lying down in cramped quarters among them, he wondered what it was about this woman that made her so different? Something unique to Rachel? Were all Jewish women this way? He could see a patch of black sky through the yurt's large vent. So dark was the moonless night that he caught sight of a meteor trailing a pearly string of light across the opening. An omen? he wondered.

If the bottom and sides of the yurt were the earth and the dome the sky, then the opening at the center of the dome was the North Star, the fixed opening to the world beyond, about which the lights of the sky revolved. Surely an omen, but what kind? His mind raced away from sleep's slow advance.

Was it her intensity? A certain unpredictability? These, yes. But there was something else: he felt that, underlying her behavior, there was an assumption, one he had never experienced before, that he would accept her as standing on the same ground as he stood. And this despite her being alone, essentially helpless and dependent on him. In others it might shade into arrogance. What's more, the assumption was not wrong. He thought her similar to certain older women in his village, those whom no man could intimidate. She was bewitching. He drifted toward a restless and interrupted sleep through the few hours of darkness that remained.

On the next day, they reached the headwaters of the Phasis River. With the night's conversation in mind, Targitus mentioned an alternative route that crossed the Surami Range and would have brought them to the River Cyrus, which flows east across the rich Iberian plain to the Caspian Sea. It was named for the man who had both divided and united them the night before. Riding side by side where the trail widened, Targitus asked, "What future do you see for Cyrus? You said you had talked to him about his family. I heard from Persians in Trapezus that he envied his brother's place, feeling superior in every way. I heard he even boasted of holding his wine better than Artaxerxes. I have an older brother. I can understand. With Darius dead, Artaxerxes will become King of all Persia."

"I couldn't get him to talk about his brother. He was close to his mother. I heard gossip around the palace that Artaxerxes hated Cyrus. I suspect life's going to change with Darius gone."

Targitus' questions about Cyrus and his brother had knocked another scab off the wound he bore. Stupid, self-inflicted pain, he thought.

In silence they resumed their ride. Targitus saw no obvious escape from his dark mood. He worried that it might scare Rachel.

He was saved by large clumps of the mellea, or honey mushroom, that he spied among the tall pine and spruce growing thick back from the water's edge. It was a sight to lift the heart of any mushroom fancier.

"Look, do you know that mushroom?"

She followed with her eye the line of his arm, but didn't see them at first, so completely had their reddish brown and yellow caps blended with the earthy hues of the groundcover. Finally, the whitish shades of the stems caught her eye, enabling her first to imagine, as one might a rabbit that had just disappeared in a thicket, and then to see, the tufts of honey-colored caps above. "Isn't it late for mushrooms?"

Dismounting, Targitus pulled a felt cloth from his ground pad

## 11: EN ROUTE TO SCOPASIS - 406 B.C.

and, instructing Belukcha to stay while exhorting Rachel to follow, he darted under, around and sometimes through the dead branches that thickened with each step he took into the forest. Rachel followed behind, grateful for the course he was opening. They got down on all fours to examine the first large clump.

"They came after the heavy rain, despite the chill," Targitus explained. Breaking off a hollow stem midway down, just below the ringed remains of the universal veil that had enveloped the young fungus as it emerged from the ground, he invited Rachel to bite off a chunk of its matted wooly cap. "It won't hurt you, I promise. Tell me what you taste."

Mushrooms held powerful associations for Rachel. As a teenaged girl, she had often been sent to collect them in the Tmolus Range. They were unpredictable, even magical, in their changing shapes, smells and tastes.

The earth was ripe and moist. Responding to the couple's tread, it exhaled earthy smells that enveloped Rachel even before she caught the pungent odor of the mellea or the now comforting smell of Targitus beside her. With shivers of pleasure, she recalled the coda to last night's long conversation. It was the same feeling she had experienced with Targitus in Sardis. She felt self-conscious next to this Altaian. Deeply so, as she recalled the bat cave incident. Averting his gaze, she followed his example by nibbling a mushroom. "You can't eat that," she cried, spitting out what remained in her mouth.

"Actually, you can, after we cook them. I admit they taste acrid. It's lost in the cooking. You'll see."

Rachel kept spitting as the unpleasant taste lingered. "You played a mean trick on me. You look pleased with yourself." She was scowling.

"I want you to experience the contrast. Come now, help me gather what we can hold in this cloth."

Still scowling, she blurted out, "For that, you must submit your head to me for a cutting."

Looking up, Targitus caught the twinkle in her eyes.

That night Rachel ate the mellea, cautiously at first, and then with abandon. It would be the last of the year's mushrooms, for, within another day, the band would begin to climb where conditions would not support them. After supper, Targitus followed Rachel back to her yurt. He wanted to hear more about her childhood. Objecting at first, she relented when he reminded her of how she had entered her home to find him there with her mother, who was telling their family history. "Your return cut that visit short," he complained, grinning.

"I was the family's firstborn, after two miscarriages. My mother was thirty-four. My father wanted desperately to have a son, and name him Jacob, after his father, who had died when my father was eleven. They named me Jacobea.

"My mother believed it was her duty to give her husband a son. She had one more miscarriage. And then, when I was eleven, she got pregnant again. I was excited, but my family insisted that all outward signs of joy be suspended. It was as if the whole community was holding its breath.

"Just after I turned twelve, mother gave birth to a son. We were happy beyond limits. There were days of prayer and celebration leading to the ceremony of circumcision. I wondered what name they would give him. They took a long time to give me the news. They called me into their bedroom. My father said, 'Jacobea, we have decided to name your brother 'Jacob'. That means your name must be changed. We're going to let you pick the new name.' I remember thinking how false his effort to sound light-hearted."

"You were then twelve? That's extraordinary. How did you react?"

"A shiver went down my spine, sinking into my stomach. I thought of my friends and the coming mortification in having to tell them I was no longer 'Jacobea.' I felt they had chosen the newborn over me. I told them I felt sacrificed. I was so miserable, I even compared it to the gruesome Hebrew rite of burning one's firstborn as an offering to Moloch, the fire god. I was overcome with self-pity."

"I've known self-pity. It drags one down. But somehow you must have escaped."

"Refuge in spinning. And time. I ran from the house that day, taking my spindle and a basket of wool. You don't know spinning, but believe me, it has a meditative quality. It laps at the edges of your mind, numbing anxieties. And in one respect, my parents were right.

## 11: EN ROUTE TO SCOPASIS – 406 B.C.

I had fun picking my own name. As word of my search spread, I became the center of attention. Particularly among my friends."

Rachel made Targitus another cup of tea. With felt pads she picked up a pot close to the fire and poured boiling water over the chamomile leaves she had put in his cup.

"Why 'Rachel'?"

"I had several interests that gave me ideas. I had heard the ancient Judaic texts many times. I knew by heart the stories of Eve in the Garden of Eden, of Naomi and Ruth in the country of Moab, of Esther in the king's palace at Susa. I thought of picking a name from among these legendary women. They appealed but at the same time frightened me."

"Too many expectations?"

"Maybe. I never figured it out. But I had a love of the garden and of cooking. That came from my mother. So, I thought of names associated with fruits, nuts and herbs. Shrubs too."

"Like what?"

"Oh, there were many possibilities. Cherry, hazel, rosemary, sage. Saffron, sassafras, sorrel and thyme. Holly and heather. Even juniper. I tried them all. And flowers. Rose, clematis, viola, hellebora, primula and iris. No mushrooms." She threw him a piquant glance.

"But my biggest love was the spindle and loom. I knew how to spin threads of wool, linen and gold; how to use vegetables and insects to extract dyes that could turn white wool flesh color, hyacinthine or blood red; how to use the vertical loom to craft fabrics for the family. And I was obsessed with becoming an artist. Once I started down this path, the choice became obvious."

"Really?."

"'Rachel' in Hebrew means 'ewe.' Actually, I first thought of 'Tavah,' the Hebrew word for spinning wool. Didn't like that sound. So I tried 'Rachel.' Once I said the name to myself out loud, it seemed to fit."

"So you re-created yourself as Rachel."

"Yes. And, you know, once I got started, the search was fun. To be in control. To have this power."

"It probably helped you grow up quickly."

"I am making it sound too easy. You have to remove one set of clothes before you can put the new set on. Getting rid of 'Jacobea' didn't happen the instant I began to call myself 'Rachel'. It took time. About as long as it took to forgive my parents. What they did to me gradually changed my vision of the future. Acceptance of my father's faith began to waver. I grew more independent. Although the world I hoped to inhabit was indistinct, it became more and more detached from that of my parents. By 'Rachel's' first birthday, I knew my world was going to be different."

She had finished.

"What a story! Amazing." Revealing too, he thought, electing to keep his insights to himself. The hour was late. Targitus retired to the Altaians' yurt, where he confessed his interest in Rachel wasn't entirely a fascination with her mind. Not beautiful to the point of Argali's perfection, to be sure. Her face was alluring not because of what Targitus saw but what he imagined would become of her still maturing features. Her eyes shone brightly despite being deeply set above wide and sharply exposed cheekbones. Her mouth seemed a bit too full. From their first meeting, Targitus had noted the curves of her upper lip.

Under rough travel clothes, he saw again her smooth olive-colored skin. Below the bat cave he had stored it all in his mind: from the line of her narrow waist up a straight and softly muscled back to her long delicate neck visible despite the skein of hair that tumbled down; from there to the curve of her neck around and down to her breasts, nipples separated by the full reach of his thumb and little finger; from there in his mind's eye he had moved down along the arabesque turn of her hips to limn the fullness of her thighs, the half-moon curve of her buttocks, the taper of her legs below and between them a dark and curly region.

Beyond these thoughts, there was plain physical need. He hadn't enjoyed a woman since Sardis, where the Satrap's attendants had discreetly provided opportunities for Altaians seeking female companionship. In the Altai, he was accustomed to sex whenever he wished. Until married, Altaian women in theory, but seldom in practice, could say no to a man's advances; upon marriage, even the theory dissolved, leaving the wife at the mercy of her husband.

## 11: EN ROUTE TO SCOPASIS – 406 B.C.

"My hair offends you?" Targitus had ridden close behind Rachel. The trail had grown steeper and the horses were being held to a slow pace. The day had started out overcast and blustery, but with the approach of mid-day, the west wind was driving the clouds away.

Rachel turned on her horse to face Targitus. "Did I say that? All I meant was, unless you want to attract birds and mice, you must let me cut it."

"I suppose you can see the need more than I can. No offense, but do you know how to do it?"

Again she turned to respond, and also to check his humor. "With a very sharp knife, yes. I often cut my father's hair and beard."

"When we stop for our meal, you shall have it." He was enjoying the banter so much that for a moment, an uncommon moment, he forgot his responsibilities. But, then, he added, "Ho, Rachel. Better not to turn around on this steep trail; your horse could easily misstep."

They stopped on a large, flat stone outcropping overlooking the Phasis ravine. Targitus took out his knife and dressed the already sharp blade on a soft stone. He checked its condition with a careful scrape of the blade against the fingernail of his thumb. Declaring it sharp enough, he handed it to Rachel and sat down. "Do you want an audience or should I send them away?" he asked.

"No need for that. A comb might help, though. And some water."

The men made a fire and heated water, enough for barley and to soften and clean Targitus' hair, which was too dense, dirty and matted to allow the use of the comb Tymnes had given to Rachel.

Waiting for the water to heat, Rachel examined the task before her, looking for a plan of attack. She sunk her fingers into his hair, trying to use them as a rough comb. They wouldn't come out. "I'll tell you right now, this is not going to be easy," she said.

When the water was ready, she ordered Targitus to lie down on his back, resting his neck on a log that Tymnes, who seemed determined to help, had anticipated a need for. She spooned the water over his head and across his bearded face, rubbing gently with her hands. For the first time since leaving Sardis, she felt in control. Wasn't washing hair something like spinning wool? And happy. Wasn't cutting hair going to be like cutting the pile knots she had tied a million times and more in making pile carpets?

"You've cleaned up well. Better than expected. Now, sit up straight and hold still." Rachel tried the comb, but it couldn't be used for such a thicket. She would just have to do her best with fingers.

The day was now bright with sunshine and warmth. A bird hidden in the forest sang a trilling melody, again and again. Targitus said, "Do you hear that thrush? Listen, it's saying: Sweet joy befall thee." Rachel pinched him in protest. "I am not making this up. My mother's story. The words fit. Listen."

"Ask Madyes to respond. We can have a duet."

Targitus nodded. But before he could summon Madyes, he appeared, pipe in hand, prepared to play.

Rachel said, "Pipe us a gleeful song, a merry one to honor the thrush and attract the skylark." The piper piped while Rachel cut. The mood was happy, content.

Rachel's knees pushed against Targitus' back as she worked the knife, using one hand to position and comb his hair for cutting. He was enjoying the quick motions of her hands on his head and face, the pressure of her body, its closeness and even her smell, which waxed strong as she grew hot under the sun, now directly overhead. And somehow, she sensed his joy, confirmed by a loud moan when she announced the job was done.

When he entered her yurt that evening, he carried a torch from the cooking fire with which to light a modest blaze in the center of the yurt. They sat cross-legged next to one another for the first time, knees touching, and sipped tea in silence. Targitus felt sure there was between them some tinder dry and ready to ignite. As for Rachel, the cutting of Targitus' hair had been at once a fulfillment and a frustration. Within a minute of his leaving her the night before, Rachel's independence, so central to her sense of self, had collapsed. She wanted Targitus beside her, touching her. Since leaving Trapezus, she had felt enfolded by his presence. Now, she was ready to be enfolded in his arms. She was surprised, almost frightened, by the strength of her desire. Was this love or merely the physical side of depend-

## 11: EN ROUTE TO SCOPASIS – 406 B.C.

ence? Was she reckless with desire because the pull of family and home were gone? Not reckless enough, she mused with a slight laugh, to be oblivious of her cycle. With the coming of blood but a few days away, she knew the chance of pregnancy was remote.

Now, Rachel saw the prospect looming at the edge of the flickering light, having rehearsed it any number of times with Vashti's help and most recently, the night before, alone. She felt herself ready, indeed, hungry.

Targitus led with his heart. Taking her hand in his, he said softly, "Shall we pick up where we left off last night?" Putting his arm around her, he lifted her face towards his and gave her a long kiss. Gently, he lay her down on her back on the felt bed. He removed his clothes. And, then, he removed hers. Whispering, she said, as much to herself as to him, "I've waited for this moment." As he hovered above her, Rachel watched him pause long enough to take her in. Suddenly, as his eyes swept down her full length, she felt self-conscious. And then, the things that should have evolved didn't. Although she knew that what he wanted was hers to give and that, since the night before, she had been eager, even desperate, to oblige, her body refused to follow the dictates of her mind.

Neither spoke. Rachel felt as if parted in two, with a great divide between mind and body, each operating entirely on its own. The more Targitus tried to win over her body, the more resistant to his touch it became. And, then, Rachel grew frightened, her mind bending to the will of her body. Her moorings gave way. She was adrift in an unknown realm with a man she hardly knew, a man who came from a very different culture far away. Taking recourse in candor, she found voice enough to whisper, "I am sorry; I am sorry Targitus. There's nothing I can do."

For minutes hers had been the only sound in the yurt, other than an occasional crackle from the fire. The tension grew. Finally, Targitus laughed. Encircling stress ebbed away. Rachel's heart slowed to a resting beat. She was able to ask why he had laughed. And he replied: "Rachel, I didn't know whether to laugh, cry or get angry. Then, looking at your face, I realized you were going to handle the crying part. So I laughed. There was nothing better to do."

Rachel gathered herself tightly, arms around raised knees, naked beside Targitus, who was seated back on his haunches. It was still warm near the fire, although the flames were receding. She stretched out a hand to grasp his. Then, with her fears beginning to melt, and all of Vashti's teachings before her, she rose to fetch a couple of dry logs from the opposite side of the yurt. Putting them on the fire, she directed Targitus to assume her former position on the felt bed. "I have an idea, Targitus, that we might try before you leave."

The next night they camped at the confluence of the Phasis and its main tributary, the Qvirila, where the Phasis turned north to commence the ascent that would lead them over the Caucasus Range almost midway between Mount Kazbegi and Mount Elbruz. During the day, they had watched cranes, greylag geese and black kites winging southeast towards the Caspian or sometimes veering southwest towards the Black Sea. The formations were as varied as the species, some in wedge, others bunched or in line and some in a magical skein that tapered across the sky. The music of their voices, not always melodious, could be heard before the birds were seen. Their multitudes quickened the collective pulse of the travelers, making manifest the coming of winter. Through that chill and blustery day, with each passing flight, horse and rider were as one in picking up the pace.

The established pattern continued that evening, with Rachel and Targitus disappearing in her yurt after supper, tea in hand. Targitus had slept a while beside Rachel the night before, awakening to an owl's lament in the pitch of night to return to the Altaians' yurt.

They sat at an angle to each other before the fire. Close but not touching, eyes directed into the flames. Targitus was the first to break the silence.

"Do you know what went wrong last night?" he asked. "I mean, I know what went right, but that came afterwards."

"I am not sure we can talk about it. It's difficult. Let me confess something: I am way beyond my experience."

Targitus could read her caution, but he sensed an eagerness to

## 11: EN ROUTE TO SCOPASIS - 406 B.C.

talk as well. He thought he could handle whatever she had to say. "Please. Let me know your mind."

Rachel saw a gentle and ingenuous expression on his face, now turned toward her. Again, she felt secure in his presence. She knew he was incapable of hurting her. Returning her gaze to the fire, she cast off.

"I am a virgin. I had prepared my mind to change that last night. Maybe I failed. Maybe my mind was ready but not my body, which got the upper hand. I don't know. Before father was killed, I was determined to remain a virgin until I married. And I would only marry for love. Cyrus tested that resolve. As much as I wanted to be an artist at the loom, I wanted children by a husband. A Jewish elder once told me the only sure path to immortality was through one's children. I believed him, although I also believe that for the artist there's another path. I still believe him, and I want that sort of immortality, desperately, I want it someday. But things changed on top of that mountain. Life grew less certain. I felt much older. I decided to be open to any good thing that came along. Like you. Maybe deep inside, change isn't so easy."

Rachel surprised herself. It was as if she were engaged in analyzing someone else's mistake at the loom. Slowly she turned her head away from the fire to look at Targitus, who wore an expectant expression. "And what about you, what were you expecting?"

"Why, the same thing. I thought you were willing." Targitus reached for a couple of logs, placed them on the embers and locked his eyes on the flames that began to curl around them. "Your reaction, it's something I'd never experienced before," he said.

Rachel winced. "Please don't take offense. You were right to believe I was eager. I thought so too. Something happened that I can't explain." Rachel turned back to concentrate on the flames, which had become an uncritical conduit for their thoughts. "Perhaps we were too hasty."

"Hasty?"

Rachel shifted from sitting cross-legged beside him to resting on her haunches, facing him. This put her head a notch higher than his.

"Yesterday, you taught me to love the mellea. Without you, I wouldn't have even seen those clumps; and even had I seen them, one taste and I would have thrown them away. You gave your knowledge to me, and that made us both happy. The lesson applies here as well." Seeing that Targitus continued to stare into the fire, she shifted her position again, returning her own gaze to the same spot. "I am afraid to speak of these things."

Targitus reached out to press her hand in his.

"As Vashti put it, men think love-making comes naturally; the better the man, the more naturally it comes. She said it's not that simple."

"The women I've coupled with always enjoyed it," Targitus said, releasing her hand and rising to rest on his haunches.

Rachel hit back hard. "Were they really free to tell you if they didn't?" Seeing him subdued, she wished she hadn't.

"Are you finished?" he asked.

"When I was around twelve, my mother trapped me one day, sitting before my loom in the middle of a pattern she knew I wouldn't abandon. She wanted to explain the woman's role in marriage. Sex was for wives one of the covenants of marriage. Like giving your husband a son. If done well, it might become a source of power. It might or might not be enjoyable. It didn't matter. On the other hand, by Jewish tradition, men were expected to give pleasure to their wives. Mother said this duty was more aspiration than reality. She thought most women's pleasure came vicariously, through pleasure given to their husbands. Vashti called my mother's ideas an excuse.

"And you? A disciple of Sarah or Vashti?" They had lifted their eyes to look at each other.

Rachel smiled, as if to show him she knew this question had no simple answer. Things were seldom straightforward. "I have a proposition for you," Targitus announced, lifting Rachel by the hand. "I'll teach you the mushrooms of the forest. In exchange, you'll teach me the lessons you learned from Vashti." Targitus was grinning, with a look that told Rachel his offer was one part serious, two parts jest.

"All right, it's a bargain." Now they were both laughing. "When do we begin?"

The mushroom season had ended. There would be no teaching

## 11: EN ROUTE TO SCOPASIS – 406 B.C.

opportunities until May of the following year, by which time, she and Targitus would be more than a thousand miles apart. The skewed bargain bemused her. But she didn't complain. Instead, gently lifting her arms to encircle Targitus' neck, she drew him to her. Lips met; the lessons began.

"Listen," she said.

> 'Kiss me with the kisses of thy mouth,
> for thy love is better than wine.
> because of the savor of thy good ointments
> thy name is as ointment poured forth,
> therefore do the virgins love thee.
> O take me with thee, that we may run away:
> for the king hath brought me into his chambers.'"

Targitus savored her words.

"How often I imagined reciting that poem to my lover," Rachel said.

Targitus held Rachel at arm's length, looking at her as if for the first time. He now understood how Cyrus could have been smitten by this woman, by her voice alone.

"It's the Song of Songs," she continued. "It comes from Solomon, a great king of the Jewish people.

They kissed again. The night passed.


The band of seven riders struggled first up and then down the narrow path that led across the Caucasus range. Targitus had been selective in responding to Rachel's questions. There were many routes, to be sure, along this east-west barrier separating the European tribes from those in Asia, but none was easy. For the mountain tribes of Colchis and Iberia, the question was simply, "Can a dog pass? Where a dog can go, there too can we."

Near the top of the pass, first, a thick mist and then, a wet snow driven by wailing winds cut off all visibility. They knew they had reached the summit only when they bumped into a tree-shrine in the narrow pathway leading north. It was a stunted conifer, gnarled and bent. Affixed to its branches were bits of clothing, each tied there to bear witness to a traveler's prayers. This spare sign of humanity revived their spirits as they waited, crouching in the wind shadow of the tree, for a break in the weather.

Once over the pass, the Altaians proceeded in a northeasterly direction across the relatively flat lands that separated the Caucasus Range from the Oarus River. Always together, sharing the preparation of meals and the other chores of survival and progress towards their destination of Scopasis, it proved impossible to maintain secrets. The growing intimacy of Targitus and Rachel was marked by the others as clearly as they felt the cold wind brush their faces or the falling snow wet their clothes. Vicariously, they warmed to the progress of this romance.

One day, Tymnes mentioned to Targitus that, whatever concerns he might have had with appearances should by now have vanished. He suggested that Targitus would get a better sleep if he just remained overnight with Rachel in her yurt. "After all, wasn't it yours to begin with?"

The couple's joy grew increasingly obvious. Radiating through the band, it became infectious, lifting all spirits. Envy grows only in those believing they might have walked in the shoes of the envied. Even Tomycharsis, who claimed to miss women more than all the others combined, begrudged Targitus nothing. He took vicarious pleasure in what he imagined was going on in Rachel's yurt and, despite being silenced again and again by the others, was ready in an instant to describe what he saw. Targitus accepted the advice of his senior aide.

It took Rachel many nights of experimentation to discover for herself, as she taught him, what gave her pleasure. She found him an eager student, who, from the beginning, had accepted the simple idea of deferring his own pleasure until he was assured of hers. He found it challenging at first, because the act of bringing her to a high pitch of excitement proved a powerful catalyst to his own arousal. After a couple of failed attempts, he grew despondent. Rachel knew of these things from Vashti. "Look, Targitus, this is normal. Don't worry about it. Tell me, since you first began, have you ever tried to defer?"

## 11: EN ROUTE TO SCOPASIS – 406 B.C.

Targitus shook his head.

"So, you've got a habit. Here's an idea. When I start to become so aroused that it threatens to spread and overpower you, think of something else. Think of crossing an Altaian river all covered with ice, or in late spring, when most of the ice is gone, holding your horse's tail in the frigid waters, trying to make it to the other side."

Targitus took her suggestions seriously. Deferral became his new paradigm, something he worked on so hard that Rachel worried he might overshoot the mark. Deferral did not mean indefinite postponement, she reminded him. Or so much work as to crowd out spontaneity.

Their nights of exuberant wakefulness grew longer as the number of days left before they would reach Scopasis declined. Targitus found belief the key to control. As they opened to one another, nothing was off limits. They found the engine of desire in their minds, which propelled their bodies forward.

"Here's something I like about you." Targitus said. They were lying between felt bedding, entwined tightly and listening to a wind that challenged the yurt with powerful gusts.

"Your recklessness in weaving. Those spreads. Without that rebellion, you wouldn't be here now."

Rachel hadn't labeled herself "rebel." But she didn't object. "In Sardis, one learned to spin, dye and weave early. That's what little girls did. At first, my mother taught me. She was good. I loved our sessions together. Then, at thirteen, I went to apprenticeship. My choice, not mother's."

"But the passion. Was it there from the beginning?"

"I remember liking the process but not the passion. I guess it grew slowly. It's a long story. Sure you want to hear it?"

Targitus nodded. Outside the wind moaned.

"I loved the class, which concentrated on spinning. We were using spindles with whorls placed low on the shaft. The one I put through your hand had the whorl up high." She threw him a sly smile. "I guess you've never tried spinning."

"It's not popular among Altaian men."

"Here's how it works." She sat up, resting on her haunches. "I need my arms. You start the spindle whirling with a quick flick of thumb and fingers, as you might a top. Like this. The whorl acts as a flywheel. It's made of clay. The idea is to use the whirling spindle to twist the wool into thread, store it on the shaft and maintain tension as the spindle is "dropped" from the hand and lowered to the floor on the thread being spun." The wind began to howl. Undeterred, Rachel acted out each movement in detail. "Look, here's my left hand feeding the wool from a bundle of supply to my right hand, which can adjust the speed of feed. The goal? Strong thread. Uniform thickness. Now, when the spindle reaches the floor, I wind the newly formed thread up on the shaft. Then, I give another flick to set it whirling, and repeat the process."

She caught him yawning. "Are you asleep yet?"

"Listen. The wind's picked up. I couldn't sleep even if I wanted to. You don't make it look easy."

"There's a knack. The right hand makes a quick downward pull on the wool supply and an equally quick release of the yarn so that it is free to form thread through the twirl of the spindle. Actually, it's more than a knack. One needs the gift of eye and hand working together. It makes a difference in spinning and weaving. It came naturally. As I am sure it did for you in handling a bow and arrow."

"That," he admitted, "and constant practice."

"I entered a spinning contest at the end of my first year of apprenticeship. I thought I could win."

Rachel noticed a quizzical smile forming on Targitus' face.

"The class had taught me something that's hard to describe. I don't mean technique. I mean how good I could be. As the year passed, I gradually realized I was different."

"Different?"

"Better than the others. My parents kept telling me a sign of growing up was knowing what you can do and what you can't. I became aware of a talent."

"And you were right."

"Not exactly. I'll tell you. I was the shortest and youngest to compete. I got off to a flying start. By the time the measuring sands were half gone, I was way ahead in length of thread spun. Suddenly,

## 11: EN ROUTE TO SCOPASIS – 406 B.C.

after a vigorous twirl of the spindle, a section of my clay whorl flew away from the shaft, followed by another and another. My speed decreased. My rhythm broke with the clay. I tried to regain control, but it was useless. I was crying. Finished."

"That's sad. You needed a hug."

"That and more. Nothing like this had happened before. My mother solved the problem, once we got home. On the way, my father insisted it was a lesson from Yahweh to his doubting daughter. Mother shut him up with a more natural, and convincing, explanation. She had noticed that, at about three yards from the walls around the room we were in, the wooden floor ended and a tile one began. I had backed up all the way to the tile floor as I spun. My spindle was hitting the floor hard, the whorl taking most of the impact. In time, the clay cracked."

Still on her haunches, Rachel suddenly felt cold. Lying down, she snuggled against Targitus as the wind continued its attack.

"Weren't you going to explain the passion? There must be more," Targitus said.

"I returned to class the next year. And entered the contest again. Like getting back on the horse that threw you. I used a new spindle. The whorl was clay, but this time, I put a rug under my feet. It was just big enough to stand on. I hoped it would hold me in place while spinning, as well as soften the spindle's fall if my feet didn't.

"But the big thing was the design. I put the whorl high on the shaft instead of low. No one in Sardis had ever seen that design before. It was my secret. To set this spindle twirling, I would roll the whorl down my thigh. I found the spin easier to accomplish this way than with the thumb and finger flick. Also quicker and more powerful. I had tried to twirl a low-whorl spindle on my thigh too. It only worked until the shaft became covered with thread.

"One day, while playing around, I caught the new spindle between my feet as it reached the floor. I must have been trying to prevent the whorl from hitting. Just for fun, I continued this trick and began to wonder whether I could use my feet to give a new twirl. If, at the same time I could lift up my arms, couldn't I draft another one to one and a half feet of thread before having to wind it all onto the shaft? It was awkward going at first, but I saw the possibility of getting a good spin with my feet. I could spin clockwise using my right foot to kick and counter-clockwise with my left.

"It worked. With plenty of practice, I want you to know." Rachel laughed.

Targitus saw that Rachel's enthusiastic storytelling would brook no interruption unless the yurt blew away. A possibility, he thought, since the wind had risen in pace with her energy.

"So, with practice and ingenuity, you won the contest."

"Not so fast. Didn't I say the story was long? My design caused a problem. Anatolian wool had always been spun with a Z-twist. For me, the most natural thigh roll produced an S-twist. So, in competition, I would produce strands of wool twisted in a direction opposite to Anatolian custom. Wool has no natural twist, left or right. We can spin it in either direction. Only force of habit explained the Anatolian preference. I was sure I had invented a better way and would prove it in the contest.

"From the beginning, I was spinning more thread than the others. Much more. With each drop of my spindle, the foot kick caught the eye of more of the audience. By the half-way point, the whole room, save for other contestants, were clustered about me, pointing and murmuring. I was thrilled.

"The parents of the second place contestant were the first to object. They claimed my high-whorl spindle was illegal. After conferring briefly, the chief judge said there had never been limits on the kind of spindle or technique used. He ruled my spindle legal.

"Another contestant complained that my thread had an S-twist, different from all the others. This point caught the judges by surprise. S-twists weren't part of their experience. Undone by the angry outcry, they ended the proceedings without declaring a result. Two days later, they announced the winner. Not me. I got a special award for 'Originality of Design and Technique.' Despite my obvious improvements, at first, no one tried to copy them. But word spread swiftly. I later discovered my design had received more attention than the workshop was willing to admit."

"I think the yurt's still protecting us," Targitus said. "But just in

## 11: EN ROUTE TO SCOPASIS – 406 B.C.

case." He moved on top of her, feigning the need to cover as much of her as possible.

Targitus wanted to see her spin. "Must I wait till we reach Scopasis or can you do it from a horse?"

"I'll try tomorrow if you'll let me sleep now."


Progress on the ground proved bittersweet for them both. The excitement of getting closer to the Scythian settlement was offset by the pain of anticipating the changes that arrival would bring.

Targitus was serious about planning ahead. He had one central issue, which he elected to raise not during the intimacy of an evening but in the course of a day's travel, when Rachel would be more focused on their destination than their next evening together.

"Rachel, I am sure we'll be offered yurts in the village. They keep some for travelers. We used them on the way to Sardis. How do you feel about our continuing to share? I mean publicly."

Rachel hadn't wanted to think about this, or any other aspect of what lay ahead. She was not ready to face an end to the beginning of her adult life so soon. "Oh, gentle curses on you, for asking that question." As usual, Targitus was bringing up the rear of the column, just behind the extra horse being led by Rachel. He had ridden up beside her, reaching a hand out to her reins to slow their progress enough so that they could speak freely. A wise precaution, since sounds carried, particularly that day with a sizeable wind to their backs. Targitus laid out his line of thought, choosing words carefully. "Look, to all appearances, you are a young, attractive Jewish virgin with a talent for weaving and a plan to remain in this village and make it your home. We are Altaians passing through. Wouldn't it make sense ..."

Interrupting, Rachel demanded to know just what "appearances" suggested virginity. "Young and Semitic." Yes, she could accept that and perhaps "attractive" as well, for hadn't Targitus and even Cyrus before him found her so. But why would a Scythian assume anything about her virginity?

"Your hair. Your long raven's black hank of hair. From the morning I met you atop the pass to Trapezus, no, no, even earlier, from the first time I set eyes upon you in the royal workshop, you have worn your hair in braids. Among Scythians, only virgins wear their hair in braids, single or double. Upon marriage, a woman's hair is trussed up. Here's my point. The best plan to assure your happiness and success in this village is for you to arrive a virgin and retain that status, at least until we leave."

Rachel wanted to resist. She had protected her virginity from Cyrus' assault in order to give it at a time and place, and to a person, of her own choosing. Having done so, there was a part of her that wanted everyone to know. His possession of this precious part of her, something that could only be given once, gave her an equal sense of possessing him. And that pleased her. Yet, while wanting hers on display, sadly she recognized that marriage was the only acceptable way for a woman to show possession. She was not so independent that losing her virginity without marriage gave her no qualms. She felt a tug of emotions from two directions.

The strength of Targitus' argument settled the matter. "You took away my virginity. Now you want to keep its loss a secret, and carry that secret all the way to the Altai. I don't like it, but what else is there?"

Targitus wanted to say this decision was hard for him, too. Very hard. But his practical bent held sway. No reason to expose his own frayed emotions except to invite attention to his own pain, something he had been taught to shun in himself, scorn in others. "So, we're agreed. Trust me, it's for the best."

Rachel tried to imagine marriage in Scopasis. Was that part of her plan, as Targitus seemed to assume? She wished he weren't so quick to give her up.

"I am an outsider. A Semite. Do you think it possible for me to marry well? Assuming I want to?"

"I don't see a problem, unless you fall in love with a prince."

"Someone like you?" She shot him a wry look.

Targitus didn't catch her humor. "I am sure the Scythians of Scopasis are like the Massagetae. You know my parents are rulers. As a prince, my marriage would need their approval. Getting it would be unlikely if the woman were not from our tribe, unless some tribal

## 11: EN ROUTE TO SCOPASIS – 406 B.C.

advantage would result."

"I must stay away from princes. So far, my record isn't very good, but I'll keep trying."

From the start of the journey, Targitus had drawn Rachel out on the subject of weaving. It wasn't difficult. Speaking of textiles was as irresistible to Rachel as peach blossoms to bees.

"We all had the technical skill. But for me it counted for little if the piece I was weaving was designed by someone else. You look puzzled.

"Think of bread without salt. Meat without spice. Weaving's slow. Take away my art and it's all drudgery. Working in the Satrap's workshop closed my mind instead of opening it. That's enough about me. If you're not as sleepy as you look, tell me something more about Altaian weaving."

They were lying beside one another in the yurt, less than two weeks' travel from Scopasis. The night was pitch black – both inside and out.

"We weave nothing more elaborate than narrow belts on backstrap or ground looms."

"But you said there are many flocks of sheep?" Rachel tried to curl up with Targitus, hoping to capture what she knew to be his excess body heat, granted to him, she guessed, by some Altaian god in recompense for living in those cold environs.

"We use wool for practically everything: clothing, housing, blankets and many other things too, like wall hangings and horse adornments. But we felt the wool instead of weaving it."

Rachel had risen to a kneelling position above him. In her excitement, the blankets had fallen away, exposing her shoulders and chest to the cold night air. Peering down, she said, "When we get to Scopasis, I'll teach you to weave on a vertical loom. You can take measurements. Then, when you get home, you can build a loom and show your weavers some new things."

"Let's get there first. Then we'll see. It could take much longer than you think to teach me weaving on any kind of loom. I doubt we'll be there long enough."

A week of hard travel passed. With only a few days left, they had retired early one night. With Rachel moving gently astride Targitus, her breasts welcoming to his gaze, Targitus lifted his head upward to touch with lips and tongue what his eyes beheld, a now familiar pattern. After a while, he laid his head back and, recalling her recital to him of her beloved Song of Songs, he spoke softly a few of his favorite lines:

> "How fair and how pleasant art thou,
> O love, for delights!
> This thy stature is like to a palm tree,
> And thy breasts to clusters of grapes.
> I said, I will go up to the palm tree,
> I will take hold of the boughs thereof:
> Now also thy breasts shall be as clusters of the vine,
> And the smell of thy nose like apples ..."

And then, he raised his head to repeat the practiced pattern.

Rachel thought of the maiden, who was "sick with love," and applied those words to herself. "When we reach Scopasis, how long will you stay?"

Targitus had asked himself this question. The goal of getting home as soon as possible. The problem of his brother. The dangers of travel in the depths of winter. And now the prospect of leaving Rachel. His mind had lingered over these concerns, enlarging them until they had crowded out all else. "I don't know."

Rachel could feel him softening. "Oh, woe. I didn't mean to take you back to the beginning. It's that snow and cold."

"No. The thought of leaving you."

"I think that decision's an easy one. You started off from the Great Ulagan in March because that was the best time to leave. The same holds now. You will stay in Scopasis until March," she announced.

In fact, Targitus had become incapable of imagining the rest of his journey without her. Each time he tried, his mind slipped away, like a thread perversely avoiding the eye of a needle. Unable to examine his emotions, he turned to logic for some way around them. He thought of the Altai's deficiencies in weaving and of Rachel's proposal to teach him the skill. Soon, a new idea was forming. Rachel

## 11: EN ROUTE TO SCOPASIS – 406 B.C.

should come with him to the Great Ulagan valley and there found a weaving center. He knew the obstacles. He would have to convince her to give up the goal she had doggedly pursued. He knew her independence and ambition could conquer the powerful bond they had established. To give the idea a chance would take time. Time for her to imagine the venture as providing greater opportunities. Time for her to convert his idea into a plan of her own.

Rachel had rolled off him. Lying close, she was stroking his chest. Thinking there was much to what she had said, he nodded, without mentioning the main reason he had decided to pass the winter in Scopasis.

Beginning at dusk the evening before what they hoped would be the last day of travel, snow had fallen, thickening as dark gathered around the party. Anticipating bad weather, the yurts' side walls, which stood over three feet and were formed by a lattice of wood, had been dispensed with. The ribs of the shelter, curving poles that sprang from the lattice-work to hold the domed roof, had been set directly on the ground to lower the profile of the yurt, which must stand against the gale they expected later that night. There was a smoke hole at the apex of the dome, held in place by a wooden ring three feet in diameter, into which the poles were socketed. A flap of felt could be drawn across this hole by hemp rope, either partially to adjust the draft, or completely to shut out the elements. Despite the snowfall, the hole had been left open, a vent for smoke from the bright blaze of tamarisk and horse dung warming the occupants at the center of the yurt. The fire's flickering light cast shadows on the felt dome, illuminating the snow as it descended through the opening to be vaporized by the heat, which rose in defense of those seated below.

After midnight, the snow had tapered off; taking its place was the first frigid air of winter. By early morning, the temperature had dropped precipitously. Awakening around two from the chill that had vanquished the fire's last warmth, Targitus pulled the flap over the smoke hole to retain what little heat remained in the yurt. By then, the wind had begun, a soft murmur at first, lapping at the rounded felt wall of the yurt. Growing in intensity through the remaining hours of darkness, it became a frightful howl. Sleep became impossible. Outside, a wall of snow fifteen feet high was being driven across the steppe. Hard grains of snow penetrated the yurt, swirling about the Altaians, numbing their faces and hands.

The travelers rose before dawn and struggled in the wind to break camp as a faint light mustered in the southeast. The day's passage required the horses and their riders to go head-first against the storm. Felt wraps covered all but the eyes of the riders. The horses rebelled, unwilling to face the brutal elements. The riders tried walking ahead with reins in hand. By mid-morning, they had barely covered two miles.

Turning Rachel away from the blast, Targitus lowered her face covering to examine her nose. White spots polka-dotted a bright red field. "Can you feel my hand on your nose?" he shouted above the roar.

Rachel shook her head.

Targitus began to rub her nose vigorously.

"That hurts. You're rubbing too hard."

Targitus could see the white dots shrink as the congealed blood in her nose, aroused by his massage, flowed to the endangered tip. "You came close to losing one of your best parts. It'll be safe for now, but you must keep rubbing it and your other extremities to make the blood flow. Keep checking. Hands and feet too. If the feeling goes, you must rub until it returns."

Struggling forward through the driven snow, which rasped against them, Scyles just missed tripping over the body of a dromedary. The giant beast was in a kneeling position, still alive but far too numb and weak to stand. It must have been there for two days or more. Only its legendary endurance had kept it alive. Death was certain, either from peaceful surrender to the elements or violent attack by wolves. The chance encounter proved catalytic, triggering a decision to wait out the wind. The horses were led to form a circle, enclosing the riders, heads facing away from the wind. Inside this equine ring the riders cleared the deep snow that had drifted downwind of the dromedary. With no outward sign of guilt over using this

## 11: EN ROUTE TO SCOPASIS – 406 B.C.

dying creature so, they sat down on the frozen steppeland, resting their backs against the dromedary's side.

Amidst the whine and swirl of the gale, communication was difficult, even within the equine fence. The riders settled down silently, alone with their thoughts, to await the end of the storm. Rachel felt particularly isolated in her yearning for a change in the weather. From the moment she saw the dromedary on its knees in the snow, the image of her father sinking to his knees had taken hold of her mind. The decision to seek shelter behind the beast filled her with horror, worse because she saw no way to escape. She felt anger, too – anger directed at the Altaians for their pitiless use of this dying animal. Keenly she saw how different from these Altaians she was, how desolate she had become.

Suddenly, as if Boreas had done an about-face, the wind was gone. The high wall of snow collapsed gently of its own weight. And the sun, which had only been masked by that snow barrier, dazzled above. The distant horizon grew clear, revealing no object between frozen earth and blue sky. The steppe was covered by an endless layer of snow, a palimpsest for the wind, which since the early hours before dawn had drawn eddies and currents of ever-changing design.

Rubbing her nose and other extremities as instructed, Rachel gasped at the miracle of sunshine and the apparent warmth it brought to the stillness that now enfolded the steppe. "I could never have imagined it."

"The steppe is famous for this. We call it the 'perishing cold.'" Pointing to the snow-covered dromedary, Targitus continued. "It takes its share of travelers. But don't be fooled by the sun. The temperature is still far below freezing. The wind's absence makes you feel warm. Keep up the massage. We should get moving again." She remained silent, wondering if the weather alone could make her feel so downcast.

Abandoning their shield from a wind that had vanished, the band mounted their horses and resumed the course that would bring them that day to Scopasis, a Scythian settlement half-buried in the bone-dry snows of the frigid steppe.

# CHAPTER 12

Scopasis – 406-405 B.C.

They arrived at dusk and were greeted by the villagers with great warmth. News that the Altaians had returned spread rapidly. Soon they were surrounded by Scythian men bundled in sheepskin greatcoats girded tight at the waist with colorful sashes. Their heads were covered by pointed caps with large earflaps drawn close around their necks. The caps were crafted of sheep or goat skin with wool facing inside, and their boots were long and lined with thick felt.

The cheers and questions, flung into the deeply chilled air, vanished before reaching the intended audience. It didn't matter. The need for shelter was obvious. With a great waving of arms and pointing of direction, the villagers led the band to a level site on which three yurts were maintained for the use of travelers. While some of the hosts took away the exhausted horses to be watered, fed and groomed, others invited the band to divide up the yurts. Targitus picked one of the two smaller ones and Rachel the other, leaving the large yurt for the remaining Altaians. Inside, tamarisk fires had been started. Fed by the abundant fuel, the flames were drawn upward, heating the air, infusing it with sweet scents.

## 12: SCOPASIS – 406-405 B.C.

Rachel had traveled some six hundred miles to Trapezus to join a weaving workshop that she then had to chase another seven hundred miles across the Caucasus Range to the banks of the Oarus. In Scopasis, the pursuit ended. She had just been left alone in her assigned yurt when a villager burst in with happy word of the workshop's presence. The news hit her like ice water. In Trapezus, she had learned of the weavers' departure with deep disappointment. Now, news of their presence brought confusion, which reigned through the night, shouldering sleep aside.

The next day, Rachel was led to the resident weavers, at work in a small shelter. There were fifteen of them, each seated before a loom. Rachel saw there were ample supplies of wool. Skeins of spun yarn hung neatly on one wall; on another were as many skeins of plied yarn. Dyed and undyed, their arrangement was a product of design, Rachel thought. Lovely. Large piles of raw wool rested on netting suspended from wall to wall above the weavers.

The women appeared busy. Rachel later learned that, after a start-up period of four months, demand for the workshop's products had grown dramatically. Orders began to arrive from points south and north along the Oarus. Later, they came from many villages along the Don River, which veered east just north of the point where the Oarus veered west, creating a land divide between these two great waterways of only forty miles near Scopasis. By Rachel's arrival, the workshop had a long list of back orders, particularly for articles of clothing.

Rachel liked the workshop's atmosphere. There didn't appear to be anyone in command. Rather, the weavers seemed to operate as a co-operative in which all shared in both burden and benefit. There was also an openness towards culture and religion. Five of the weavers were Jews. The others were a sprinkling of Scythians, Greeks and Persians. Origin and faith held little interest. The important thing was one's skill with dyes, drop spindle and loom. Rachel heard how gladly she would be welcomed into the company of this female workshop. Given the backlog, she was needed. But she would have to prove her skill. The success of this workshop had been due to the uniform quality of its products. That reputation had to be preserved. In a few days, she would be tested.

On the Altaians' fourth day in Scopasis, Rachel went to the workshop to show what she could do. In the privacy of her yurt, she had practiced a bit with her golden spindle but decided not to bring it to the workshop. Targitus had never seen her spin, her promise to spin while riding having been a casualty of the weather. He went with her.

The leading spinner in the workshop handed Rachel a spindle and distaff, together with a quantity of medium-length wool combed into tops. The spindle was of the high whorl variety. "Have you always used the high whorl spindle?" Rachel asked, as she put some of the wool on the distaff and prepared to spin.

"No, just for the past two years. A weaver came through with news of a new development in Sardis. Something the Satrap had invented. Speeds up the process. We have low-whorls if you prefer. We thought you would know the new technique."

"I do," Rachel said, and commenced to spin.

Targitus stood outside the semi-circle of weavers, watching. He thought she'd be out of practice, and indeed, she was, to a degree. But the engrained motions were still in place. Like a horseman born to the saddle who starts riding again after a year away from horses. It was mainly the rhythm that needed work. It was going to take a little practice to recapture. The warm-up lasted only a few minutes. The regular sequence of sounds from the twirl of the spindle to the gentle bump when it hit the floor told the audience that Rachel was ready.

By the time Rachel had finished fashioning yarn from the hanks of wool she had been given, all neatly wrapped around the spindle with virtually no space for more, the room was still. Targitus was about to speak when clapping broke out. The applause lasted too long. Looking embarrassed, she bowed once, then raised her arms, palms facing the audience and fingers extended. "I've always loved spinning," she said. Targitus couldn't conceal his pride.

## 12: SCOPASIS – 406-405 B.C.

After conferring briefly, the senior member of the co-operative proclaimed an end to the test. "You have good reason to love spinning. You are now part of our workshop. Join us for tea. We have fresh bread and, best of all, nardek from the region you just left. And Targitus, there, who seemed so amused by something, I hardly know what, should join us."

Some of the weavers set about organizing the chairs, others the cups, while food preparers brewed the tea, cut the bread that mysteriously appeared and explained to their curious guests that the ceramic jar of nardek, a specialty of Trapezus, was a marmalade made of grapes and beckmiss, a syrup consisting of various fruits crushed into a puree and heated with honey. All was laid out on a low wooden table, around which the group gathered. In the bustle of the moment, Targitus drew within whispering range of Rachel, took her hand in his and shook it in what, to a close observer, might have hinted of more familiar greetings. Despite his urging, she refrained from disclosing her role in the new technique. Like the golden spindle, there would come a time for sharing that secret. Not now.

As tea was poured, the questions began. "Rachel, your parents picked the right name for you. Tell us why you left Sardis. And how you met this hirsute companion. And all the rest. What an adventure you must have had."

Targitus knew Rachel's instinct for privacy. He decided to follow her lead, adjusting to whatever she chose to reveal. The story they told was a tapestry of minor scenes woven in muted colors.


Rachel threw herself into the life of the weavers' co-operative. Her enthusiasm for work, measured, for example, in time spent at the loom, surprised everyone, including herself. She seemed driven to expend her energy in the workshop. Of course, she saw the Altaians. The village was small and they were living in two guest yurts near hers. But, by mutual agreement, she and Targitus had avoided behavior that might have suggested intimacy. Rachel wore her hair in two neat braids, hanging long down her back. Shimmering black against the cover of snow drawn snug around the village for the winter, the ds at a distance could easily have been mistaken for twin black snakes, wriggling in the pleasure of Rachel's company as she strode briskly to and from the workshop. As she became known in the village, young Scythians took notice. Targitus began to worry.

The Scythians celebrated the winter solstice with koumiss, a brandy distilled from the milk of mares. On this, the shortest day of the year, they engaged in a collective ceremony centered on the fermentation of buttermilk over fires of cattle and camel dung, the fuels of choice in winter because of their availability and steady clear fire. Everyone in the village was expected to participate. The formula was simple: one-sixth warm water, five-sixths mare's buttermilk. Add some old koumiss as yeasty catalyst. Then heat. Agitate. Finally, step back, take a cup of the old koumiss and, in the company of others, watch the fermentation proceed.

There was plenty of roast meat for the occasion. Tradition called for sheep and goats, and fish from the Oarus. But it was koumiss that put everyone in the mellow mood necessary to face the long darkness of winter with patient expectancy of lengthening days and other glories of spring and summer. From sunrise to sunset, the village was astir with celebratory contests. There were horse races over a snowy course, eagle hunting for fox and hare, archery at full gallop. And a game called baiga, which always caused the greatest excitement.

Anyone with a horse could participate in baiga, which began with the slaughtering of a sheep or goat. The game itself started with a contestant galloping off with the carcass laid across his horse. The other contestants followed in pursuit. When all were at full gallop, the leader would cast the carcass to the ground, triggering a free-for-all to gain possession. The winner was the rider who finally seized and held the trophy long enough to make his way to the judge and drop it before him.

Rachel could hardly believe the high spirits rippling through the village. The Altaians were going to play. They had gathered together with their horses, whose shaking heads and pawing hooves caught the build-up of excitement. The day was clear, almost windless and cold. To the East, the steppe offered the contestants a limitless field covered by two to four inches of light, windswept snow. Neither mountains, woods nor stones marred the perfectly level line at the horizon where white met blue from north to south.

Targitus proposed that the Altaians work together with a plan, an innovation in this game, where by custom every man fended for himself. The absence of rules, other than one against the use of weapons, made anything possible. Targitus was outlining his plan when Rachel entered their tight circle in the snow. She caught the last of his words. "The time to attack will be after the initial flurry. We must save our horses' energy. If the carcass gets torn in two, so much the better for even the larger part will be easier to handle. My finger whistle will be the signal. Any questions?"

Rachel asked, "Aren't you afraid of getting hurt? Look at that horde. There must be three hundred riders. You have a long journey to the Altai. They live here. None of you need prove your prowess. I am ..."

Frowning, Targitus cut her off. "Baiga's something Massagetae do. It's as simple as that. But to reassure you, in my experience, only the sheep and a horse or two get hurt."

Rachel dodged the instinct to pout, recognizing her outburst had been a mistake.

The Altaians mounted in preparation for the starting signal. Looking up at Targitus, Rachel said she needed to talk with him when the game was over. Would he stay for the celebration? He gave her a vigorous nod, noticing that she had traded her maternal look of concern for something closer to pride.

The senior player swung the sheep into position across his horse and moved at a gallop away from the contestants. With a loud roar, the horde tore off in pursuit. The leader tossed the carcass to the ground. In the space of a few seconds, it had been picked up by the leading pursuer, who bent down gracefully at full gallop and with his right hand seized the sheep, his left hand clutching the horse's mane for support. He swung it in an arc up and over his horse's neck, muscling it into position with both hands.

With pursuers gaining ground on both sides, the rider in possession was forced to gallop directly away from the staging area, where the judge awaited the winner's return. For Rachel and the villagers gathered to watch, the participants grew harder to distinguish as they dashed away across the steppe. Snow covered many of the marmot holes dotting an area through which the leader would have to pass unless allowed to turn. Riders advancing on each side of him came within striking range. There would be no turning. Blows came from both flanks. Striking back, the lead rider used his legs to kick first one and then the other assaulting rider's horse in the neck. The technique worked, causing both horses to break stride and fall behind. But, in their place, two other pursuers had advanced. The one on the right, now riding knee-to-knee, attacked the leader savagely with fists. As the leader's arm went up to guard his head, the pursuer sought to grab it and pull him off his horse. That proved unnecessary. The leader was gone. Looking back, the pursuer saw him on his back in the snow, his horse having crashed to the ground with a broken leg, victim of a marmot hole. The carcass had come to rest midway between horse and rider.

It was easy for the second pursuer to rein in his horse and scoop up the carcass. As he headed to the north, hoping to escape both pursuers and the marmot field, he could see the look of frustration on the closest pursuer's face, still sitting his horse to take in the scene just behind him. And he could hear the horde as it wheeled in a tight arc to the north. The new leader didn't last long. The next rider was closing the gap quickly. Ferocious grappling began as the two horses raced stride for stride. The leader tried to use his foot to separate the horses. Seizing the foot, his combatant unhorsed the rider in one easy motion. Grabbing the other horse's reins, he kept the horses together just long enough to maneuver the carcass over to his own horse, which he then directed in a broad turn back toward the village. It was at this point that the advanced elements of the horde engulfed the new leader, knocking him and the carcass to the ground.

Aroused horses and riders thrashed about in search of the carcass, lashing out at everything they could touch in the process. At the height of this confusion, the Altaians, who had only just caught up with the horde, heard the whistle summoning them to action. With Targitus in the lead, the six formed a tight wedge to move at a

## 12: SCOPASIS – 406-405 B.C.

steady trot toward the place where the carcass was being fought over. Horses had to be pushed, pulled and pried out of the way. Once there, they crashed their horses against the horses of the two combatants who were tugging at the carcass suspended between them. On impact, the carcass split in two. The larger part slipped from the grip of one contestant, but before reaching the ground, it was snatched away by the swooping Targitus. Now the Altaians encircled their chief and the band launched into a gallop towards the village. Working together to sweep other riders aside, they were able to clear a path out of the melee. Once free, they put a little distance between themselves and the horde, now in full pursuit.

They knew the lead couldn't last the entire distance back across the steppe. Particularly because their plan called for them to stay together as an advancing line, with Targitus, carrying the carcass, at the extreme right. As the first pursuer reached him, Targitus lifted the carcass up and threw it to the next Altaian riding knee to knee beside him. He dropped back to interfere with the oncoming horde for as long as he could. He then worked his way over to the left to rejoin the line of Altaians. The process was repeated with the carcass shifting each time the rider carrying it became threatened by pursuers. So novel was this technique that the pursuers failed to anticipate the next transfer. By the fifth transfer, however, they were better prepared to go after the sixth, which would renew the cycle with Targitus receiving the handoff. But by then, the judge's table was in sight. Rachel could see that the Altaians were bunched in a semicircle around Targitus, providing effective interference to the rear. She heard the clatter of hooves and cries of the Altaians and their pursuers, now strung out across the horizon, grow in intensity as they approached, white clogs flying. She realized the Altaians might win and started cheering. And then it was over. Well protected by his comrades, Targitus was able to slow from gallop to trot to walk and then to deposit the larger part of the severed carcass just in front of the table. A loud cheer arose from the audience, who had stood stamping their feet in the cold throughout the game. The Altaians, breathing quick upon their victory, fists raised in triumph, joined in the cheering.

When the mounted contestants had gathered around the judge's table, Targitus was summoned to receive his award, a plump sheep ready for slaughter. The horses were snorting in small gasps. They were covered thick with a frozen lather of sweat. The ice produced a loud tinkling sound as it softened against their heated bodies and cracked, dropping to the ground. As befitted his success, Targitus called up his companions, declaring that it was the band that won and the band that would share the prize.

The game of baiga was the last of the day's contests. As the sun began to sink across the frozen Oarus, the drinking of koumiss and the feasting resumed in earnest. The gathering around the judge's table dispersed. Rachel cornered Targitus. Quietly, unobtrusively, while enjoying the feast, they talked.

"I am having trouble sleeping," Rachel said.

"I am having some trouble too. You're getting to be known in the village, just as we planned. I am starting to have thoughts of you with another man. It's keeping me awake."

It was Rachel who offered a plan. She thought the fiction that they were just friends could be preserved if they only saw each other in her tent occasionally, after dark. Needing him more than she was prepared to admit, she devised another fiction for their personal consumption: surely they could see one another in this way without having it affect any long-term plan. She presented her idea and Targitus agreed. They were deceiving themselves, and they knew it.

"If we're not going to get close enough to talk, how will I know when to visit?"

"That's easy," Rachel replied, a smile creeping in at the corners of her mouth. "Since I have the most to lose if we are discovered, or if we pick the wrong time and I get pregnant, I'll be in charge of scheduling. On a day when I want a visit, I will wear my hair in a single braid. Otherwise, there will be two braids, like this." She twisted her head and shoulders, making the braids swish this way and that. "You must come only after dark, taking care not to be seen. And only on one-braid days. Even your men mustn't know."

"That's not possible, Rachel. I will have to tell them. They keep secrets."

## 12: SCOPASIS — 406-405 B.C.

For Rachel and Targitus, the winter seemed to pass more quickly, even as the days lengthened. A paradox, due perhaps to the longing to be together that grew between the days on which Rachel wore her hair in a single braid. Or the lessening hours of darkness that made them conscious of their dwindling time together.

Gradually, Rachel expanded her circle of friends among the villagers, a migratory process that began with acquaintance and moved towards friendship as opportunity allowed. Rachel was not one to push herself forward to claim a new friend. Valuing for herself a reserve of privacy, she was careful to avoid penetrating the reserve of others without some clear sign. However, there was about her an openness to others, something that she wore transparently on her face and in her dark, laughing eyes, something that she projected not just in speech and gait, but mysteriously, by an inimitable presence. Rachel made the person with whom she was interacting feel that all her attention was focused on that person alone. And, in fact, it was. Hers was an inviting contact, a presence that enveloped without touching.

For Rachel, the weavers' custom of opening their workshop to all comers for afternoon tea and bread proved catalytic in hastening friendship. This was the case for Kolaxis, a shepherd who provided both sheep's parts to eat and sheep's wool to spin and weave. Rachel had become one of his customers, and not long after, he had been drawn to tea because he wanted to learn more about this Jew who, surprisingly, had left the soft city of Sardis to settle down in his harsh village as a weaver. It was from Kolaxis, one afternoon, that Rachel learned the story of Anacharsis. It had come up in counterpoint to a comment made by one of the weavers, who expressed the group's opinion that the Scythians of Scopasis had been wonderfully accepting of their foreign ways. Kolaxis was quick to rebut the notion that Scythians were comfortable with the practices of other peoples.

"Anacharsis lived many generations ago. He was a member of the Scythian royal family. He was wise in the ways of the world, having traveled to many lands, including Greece. As the story unfolds, he is returning to his homeland after a long absence. Near the Hellespont, he stops at Cyzicus, a Greek village whose people worship the Mother of Gods."

Rachel recognized this Greek God, whom she knew to be the most important God in Persia, the one known as Cybele, for whom an altar was built at the goldworks in Sardis, the one at which her mother sacrificed to gain a son.

"Watching the Cyzicienes engaged in a magnificent festival celebrating the Mother of Gods, Anacharsis vows that, if he ever reaches home, he will devote a similar ceremony to her. Upon crossing into Scythia, he goes to a thickly wooded region, Hylaia, and, as piety demands, prepares a celebration in honor of this God. He hangs images of the Goddess from his neck and proceeds to dance while banging on a drum and clanging a tambourine, imitating the rites and observances of the Cyzicienes. Now, the Mother of Gods is not among our deities. We have been taught that this Goddess breeds effeminate behavior, weakening our men. Anacharsis, who had been sent by his father to learn Greek ways, is seen by a Scythian, who summons King Saulius. Watching Anacharsis engaged in tribute to the Mother of Gods, the King is angered. He draws his bow and kills Anacharsis.

"There is another aspect to the story. Saulius had succeeded his father, Gnurus, as king. Gnurus had two sons, the other being Anacharsis. King Saulius had killed his brother for adopting foreign ways. A tragic tale. Yet one that's true to our people."

Rachel had listened carefully. She wondered whether Targitus knew the story. That night, when he came to her yurt, she asked.

"Oh, so you heard that old tale. We Altaians know it well. I've always questioned whether Saulius killed his brother because of his foreign ways or just because Saulius had inherited the Kingdom in his brother's absence and feared losing it if Anacharsis were allowed to return." The familiar vision of Ishkapai appeared. He struggled to attend to what Rachel was saying.

"Kolaxis used the story to challenge our happy belief that Scythians were accepting of foreigners and their strange ways. He convinced us that the weavers' treatment by the village was an exception."

"Rooted, no doubt, in your contribution to the comfort and wealth of Scopasis."

"How often in royalty there are brothers at war with one another. There were constant rumors in the palace that Cyrus would kill his brother and assume the Persian throne."

Targitus listened, deep in thought.

"But there's something personal in this tale that I want to tell you. Something I forgot to mention when we exchanged stories of growing up. It's about the Mother of Gods that Anacharsis was honoring when he was killed. My mother joined that Goddess' cult for a time. It probably changed my life."

"More about your family? I am ready."

"You remember that, after my birth, my mother tried for nine years to have a son. There was a lot of praying to Yahweh. Father spoke often of her duty to give him a son. She was getting desperate. After another miscarriage, she was about to give up when a Persian neighbor offered advice. He urged my mother to pray and offer sacrifice at the altar of Cybele, the great mother-goddess of all Anatolia, and the goddess of fertility as well. He broke through my mother's resistance by asking how Yahweh could be offended if her prayers to Cybele were answered with a son, who would be taught to love Yahweh with heart and soul. My mother's faith was softer than my father's, less sure, more forgiving and pragmatic. Without telling my father, she sacrificed a fine goat on Cybele's altar and prayed. By the next full moon, she was pregnant. You know the rest."

"Did your mother tell you?"

"The priests were sworn to secrecy. Apparently, my mother was not the first Jew to appeal to this goddess; they were accustomed to keep such matters private. For a price. They took the best parts of the goat and two gold staters besides. And they were discreet. But a friend of mine happened to be the daughter of one of the priests. She overheard the story at home and told me some years later. My father never knew and my mother never found out I knew."

When Rachel had finished, Targitus gently brushed back the wisps of unbraided black hair that had gathered at the corners of her eyes, then tenderly stroked her forehead, passing his hand down the fall of her hair to trace the reversing curves of head and nape of neck. Catching her eyes in his, he remarked on her story and the links they each had to the Mother of Gods. Rachel saw sadness in his face.

Earlier Rachel had considered the same point, deciding not to bring it up. Since Targitus had done so, her pleasure in analysis shoved judgment aside. "Yes, I thought of that. Cybele, giver of life for my people; taker of life for yours. Exactly the same as Cyrus. Is there a pattern here? A message?"

Targitus sat mute. Rachel reached out to take his hand, trying to redeem the evening. It was too late. Despite shared expectations, an unaccountable mood, solemn and uninvited, had intruded.

Rachel's skill and energy in the workshop was appreciated. So great was her efficiency, that early in the new year, she was allowed to devote time before the Altaians departed to weaving something for them.

What Rachel chose to weave for each of her "Altaian Family," as she liked to call them, was a yurt band of unique design tailored for the individual recipient. These bands served a functional purpose. They were attached to the corners of the large pieces of felt that covered the yurt's dome. By pulling them tight, one could secure the felts in place across the inside of the dome. There were typically three to a yurt. Their extra length made arcs from one side of the yurt to the other, affording scope for artistic expression. Indeed, artists had been inspired to use brightly colored wool to weave these bands, typically in twill flat weave, choosing geometrical designs in red and blue. Rachel imagined a band of greater complexity.

Targitus and his men began to worry about the amount of time Rachel seemed to be devoting to the workshop. One evening Targitus broached the subject. "I know you thrive on work, and love making textiles, but we are concerned for your health. Do they insist on these hours? Winters on the steppe should be a time for rest and reflection."

"There's no time for that. Look around you. Who's resting and reflecting? Men. Drinking koumiss to divert their minds from the work going on around them. I am lucky. I just have to tend to my loom. No children to care for. No husband."

Targitus looked hard at Rachel. Was she challenging him to a fight? He let the comment pass. "It's amazing what you've accomplished. How hard the men or women of Scopasis work doesn't mean a thing to us. But we notice your hours and can't help contrasting that with our leisure. To speak plainly, it makes us uncomfortable."

"I am sure you'd rather I worked from dawn to after dark than spend time with some of the young Scythians who follow me with their eyes."

"Rachel."


It was the first of March. Rachel was within a week of finishing the last of the yurt bands. The Altaians had intended to depart by the third week of the month. She planned a celebration in her yurt on the tenth. A rite of passage, bittersweet. Through the first ten days of March, the chill of winter persisted despite lengthening days. In early evening on the tenth, the Altaians arrived at Rachel's yurt with a freshly slaughtered lamb and several goat skins full of koumiss, entering the shelter in exactly the order of march that had been their custom on the long journey from Trapezus. They were infused with the strong odor of sage. Targitus entered last, greeting Rachel with a hug that bespoke well worn affection. From head to foot, the guests looked uncommonly clean. Even Tomychasis, whose penchant for foul language was matched by one for foul smells.

The yurt was warmed and brightly lighted by the fire centered under the dome. A low table adequate for seven was positioned nearby. Candles burned on pedestals around the circumference of the yurt. On the ground as well as the sides of the yurt were brightly colored felts, some bearing designs of appliqué. Three serviceable bands pulled snug the great felts covering the dome, their ends hanging in graceful arcs above the heads of the guests.

While skins of koumiss were passed around, Rachel brought to the table dark bread baked that day by her weaving colleagues. The lamb was butchered on a side table and cut into pieces. It was then transferred to the large iron cauldron resting on a circle of stones over the fire, which had long ago brought water to a rolling boil. The meat would take over an hour to cook. In the meantime, Rachel had prepared a salad of grains and hard-boiled eggs. And the koumiss, uct of Altaian foresight, would loosen tongues and engage spirits.

Before the salad was touched, the practical ceremony of handwashing took place. Rachel poured the water from a copper ewer, held above a pot set off to the side. Next, honoring Altaian custom, the ritualistic burning of a dried sprig of sage, whose cleansing aroma was claimed to drive off evil spirits. Since plenty of sage came in with the guests, Rachel wondered what more a burning sprig could do. As for the spirits, she was full of doubt, especially tonight, in this festive yurt.

As the waters covering the lamb resumed their boil, the group's musicians offered a serenade. Tymnes had brought a four-string harp, Scyles a one-sided drum and Madyes, the pipe.

Marsyas, the youngest, was lead singer. He commenced with a soft droning in 4ths, 5ths and 6ths, accompanied by the instruments. The sounds lapped at the ears. As the musicians continued, a trance-like condition overcame the group, lowering their heartbeats, expelling anxieties. Rachel had experienced these effects once before and was happy to be exposed again. Without warning, the players changed to songs of melody and verve. One had a refrain of "Hoy, Hoy, Hoy." By demand, it was repeated twice.

Rising to check the lamb, as its aroma spread from the cauldron, Rachel decided there was just time for her presentation. Thanking the musicians, she announced a surprise. She lifted a cover from six bands, each rolled up tightly and held in place by yarn brightly colored in red, yellow and blue. Carefully Rachel picked them up, one at a time, and handed them to the Altaians. Watching closely as the bands were unwrapped, Rachel beamed with pleasure. Her artistry could not be compassed at once. What the Altaians could see plainly, on all the bands, was the brand mark used by Altaians of the Great Ulagan Valley to identify their flocks. A double cross within a diamond, it had been neatly constructed in wool pile dyed pinky orange-red with madder root.

In each Altaian's band she had incorporated some personal identification with a subtlety not used since her days in the palace workshop. The bands were six inches wide and about fifteen feet in length.

The Altaians sat in silence, fingering the weavings.

## 12: SCOPASIS – 406-405 B.C.

Rachel stood. "You're pleased. That makes me feel good. It's my reward."

As if on cue, the men rose to their feet and, lining up, embraced her in turn, bringing tears that continued to flow when Targitus, last in line, clasped her tightly. She whispered close to his ear, "I am so happy." For some moments, they clung together near the center of the yurt. And, then, he released her. "Come," she said, exhilarated. "Put those bands away and help me bring lamb to table. We have some eating to do."

The sheep's parts were carefully lifted from the cauldron and distributed around the table. Included were sections of loin, two thigh bones, a piece of the fat tail and, in front of Targitus, the whole head, the hair from which had been scorched off by the Altaians before they had arrived at the yurt. Despite its dubious appearance, the head contained ears, cheeks and tongue, the most delicate parts. The group was hungry. Conversation yielded to feasting. After they had their fill of meat, they were served bowls of the broth in which the sheep had been boiled, now thickened to concentrate the flavors. Rachel had saved one loaf of bread to sop up the last drops.

With another washing of hands, the evening came to an end. Not a moment too soon, Targitus thought, as he reflected on the energy Rachel must have expended on preparations. Exhaustion had begun to show in her face. He knew better than to stay behind. On kissing Rachel good evening, he found a willing ear in which to whisper, "I hope soon to see your hair in a single braid."

As Marsyas was about to leave, he spoke to Rachel, pointing to the band held tight against his chest. "Now we understand. Your long days at the workshop were for us. I am not sure whether we should feel less guilty at our leisure than before. Or more."

Two days passed. On the third, Rachel walked by the Altaian yurt just as the men were returning from exercising their mounts. Targitus noted her single braid, shining a luxurious black in the midday sun. On this occasion, she wore it turned up in a loop just below the neck, held fast against her head by a leather clasp pierced by a pin of polished bone. She used this arrangement when she expected to do a lot of walking. Targitus found it elegant. He was particularly fond of the way the last few inches of the braid, above the pin, fell away from her head, held together by a wisp of white yarn.

Rachel was headed for the workshop, having slept most of the morning to recover from the long exertions of the past two months. There was a bounce in her step. Targitus' joy gave way to anxious tension. Tonight would be his last chance at persuasion. The prospects were not good. Twice since arriving in Scopasis he had broached the subject.

The first time was in the yurt, after making love.

He had started by thanking her for persuading him to winter over. She looked pleased. But when he began to present the case, her face assumed a look of surprise and distress. Cutting him off, she said she didn't want to talk about it; that they both knew it wouldn't work; that their cultures were too different and so were they.

"You're a prince; I am an artist. It's impossible." She begged him not to torture her with argument.

The second time was in the weaving center, where he had joined her for tea and the good bread on offer there. He hadn't even finished his opening when she interrupted, threatening to leave the room if he pursued the matter.

Targitus had trouble accepting the fact that she was refusing to take the possibility seriously. He knew the coming separation was, for her, as it was for him, a painful subject. Too painful, he guessed, for her to weigh the alternative.

The thinking necessary for her to reach the right answer had not even been tested. And time was running out.

Targitus arrived in Rachel's yurt soon after dark. A fire cast flickering shadows on the felts spread across the sides and dome of the yurt. From the beginning, they were at cross-purposes. Rachel was bent on passion, hoping Targitus could bring her to that point where the body took charge and cognition ceased; for his part, Targitus was bent on persuasion, his mind edged with sharpness, alert to the night's requirements and the strategy devised to meet them.

In the Great Ulagan, he had been remarkably successful at persuasion. At first unconscious of technique, the exercise of these powers gradually made him aware. Earnest and self-effacing, he was

## 12: SCOPASIS – 406-405 B.C.

able to present his case with the appearance of dispassion. He convinced others of his absolute objectivity, sowing seeds of trust. In truth, he had become a consummate manipulator, using his feelings, which were genuine enough, as the principal tool. His only false note was to wrap those feelings in the guise of complete disinterest.

Targitus knew precisely what he had to do. They lay down on felt blankets beside the fire. Rachel began to undress him. He offered no resistance. When naked, they pulled another felt over them, and Targitus began, very slowly, to help Rachel undress. As he did so, he opened the well rehearsed conversation.

"You've never admitted it, but I know you have a great memory. We're both gifted. I suspect yours exceeds mine. Look at your command of Jewish legends and poems. Possibly our being brought together is an accident. But might there not be more to it? Your God, Yahweh, could he be responsible? Could he have some purpose in mind?"

Still focused on her goal for the evening, it took Rachel a moment or two to understand his point. She had never boasted of her skill. But his interest in the Jewish stories had brought forth nearly all the material she carried in her head, some of it more than once. While not surprised by his appreciation of her ability, she was amazed at his effort to make a connection. "I don't know why we met. Probably mere chance. Like the drone a queen bee chooses for her mate, among thousands of airborne suitors. Perhaps a contrivance of Yahweh. Or Cybele. Or the Gods your people worship. Or a force beyond our ken. Should it matter? We'll never know for sure." While talking, Rachel was trying with her fingers to raise some stirring. Lack of success eroded her own ardor.

"We wouldn't be together now if your father hadn't been killed. Might our meeting above Trapezus give meaning to his death?"

"It's too simple. How can there be any good purpose to a violent, unprovoked killing?"

"You know, I am not a deep believer. But I am convinced we were brought together for a purpose. And for what purpose if not marriage and family. It was our powers of memory that got me thinking. And there are many other ways in which we are a match. Not an accidental one, a match made by design." Targitus could feel his argument gathering strength, his mind letting go of the reins. "And I am not only speaking of our physical attraction for each other. That, by itself, is stronger than anything we are likely to find elsewhere. You've said so yourself. But there's more to what we've become than just passion. I think I've found a way for us to hold on to it."

"My dearest one, I want to believe. But listen to me. You're forgetting something. Your people could never accept an outsider, even from a nearby village, unless the marriage furthered the political purposes of your people. You told me that long ago. For us, marriage is out of the question. My status, were I to come with you, would be ambiguous. I'd be and remain an outcast. Mistress to a prince. I had a chance for that in Sardis. Here, there are a number of Jews in the center. And I am not involved with a prince."

"You're right. That's what I said. Almost. I said a marriage outside our tribe would need some special benefit. But it doesn't have to be political. That's the usual benefit. The answer for us has been too obvious for me to see until your weaving of the bands forced it upon me. The benefit of our marriage will be the gift of your talent to my people. Weavings that meet practical needs, weavings transformed into art. This will capture the spirit of our people as well as any political union."

Targitus thought Rachel had been moved but not convinced.

She said, "But how about the Anacharsis tale?"

"An ancient story. Remember, too, that the "foreign ways" explanation may have been a disguise for fratricide. Scythians have changed. They're less insular now. Here's the proof, right here in this village, where you and the other weavers are accepted and much loved. And why? Because you bring benefits. The same will hold for my village."

Rachel sat up, drawing knees to bare breasts and holding them there with arms wrapped tight, hands clasped together. Questioning still, she looked deep into his eyes for answers.

"And there's one other thing. Children. We both want a family. By the time you've begun to nurse our first baby, the village will be yours."

With eyes open wide, pupils large in the dim light of dying

## 12: SCOPASIS – 406-405 B.C.

embers, she said, "How can we be sure?"

Targitus sat up too, legs crossed. He wrapped the felt cover around Rachel's shoulders. "Ah, Rachel, now you ask for certainty. What certainty did you have when you left Sardis? The night your father was killed? After we got to Trapezus to find the weavers gone? The certainty I can offer is no more, but no less, than a princely promise: first, to marry you in the Great Ulagan valley, before all of my people, with or without parental blessing, second, to do all in my power to secure those blessings; and third, to do my part to assure the gift of children. Isn't that enough?"

Lying beside him, she could see his eyes straining for some signal from her. Suffused with emotion, she idled her tongue. Tears rolled down her cheeks, salting her lips.

"One more thing. The story you've told me, at least twice, about Ruth, the Moabite widow who followed her Jewish mother-in-law, Naomi, back to Bethlehem. I know you're moved by that tale, as I was by your telling. I believe my people will give you a real welcome to the Great Ulagan valley, one that might, in time, cause you to say to me, as you taught me Ruth said to Naomi:

>'Entreat me not to leave thee,
>or to return from following after thee:
>for whither thou goest, I will go;
>and where thou lodgest, I will lodge:
>thy people shall be my people.'"

Holding her tightly, in a yurt now darkened, Targitus remarked that it was lucky the felt beneath them was so thick. "It can soak up a sea of tears." Ignoring the work of adding another traveler to the group, work that would now have to be squeezed into a few days, Targitus and Rachel turned to the possibilities of spending a night together.

# CHAPTER 13

En Route to the Great Ulagan Valley – 405 B.C.

Weather on the steppe was notoriously changeable, particularly in March. They departed at sunrise, followed for a short distance by the curious dogs that patrolled the village throughout winter in search of food. The entire work force of the weaving center turned out to bid farewell to the Sardian, whose unexpected arrival in their midst they had begun to call a deity's gift, as unlikely as it was generous.

The weavers had brought something for Rachel, a present they knew she could use in the Altai. Neatly tied with brightly colored woven bands, this bundle of wood was not recognizable to the Altaians. For Rachel, however, it held no secrets. "My loom. Oh, my loom," she cried. "Thank you, thank you. This will be the model for my center." Plunging into the group of weavers, Rachel hugged them each in turn. Tears flowed. The milling dogs began to howl.

"Will we see you again?" someone asked.

Another exclaimed, "Oh, yes. You must."

"Of course I'll be back. On my way to Sardis." She shot a glance at Targitus, who had heard the exchange. His expression revealed

## 13: EN ROUTE TO THE GREAT ULAGAN VALLEY −405 B.C.

nothing. She thought of her mother and Jacob, how far from her they were, how little of her they knew and she of them.

Leave-taking, even from a jubilant crowd, can turn lonely and sad, she realized.


They rode into a clear sky and warming sun. Off at last on the final leg of a year's journey, after a four-month wait, both horse and rider felt a surge of excitement.

By noon, they had traveled thirty-five miles across the perfectly flat steppe, the horses eagerly advancing at a steady trot, from which they often tried to break into a canter. It was as if they could smell the stable. Dropping back to ride side-by-side with Targitus, Rachel asked about the length of the trip, a question she had been reluctant to pose until they had left Scopasis. "A bit farther than from here to Sardis. But the going's easier, at least until we get to the Altai. From east to west, it took us almost seven weeks. With the prevailing southwest wind, and some luck on the weather, we should do better going home."

In the afternoon, clouds appeared in the north. Pointing in that direction, Targitus got Rachel's attention. "Look. Feel that wind? We're in for bad weather."

The temperature was dropping slowly. They saw snow in the distance, at first, just a lightened version of the dark clouds coming towards them. As it advanced, they could make out a swirling mass of whiteness, chased across the steppe by a driving wind directly into their path. The travelers added extra layers of clothing. To the bite of the wind, which they had felt for some time, was now added the sting of driven snow. As the storm grew, Targitus signaled a pause. Experience told him the storm would pass within the hour. They had best turn their backs and wait. Facing south, they sat their horses, quietly watching the wind scour the snow and tickle the dry feather grass, preventing drifts from forming across the level sweep of land.

The snow stopped as suddenly as it came, leaving a cover of white. The sun broke through scudding clouds to the west, turning the landscape into a carpet of crystals. The temperature was frigid.

The wind continued to blow. The fresh snow, lighter than lint, swirled over the ground, gathering speed to be sucked up to the sky, cyclones of white.

Rachel had been asking for a description of the journey ahead. That night Targitus gathered the band in his yurt. He explained how they would follow the Eurasian steppe zone all the way to the foothills of the Altai mountains.

"There's a good side to this weather," Targitus said. "If the ice cover holds on the rivers, we could better our estimate of seven weeks."

From early childhood, Rachel had been afraid of rivers. Living beside the Pactolus, her parents had warned her over and over again, using cautionary tales of friends who had drowned.

"What happens if the ice breaks up, or is too thin to support us?" Rachel asked, hoping to allay her main fear. On the morning of their departure, Rachel had learned from one of the village elders, a concerned friend, that the delay had put them at risk that the crossings would require open-water passage. She had concealed her concern, but it gnawed at her after Targitus described the four great rivers they would have to cross. Targitus paused a long time before answering. He could try to relieve her anxieties. Twisting the truth, however, would sooner or later be discovered. Avoiding the question could worsen her concerns. He chose directness, aware that many days would pass before they would come to the first river, allowing Rachel time to anticipate the crossing and, perhaps, calm her nerves. "When the ice breaks up, you're right. It's a dangerous time to cross. We search for the best spot, level and shallow. We equip ourselves with floatation, tying it about our chests. We then send the horses into the water, holding onto their tails. The trick is to keep the horse moving, keep it calm and hang on until it reaches the far bank."

"What floatation?" she asked.

"Goat or sheep stomachs. We inflate them, then tie off the opening. They work," he added with emphasis.

"Did you do water crossings on the way to Sardis?" Just imagining it made her shiver.

"There was the Oarus. We had to ford it."

## 13: EN ROUTE TO THE GREAT ULAGAN VALLEY −405 B.C.

"But there you had the support of a whole village. I am not sure that counts."

"Look. There's no point in worrying about it. If this weather holds, we'll be on ice. If not, we'll still be all right. Altaians used the technique long before I came along."

Sadly, Rachel concluded that not even Targitus could understand her fears: of knowing she could barely swim, of losing her grip on the pony's tail, of sinking in frigid waters, of being too cold to move. Rachel saw no option but to turn her unrelieved fear inward.

On the day they approached the Ural River, beyond which lay Filippovka, they happened upon a Scythian chief and two attendants, who had dismounted and seemed to be circling something on the ground. As the band came closer, they could see that the men were working to mew a great golden eagle that intermittently flapped its giant wings to maintain balance atop a mature red fox it had just subdued by a swift strike from the air. Calling out to those in front of him, Targitus suggested they stop and watch. The attendants had just succeeded in attaching a leash to the bird's foot and were struggling to place a plumed hood over its head.

Targitus helped Rachel move in close to the circle just in time to catch the flash of this noble creature's eyes before the hood was pulled down. Here was an eagle trained to hunt. It stood thirty inches high, its colors ineffably complex in varying shades of black and brown, with bits of golden yellow on the nape and back of its neck. Rachel only knew eagles as expressions of art; she'd never been so close to a live bird. Just as she was weighing possible dangers, the bird struck a docile pose and dropped its hold on the fox. Rachel exclaimed, "Look at the size of those claws. And the legs. Its feathers go right down to its toes."

The fox was dead, killed instantly when the eagle struck, fixing its talons at the back of the neck to pierce through the soft base of the skull and into the brain. It was this technique, favored by the eagle for its swiftness and by the eagle's handler for the absence of damage to the pelt, that made these magnificent birds so valuable.

Targitus said they were worth at least three good horses in the Altai, where they were even more abundant than along the Ural River. He asked the chief where he got the bird.

"In the nest after it had fledged. Kept it hooded as it grew," the chief replied. "It's a female. She's larger than the male and by far the better hunter."

"How do you get the eagle to do your bidding," Rachel asked. "If you want fox, how do you stop the eagle from going after hare?"

"We can only do so much. We fast the eagle for about twenty days. Being hungry, she will strike the first quarry sighted, rather than hovering until her favorite food comes along. We still have to time the release so that her first sighting is a fox. And there's no assurance on that. None at all."

As they resumed the journey, Rachel mused out loud about efforts to domesticate the eagle. And other animals. Why is it, she wondered, that sheep and goats, horses and dogs can be bent to our will while other animals, like deer and leopards, can not?

"You're the leader. What's your answer?" Rachel asked, her voice a challenge.

"I wish I knew. God's will or man's striving. In our village, efforts to domesticate the deer have gone on as far back as memory serves. I suppose we'll keep trying."

"I like that."


It was afternoon. A desultory day of riding was coming to a close. About eight miles beyond Filippovka, Targitus, in his customary spot at the rear of the column, heard approaching hoof-beats. Turning, he looked west, into a sun four fingers above the horizon. The steppe concealed nothing. When his eyes had adapted to the sun, he recognized a group of ten riders approaching at the gallop. They didn't appear friendly. He cried out to his men, instructing them to shift from steady trot to rapid gallop. He then rode up beside Rachel, telling her to stay with the group, and asked Tymnes to hang back with him. Looking again to the west, he could now make out flashes of sunlight on swinging swords as the horsemen closed the gap.

## 13: EN ROUTE TO THE GREAT ULAGAN VALLEY −405 B.C.

Tymnes and he were moving at a gallop, but much slower than the others in his group, who now pulled ahead. Taking his bow from its gorytoi, he braced it on his foot and leg, a feat of unusual coordination and strength at the gallop. Tymnes did the same. Each then drew an arrow. Unique decoration of nock and shaft led each rider to the arrow he wanted.

Although the range of the Scythian composite bow was one hundred and fifty yards, Targitus knew an arrow released from a galloping horse was only accurate to fifty yards. His plan was to continue at a pace reckoned to allow the pursuers gradually to come within range while enabling their friends ahead to widen the distance between them.

The pursuers were closing fast. They appeared unconcerned by the actions of the Altaians ahead. Targitus assumed their numbers made them fearless. Their bows remained in their gorytoi, unstrung. They were spread out across the steppe, with two, the leaders, riding abreast at least three horse-lengths ahead of the others. They held short swords in their right hands, which moved up and down in rhythm with the long strides of their horses. As the gap narrowed, Targitus could hear fierce cries from the leaders above the hoof beats on hard ground. On cue, each Altaian nocked the arrow to his bow, turned his chest to the left with a gentle twist from the waist so that his shoulders lined up with the horse's croup, canted his bow above the croup and drew it smoothly to the full-drawn position, ready for sighting and release.

Accurate shooting from horseback required the practiced co-ordination of eye, hand and horse. The pull at full draw was over sixty pounds. The archer must hold himself at the draw, still as an eagle that holds its wings motionless in flight, while taking aim at the target to his rear. The horse must remain in full stride at the gallop. The arrow must be released when the horse is in mid-career. At the instant of release, the bow-hand must move directly toward the target, while the elbow of the drawing hand must thrust back in a jabbing motion. The Altaian warrior's exceptional abilities rested on a high level of athleticism. But ceaseless practice was the key to success. Targitus had rehearsed this moment hundreds of times, as had his companion.

Now the two leading pursuers were within forty yards. Bows bent, they took aim and released. Arrows hissed as the fletchings spun the shafts towards their targets. Both arrows hit their marks. Pierced through by the arrow's triangular head, one of the riders fell instantly to the ground. The other, wounded, clung to his horse, struggling to bring it to a halt. The remaining pursuers reined in their horses, apparently shocked by the sudden change of fortune and loss of leadership. Seeing the success of their first flight of arrows, the Altaians wheeled about. Targitus said, "We're in luck. Two hits and still they haven't strung their bows. Let's approach at the walk to within range and take two more down."

Swiftly, the Altaians drew and nocked two more arrows and, with deliberation, walked their horses toward the eight horsemen, now halted beside their two leaders. The wounded rider let out a sharp cry and fell, head first, to the ground. Confusion reigned. Some of the pursuers started to dismount and tend to their leaders. All were aware of the archers who again were within range, bows drawn. With a nod from Targitus, they took aim; again, the releases were clean. And again, the arrows found their marks. Two more riders were hit, one fatally, the other through the shoulder.

From a fixed position, a skilled Massagetae could shoot an arrow every second. With the loss of four of their group, the remaining pursuers turned their horses, urging them into a galloping retreat.

Three pursuers lay on the ground, abandoned by their horses, which followed the others. The Altaians rode up to them. Covered by Tymnes' drawn bow, Targitus dismounted. Verifying that two were dead, he bent low over the third. "Why were you pursuing us?" he asked. "We had nothing worth stealing."

The man looked with pained disbelief at Targitus. His breath came in short puffs. The arrow had pierced his lungs, its head protruding from the cape on his back. Targitus pulled the arrow through, then returned it to his gorytoi. Blood spilled out of the man's mouth. Speaking with difficulty, the man said "Gold."

"Who told you that?"

The man might not have heard the question. For just then he

## 13: EN ROUTE TO THE GREAT ULAGAN VALLEY -405 B.C.

died. Targitus remounted. Turning their horses to the east, they trotted off in the direction of their companions, who appeared as specks on the bleak horizon.

Although she had heard the story as soon as Targitus and Tymnes caught up with the others, Rachel insisted on a re-telling in the privacy of their yurt. It brought forth goose pimples up and down her spine. Within the yurt's ring of apparent safety, Rachel could be joyful, participating vicariously in her lover's prowess. Yet, she would always remember the fear that had seized her as the attack began, a trembling that persisted long after the immediate threat was far away. She had recognized her fear as similar to what she experienced the day her father was slain, only much stronger. Implacable. She couldn't master it precisely because the events were taking place beyond her sight. Exposed to unmeasured dangers, sometimes her fear could not be contained. It had to exhaust itself.


For Rachel, the endless steppe was manifestly more than an overused expression. She was losing hope that it would end. She lacked the experience of the Altaians, who knew to a certainty that the great Altai range of mountains would finally come into view. Day after day she would look eastward, straining to see some rise in the land, some cloud concentration, anything to indicate the end of the steppe. As hope ebbed with the passage of weeks, she searched the eastern horizon less and less. And then, deliberately, not at all. Only the cheerfulness of her companions kept despair at a distance, somewhere near the receding horizon.

When they broke camp one morning, a low cloud bank extended to the horizon in all directions. The air was surprisingly still, threatening cold rain. Rachel's spirits mimicked the weather.

Targitus wasn't born to banter and amuse. At a time like this, he longed for those skills. Or just a clever way to bring Rachel's future into focus for her. He knew weather on the steppe, however, and that, plus a sense of where they were, was enough.

"New weather is coming fast from the northwest. Look behind you."

Turning, Rachel saw a brightening sky near the horizon and, in front, a sheet of rain coming towards her.

Given her mood, Targitus knew she'd concentrate on the rain. "We're coming to the Irtys. I am going to make a prediction. This weather will clear the sky ahead. When that happens, we'll see the foothills of the Altai Range. If I am wrong, you can cut my hair again."

"That's a bold promise. Almost reckless coming from such a cautious leader," Rachel said. And, then, laughing, she added, "I must look awfully sad to make you so desperate. As for that shaggy mane, I am going to give you a cutting whether we see the foothills or not."

The Irtys proved an easy crossing on solid ice. By the time they reached the far side, a clearing sky had brought the foothills in view. A loud cheer from the band confirmed its leader's sense of place.

"Wait," Rachel yelled out as Targitus was in the act of mounting Belukcha. Twisting in mid-air, he cleared the horse to land on the other side, facing its rear.

"You wanted me to wait?" he said with a touch of triumph in his voice. "I am at your command."

"Good. Stay right there," she said, starting to sprint. She hit him at the run, landing in his arms. "I wanted to hug you for bringing me to the Altai, for protecting me, for many other things besides." He swung her around. She shot him a look.

"To thē Altai," he said.

Her laughter, rising like a brook from heavy spring rain, continued until she reached her horse and mounted.

From the Irtys, they turned northwest to where the Ob is formed by the confluence of the Katun and the Bija, two of the greatest rivers flowing north out of the Altai Mountains. Crossing the Katun on ice of questionable thickness, they went single file, ropes at the ready for rescue. For maximum safety, Targitus decided that Rachel should be the third to go. When all had reached the far shore of the Katun, the last of the big rivers they had to face, someone pulled out the rest of the koumiss to celebrate. All that remained was the long ascent to the Great Ulagan Plateau, a distance of some three hundred miles.

## 13: EN ROUTE TO THE GREAT ULAGAN VALLEY −405 B.C.

The prospect of leaving the steppe made Rachel impatient. She wanted to get into the enchanted land of lush green foliage and towering pines that Targitus had promised. They had traveled about seventeen hundred miles since leaving Scopasis on March 15th. They crossed the Katun on April 29th, just two days before the beginning of May. The breakup of the winter's ice was near. The banks of the Katun were bursting with signs of spring. The sky was alive with birds. Only about ten days of travel remained. Feelings of happy anticipation rippled through the band.

They chose the north side of the Katun for travel because its south-facing slope was dry and sparsely covered with growth, separated by rushing waters from the lush, dense taiga found opposite. They would follow that river to the Inja village, where, with constant roar, the Chuya emptied its green, silty waters into the Katun. From there, they would follow the Chuya on its north bank, often along a narrow plateau far above the river.

Arriving late one afternoon at a place called Kolbackash, Targitus led the band to a well-used campsite, where the yurts were thrown up, fires built and food prepared. Here, Targitus had claimed, there was ground hallowed by Altaians through mystery and legend. The days had lengthened since they had left Scopasis. By afternoon, there was often warmth in the air. The nights remained chilly, particularly as the band gained altitude. By Altaian tradition, the mystery of Kolbackash was viewed at sunrise. Targitus turned away Rachel's questions

"You're set on keeping this a secret. It better be good," Rachel declared, feigning disgust.

The fire had long since grown cold when Targitus gently pressed against the length of Rachel's prone body, conforming his own to the fetal position she often assumed while asleep. Touching her ear with his mouth, he whispered that it was time to rise. She awoke to the wetness of his tongue and the warmth of his body, radiating from neck to toe. She sat up. It was still dark outside. Wistfully, Rachel recalled the moment of awakening, when it seemed she held happiness in the palm of her hand.

"Follow me closely, or you'll fall. It'll take us about ten minutes to get to the sacred ground. From there we should see the first signs of dawn."

Rachel recalled his many claims that the endless steppe was ending. She was preparing a nasty remark when Targitus whispered, "See, she breaks."

As they watched, the speck of eastern light grew. Soon Rachel could make out the shapes of rocks directly in front of her. They were formed from sediment compressed for eons under immense pressure to form a green slate that had been thrust up to stand perpendicular to the ground. Light had now advanced enough to uncover the surprise. Rachel could make out petroglyphs on the slate. Targitus had to restrain her from putting her eyes up close to the nearest one. Pulling her back to enfold in his arms, he said, "There's a process to this. We wait for the first rays. When they hit the slate, we burn sage, to ..."

Rachel finished his thought, mouthing each word for emphasis. "Drive—off—evil—spirits."

Targitus frowned. Was she mocking us? Just jesting with me? Not the time for a fight.

Rachel caught the change. She knew the smile was forced. I've hurt his feelings.

In the cold, time passed slowly. And for Rachel and Targitus, awkwardly. At last, the first glint of sunlight appeared high up on the mountainside. Creeping, it made its way down the mountain. At last it struck the top of the green slate, which responded with a soft glow. The petroglyphs facing east grew distinct. Targitus had kindled a small fire, too small, Rachel noted, to cut the chill. It's purpose was just to light the sprig of sage. "It's time, Rachel."

Some of the drawings were made by pounding the slate to create tiny indentations. Others were simple line drawings etched in the slate with a sharp tool. The sheer number was astonishing. There were depictions of bison, reindeer, elk, sheep and mountain goats in many variations. Some had exaggerated horns, beautifully rendered to arch back over three-quarters and more of the animal's body. There was a bull with mighty horns zigzagging like twin lightning bolts above a noble head.

One horse caught Rachel's fancy. The artist had depicted a play-

## 13: EN ROUTE TO THE GREAT ULAGAN VALLEY −405 B.C.

ful animal, tail up, legs splayed out. There was only one scene of a horse with rider. And only one showing a man with bow drawn, arrow pointing toward his prey.

Rachel came to an extraordinary human-like figure with an eye and two arms reaching up, fingers extended, as if in supplication or wonder, with a pointed head and long rectangular strips at the base of what appeared to be the figure's body. She turned to Targitus.

"No one knows for sure. The strips are a kind of skirt. Perhaps it's a goddess of childbirth. Even in this cold climate, young women wore short skirts to announce they were ready."

"They have a primitive look. Do you know how far back they go?"

"From tribal memory we know nothing. As deep into the past as our collective recall goes, it's always been the same. The drawings came before."

Moving swiftly from rock to rock, Rachel continued to examine the immense display, finding at last the most profound collection of all. There, on the green slate facing her, were at least sixty images of deer, reindeer, elk and mountain goat, varying only in size. Appearing in their midst were six human-like images, identical except for their varying sizes. They were frontal views of a riveting figure, head curved like the profile of a mushroom cap, perhaps intended as a helmet, one arm at the side, the other splayed out with hand at hip, holding an object, a gesture radiating confidence and power. To enhance these features, the artist had adopted a distinctly triangular shape for the figure's chest. From the waist down the figure was diminished, legs too small in proportion to the shape and size of the upper body, and bent as if sitting.

"What do you make of this? Obviously the work of a single artist. It has a joyful quality. An insistence, too."

"I don't know. Many have tried. Your people might look at them and see Yahweh. Altaians might see hunter-gods. Who's to say? We see what we want to believe."

Rachel moved closer to the figures. Closing her eyes she traced the shapes with her fingers.

Targitus watched her and suddenly a warmth washed over him, producing shivers.

Rachel opened her eyes in time to catch his stare.

Targitus blurted out something.

"What did you say?" She had read his expression.

"I said you've tied a knot in my heart."

Rachel acknowledged this declaration only with her eyes, which answered him where he stood, some feet away from the slate. Smiling awkwardly, she turned to face the slate: "There's energy here. I feel it as a celebration of life."

They stood still, staring at the display. The sun's warming rays had finally eclipsed the chill. Rachel reached for Targitus' hand, placing her own like a small round jewel in his palm to be squeezed tight. Turning away from the petroglyphs, they moved toward the campsite.

"Well?" Targitus said, "Better than good. And you know what I like? The ordinariness of the drawings. These were people like you and me. Of course, we are more advanced today than they were, in some ways. But, still, in what counts I can't believe these people were different."

"Does that discourage you?"

"It's reassuring."

"It's the petroglyphs. Every time I come here, they set me thinking."

Rachel turned toward him, threw her arms around his neck and kissed him hard. "For bringing me here," she said. "Tell me."

"You captured it with that celebration idea. We live and die in such a brief span of time. Yet mankind doesn't die. And here's the point: mankind's enriched by what people, in their brief time, can do. The petroglyphs reach across the span of time to help us understand who we are.

It was Taiga, Targitus' dog, that sounded the first warning of their approach. She scampered across the ice on the Bashkaus, hurdling spots of open water, barking the whole way.

Once on the far side, Taiga had dashed straight for Belukcha. She raced back and forth in front of the piebald gelding, shaking, nearly

## 13: EN ROUTE TO THE GREAT ULAGAN VALLEY −405 B.C.

delirious with excitement. Dismounting, Targitus approached her. Dancing wildly before him, she hurled herself this way and that, wagging from the shoulders back. Turning to chase her tail twice round, she then scraped her bottom across the ground in that familiar demonstration of obeisance, face uplifted and radiantly happy, tongue ready to lick the hands of her long absent master. "Taiga, that's the best of greetings," Targitus said.

Taiga's signal alerted the village. Word passed like fire. As the travelers gathered along the river's edge, near the hemp rope bridge that spanned the waters, the whole village came out on the other side, waving arms and shouting greetings. The day was blustery, with bright sun and scudding white clouds. It was the wind that kept spring at bay, despite the calendar's insistence. Looking up, Rachel watched as two kestrels, flying north wing-tip to wing-tip, cried out loudly, then paused in flight with uplifted wings and lowered tails, hovering in mid-air. Why did they hover just then? She imagined they had arrested their passage to join in honoring the band's safe return. Taking Rachel's reins to move her horse closer to his, Targitus gestured to point out Sparetra, his mother, who was a bit back from the crowd, surrounded by a group of village elders.

"And your father?"

Searching the lines of villagers gathering on the far shore, Targitus couldn't locate Maytes.

Rachel noted the colors of felt clothing worn by the gathering crowd. There was plenty of vermilion, as well as whites, yellows and blues, displayed on capes, aprons and the nearly universal hats that covered nape and ears, with two side flaps, drawn tight against the wind. She could make out rhomb patterns of cut-out leather on shabracks easily visible on horses whose riders stood beside their steeds, reins in one hand while waving wildly with the other. Here, she realized, amidst this strange throng, in this foreign society, she must begin a new life. The unfamiliar can frighten. New places and people can make one long for home. A pang of loss struck deep as she thought of her family. So far away and out of touch. And, she feared, beyond hope of contact. Wasn't this village at the farthest end of the world from Sardis? Recalling her departure from Scopasis, she again felt strangely alone on the far side of the river, immersed in sadness.

They crossed the bridge, leading their horses to the edge of the Bashkaus and then into the ice that partially covered its waters. Solid ice or none at all was safer than the combination of thin ice and open water in a fast-moving river. Fortunately, the bridge had been located where the river widened to become less vigorous and deep. Still the horses had to be strongly held lest they lose footing and be drawn downstream, where they might be sucked under ice strong enough to prevent them from surfacing. To guard against this risk, extra ropes had been tied around their necks and bodies. The rope ends were stretched to either shore, there held by villagers familiar with the process.

There were fifteen horses in all. Rachel's favorite horse, a bay gelding, entered the river well enough, stepping carefully into the deepening waters, leaning against the raging current with neck arched and ears cocked. Rachel could see him quivering from head to tail as he felt the first shock of icy water. As he advanced to her calm voice of encouragement from the bridge above, a voice in contrast to the frantic, shrill cries of those on either shore, she could see his nostrils expand in alarm and hear impassioned neighs. She held the reins and one of Targitus' band held the rope tied around the horse's neck. There was a wrench. Reins and rope were pulled free by the animal's weight as he slipped on the unseen riverbed and plunged into the water on his side.

Men on either shore held the remaining rope but had no way of righting the animal, which was flailing desperately in the swollen waters as the current swept against his bulky frame, exerting a growing pressure on the hemp. Rachel cried out again and again, as helpless as her horse. The animal's only hope was to regain its footing, but he could not. The rope around his waist broke. With restraint gone, the horse was quickly swept out of sight beneath the ice by the torrent of water. Moments passed. Then, some distance down stream, where open water returned, the horse surfaced, lifeless, careening from boulder to boulder until its momentum was arrested by a back eddy. Frozen on the bridge, Rachel could see an excited crowd gath-

## 13: EN ROUTE TO THE GREAT ULAGAN VALLEY −405 B.C.

ering around her late companion. She completed her crossing to walk slowly downstream in a state of shock. Targitus, who had been with his mother, broke away from her clinging arms to join Rachel, his crestfallen face mirroring her own.

Pulled, rolled and pushed to the water's edge by as many villagers as could apply useful hands to the task, the ankles of the animal were immediately cut to drain its still warm blood into clay vessels, which were then passed around until the last drop had been consumed. Rachel was surprised at this custom but took her share of the dark, life-sustaining fluid. How dependent she had been on this wonderful animal, so sturdy across three thousand miles and more of travel and yet so vulnerable in the spring torrent of the Bashkaus, just yards from the safety of home pastures in the Great Ulagan valley. First, the hovering kestrels, then, the fallen horse. Omens, good and bad. Given the choice, she'd pick the returning flight of raptors in search of a place to nest. Of course, she admitted, there were other interpretations, but why not grasp the most hopeful one?

Looking around at the crowd of Altaians who had participated in the recovery of her horse, she saw in their faces the human reflection of their homeland: all crags and promontories, cascades and rills.

# CHAPTER 14

Great Ulagan Valley – 405 B.C.

They had their own yurt on the northern edge of the village, somewhat apart from others, at the confluence of the Great Ulagan and Balyktuyul Rivers. Targitus had picked the site, which held important associations for him as a child free for the first time to ride by himself. It was a favorite haunt in those days, just enough removed from the village to give him the excitement of being an explorer alone with his horse. As he returned to this spot again and again, he dreamed of sharing it with someone important. By the time the child's dream had come true, to the adult's mind, it had become a carefully laid plan fulfilled.

Rachel had taken it all in. The valley was flat, with tall larches touching the sky to disperse both sun and rain upon multitudes of wildflowers carpeting the ground. Almost as wide as a woman was tall. These giants were often found in isolation, towering conical sentinels. Rachel thought their deciduous needles, freshly grown in shades of pastel green, drooped down like feathery eyelashes blinking beneath limbs and trunk, all dark. At the river's edge, she found aconitum and delphinium, flag iris of deep blue, violet and yellow, as

## 14: GREAT ULAGAN VALLEY – 405 B.C.

well as nepeta and monarda of varying colors and scents. Under the filtering larch, she saw geranium in waves of blue and white with pinkish veins, white scabiosa and the aromatic yellow flowers of smokey tea.

To the north, hills rose between the two rivers, the highest forming a spur commanding the Great Ulagan Valley to the south and the mighty white peaks beyond. Targitus had told her of his ride to that spur two autumns past to face the rising sun on the day he resolved to let his brother lead the mission to Sardis. Now she saw it with her own eyes, but in a different season. Covering those hills to form a palette of sprightly hues were masses of the gentle alchemillea in pale yellow, the bright pink of creeping thymus, the bold blue of veronica, and the varying whites of alpine paeonia, artemesia and edelweiss.

Lying together one night a few days after their arrival, they listened to the gentle gurgling sounds of the two rivers as they swept toward a confluence only yards from the yurt. The hot embers of their fire were just adequate to keep out the chill of a spring evening. Rachel marveled at her sense of comfort and safety, at the swift displacement of the many anxieties she experienced on the journey from Scopasis and even the pangs of homesickness at the bridge, where she had stood on the cusp of her new life.

For Rachel, looking back from the safety of Targitus' village in the Great Ulagan Valley, the journey seemed a blur, surprising to one accustomed to perfect recall. But memory didn't function automatically; it required purposeful concentration. Rachel's journey spanned two lives. Her goal was to manage the crossing as quickly and gracefully as possible. If a blur overall, particulars of the journey, good and bad, were still vivid.

Isn't it strange, she thought, how quickly one's perception of what's normal can change. "On the journey," Rachel whispered, "anxiety was a constant. Now, in this strange village, I've lost all fear in only three days."

They were facing the same direction, resting on their sides. She pushed her body backwards against his, pressing hard as if bent on gluing one thing to another.

Targitus enjoyed encasing her within the curves of his own frame; catching the smell of her hair, freshly washed that afternoon in the natural bathing pool nearby; and recalling the sight of her, naked and cold in the filtered sunlight at the edge of the pool, a nymph in black and white about to become colder still in the dark pool at her feet. "Where does your optimism come from? And these sudden enthusiasms?"

Rachel implanted kisses on her fingers and then, reaching back, affixed them to his face. "First, tell me where we come from; then, I might answer your question. But here's a caution. Mother said never examine happiness lest you drive it away. This might apply to other feelings as well. Let's just enjoy being ourselves, together."

Targitus was seldom more playful than purposeful. "Be careful," he responded. You're the one who believes in cycles. Too much contentment can be dangerous. Here in the Altai, fortunes change swiftly, like the weather."

"Oh, Gods of the Altai, help me. Help me with this man. His capacity for romantic indulgence needs nourishment." She had puckered up her lips, eyes wide, scanning the sky through the yurt's opening. "But I am sure you're right. Change can be just that swift; consider my horse."


A week passed before Targitus took Rachel to meet his mother. In those confused moments after crossing the Bashkaus, Targitus learned that Matyes, his father, was confined to bed with a strange sickness. Sparetra was ecstatic and tearful at her son's safe return, but Targitus sensed she was in no mood to meet a strange woman from a faraway land. He chose not even to mention Rachel during the first few days, while he visited his father, consulted with the healers and reported the results of his trip to the elders of the village.

To help Rachel get settled when he was otherwise occupied, Targitus called on Tymnes for one more service. He was to shepherd her around the village, introducing her as an accomplished Sardian weaver whom Targitus had brought to start a weaving center and to become his wife. He should involve the rest of the band in making

## 14: GREAT ULAGAN VALLEY – 405 B.C.

her feel comfortable.

Rachel couldn't hide her disappointment at not being taken to Sparetra straight off. She tried to understand Targitus' strange caution. "After all," she said, "Sparetra must know something. She was there at the river. She saw me with you, as you pointed her out in the crowd. She must know we live together. Surely she'll hear how Tymnes is introducing me. Maybe I could help your family in some way."

"I want to get control of my father's situation first. I've got to plan the meeting. Things aren't right yet, believe me."

As Maytes' condition worsened, Sparetra demanded that Targitus stay overnight with her in the family yurt. She seemed to be forcing him to choose between "your Semite," as she had begun to call Rachel, and his parents. Each night was a battle. Sometimes he stayed; sometimes he returned to Rachel. His explanation was always the same. "My family needs me. I know you understand."

But Rachel couldn't. And it hurt. What he didn't appreciate, she believed, was how helpful she could be. Hadn't she opened the way to the Sardian secrets? Desperate to recapture Targitus' attention, she longed to tell him how she pled his cause with Cyrus. That she did it for him and was successful. Each time the idea surfaced, she would hesitate. What would he think she had done to persuade the Satrap? Could she convince him that it was not much at all, just a kiss and hug? For if she were responsible for unlocking the secrets, Argali was not. Argali must have failed, despite having given so much more of herself to the Satrap. But, if she were really honest, might she have to admit to the possibility that she did it not for Targitus but for herself. For the pleasure of testing her power over the Satrap? Or to see if he might become jealous? Disclosing the episode would cut, like a Scythian sword, in many directions. A sense of shame restrained her.


The whole village thought of nothing but the declining health of its beloved leader. Targitus soon heard many suggestions from earnest villagers intent on curing his father, whose symptoms were widely misunderstood. Targitus questioned his mother closely. "When did you first notice some change?"

"I am not sure, exactly. He was healthy when you left for Sardis, wasn't he? In the spring, he began to develop tremors. He had tingling in his fingers. Then brief flashes of light in his eyes. Of course, he noticed these things and asked me. I thought it might be his diet. Or too much koumiss."

Sparetra was trying to sound analytical, but her face, a mirror for her heart's despair, defeated the effort. Looking at her, Targitus saw a different face, skin drawn tight, eyes drooping dull, hair awry, lower lip in motion. She turned away too late to conceal her sobbing. Targitus reached out, drawing her to him. Her forehead sought the solidity of a shoulder to support her pain, which now flowed audibly, filling the yurt, while she collapsed in her son's tight embrace.

Between sobs she tried to continue. "We stopped the koumiss for a while. Cut back the meat. More yogurt, that sort of thing. We tried tapping the blood of our best ponies. The tremors increased. And, slowly, other problems appeared. It felt strange to mark the progression. Like watching the effects of fungus on a tree. We knew the way things were going." Sparetra's composure was back.

"It must have been torture."

"He grew frail. Standing was difficult. His balance went. Often, he would fall, stiff and straight, like a glass tipping over. He began to slur his words. Then mental confusion. He forgot the name of his horse. And his servants. Lucidity would return at times, only to vanish again. But he never forgot me. Nor his belief that communion with the spirits would speed his recovery."

"You mean the hemp-smoking ceremony? He kept up with that?"

"As health declined, hemp use increased. Well, you know we've always believed in hemp for purification and protection. But he's turned to it more and more. And our shamans encourage him. At least once a day. Sometimes twice. It puts him in what he calls a floating state. He says hemp smoke puts his mind at rest, takes it to a place beyond harm." Sparetra got up to boil water for tea. Targitus saw that color had returned to her face.

"But aren't the effects just temporary?"

"The more he uses the cauldron, the more he seems to need it. And his health keeps deteriorating. His memory loss seems

## 14: GREAT ULAGAN VALLEY – 405 B.C.

permanent. He has more difficulty sleeping. And he's unable to eat. In truth, the ceremony's all he's done in the past few months."

"The censer is different from the one he used. Much bigger."

"Oh, that cauldron was made to the shaman's specifications about four months ago. Matyes complained he wasn't getting a rich enough dose of hashish because the hot stones cooled too fast. He wanted a bigger vessel to hold more stones and hemp seeds, and a way to keep the heat coming until the seeds were exhausted. The new cauldron works just as your father wanted it to."

"Why does he wear that dye on his face and arms?"

"Another idea of Idanthyrsus. Chief shaman. Red for fierceness, red for strength, as in blood."

"It's a warriors' dye, to bring victory," said Targitus. "Not a medicine."

"Idanthyrsus came in one day, all excited, claiming that it will bring your father victory over the creeping illness. I pointed out that Matyes already had tattoos covering much of his body that used the red dye as pigment. The shaman was dismissive. Insisted we use the dye, that it would work." Sparetra poured tea for them, then started sobbing again as she tried to explain that Matyes, in his few lucid moments, believed the bright colored dye was a success. He insisted it remain on his body, renewed daily.

Again, Targitus gently enveloped his mother in his arms until the sobs had run their course. And, then, with caution in his voice, he asked the question he had been holding back. "Does Ishkapai know of father's condition?"

Sparetra stiffened. "He does now. For months, I didn't send word, not wanting to worry him, still believing there was a cure. A couple of months ago, when Matyes' loss of memory was matched by his loss of weight, I began to give up hope. I sent word. Your brother wants to come home."

Targitus appeared calm, having anticipated her answer. "What do you think?" he asked.

"Matyes won't recognize him. He didn't know you until I got through to him at a semi-lucid moment just as he emerged from a hemp session. But for Ishkapai, it's important to see his father, even in this condition, before he dies. It's up to you. That's what your father would say, if he could remember. So it's up to you. Think carefully. The implications extend beyond your father's life." Targitus searched his mother's face for a clue as to what she thought. Finding nothing, he said, "I'll consult the council."

Targitus was on tip-toe in preparing his mother to meet Rachel. He would not disclose their intention to marry. Again, Rachel believed him overly cautious, and said so, but to no effect. Targitus believed it best to describe Rachel as a woman he was living with because it pleased him to do so, a woman of artistic accomplishment who had come to the Altai to create a weaving center. He would ask for Sparetra's support. As he labored to explain Rachel to his mother the day before their meeting, Sparetra appeared intent on following every word, like a puppy dog showing its training. He was pleased with his approach. If he had known more of his mother's powers of understanding, or been less enthralled with his planning, he might have caught a glimmer of dark amusement in her eyes, a certain movement of the lips inward against the teeth, for, in fact, she found much to laugh about.

Targitus ushered Rachel into his mother's sturdy cabin of larch logs neatly notched to fit tightly at each corner. And so they met, facing each other at a distance of two or three feet, Rachel open-eyed and friendly, Sparetra dignified and distant, each taking the full measure of the other while pretending not to. They sat together around a low table that stood in front of a fireplace at one end of the cabin. Sparetra served tea. Conversation was natural and unchallenging. Rachel talked about her plans. Sparetra spoke of life in the village. Asked about life in Sardis.

"And the Satrap? Did you get to meet him?"

"Mother," Targitus interjected, "of course she did. It was his workshop. He often came to see the weaving."

They continued to converse. Targitus finished his tea. With a serene smile, he declared the meeting over and rose to escort Rachel out.

"Rachel," Sparetra said. "I assume you came to the Altai to

## 14: GREAT ULAGAN VALLEY – 405 B.C.

marry. Tell me your plans."

Targitus sat down.

From her earliest years, Rachel was accustomed to speaking the truth. Not from any moral imperative, although she respected Jewish teachings. She knew how to lie and could do so if it served her interests. The instinct to speak plainly was stronger. It sprang from recognition of the many ways in which she was different from those around her. She was unrestrained, no matter how angular her opinions might appear to the straight-forward consensus. She would speak her mind because she valued her thoughts and was eager for others to value them as well. And so it proved impossible for her to dissemble, or deflect the question to Targitus. In fact, so eager was she to answer Sparetra, that she didn't consider its impact on him at all.

"My plan is to live out my days here. To serve the community through weaving. To serve your son as wife and mother to his children. We are betrothed." Rachel looked only at Sparetra as she spoke. Sparetra's only answer was a wry smile.

Awkwardly shifting from one foot to the other, Targitus muttered acknowledgement. And then, motioning to Rachel, he gave his mother a hug and moved toward the door. Rachel followed, extending her hand to a woman who now seemed more distant. At the same instant, Rachel wished she could have felt comfortable in embracing this woman, whose love and support she not only wanted but knew she had to have.

Outside the cabin, they mounted horses in silence and, at the trot, began the ride north to their yurt. Targitus broke the silence, which had grown uncomfortable. "I am not sure which of my two women surprised me the most."

"I like your mother. I don't know how she felt about me. Ought I to worry?"

"You'll have her support. Without a doubt, you will. It's just going to take some time."

As they talked, each stared straight ahead. Then Targitus said, "I knew you would handle her perfectly." He threw her a wry glance. She broke out laughing.

Targitus knew the answer before conferring with the council. It was his nature to act, where possible, with as much support as possible. From watching his father over the years, he knew that spreading responsibility helped. By bringing his brother back from exile only with their approval, he would implicate the elders in any unhappy consequences. With Ishkapai, one could never predict. Nor, he thought, could one be too careful.

As the family awaited Ishkapai's return, Matyes' condition worsened. Those parts of his skin not already covered with tattoos or the constant application of cinnabar dye developed pink discolorations. He began to experience bouts of severe sweating, a condition that was exacerbated by his twice daily visits to the hashish tent. Hearing, speech and vision grew worse.

Despite his pleas for patience, Idanthyrsus came under growing pressure. At last, he produced a handful of reddish pills composed of ground-up cinnabar, which he directed the patient take three times daily with water. Sparetra asked if the remedy was tested. With the annoyance of someone having special access to life's mysteries who is suddenly challenged by a common mortal, Idanthyrsus reminded her that Altaian warriors had always used cinnabar. Holding up one of the pills as if it were an elixir, he intoned: "If cinnabar paint gives strength to a warrior, even more will come from grindings. You must administer the cure."

Taking Targitus aside, Sparetra said. "The worse your father gets, the more omniscient he behaves. I'm afraid."


Rachel had no obvious role in this family drama. Not wanting to appear callous or indifferent, she felt relief at not having been assigned a task. She was still a stranger within Targitus' family. In the village, she was a curiosity, except to the band who had returned with her to the Great Ulagan valley. Led by Tymnes, they found ways to help her make of the village a new home. They would always greet her warmly on the street. They took turns escorting her to find food and supplies. And they made sure the prominent families of the village met her and heard her story. Targitus was consumed by his

## 14: GREAT ULAGAN VALLEY – 405 B.C.

father's worsening condition and the family's loss of confidence in the shaman. Rachel knew nothing of shamans or Maytes' strange sickness. With a woman's intuition, she knew all she could do was make Targitus' life easier by providing food and comfort when he had time to accept it.

Targitus wanted something more. It proved to be the source of their first fight in the Altai. He asked her to remove the beeswax pessary protecting them against pregnancy. It wasn't an easy decision. If Rachel knew anything about her family's culture and religion, it was an absolute insistence that marriage come first. Targitus claimed that, in the Altai, it was natural for a couple to start with a family, then to move to marriage. He pressed her hard.

At first, while accepting that pregnancy could be a route to marriage, she told him it would not be her way. Targitus listened. He continued the pressure. He excused an uncommon abruptness in the matter as due to stress from his father's condition.

In time, she realized that giving him a child might be the only route to marriage in the Altai. He never said so. But marriage was like the ever-distant horizon she remembered so well during the journey across the steppe. Once the pessary was removed, Targitus relaxed, content to let nature take its course.


Rachel resolved to bring the weaving center to life as quickly as she could. After all, it was the final, and successful, argument that Targitus used to get her to follow him to the Great Ulagan valley. To proceed apace, she rationalized, would be to serve both her lover and his family and the whole village.

While encouraging her to proceed, Targitus had time for nothing more tangible. But it was enough to allow her to develop a plan and start to implement it. In this effort, the support Sparetra gave was invaluable. Rachel guessed that Sparetra found this diversion from the unrelenting role of care-giver a blessing. She also supposed that, without Sparetra's visible support, some villagers might have quickly found fault. Foreign ways were not always welcome, even in cosmopolitan towns like Sardis. Surely in the Altai, her plan would have been rejected at once without Sparetra's shield.

Luck also played a part. There happened to be an unused building well suited to Rachel's needs. Tymnes led her to it, lugging the package of loom parts for her to assemble. What she was being given was a rectangular structure situated a short distance from the village square, within sight and sound of the Bashkaus. It had a raised floor of larch planks resting on layered stones interlaced for strength and lateral stability. It was large enough, Rachel thought, to house six vertical looms and supplies. From its site on flat ground not more than a stone's throw from the river, Rachel could listen to the energetic rush of waters outside the felted walls. Later, as the weather grew warmer, she would be able to roll the sides up tightly, tying them in place with the straps that hung down from the ribs of the structure. Then she could look out at the frothy river and farther south beyond the river, where the mountains rose, she could see the peak of Kis-Kishtu-Aik, white with snow throughout the year. There was plenty of room to add additional structures as needed. It would even be possible, Tymnes suggested, to join one building to another so that weavers could move from one to the other protected from the elements.

Rachel was assembling her loom the next morning when a middle-aged woman appeared at the door.

"I understand you're looking for volunteers. My name's Paralata. Mother of Marsyas. He insisted I come. Did you know he worships you?"

"Mother of Marsyas, he of the giant heart," Rachel said, putting down a piece of the frame and rising to greet her first volunteer. "You did well with that one. Come in."

Rachel resumed the assembly of her loom while Paralata talked. She was one of a group of artists who worked in wool and metal. "I spin and felt mostly," she said. "I've done a little weaving but not on anything as elaborate as that," she said, her voice rising for emphasis as she pointed at the wooden pieces neatly spread out in an arc on the floor.

Marsyas was Paralata's youngest. She had time to help. And desire to learn. Among her friends, many, she told Rachel, would want to join the project.

## 14: GREAT ULAGAN VALLEY – 405 B.C.

In the days that followed, Paralata's prediction proved correct. There was no shortage of volunteers. All were women, some as young as Rachel, others much older. All were practiced in design and fabrication. From the works of their hand that Rachel saw, it was obvious they were artists of accomplishment, who expressed their art through a variety of utilitarian objects.

The sculptors, whether in wood, horn, leather, felt or metal, were usually men. They fashioned objects in the round as well as in high or shallow relief. Virtually all objects of everyday use expressed the Altaian aesthetic. They depicted animals, real and imagined, in violent combat on saddles, bridles, croups, tables, stools, chairs and coffins.

Altaian women were skilled at spinning with wool and vegetable fibres, such as hemp and kendyr. The dominant use of wool, however, was for felt, where sheep's down was preferred. In all the spun yarns she saw, she noted the consistent use of the Z-twist. "It's been our way for as long as anyone can remember," Hestia, the eldest among them, said. "It feels right."

These women had mastered the art of making large pieces of uniformly thin felt material and of dyeing it in a wide variety of fast colors. Felt was used for caftans and stockings, as a base for leather head decorations, for wall hangings and in the shabracks that served as horse coverings, where applied felts of different colors were used in inventive and arresting patterns.

Mastery showed in their stitching, whether in wool, used chiefly in felt appliqué, or sinew, used to work in leather, wood and metal. But Rachel soon discovered that Targitus had been right. The Altaians lagged far behind the west in both the art and technology of weaving. Hylaia, generally acknowledged to be the village's most accomplished weaver, gave Rachel a demonstration of Altaian weaving technique.

As all weavers know, the most basic function of a loom is to hold taut one set of threads, the warp, so that the other set of threads, the weft, can be interlaced with them to form a textile. Hylaia explained that only one type of loom, a narrow body-tensioned one, was in regular use. She used one in the demonstration. This simple instrument consisted of two stiff rods to which the two ends of the warp threads were tied. One rod was then hitched to the weaver by a strap around the waist and the other, the warp beam, to anything fixed, such as the wall of a building or a tree or post. Tensioning of the warp threads was achieved by the weaver's weight and was adjustable by her movement forward or back. The work progressed from the weaver toward the warp beam with the rod strapped to the weaver being turned to roll the finished textile out of the way.

The weaver used wooden bars lying across the top of the warp to create openings, called "sheds," through which the weft thread was fed under or over the warp threads as required by the particular weave. Each bar was attached to certain of the warp threads so that, when lifted up, the attached threads would also be pulled up to create the shed. For the simple "over and under" plain weave, only two bars were needed. For the twill weave, which was popular for clothing in the Altai and the one being used by Hylaia in the demonstration, four bars were required.

Since the weaver was not free to move about a body-tensioned loom, her arms defined the maximum width of the textile, about eighteen inches, that could be woven. It served the Altaians for needs not readily met by felt, such as belts and straps for cinching and girding. Paralata said it would be hard to exaggerate the importance of wool in the Altai. However, she emphasized, the fabric of choice for making woolen objects had always been felt, because of its warmth, weatherproofing, malleability and ease of fabrication.

For Rachel the limited development of the weaver's craft in the Great Ulagan bespoke need and opportunity. There was a gap to be filled, bigger than she had imagined. Sitting alone in the empty yurt, she considered the possibilities. Was she really free to put her mark on the center?

Targitus appeared at the door. Rachel was seated on a low bench in the middle of the room. "You look lost in thought. Where are your helpers?"

"Gone for the day. But do you know how I feel?" Her face became animated. Then exultant. Jumping to her feet, arms over her head, she said, "Exactly as the first weaver to discover the royal purple

## 14: GREAT ULAGAN VALLEY – 405 B.C.

dye must have felt. And not just that," she quickly added, "Just like the first to reap the benefits of growing sheep for wool, not meat."

"Your stories. If that's how good you feel, I am .... I am happy too."

Rachel plunged into her lover's world. She could see he'd had another difficult day.

"What news?"

"More of the same. He's dying. I will stay with them tonight."

Rachel moved close in front of him, seizing his hands in hers. Looking up at his sad face, she said, "I wish there were some way for me to ...."

He cut her off, as he always did when she tried this appeal.

"There is. Right now. Finish telling me why you're so excited."

Rachel knew he was burdened not only by Maytes' decline, which he would openly discuss with her, but by the imminent arrival of his brother, a subject on which he would not be engaged. There was nothing to be done. She would try to distract him.

"I had an interesting thought yesterday. A question really. Maybe you can help me. I tried to imagine the first steppe dweller to mount a horse instead of killing it." She had moved close to Targitus and put her hands on his shoulders, holding him there as if by doing so she could fix his mind in place too. "I am sure he would have lived among your forebears. Haven't the Massagetae been great horsemen for a long time?"

"A Massagetae? Surely. One with great vision," he said, looking deep into her eyes.

"And brave to climb onto the back of such a large, dangerous beast."

"A moment of grand possibilities," Targitus said.

"That's it, and precisely how I feel today." Dropping her hands, she hugged him tight.

He had to arch his back to look at her, his expression more of bemusement than pride. "Effulgence. That's the word for you. For as long as I've known you. It's what your enthusiasms do for you."

After another embrace, she fetched her horse and returned to their yurt, leaving him to attend to his parents.

Ishkapai arrived too late. The pills had hastened his father's descent. On the third day of treatment, he died. Immediately, plans were made for a burial befitting his royal status. Custom held that interment must take place at the beginning of summer or await the arrival of autumn. The family decided there was just enough time to complete a proper service before the end of June. Embalming was the first step, a process entrusted to shamans. Idanthyrsus appeared at the king's home to offer his services. The shaman was confident, full of energy and insufferable pride. He carried a great bundle of willow rods that he spread on the ground before the corpse, taking care to separate each rod so that it touched no other. He then began to prophesy, collecting the rods one by one as he spoke in obscure phrases that at times were impossible to understand.

Targitus was able to discern that Idanthyrsus blamed the death on an unnamed relation of Maytes, one who had left the village in disgrace. This person had been issuing repeated oaths of vengeance against Maytes, invoking the spirits to destroy him. These oaths, Idanthyrsus claimed, grew in power until they overcame the cannabis and cinnabar. He closed the ceremony by imploring the family to root out the villain and behead him. With that, the shaman left, bundles of willow rods tucked under each arm, to prepare for the embalming.

Targitus and his mother stared at one another across the nearly naked body of Maytes, still lying on his death bed. Targitus felt doubt and horror in equal measure. Looking at Sparetra, he thought she shared his emotions. Neither spoke. At that moment, Ishkapai burst in, tears on his stricken face. Always a little larger than life, Ishkapai filled any room he entered. Targitus was standing nearest to the entrance. Ishkapai flew to him first, large arms wrapping tightly about him in an emotional embrace that Targitus reciprocated, on instinct alone. Ishkapai said, "Brother, I welcome you safely home as I know you do me."

Targitus felt degraded by the touch of his brother. He remained silent, his conflicting emotions too tangled to sort out. Later, he would curse himself for failing to prepare.

Releasing Targitus, Ishkapai turned to embrace his mother, whose tears were a match for his. The greetings over, Ishkapai asked

## 14: GREAT ULAGAN VALLEY – 405 B.C.

for tea, then seated himself before the corpse to hear the story.

As attendants brought birch and mint tea, Sparetra and Targitus took turns telling of Maytes' ebbing life. Sparetra brought the story current by reporting that the chief shaman had claimed his medicine failed because "someone from the village unknown to the shaman" had inflicted a series of curses on Maytes. Ishkapai's countenance darkened as the tale unfolded. Rising to his feet, he moved to his father's corpse and began examining it. "When did father add these tattoos?" he asked.

Sparetra said they were applied about a month after Targitus had left for Sardis.

"Why cinnabar?"

"Your father insisted. For the same reason it was applied to his face and ingested. Strength."

Targitus hadn't examined the tattoos. Now, reacting to his brother's attention, he looked closer. What he saw was an abundance of artwork covering his father's arms from shoulder to hand, his legs below the knee and his torso, front and back. Mountain sheep, horses, fish and fantastical horse-like animals being pursued by eagle-griffins. The colors ranged from vermilion to crimson, depending on the place and depth of puncture.

"Did anyone urge cinnabar on father?" asked Ishkapai.

"Oh no," Sparetra replied, "it was his idea, which he forced on the artist, who had never used that dye for tattooing."

"What about Idanthyrsus? I thought you said he pushed it as a cure."

"Yes, but that came later, after your father grew ill. He suggested it as medicine. And Maytes agreed, emphatically."

Targitus didn't understand. Remembering the shaman's prophecy, he wondered if Ishkapai might be trying to divert their attention. Before he could ask the right question, Ishkapai laid bare his thoughts. The three were standing in a circle around Maytes. Ishkapai spoke softly.

"Cinnabar killed our father. As a dye it can be smeared on the face without harm. But used inside the skin as a tattoo, or even worse, ingested as a pill, it will kill." Ishkapai looked at the family to left and right. "I see you don't believe me. Let me tell you a story I heard on my way to banishment. We were passing Dead Lake, just north of the Red Gates. Mother, you may not remember, but I am sure Targitus, who recently passed those gates, will. The Red Gates are the mountain pass through which one descends along the Kara-Ozok River to its junction with the Cuja. On either side of that pass are high red peaks of cinnabar. I remarked on the oddity of this lake; that nothing lived there even though all the other lakes, and there are a string of them running north through the valley, had fish and fowl in abundance. One of my guards claimed that cinnabar was the cause. But, trust me, it was more than a theory. His wife was an experimenter with herbal remedies. A woman famed in the village for taking a chance, although some called it foolishness, in the face of the unknown. She was given to nibbling untested mushrooms. Some thought her a witch. Others thought her seized of mysterious powers. Her husband knew she was neither. Just an excessively curious human being. She developed the theory that cinnabar might cure headache. Dissolving the vermilion material in water, she used it as soon as she could on a young volunteer suffering with severe headaches. The headaches persisted. The dosage was increased. Within three weeks, the woman had descended into a coma. In another week she was dead.

My guard's wife was exonerated of guilt through a lucky coincidence. The woman killed by cinnabar was discovered to have lied under sacred oath to her husband. Her death was attributed to the Gods. The excessively curious woman was neither reformed nor repentant. Suspecting that cinnabar had poisoned the woman, she examined Dead Lake, taking samples of the water to compare with her own cinnabar solution, which had been taken from the Red Gates. Using minnows as a test, she found that both solutions killed."

Ishkapai's story rang true. Its implications sunk in. Sparetra and Targitus saw the ease with which Maytes' illness and death could have been avoided. Simple grieving turned to horror. A husband and father had poisoned himself and been finished off by shamanic ignorance.

Anger quickens the tempo of life. Idanthyrsus and his two principal colleagues, who had formed the triumvirate of shamans respon-

## 14: GREAT ULAGAN VALLEY – 405 B.C.

sible for treating Maytes, were seized. Soothsaying was a risky vocation, as uncertain as soldiering. One could live well so long as one performed. Punishment for failure was harsh. Gagged and bound hand and foot, the three shamans were placed deep in a cart, which was then filled high with sticks and harnessed to a team of oxen by a long pole. The oxen were led about the village to achieve maximum deterrence. The sticks were then ignited and the oxen chased away at a run. By the time the pole burnt through, allowing the oxen to escape the mobile pyre, the shamans had been consumed.

His mind was beyond control. As the day of burial grew near, Targitus kept rehearsing each step of the ritual demanded by tradition for the burial of an Altaian king, as if by repetition the after-shocks of a father's death could be dampened.

He imagined the newly appointed shamans embalming his father. He could see them trepanning the skull, removing the brain, entrails and musculature. In trying to finish quickly, before the aroma of decay grew unbearable, they would be rough, confident Maytes was beyond pain. Targitus winced. Pain belonged to those left behind.

The shamans would insert pine needles, larch cones and such traditional herbs as galingale, parsley seed, anise and smokey tea. Targitus knew the smell of each and their purpose in masking the stench, which had announced itself before the shamans took Maytes away. They would sew him up with cord twisted from plaits of horsehair.

This preoccupation must have affected his riding, for with head shakes and an ornery disregard of signals Belukcha was trying to get his attention.

"Be-lu-Be-lu, I know what you're thinking. You're right. My mind's far away." Targitus placed his head against Belukcha's mane and, stretching both arms out, rubbed the sides of his horse's head and neck. In response, soft nicker.

Targitus hadn't explained the tribal rituals to Rachel. He knew enough of her culture to be concerned. Days passed. On the eve of the burial, Rachel said, "I know there are rituals. My weavers told me that much. They're surprised you haven't told me what to expect.

I feel the foreigner again."

Targitus had prepared an excuse. He would say that, consumed by his loss, he had simply overlooked the need to prepare Rachel. He would apologize. Instead, he blurted out something else.

"I am not good at talking, especially about this."

"I know that." Rachel concealed her surprise.

He began to describe a king's burial in the Altai and the turmoil in his head. They were standing at the confluence of the two rivers near their yurt, catching the cool air stirred up by the cold waters and watching the sun dropping behind the steep hills to the west. When only an after-glow remained, they returned to the yurt. Once started, Targitus felt a need to cover every detail.

"It's an ancient custom of our people. The idea is to have the dead man retain contact with his life-bearing organ. In this way, our ancestors believed, he will find safe passage and a kind of rebirth in the next world." Targitus was describing how the shamans would bind the index finger of Maytes' right hand at the nail with a thread that would then be attached to the skin of his pubic area.

"Do you believe that?"

He felt challenged, without knowing whether that had been her intention.

"I accept what I've been taught."

Rachel remained silent, responding only with a quizzical glance that Targitus recognized as an invitation to debate. He resumed the description.

"The embalming was finished a week ago. It's all done out of sight, although it's no secret to villagers." He dropped his eyes in embarrassment. "I didn't want to talk about it. They placed him in a wagon to be drawn through nearby villages. By now many crowds will have witnessed his passing. And many will have joined the procession, which returns tonight. The burial site is north of here, above the spur we rode to. They've dug a huge tomb shaft. You'll see."

At dawn the next day, Targitus and Rachel set out to join the cortege where it had stayed the night in the village. Targitus noted many Altaians from other villages, camping in place to await the final procession to the burial site. By their costumes, he knew they came

## 14: GREAT ULAGAN VALLEY – 405 B.C.

from many villages, some far to the west, in the foothills of the Altai and even the steppe beyond.

Soon his mother and his brother arrived, riding stiffly, solemn gray forms against the lighter gray of the eastern horizon, their horses dressed in accoutrements as fine as those he and Rachel had placed on their mounts. Targitus knew the day would soon brighten with the sun's life-giving rays, oblivious to the grief that would persist among his family well past sunset. He wished it were otherwise.

The order of march put the wagon bearing his father first. Twenty-eight horses followed, magnificently caparisoned and led in single file from the left by an equal number of grooms. The family came next. Rachel had positioned herself beside Targitus, just behind his mother and ahead of his brother. Turning in her saddle, Sparetra looked at Rachel as she said, "Should my sons ride side by side?"

Neither son spoke. Rachel knew her question was an order. Breaking away, she moved to the rear of the family. Looking back she saw an almost endless stream of riders starting to move forward. The cortege had begun its final day's travel.

As the family neared the tomb shaft, Rachel heard the slow, incessant beat of a single drum. She saw her father, face up in the shallow grave. She remembered the arrow and felt this mournful dirge in the pit of her stomach.

Lining the outer edge of the shaft to pay their last respects to King Maytes were a group of burial workers. Rachel noticed antler picks and wooden wedges, mallets and shovels strewn about the site, each battered and broken in battle with hard boulder clay. She could make out still serviceable versions of these tools resting in what she knew would be the blistered and bloody hands of the exhausted workers.

She was struck by the certainty of the ceremonial process. As with her own people, custom was deeply etched in the collective memory of these Altaians, extending far back in time, for the death of an Altaian king was not a frequent occurrence.

As she watched, the crew of handlers from the cortege gently laid Maytes on his back, arms and legs extended, in a coffin made of larch, a tree trunk three feet across. Dressed smooth by axe on the outside, the coffin had been hollowed by adze. Around its sides were leather cut-out silhouettes of deer running in a counter-clockwise direction. Foil of hammered tin had been stuck to the leather surface and each cut-out had been secured to the coffin by tiny iron nails.

She couldn't prevent herself from processing the coffin with an artist's eye. She was having difficulty sharing either the pain or sorrow of others. Something seemed to be missing from her inventory of feelings.

The family was invited to take one last look at Maytes, who had been surrounded by gold adornments: a torque of six spirals ending in griffin heads, a matching bracelet, the dynamic figure of an Altaian horseman mounted on his steed, bow drawn taut, arrow nocked, and an exquisite figure of a reindeer captured in full stride, tongue extended and antlers soaring above its frame from head to rump.

Sparetra rode forward with her two sons to the edge of the coffin. Dismounting, they knelt beside Maytes, moving together as if they had rehearsed the scene many times. Their faces were essays in emptiness and grief. Watching these expressions, Rachel felt a chill of guilt. A shiver ran down the length of her back, as if to challenge the heat of a sun now high above. She was falling short and they all knew it.

So much gold, she thought. Then came the realization that it could not be pure gold.

This thought propelled her back to Sardis, to her first sighting of Targitus at the door of the weaving room, to her encounters with Cyrus, to her successful plea on behalf of the Altaians. She longed for the day when she could reveal to Targitus her role in prying loose the secrets. What was she waiting for? Marriage? A family? When the process had proved workable? She wondered when any of these things might come to be.

While her mind wandered, her eyes were held by the coffin, where shirts, breeches, fur-lined headdress, belts with silver plates and felt appliquéd capes had been piled neatly beside Maytes, who was unclothed except for footwear. An ox-horn drum had been placed at his feet. All signs of cinnabar had been removed, save that used in the tattoos.

## 14: GREAT ULAGAN VALLEY – 405 B.C.

Were all these things necessary, she wondered, comparing how she had laid Benjamin to rest with only an arrow for company. Catching a scent, she decided that a ripening body, with more accoutrement or less, will become nauseous.

At a signal from Sparetra, a larch lid was placed over the coffin and secured by four square pegs that passed through both lid and coffin at the corners. A crew of four then lowered the coffin into a burial chamber within the shaft by heavy hemp cords, which were passed through holes in the two pairs of large lugs carved at each end of the coffin. From their loud grunts, strained faces and taut bodies, she could see the men were being stretched to the limit. Brief passage. First leg of a long journey. For the rest, she wondered, who would help the King?

The day had grown unseasonably hot. How long would the family remain at graveside? How long could they? I never knew Maytes. I could grieve with Targitus, and for him, if only he would open up a little.

"It won't be long now," Targitus said. "Look, the crew is taking things down."

Rachel could make out some of the personal effects and adornments being placed in the chamber around the coffin: a wooden stool, two low tables with detachable legs carved in the shape of elongated tigers, heads facing upward, Maytes' favorite bronze censer, his leather flask, filled, she was sure, with hemp seed. Goat- and horse-meat and quantities of cheese were placed on the tables, together with iron knives. Two tall earthenware bottles stood between the two tables, resting on circular felt stands. "Koumiss?"

Targitus nodded. "We try to give him what he loved and what he will need. You look doubtful. From experience, that's how we know. No one's returned, so that should tell us we are doing it right don't you think?"

Rachel couldn't tell if Targitus was joking. It was not his habit, even in less stressful circumstances. She let the subject rest.

When the burial chamber was complete, Rachel and Targitus turned their horses to ride slowly to the spur overlooking the Great Ulagan valley, less than a half-mile from the burial site. Rachel felt relief. Like escaping alone from a severe snowstorm into a warm room full of friends. Now, sitting their horses, they took in the view of the valley, deeply green with mature growth, the ridges on either side flanking the two rivers that joined in the copse where they could just make out their yurt. Kis-Kishtu-Aik glistened white in the center of the mountain range beyond the village.

"Killing those young horses," Rachel said. "The image of them lifting the axes makes me wince. I couldn't have watched."

"Just a quick blow. My father's best riding horses. They'll be buried in full parade harness. He will ride them in the next world," he said, half defiant, as he caught Rachel's side-long glance. "That look again."

Rachel tried to attract his eyes, but they were now downcast.

"I am sorry," Rachel said. "It's your father's funeral and I am grieving for his horses."

Targitus started talking, eyes straight ahead.

"I tried to prepare. Often. Unlike you, I had the time." Targitus bent forward to stroke Belukcha, then glanced at Rachel. He felt the warmth of tears in his eyes. Looking away, he continued stroking his gelding, whispering softly, "Be-lu. Good horse, Be-lu."

"Not once did I imagine he would die before his time, as much by his own hand as by any other. I am not good at grieving publicly, when everyone expects it." Belukcha let out a loud whinny, shaking her head at the line of mounts far below, carrying villagers back to their homes.

"I am going to miss him not all at once, where one can grieve mightily and then get over it. The loss will come in small doses, again and again, so long as memory holds. When I have a question and turn to find he's not there. When the first cranes of Spring circle low over the Bashkaus. So powerfully did he connect the sighting of those wondrous creatures with being alive."

Rachel tried again to catch his eyes, to lift them up to meet her own. "I wanted to share your grief. I failed. Vicarious grieving doesn't work for me. Perhaps I need more practice. Perhaps you do too, in helping me understand."

Targitus turned Belukcha until he was looking at Rachel's mount, just inches away.

## 14: GREAT ULAGAN VALLEY – 405 B.C.

"What you just said about your father fills a gap. It was beautiful. You can look at me now." Rachel smiled, her face wet for the first time that day.

"I must tell you something. Even though I fear you'll think less of me. Through this whole burial ceremony I've been wishing for pregnancy to come, hoping for a sign that I was carrying your son. All week I've waited. My timing was off." Rachel looked crestfallen, at last a match for her companion, whose only response was to keep his eyes on hers as tears gathered on his sharp cheekbones to roll, two by two, down his face.

With a signal to their horses, they began the descent, pointing their mounts toward the corpse extending halfway up the spur. The larches stood tall and solemn, their blackened bark a foil for the soft pastel green of fresh needles. Despite herself, Rachel was cheered by the summer's pleasure that enclosed her beneath the trees. There, nourished by moisture collected in the draw, were throngs of peonies, now robust with full bloom, bursts of white against the deep green of their leaves.

Rachel now spent all her days at the workshop. She had set up the vertical two-beam loom that the Scopasis weavers had given her in an area of the yurt where it was possible to introduce plenty of light by pulling back the felt coverings. She had begun to teach from the loom and, with Tymnes' help, had engaged a skilled carpenter to make five copies for use by the growing number of women seeking to learn her way of fashioning textiles from wool. There were many advantages to the design of her loom. It allowed the weaver to sit rather than stand. One or two weavers could manage it. In contrast to the body-tensioned loom, it could accommodate textiles of great width. In contrast to the horizontal loom, it occupied less space, a valuable feature in a climate such as the Altai, where rain came intermittently throughout the summer and snow from early fall to late spring. The weaver moved from bottom to top, packing the weft threads tight with a downward motion favored by gravity rather than the upward one required on a warp-weighted loom. As Rachel explained to her class, for tying knots to make a pile carpet, there was no satisfactory alternative to the two-beam vertical loom.

This last point turned out to be especially important. For several weeks after the burial, Rachel had been mulling over the question of how best to use her loom. The copies were going to be ready soon, and she would then be able to teach weaving with five additional looms. Interest among the Altaian women was high. She would teach in two daily shifts, so that the ten students selected for the initial training session could each take a hand at one of the new looms. There was much eagerness to get started.

She imagined using her own loom not for training exercises but to demonstrate the skill. She would try out this idea on Targitus. By the time she reached their yurt, a twenty-minute ride from the workshop, the seed had grown beyond germination. Bursting into the yurt, Rachel found Targitus sitting in his customary place, deep in thought. Taiga lay quietly beside him, hind legs splayed out, head on the ground. Taiga pricked up her ears and raised her head.

Rachel sank to her knees in front of Targitus and, leaning forward, encircled his neck with her arms, pulling his distracted face forward. The kiss that followed was one of custom more than craving. As their lips parted, she held him close. " I don't know what's on your mind, but put it aside for a moment and listen."

"Do I have a choice?" Targitus replied rhetorically, erasing his distant expression.

She reported on progress at the workshop. And, then, she said, "I'd like to use the Scopasis loom for my own work to show the students what the loom can do. To inspire them."

"And engage the village. Very good.

"It will keep you from getting bored, at least till we have a baby. Can you do both?"

"Oh yes." Rachel beamed at the thought. "Remember, spinning and weaving are mothers' work."

"Your project will challenge?"

"Yes. It must. Here's what I want to do."

"Before you tell me, Rachel, how about releasing my neck. My back's beginning to feel your affections."

## 14: GREAT ULAGAN VALLEY – 405 B.C.

"I keep forgetting you're not as flexible as I am. There." As if to prove the point, she leaned far forward to kiss him gently again as, released from her hold, he straightened up. "Now, beyond showing off the loom, I have two other goals. First, the weaving should honor your father. And second, it should honor our marriage, which, as you put it, will take place at the 'right' time. It could be my present to you.

"Unless it gives you an excuse to postpone." She laughed.

Targitus rose, engaged Rachel's hands, pulled her to him. "It's exactly right. For you. And for us." He held her at arm's length. Her laughing eyes gleamed.

"I've come a long way to escape the palace workshop. Now, with this project, I feel free. It's a little frightening."

For days she had been sketching on tablets of stone in the workshop and on one less obvious in her head, each a palimpsest for many ideas that were taking shape. Now, as she retraced her steps for Targitus, what the first fruit of her workshop should be became clear.


A month after the burial, Rachel missed her bleeding. A second month passed. She knew. Soreness in her breasts. Occasional nausea upon waking. She didn't tell Targitus and didn't have to lie because his attentions were drawn to village matters.

She held the secret tight. If anyone else knew, it could only have been the babe growing inside. The added joy she felt among her students, the little extra lilt in her voice as she spoke to them of weaving, the tiny extra smile on her face as she described the creative process of design, all went undetected. When alone she spoke to the babe, calling him, for she was sure of a boy, "my little larch." She sang to him too, and hummed an air, confident he was responding in kind.

She was well along the path to childbirth, a path leading thence to marriage. One afternoon in the third month, before Targitus returned, she was sitting among flowers near their yurt. A powerful wind filled the trees. The sky was clear, the air dry. She watched the lowering sun cast light through the unspoiled leaves of early summer. The trees swayed with each burst of wind, pulsating, vital and urgent, driving through the trees, making rushing sounds that distilled her senses in two directions: one, a sense of absolute well-being; the other, a sense of nature's danger. Suddenly, she felt severe cramps. The pain caused her to stretch out, roll over, stand up, searching for relief. She began to bleed. Slowly at first. As the flow increased the pain from cramps subsided. By the end, the bleeding had been profuse. Heavier than any she'd ever experienced.

Again, she knew. With crushing certainty she knew. And was consumed with shame. Thank the stars she hadn't told Targitus. He must never know. In the days that followed, anger mixed with her sense of failure. She was sure this miscarriage had everything to do with not being married. She cursed herself for being weak, for submitting to his pressure, despite her instincts, her sure sense of what her family would have advised.

# CHAPTER 15

Great Ulagan Valley – 405 B.C.

While Rachel was absorbed with her weaving center, Targitus was caught up in the politics of choosing a new leader of the Altai. The council of elders had begun discussions soon after Matyes' death. After the funeral they summoned his sons. They planned to meet with them separately. When a king died in the Altai, custom empowered the council to pick the successor. By asserting its power swiftly, the council could fill the vacuum, achieving tacit recognition of its legitimacy. Of course, the blood line of a king, particularly one as revered as Matyes, was not irrelevant. Barring something extraordinary, there was a presumption that the son of a deceased king would be picked.

Ishkapai, now twenty-six, was called first to the council's yurt, located in the central square. The council was drawn up in a semicircle with all chairs filled save the one in the middle, Maytes' seat. There was a stool for Ishkapai, facing the others. Before the questions began, mint tea was served. The day was hot, and the felt flaps were pulled away from the center to encourage a breeze. Ishkapai took little time to convey both his desire to succeed his father and his conviction that he should. Baldly dismissing his banishment as the result of a minor intra-family dispute, he noted that he had been summoned home by both his mother and his brother. He pointed out that he was the only person in the village who had divined the cause of Matyes' illness and death.

Scyles, a recently appointed member of the council, suggested that Ishkapai had found growing up especially difficult. He asked if Ishkapai considered that process concluded or was there still work to do?

"I've been told I am too erratic and unpredictable to lead. Some years ago these would have been weaknesses. But I've put all that behind me. They're gone." Rising from his stool, Ishkapai drew himself up in front of the council. Tall and strong-limbed, he was imposing. His beard was black with tints of red and a sprinkling of white. His eyes, deeply set in a sharply chiseled face, were cornflower blue.

"I love my brother. Some of you, I know, are thinking I haven't always acted that way. You'd be right. We grew up fighting. Our father encouraged us. He said fighting ran in our veins; that we would be good at it; that by fighting each other, we would learn the skill and the ability to control ourselves. What we did within the family, he said, was private, of no concern to others.

"I have nothing to say against Targitus. The soft Sardian influences will erode with time. All save one. I feel sorry for the Semite. You and I know that we Massagetae aren't comfortable with foreigners. That's been our history, across the steppes. She hasn't been accepted here, and that must explain why my brother hasn't married her. I have trouble, perhaps you do too, imagining how she would cope if my brother were picked to rule. Or how we would feel if she became our queen. As for me, I'll marry in good time. I'll pick an Altaian. One you will never have to question."

Taking a step forward, he extended both arms and used his index fingers to point at pairs of the ten councilmen in turn, from the outside in, until he got to the empty chair, at which his fingers continued to point. As he moved in twos to the center, he declared with force, "I am the strongest, the boldest, the most natural leader within my family. I want to be your king. I expect to sit in that chair."

Whereas Ishkapai would be happy to wrench the prize out of the reluc-

## 15: GREAT ULAGAN VALLEY – 405 B.C.

tant hands of the judges by brute force, Targitus' style was calculation and ingenuous guile. He would seduce them into insisting that the prize be his. Playing on what he assumed would be his brother's approach, Targitus talked of his long preparation for this responsibility, not because he desperately wanted it, but out of a sense of duty. His father had worked hard to prepare him to receive the post if asked. He reminded them of his reluctance to go on the Sardian trip until they insisted.

He allowed himself a little boast about discovering the secrets of gold purification. Reminding them that it was his idea to take Argali as a princely gift for Cyrus, he said it had not been easy to bring her over 3,200 miles to Sardis in condition for delivery. Once in the Satrap's palace, he claimed subtlety in transforming an explicit gift into an implicit exchange. He led them to believe, as he did, that without Argali the secrets would never have been shared.

Reminding the elders of the ancient tribal custom by which family power naturally descended to the youngest son, he intoned that it would be unfair if he were picked for that reason alone. He urged them to consider the wishes of his father. He knew these wishes had never been expressed except by implication, and he also knew that the council, to a man, would assume those wishes pointed to Targitus. He urged them to consult his mother. He asked them to consider the role Rachel had assumed in the village, claiming that her popularity was growing faster than the wild geraniums now blanketing the valley with bluish-pink blooms. Turning to the council, he spoke of consensus, the importance of working with the council, of being as one with them, a team on which he was first among equals, no more and no less. And finally, he spoke of honor and duty, of his willingness to respond to the council's will, to accept its decision peacefully and, if the high office became his, to do his utmost to justify the trust placed in him by the council.

At the conclusion of his statement, which he had risen from his stool to deliver with quiet earnestness, Targitus bowed deeply and quickly left the yurt. He felt good. He had played the council like a harp, following to the final note the score he had carefully composed. Sure of the outcome, he had begun to consider how to address what he knew would be his brother's fury.

Rachel was preoccupied with the first Altaian product of her loom. It would be a monumental carpet, using the full size of the loom to achieve a six-foot width. The beginnings of design took shape as she explored with her mind's eye a myriad of motifs, fields, borders and dyes. In the workshop, she had placed on low wooden posts three large tablets of thin green slate procured for her from nearby mountains. The intricacies of design could now be tested on stone. Large pieces of leather had also been gathered for her use. By drawing squares on these surfaces, she could rough out knot schemes. Rachel preferred not to follow a cartoon strictly by the precise counting of knots, although she could do so, having been trained in that technique.

With a vestige of distaste, she recalled the Sardian routine, based on division of labor. The designs were rendered on line squares by male specialists. Female weavers were expected to render the repeating motifs exactly as displayed on the cartoons, by counting knots. Her plan was to use the cartoon as a pattern guide to replicate motifs based on their shapes rather than precise counts.

How does the weaver settle on a design? Rachel knew she didn't have the answer to that question. And doubted with honesty anybody else did. What did she know? That frustration is often the product of a too determined mind; that in the creative process, as in making love, the best results often came by stealth, when one least expected them; that like night vision, creative solutions are often found off-center, by approaching the problem from an angle.

Knowing this much didn't mean Rachel ceased consciously to think of design. She was simply patient. And soon enough, she settled on the major motif, an endless procession of horses and riders on the wide outer border of the carpet. It would be a solemn procession inspired by the one she had watched moving slowly from the Great Ulagan Valley to the King's burial site. A desire for balance suggested an equal number of horses and riders on each side.

But how many? She had no conviction until a dream intervened. She was with her father, who was telling her about Gilgamesh, a favorite among Sardians, whose tale was often used to prove one thing or another. Benjamin could recite the whole story. His voice came and went in her dream. She heard him say of Gilgamesh's

## 15: GREAT ULAGAN VALLEY – 405 B.C.

friend, Enkidju, that he drank ale, full seven goblets, and that mother, Ninsun, went into the bathhouse seven times to bathe in water of tamarisk and soapwort.

By being the first to expose Rachel to its rich imagery and lyricism, Benjamin had hoped to give her a stronger faith in Yahweh. But Rachel was now telling him that the story taught a different lesson. She interpreted Gilgamesh's futile search for eternal life not in terms of his having invoked the wrong gods, as Benjamin claimed, but as the blunt truth that death comes to all mankind, regardless of faith or glorious deeds; as Gilgamesh put it, "Man is snapped off like a reed in a canebrake."

The scene shifts. Now she is much younger and Benjamin is teaching her about the genesis of heaven and earth, made and blessed, as he put it, in seven days. He tells her of Noah, to whom God granted seven days in which to gather those to be spared, and of Joshua, to whom Yahweh promised Jericho. She hears Benjamin reciting His explicit instructions to Joshua: "And seven priests shall bear before the ark seven trumpets of rams' horns; and the seventh day ye shall compass the city seven times, and the priests shall blow with the trumpets."

Upon awakening, the dream's vividness startled her. So too the certainty she now felt about the number seven. It was a spiritual number, bringing good fortune, protective of life. It would be the measure of horses and riders she would weave on each side of the carpet's largest border, a shield against perils for the deceased Maytes during his journey to the next world. And for the living as well. For those who use the carpet, who stand or sit within the procession.

For most of that day, Gilgamesh remained in her thoughts. As a weaver, she took comfort in the ending, where Gilgamesh found redemption in the monument he had built and was leaving behind for others to enjoy. As a woman, she was sure he would have felt even better if he could have left behind children as well.

Rachel had urged Targitus to come by the center so she could show him her sketches. When he did, and saw the procession, he had doubts. He would have kept them to himself had Rachel not pushed him for some comment that evening, when the only sentient creature within earshot was Tiaga, whose curved form, head resting on her left front paw, ears folded down, confirmed a deep slumber.

"It's your design. But, if you insist, I'd like to see the riders mounted. They look like grooms."

Her sketches showed the horses being led by riders on foot. "I have reasons for this. I want to ornament the uncovered shabracks on the horses' backs. Use different motifs. Carpets within a carpet. Also, if mounted, the height of the riders would make the border too wide. Anything else?" She seemed sure he had accepted her argument.

He suggested having some riders mounted, others on foot. "After all, you've got twenty-eight horses and as many riders."

"That won't solve the spacing problem."

He claimed the problem could be solved by ignoring it. "Put all the heads at the same height, regardless. People come in all sizes. Make the tall ones walk and the short ones ride."

"I've got your point. More?"

"Well, the horses. They're too massive to be Altaian."

"I knew you'd notice. Remember, it's a protective ring. Size over speed."

The evening's discussion opened Rachel's eyes to a reality she hadn't considered in seeking Targitus' opinion. Unqualified approval was what she really wanted. Suppose she didn't get it? Targitus had been wise, she realized, in keeping his thoughts private. In the future, she would not press.

The size and shape of the horse and rider motif determined the overall dimensions of the carpet, roughly six feet wide by six and one-half feet long. Rachel was familiar with the large felt wall hangings and carpets made by Altaians for use in the yurts. Many exceeded the size she imagined for this weaving. However, in comparison with any textile woven in the Altai, the carpet would be large.

The horses would move as sun and moon, as the swirl of water and wind. This direction seemed apt for the dominant border among several she planned to frame the central field, which she had yet to imagine. She tried to think about the central field. Sitting in front of her green slate tablets, her mind wandered. Weaving is a solitary pursuit. And yet, the result is intended for as broad an audience as have

## 15: GREAT ULAGAN VALLEY – 405 B.C.

eyes to see. And so, she put the question, when those eyes turn to gaze at the center of this carpet, what do I want them to see? A place of refuge and peace, protected by several borders. A sacred place where one's spirit would be nurtured, where the composed energy of her art would be felt.

The goal was settled. How to express it took time, and many sketches. In the end she decided on four-rayed stars in diagonal, superimposed on straight crosses terminating in lotus blossoms. At the center of each cross, a diamond-shaped dot. This cruciform motif would be enclosed in a perfect square. Twenty-four squares would comprise the central field, running four across, six down.

She wanted twenty-four for a reason. Her father had taught her as a child that twenty-four was magical. He had called it an "abundant" number because the sum of its divisors, thirty-six, exceeded the number itself. And Hestia said that the number twenty-four held mystery for Altaians as well.


Rachel was spending long hours at the workshop. One evening, as she was preparing to walk home in the lengthening light of early summer, Paralata appeared at the yurt's entrance, asking to see her. Rachel would often remain long after her students had left in order to work on the design.

"I've come to warn you," Paralata said, her voice hushed.

She was soaked from a thunderstorm that had passed swiftly over the village, sandwiched between bright sun and white cumulus clouds. "You're shaking with cold," Rachel said. "Make it quick. Then get home to dry clothes. The evening's turning chilly."

"You know the council still hasn't acted. And Targitus is being put forth as a coward. A small group seems to be planting the seed, inciting others to oppose him."

Continuing to study the squares she had just laid out on the slate tablets, Rachel said, "But they're wrong. He's no coward. Altaians will prosper under his leadership. Don't worry. And tell that to those who do."

"You don't understand. They people want Targitus and Ishkapai to settle the issue by combat. People are stirred up. They mean to pre-empt the decision by forcing the brothers into a fight. They might even override a decision."

Rachel whirled around to face Paralata. "Who are these people?" she whispered.

"A few might be close to Ishkapai. But most are just ordinary villagers willing to believe what they hear. Naturally, they despise a coward. A rumor starts. Someone believes it and begins to worry. This starts others. It's contagious."

Rachel stood in shock, gripped by fear and helplessness. And not just for Targitus. She knew her fortunes in the Great Ulagan were tied to his star. If it fell, she would fall with it. "What do you think we should do?" she asked, as much to herself as Paralata.

"I came only to warn. Tell Targitus. He'll know."

Rachel gave Targitus the news as soon as she had reached the yurt. He had been expecting the elders to announce their decision at any moment. He had learned from Scyles that the rape, known to all but openly discussed by none, would disqualify his brother. Being edgy about Ishkapai, the council hadn't planned to tell him. Its decision would rest on many unspecified considerations.

Confident of the result, Targitus had rehearsed his acceptance speech. Rachel's story was a jolt. Although he had heard none of the rumors, it was entirely believable. He knew his brother. One of Ishkapai's strengths was knowing how others saw him. Not that his insights had ever caused him loss of sleep or nurtured a resolve to change his ways. From early childhood, Targitus had marveled at how comfortable his brother seemed in his own skin, how utterly indifferent he was to the opinions of others. A contrast to Targitus' strivings to serve and be respected.

Targitus was sure that those suggesting combat were in league with his brother. "The council's going to be influenced by the lie," Rachel exclaimed.

"No. The council's going to choose me. There's no question about that," Targitus said.

## 15: GREAT ULAGAN VALLEY – 405 B.C.

Rachel was confused. "How can you be so sure? He's the eldest and looks the part of a ruler."

"Trust me. I know the council's not going to pick him. But that won't solve the problem. As between a bully and a coward, many would prefer the bully."

"What will you do?" Rachel asked.

"We must find out how widespread this idea has become. It's tricky, because the more I insist on abiding by the decision of the elders, the more I feed the calumny. Ishkapai may have trapped us."

"Is there no way other than combat to prove you're not a coward? You have brave tales to tell. Don't you?"

"My reputation rests on intelligence, judgment, service. Of course, I am not a coward, but there's no recent proof. Once this rumor spreads among those willing to believe, it will be hard to drive it from their minds. Short of an act of bravery."


That night Targitus had a vivid dream from which he awoke disturbed enough to wake Rachel.

"I am looking up at the sky. I see something dark, shaped like a rabbit. It's pierced by an arrow. I can see both ends sticking out. It's gently circling around me, silent, motionless. I feel detached from my body. I know it's going to land nearby. I run off to retrieve it. I imagine a hunter searching for it too. I think he must be an excellent bowman. I must find the object before the hunter does. It's urgent. I search desperately through the forest. I can't find it. I awake in fear."

"I am not good at dreams." Rachel moved in close to him, hoping her body might ease his tension.

"I don't know either. But it means something."

They were lying beside one another, on their backs, looking through the opening at a fistful of stars. Rachel turned to run her hand through his hair and give his cheek a sleep-inducing kiss for them both.

"Maybe in the bright daylight, all will become clear."

His last waking thought was a vague sense that he knew this story; that he had possibly dreamed it before.

Early the next day, Targitus went to see the elders. He wanted to know the timing of their decision and whether they knew anything about the rumor Rachel had reported the night before. All but Scyles declined to talk. Their discomfort was palpable. In confidence, Scyles said the rumor was true. Some villagers were demanding trial by combat. Ishkapai was thought to be behind the rumors but had repeatedly denied it. The elders feared their decision might be rejected by the people. Although individually most of the them were brave, collectively, they were a cautious lot, bowing to the most risk-averse. As a result, they had resorted to delay.

"How do you expect it to be resolved?" Targitus asked, exasperation showing.

Scyles shrugged off the question. He shifted weight from one foot to the other, looking forlorn, then walked away.

Later that day, as Targitus emerged from Rachel's workshop, a crowd of villagers gathered around him. Women as well as men. Someone yelled "Trial by Combat." Others picked up the words, which quickly turned into a chant. Targitus raised his hands to quiet them. Their voices trailed off. He spoke.

"I've heard some croaking raven is spreading a falsehood about me. That I am a coward. That, because I am a coward, I can not lead. That I should not be selected to succeed my father." The crowd nodded. Some cried "Yes. That's it."

"I would like the one who started this rumor to come forward. If you know him, tell me his name. I will deal with him directly. And, then, you can judge whether I am a coward." Targitus paused to let his message sink in. To allow his dare to go unanswered, as he believed it would. "If he won't come forward, that's proof that he's the coward in our midst." Murmurs of agreement. "Your concern's important. But mortal combat is no solution. Whatever the outcome, it deprives you of a valuable member of the community. The real solution is to be sure the council take all factors into account, including the matter of cowardice and bravery." The murmurs grew louder. Targitus was in control. He had only to channel the crowd's energy.

"A delegation should go to the elders. Insist that these matters be considered. Who will it be?" The crowd was showing acquiescence.

## 15: GREAT ULAGAN VALLEY – 405 B.C.

From those in the front ranks, a trio of men volunteered. The crowd was starting to break up, when a tall, powerfully framed figure came forward to face Targitus at less than an arm's length. He had a baleful look.

"I am the raven you seek. I croaked 'coward.' And I will do it again to your face in front of these good people. I heard your challenge. I accept it."

Targitus knew instantly he had no choice. In front of this crowd he could show no sign of weakness or confusion. Trapped by his rhetorical skills, he replied bravely, "Tomorrow morning, then. Trial by combat. I will wait on the plain south of the village, near the Bashkaus. We begin two hours after sunrise. Agreed?"

"Agreed," Ishkapai replied.

The crowd melted away, the protagonists as well. Targitus marveled at the swiftness with which his fate had been sealed. Was there some celestial power at work here? Could he have talked openly of the rape? Might things have been different if he had?

The powers of fate hung heavy over the day's events. As he mounted Belukcha to ride to his yurt, he recalled with bitter amusement Rachel's solution to the council's failure to act: an archery contest or horse race. Anything other than combat, she had pleaded. What held him was the paradox of her ideas: at once so eminently reasonable and hopelessly impractical.

Later that day, the wife of Idanthyrsus, the shaman put to death by Sparetra for his role in Matyes' death, came to see Ishkapai. She believed that Targitus had made the decision to put the torch to her husband. She hated him for it. While she didn't much like Ishkapai, it never occurred to her that he too might have been involved, since he had been away from the village when her husband was treating the king. Ishkapai hardly knew her. He couldn't imagine her purpose.

"I am here because I want to support you. I am going to pray to our gods tonight."

In wooden tones he thanked her. Then, getting to his feet, he was about to usher her out the door when she said, "I can help you in other ways."

Ishkapai turned his back to her and moved away from the door. "Have you ever seen a horse after it's eaten hemp leaves?"

Rachel stood outside the yurt to greet Targitus. Catching sight of him at a distance, riding towards her, she sensed something amiss. After hearing the story, she tried another idea.

"Share power. Offer Ishkapai the olive branch. Why wouldn't he accept it? Why wouldn't the village? It needs you both."

Targitus listened in sadness, hollow-eyed. "The olive branch?"

"You know. Emblem of peace. Takes fifteen years and more of care to bear fruit. In Sardis, the loss of an olive tree is a family tragedy. It hurts for a long time. Tomorrow's loss of a prince will become a village tragedy, made worse by being so unnecessary."

His voice heavy, Targitus said, "There are no olive trees in the Altai."

Preparations consumed the night. Weapons were checked. Arrows, short sword and lance. The bow and its string. Targitus owned two bows, one that belonged to him from the day it was built, the other his father's, brought to him by Sparetra soon after Matyes' death. He had wanted Targitus to have it.

Targitus sharpened blades and arrowheads. He inspected bridle and saddle covers for weakness. He checked the two bows and their strings. Rachel couldn't watch. She went outside to find Belukcha. She rubbed him down, watered, fed and tethered him. When all was in readiness, they ate. Conversation was strained. Rachel knew the odds in a fight between these brothers. She had heard about the fights of childhood and adolescence.

Taiga, sensing tension, moved back and forth between Rachel and Targitus, seeking more comfort than either could provide.

After dinner, they took a walk along the flat pasture land beside the deep banks of the Great Ulagan River. Hand in hand, they moved slowly against the gentle current. The sun had set to the southwest, leaving a bright glow to challenge for a time the oncoming night. The air was cool and crystalline. The sky, unmarred by cloud, was pale

## 15: GREAT ULAGAN VALLEY – 405 B.C.

pink at the horizon and a pale blue above, becoming progressively darker until it reached a limpid blue-black overhead. On the western horizon, they saw low in the darkening sky a new moon, and, a finger-width above it, the evening star. Nothing else. Rachel recalled that Sardians thought the sky an immense dome separating their lives on earth from an after-life arranged for them by the Gods.

"Matchless," she declared as they both looked up. See that tiny crescent. There's a faint ring extending all the way around. Pale silver, it makes the moon look so delicate, like the head of a spent dandelion that could be blown away by the slightest wind. The star's different, large and bright. It's the promise of growth, of the next day and the one after that. An omen, love, for you."

Ahead of them, to the north, herds of horses appeared as dark shapes, noses to the wind, on either side of the river. All was still until a kite far above in the twilight let out a long, tremulous trill. To one not raised to know this bird, it sounded exactly like the distant neigh of a foal. So fraught with possible meaning that they each pretended not to notice.

Again the evening's peace was disturbed, this time by Taiga's distant barks. "She's treed something," Targitus said. We should turn back."

In uneasy silence, they walked to the yurt.

Yielding to the need to talk about something, Rachel said, "Have you decided on the bow?"

"Father's." He picked it up as if to show her, again, which it was. His hand rubbed its surface, an affectionate gesture exactly like the one used daily on Belukcha's head. I am comfortable with it. It never failed him." Targitus launched into a description of how a composite bow is made, as if he needed a neutral subject to distract his mind and hers.

"It's our proudest invention. In battle, unmatched." Rachel had the look of one who's heard it all before. "What you don't know is how it's made. It takes a year. The bow's four feet, nock to nock. Made from wood, horn and sinew in five separate pieces."

Rachel broke in. "I've learned enough about bow construction for one night."

"Let me finish. Have you ever noticed those splices?"

"No." Rachel was having trouble listening. She knew he needed this. "But I am willing to be taught. Skip that; tell me how the bow string is made."

"All right. Here, look at the string. Can you see?"

Rachel rubbed the string between her fingers. Smelled them. "Horse-hair, I'd guess."

Targitus nodded. He looked gaunt. She wondered how much longer he could keep talking.

"Will you come tomorrow?" Targitus asked.

Rachel shook her head, almost violently. "I'll go to the workshop. It's the place for me. Being an uncertain believer puts me at a disadvantage."

They had run out of easy things to say. The hard ones were better left unspoken.

As he rode to the site, Targitus sought to reconcile fear with bravery, for he held them both, as it were, in the palm of his hand. He tried hard, hoping one could co-exist with the other, that he could feel fear and yet, act bravely.

At the designated time, the brothers faced one another on horseback. Each held a lance and was armed with a short sword, or akinakes, sheathed about the waist, a strung bow across his back and a gorytos containing arrows tied to his left side. Ancient custom dictated the rules of combat. They would ride one hundred yards apart, then turn to face each other. When each had raised his right arm to indicate readiness, the battle would begin. There were no boundaries. Nor were there restrictions of any kind. The object was to kill or be killed. Disgrace would accompany the combatants should both leave the field of combat alive.

Targitus believed his best chance lay in keeping at some distance from his brother, using the turning abilities of Belukcha to maneuver until he could be confident of a hit with his lance. Ishkapai's superior strength would give him a large advantage in sword-play. It would not count as much with the lance or bow, where timing and accuracy

## 15: GREAT ULAGAN VALLEY – 405 B.C.

were the central elements.

At a gallop, the horses approached each other, their riders rising at the knee with lances poised. At the last moment, when he saw his brother about to hurl the lance, Targitus drew Belukcha away and lowered himself to place his body behind the croup of his horse. He had hoped to time this maneuver so that Ishkapai would hurl the lance at a disappearing target. His brother wasn't fooled. Lance still in hand, Ishkapai wheeled around in quick pursuit. The horses flew across the plain, either towards one another or away, alternating between chasing and being chased. In this game, one got only one throw of the lance. The brothers were equally bent on making the best of their chances.

In time, the steeds began to show signs of tiring. Targitus noticed that each time he broke to the side when being pursued by his brother, Ishkapai rode past to begin a circle trying to end up in an attacking position behind Targitus. He resolved to take the chance of throwing his lance as his brother rode past his standing horse. The difficulty of hitting the swiftly moving target meant that Ishkapai wouldn't be expecting a throw from that angle. Targitus thought the difficulty not all that great, however, given his knowledge of how to lead when using a bow. And he feared Belukcha might be the first to weaken, giving his brother maneuvering advantage. He soon had his chance. Ishkapai was behind, in full pursuit. Turning his horse to the right, Targitus brought it to a standstill. Ishkapai's momentum carried horse and rider straight ahead. As Ishkapai rode past Belukcha, trying again to circle in behind his brother, Targitus hurled the lance, leading the target by a couple of yards. The aim was true. The lance covered the distance of twenty yards and would have hit Ishkapai in the body had he not reined in his horse just in time to allow the lance to pass between his body and the horse's neck. From this point on, Targitus knew, there would be only one pursuer.


Rachel waited inside the workshop. She was too anxious to work. Or to sit still. Walking outside, she moved slowly toward the Bashkaus where it roared past the workshop, far upstream from the place of combat. The sun, now bright above the horizon, sparkled on the waters that crashed against rocks and swirled in pools and back-eddies, white with foam. Beside the river stood a giant larch with blackened and deeply etched bark below its lowest limbs. As she approached the tree, a small bird hit its trunk with a muffled thud and fell to the ground. Rachel was nonplussed. Birds don't fly into trees. But this one had. There must be a reason. Looking beyond the tree, she was blinded by the sun's reflected rays coming off the waters. A glint of light must have momentarily blinded the bird, just long enough for its great speed to slam it against the tree.

Rachel picked up the warbler. One side of its tiny head had taken most of the blow, the eye almost shut. The other eye was wide open, but motionless like the rest of its body and stick-like legs, with their defined and delicate feet. She held the bird tight in her hand, hoping its warmth would restore life to the stunned creature. For just an instant, her longing to play Yahweh worked tricks on her imagination. Is that the beat of a miniature heart she felt in the palm of her hand? Or merely her own heart projecting itself through still feathers. She opened her hand, looking for signs of life. There were none. Its body was merely a foil for the warmth of her hand.

Giving up, she gently stretched out the bird's wings to admire their stilled perfection. "Why stilled?" she asked herself, suddenly aware of the possibility that this bird was another omen. "God's will or blind chance?" The same unanswered question that she had asked herself upon the death of Benjamin, that Targitus had asked upon the death of Maytes.

Rachel buried the warbler under the tree that took its life. Digging a small hole in the ground, she felt the sadness that comes from failing to prevent something that needn't have happened.

As she retreated from the Bashkaus towards the center, her home close by the Pactolus came vividly to mind, adding to her sadness an acute longing for family, a kind of emptiness she had usually been able to keep at bay.

Belukcha had tired. Targitus was being overtaken. He must induce Ishkapai to hurl his lance. And avoid its sharp point. As his brother drew near, Targitus veered to the left, trying to escape. Belukcha

## 15: GREAT ULAGAN VALLEY – 405 B.C.

came to a standstill. Instead of riding by as before, Ishkapai wheeled to the right in a tight circle and hurled his lance at the first chance, catching his brother off guard. Targitus yanked on the reins; Belukcha raised his head, taking a backward step. The lance pierced the horse's neck. Belukcha lurched forward and fell to his side before Targitus could remove his leg, which broke from the weight of the horse.

Belukcha was in the spasms of death. Targitus seemed trapped beneath him. But with a lurch the horse rolled away from Targitus, freeing him to prepare as best he could for what was coming. He still had his sword. And his bow, still across his shoulder, unharmed. Targitus did his best to conceal the break. If Ishkapai had known Targitus' leg was broken, he would have dismounted and slain his brother with the sword. Targitus got to his feet, adrenalin masking the agony. He took the bow from his shoulder and looked for the gorytos. It was gone.

Ishkapai was watching his brother closely. He grew deliberate in his movements. Taking his bow from across his back, Ishkapai drew an arrow from his gorytos, nocked it to the bow and moved his horse forward a few feet. His dust and sweat-smeared face betrayed neither pain nor pleasure. Targitus could not run. Nor could he kneel. Without an arrow his bow was useless. Sweat poured forth, dripping from his face, getting into his eyes, mixing with the dirt tossed up by the violence of Belukcha's death to coat his face. Drawing his sword, he prepared to throw it at the slowly approaching horse and rider. A futile plan, he knew, because the work to be done by his brother need not bring the horse within range of a thrown sword. Might he use the sword to deflect the arrow? That would take much luck. His brain was split down the middle: one half accepting the certainty of imminent death; the other half refusing, bent on summoning a miracle.

To Targitus, right hand holding his sword, left hand his father's celebrated bow, the movements of his brother were conducted in slow motion and with perfect discipline: drawing the arrow, nocking it to the bowstring, locking the fingers on the bowstring, drawing the bow, sighting to the mark and holding at full draw to assure a clean loose. Targitus knew each of these movements in meticulous detail. The horror of what was about to happen dovetailed in his mind with reflexive appreciation of his brother's skill.

Ishkapai released the arrow. There was no doubt in Targitus' mind that this final step in the ordered sequence of movements would drive the arrow through his heart. Yet, instead of hissing as it spun away from the bow, the arrow limped slowly, dropping to the ground only a few feet from where Targitus stood. He had seen the bow wrench in Ishkapai's hand at the moment of release, returning violently to its C-shaped reflex position. One tip had struck Ishkapai a glancing blow to the head.

The bowstring had broken exactly at the moment of release, when the tension was at its greatest and the temptation of an aggressive archer was to pull ever so slightly more before releasing it.

In an instant, Targitus had reached the arrow. In another, he had nocked it to his bowstring. Ishkapai had turned and was trying to get out of range.

The horse was responding with all the energy it had left. Locking fingers on the bowstring, Targitus concentrated his remaining strength to draw the bow and hold steady just long enough to sight and loose the arrow. It twisted in flight, hissing to its mark. Striking his brother square in the back, it pierced his body. Ishkapai fell from his horse. By the time Targitus reached him, using his father's bow as a crutch, Ishkapai was dead.

Targitus stood still, staring down. His head felt close to bursting. Pain reasserted itself. Fainting, he fell to the ground beside his brother.

# CHAPTER 16

Great Ulagan Valley – 405 B.C.

The man who ran into the workshop found Rachel alone, spinning wool. Her spindle had just hit the floor, attached to thread held in her hand.

With a widow's pallor, Rachel turned to greet Tymnes. She was prepared to hear the bird's omen fulfilled. Time stopped as Rachel waited for him to catch his breath.

"Targitus lives," Tymnes cried.

Her tension dissolved. Tears gathered in Tymnes' eyes. She had questions. He did his best to respond.

Rachel wanted desperately to find Targitus, to hold him in her arms and tend to his injuries, to hear him describe the combat, to ask him to tell the story again. And again. Before she could mount her horse to ride out of the village to the ground of battle, Targitus appeared at the workshop, carried on a framed stretcher pulled by his brother's horse. Beside him on the stretcher lay Ishkapai, whose face appeared flush with dried sweat and dirt. Resting harmlessly on his chest was the arrow that had felled him. Its shaft bore the markings of the man it had pierced through, the man in whose grave it would be laid.

Rachel and Targitus stared at each other. They smiled weakly, through tears.

Rachel led the procession of villagers to their yurt. The shamans came too, for the purpose of setting Targitus' leg. All Rachel wanted was their practical experience with broken bones. And, miraculously, that was all she got. Due to the cause of injury, the shamans made no effort to drive out evil spirits or engage in séances with the nether world.

Targitus was in pain throughout the night. To palliate the sharp, stabbing aches, the shamans had urged him to use the bronze censer and the pile of hemp seeds they left behind. His father's consuming need for the vapors at the end of his life caused Targitus to refuse the tent until, towards morning, agony overcame reluctance. Rachel prepared the censer, built a fire beneath and helped Targitus position himself to inhale the fumes it began to emit. She draped the felt cover over Targitus' head. It contained the vapor long enough to be caught by his deep inhalations. In its pain-effacing properties, the cannabis was miraculous. From Rachel's point of view, its side-effects were almost as rewarding. They had loosened his tongue.

Lying back, Targitus felt strangely detached. He visualized the pain in his leg retreating before an encircling wave of happiness. He felt Rachel's hand in his. Opening his eyes, he saw her beside him, sitting on her haunches. He began to talk.

"Strange how alert I feel. On edge. I should sleep. Rachel, I want to tell you about Ishkapai, something I've told no one else."

Despite the calming effects of the narcotic, talking about his brother's attack proved difficult. His speech was halting, his breath heavy, as he tried for the first time to find the words and assemble the sentences needed to describe what he could still both see and feel in lurid detail. By the time the story was told, he was wet with sweat. He cried.

So did Rachel, having no words to respond. It was too horrible, too brutal and bestial, to speak about. She felt like rending her clothes and wailing. Aghast over his revelation, she had a flash of anger as she realized he had kept it from her for so long. The only person in the village who didn't know, she realized.

## 16: GREAT ULAGAN VALLEY – 405 B.C.

"Today changed things," Targitus said. It's not logical, but my feelings of disgrace at being debased ended with my brother's life. 'Debased.' Too weak a word for the scene I've replayed over and over again. I was raped, Rachel, but until now, I couldn't think of it in those terms. Death opens blocked passages. But I needn't be telling you that." Targitus was speaking slowly, without anger or self-pity.

"Allowing him to return seemed the only choice at the time. Our father was dying. I didn't imagine Ishkapai would claim the throne. I underestimated him. Not for the first time. I couldn't imagine the elders turning their back on me. Another mistake. Returning a hero, I was floating on a cloud of self-confidence. Until danger struck, I was unaware. The great planner, caught unprepared." He smiled ruefully.

"Do you feel revenged?" Rachel asked. She was holding his hand in one of hers while gently massaging his forehead with the other.

Targitus' state of mellowness had waxed as the narcotic, now in his bloodstream, continued to circulate. He had been close to sleep when Rachel's question channeled him into a replay of the day's events.

"I don't know how I feel, beyond being lucky. Give me a night's sleep."

The more Targitus tried to sleep the wider awake he became. Lying on his back with eyes open to the yurt's darkness, he relived every second of the day's battle. Not once but over and over. The outcome had everything to do with chance. Or forces beyond his ken. Was he the instrument chosen by Altaian Gods to punish Ishkapai? He wanted to believe his father's spirit was guiding his use of the great bow. But by whose grace was he handed his brother's arrow? Rachel had prayed for him. Sparetra prayed. And so did he. Were any of those prayers answered?

Rachel lay beside him, also awake in her thoughts of the day. Anger at not being told what Ishkapai had done drained away as she considered the misery Targitus must have experienced for so long. That he did not tell her was proof of the depths of his humiliation. If Ishkapai weren't already dead she would kill him. She'd find a way. Was it chance? Was Abel just unlucky to be slain by his unworthy brother? Or did Yahweh play a role? If he arranged Ishkapai's death, he picked the right man this time.

Already delayed, the marriage that Targitus had promised was preempted by an elaborate funeral for Ishkapai, followed by the installation of Targitus as king. For many villagers, Rachel's position was disturbingly ambiguous. Beyond the circle of students, her efforts to build the weaving center created resentment among some, jealousy among others, in the tight community of artists, who saw her as a threat to the respect they enjoyed in practicing traditional skills. Many saw no need for new ways of using wool. Were Rachel not so intimately connected to Targitus' family, her project would never have passed beyond the planning stage. For those inclined to be critical, her unmarried state and the lack of any announced schedule for changing that status provided a pretext for talk. So too did the lack of a family.

Those close to Targitus and Sparetra, and the few in the village who had come to know Rachel, were forced by village expectation and custom to consider them, in effect, married. When the subject came up in village gossip, they would say, "Why, of course, there will be a proper wedding, but the time must be right." This never seemed to satisfy those who thought something amiss. And this group was growing.

Sparetra came to the workshop armed with some food to offer Rachel for the mid-day meal. The burial of Ishkapai, which would occur the following day, was the cause of her visit.

"I understand the purpose of embalming, to preserve the corpse for its future journey, but I don't know how it's done," Rachel said.

"I'd take you to watch, but the shamans would refuse. They do this work in secret. They want a spiritually pure environment for the opening of the body. They claim the presence of anyone not of their class might introduce an evil spirit, polluting the air around the corpse and risking entry." Rachel was at the cusp of disbelief. "That's what they say," Sparetra declared, averting Rachel's steady gaze.

"Are you able to talk about this? I mean, as a mother?"

"That's really why I came. It's our custom. I've been around it all my life. For a foreigner, it may take some getting used to.

## 16: GREAT ULAGAN VALLEY – 405 B.C.

"I'll try," Rachel said. "Please go on."

"First the nails on both hands and feet and the hair on the head are cut and the cuttings placed in a leather bag for burial with the corpse."

Rachel looked puzzled.

"Life clings to nails and hair. They continue growing. The fear is that anyone possessing a deceased's nails or hair could control his future. The shamans protect these things until burial." Rachel concealed her surprise and doubt, nodding for Sparetra to continue.

"Next, the scalp is cut and folded back over the right side of the crown. The skull is then opened by cutting out a piece of bone. The contents are removed and discarded. The cranium is filled with aromatic herbs, pine needles, larch cones and moss. The bone is then fitted back and the scalp sewn in place."

Rachel tried to visualize this procedure. She felt Sparetra was bringing unusual energy to her description, almost a strange enthusiasm. It was hard not to believe Ishkapai was suffering, at this very moment. He's dead, she kept reminding herself. "The body comes next. They cut the abdomen lengthwise and remove the viscera. Into the cavity go the same materials. The belly is sewn up. Then, long cuts are made from the buttocks to just above the knees. All muscle is carefully removed and set aside. Again, the stuffing materials are used to fill the cavities. Finally, slits are made throughout the body and salt introduced."

Rachel pictured the shamans, bent over the corpse of Ishkapai. It became too vivid. She grew uneasy. Something vaguely fearful began to turn her stomach.

"You say the muscles are put aside?"

"For the rites tomorrow morning."

Rachel's stomach seemed poised for upheaval. She knew it would be the food she had swiftly devoured just minutes earlier. At risk, she pressed ahead, feeling driven to hear the answer, to put it all behind her. "Tell me about the rites," she said, trying as best she could to sound woodenly matter-of-fact.

"Didn't Targitus tell you? When a warrior of the tribe is killed in battle, we celebrate his death with particular ritual. It starts before dawn. We gather at the burial site. A sacred cock crows to herald the dawn, driving off dark spirits of the night. Immediately the shamans slay a sheep and cut its best parts into chunks, which are mixed with chunks of the warrior's muscles and then boiled in a large cauldron near the burial site. The meats are eaten first by the warrior's family, then by the tribe's leaders and finally by the rest of the village."

Rachel tried to imagine herself participating. "But why do such a thing?" she cried.

Sparetra responded without emotion, as if lecturing a child whose loss of control was best handled by ignoring it. "Nourishment. Daily, in the world of animals, we see the continuity of life pass before us. This is our way to honor slain warriors."

Rachel excused herself. Lurching to the open window, she reached it in time. Sparetra followed, putting her arms around Rachel's waist to hold her tight while her body responded to the place in her mind over which she had no control. Rachel felt discomfort at Sparetra's touch, the first since the day they met. She guessed her reaction was due more to the ritual than to what she thought was Sparetra's lack of feeling over her son's death. "We're so different," she moaned to herself, just as Sparetra cautioned against rejecting Altaian ways.

"If you're going to live here, you're going to have to accept."

"I am better now," Rachel said, turning sideways to Sparetra and unclasping the hands that held her. "Please sit down. I must ask you something else. Ishkapai was a bad person. I am not the only one to believe that. He committed horrible acts against Targitus. Even if I could accept the way you honor warriors, I wouldn't understand why Ishkapai."

Seeing her flinch in shock, Rachel guessed Sparetra must still consider it a family secret.

"He had bad parts. But not all bad. He took longer than most to grow up, and the process caused much pain. Even to himself. Complicated, yes; but not head-to-foot evil. And at the end, he proved himself."

Although her face was still drained of color, Rachel was feeling better. But her mood was souring in counterpoint to her physical recovery. "How do you mean?"

## 16: GREAT ULAGAN VALLEY – 405 B.C.

"I wasn't going to speak of this. You remember the shaman, Idanthyrsus? Well, his widow hated Targitus. The night before the battle she offered to poison Belukcha so that he would become disabled on the field the next day. Ishkapai refused her. He told the woman, 'This fight must be fair. Don't worry about me.'"

"And you heard this from the widow? Does Targitus know?"

"I haven't told him, and I doubt he'd hear it elsewhere. She swore me to secrecy. Many in the village like her. Even more feel sorry for her. There's fear that Targitus would kill her if he heard the story. Keep it to yourself."

Rachel remained silent, thinking. A man of character? Or overweening arrogance. He'd spurned the council. He'd never lost a fight with his brother. He could see no risk. Hardly proof of character, she concluded.

Returning home that evening, Targitus could see in Rachel's distraught eyes that something was amiss. With customary directness, she confessed her problem before Targitus could sit down. "I implore you not to consume your brother's body. Bury it all. Eating the remains of a human is barbaric."

His manner parental, Targitus said, "It's what Altaians have done for as long as memory serves. It's the natural thing to do."

Rachel grew more animated. "We have animals to eat precisely so that we don't have to eat one another. Have you ever heard of a deer eating another deer? Or a mountain lion eating its own? It's an offense to nature."

"When I brought you here we agreed you would accept our ways. Ruth's story, you'll ..."

"This is one of your ways I was not told about," Rachel said, interrupting his speech.

"It's an essential part of Altaian life. You may not object." Targitus was becoming angry, ambushed by Rachel's persistence. He had not seen this side of her on their long journey. He had boasted to her of an equality between Massagetae men and women that exceeded reality, something he now regretted.

"I can't abide your ceremony. I can't explain how awful just thinking about it makes me feel. There's almost nothing I wouldn't do if you asked me. But I can't participate in your brother's burial rite."

"If you love me, you'll be with me tomorrow." He shot her an odd look, half imploring, half imperious.

"If you love me, you'll respect my feelings."

They were standing close to one another, but not close enough to prevent this issue from coming between them. It had not been resolved by bedtime, and the tension they felt made sleeping fitful. Matters grew worse when Targitus left the yurt before sunrise the next morning. He traveled to the burial site alone, a fact that was not unnoticed by the crowd gathered there to participate in rites of passage.

In the week following Ishkapai's burial, Targitus and Rachel spoke not at all about the event. Outside the yurt they pursued their separate tasks with virtually no contact. Inside, the atmosphere was fraught with anger. They interacted with civility but no warmth. Neither seemed capable of getting beyond the hurt caused by the other. Rachel's natural openness was blocked by emotions she couldn't fathom. She hoped to punish Targitus by refusing to mention the burial, lest he have the satisfaction of describing what she had missed. For his part, he was trying to punish Rachel in the same way, on the assumption that she wanted to hear about the rites but was too proud to ask. Two days passed. They needed urgently to hold each other tight, to release swollen emotions. And, yet, nothing happened.

On the third day, Targitus didn't return to the yurt, sending word that Sparetra had insisted on his staying overnight with her. Rachel wondered if Sparetra could be making matters worse. Once this possibility had intruded, it gnawed away at the platform of support Rachel had so carefully constructed. Shadowy doubts arose about the meaning of Targitus' behavior of late. The harder she tried to think positively, the greater her anxiety became.

The next day, Sparetra came to the workshop, again bearing food for the mid-day meal. Rachel was surprised to see her; then glad at

## 16: GREAT ULAGAN VALLEY – 405 B.C.

the chance to confront the turmoil. They went outside, seeking a place in the sun near the swift waters of the Bashkaus.

"I fixed something different for us today." Sparetra removed the cover from her rush basket, revealing a variety of cheeses, some boiled lamb meat, and two narrow-necked earthenware bottles filled with koumiss.

"I am feeling hungry. But so much food. You have much to discuss?"

"Just one thing. Let me be frank, as you've been with me. I've seen Targitus twice since Ishkapai's burial. Once he came for no apparent reason. Another time, he stayed overnight at my request. He's miserable. I asked him to talk, but he couldn't. All he would say was that you and he had bumped into some hard differences. He used the word 'frozen.'"

Summer's sun was hot on this, the longest day of the year. The sky around them pulsated with insect and bird life. Rachel envied all this airborne activity. She remembered a similar moment in the courtyard of the palace at Sardis. She wished Vashti were here now to listen to her complaints and advise. Her thoughts were stepping stones, leading to an unfamiliar place of homesickness and sorrow. Had Sarah received the message she sent from Trapezus? Rachel winced at the thought that her mother might still not know what happened. Was there any chance of getting word to her now, so that she might send back news of family and friends? Rachel knew how remote these possibilities were, which is why she hardly ever lingered over them. Birds always seem to be going somewhere, she thought, looking skyward. Why not to Sardis, bearing messages?

In her present condition, sorrow slid easily into self-pity. That Sparetra, a possible source of her problems, was the only person available to listen, just increased her anguish.

"I miss my family, my friends. I never expected to feel it so much. Until this week began, I hadn't had time to think about them. We have a problem. Targitus insists I am beloved by the village, more so every day. I don't feel it, except with my weavers. I don't see it. I don't believe it. At times, I don't even feel accepted. He expects me to embrace his people as my own. It sounded simple when we exchanged promises in Scopasis. But I can't do it. The rites for

Ishkapai were repugnant. Refusing, I wounded him. Rejecting my feelings, he wounded me. So here we are, frozen in place, despite this hot sun." Rachel smiled faintly through tears, eyes downcast, avoiding Sparetra's look of surprise.

"Is that it?"

"It's enough, don't you think? But, no, there's something else. Freedom. Targitus keeps telling me I am free to do as I please. Perhaps he's right in a strict sense. With his backing, I can probably do anything. The trouble is, I don't feel free."

"I am beginning to understand. I'll see Targitus this afternoon."

Rachel could suppress her darker thoughts no more. "There's something else here that you might not understand. I've been hesitant to bring it up because it's awkward and, in truth, I may be wrong. Sometimes I think you and I are competing for the same man. It drives me to despair. I had to tell you. I have to know."

Sparetra recoiled at Rachel's words. Tears welled up in her eyes, making them glisten in the bright sunlight. Moments passed. Finally, Sparetra answered in a voice heavy with emotion.

"Since you came to our village, I've lost a husband and two sons. You're not Altaian and that can't be changed. If it could you'd be pregnant by now, giving me the promise of a grandson. Our Gods don't favor you. Of course I want Targitus back. Wouldn't you in my place?"

Sparetra's words stabbed Rachel, cutting deep. She responded in kind. "It's not the Altai that denies me a babe. It's being kept separate from the family of the man who brought me here. Give me your son in marriage and I will give you a grandson." Rachel's eyes flashed, the cause of her miscarriage never so clear. "There's enough of Targitus to share. We have different roles to play in his life." Seeing Sparetra's face awash in tears, Rachel too began to cry.

"You've given me something to think about. Enough for now." Sparetra rose and quickly departed, her eyes averting Rachel's. She left behind the rush basket, its contents untouched.

That evening Rachel was preparing the meal when Targitus arrived. The tenseness on his face was gone. He appeared self-confident and

## 16: GREAT ULAGAN VALLEY – 405 B.C.

happy. A big contrast, she thought, to her own state. While her talk with Sparetra had released a pent-up need to confide and confront, it had solved nothing.

"I have a proposal, Rachel. You'll never guess." They were standing in the yurt. Taiga was close by. She had rolled over on her back and with paws limp was shamelessly begging one of her keepers to rub her tummy. Targitus said, "In a while, Taiga, I have an unfinished project first." He moved a step towards Rachel, taking her hands in his. It was the first purposeful touching between them all week. She struggled to preserve an anger that was beginning to melt away from the heat of his hands and the smile on his face.

"You're going to escort me back to Scopasis?" she said, a broad smile crowding out the last vestige of tension.

"Something quite different. I propose that we marry in a village ceremony exactly one month from today. I will announce the date tomorrow so preparations can begin. Will you allow it?"

His words formed a key to her heart. She felt released from invisible bonds; she soared, weightless before him. She dropped his hands to wrap her arms around his waist, squeezing tight.

The month passed swiftly. Rachel and Sparetra spent much time together, planning the wedding. Although neither spoke of it, Rachel knew Sparetra shared her belief that their exchange had rescued the relationship from a downward spiral. Sparetra detailed the marriage traditions of the Massagetae. Rachel appeared accepting. Targitus was kept at a distance. The fight over Ishkapai's last rites, though unresolved, seemed to diminish in importance with the passage of time and the excitement of wedding preparations.

Progress on the carpet was a casualty. Sparetra raised the subject of children. Targitus responded with enthusiasm, as if the thought had just occurred to him. Rachel was silent. With marriage less than a month away, she could look back on the miscarriage with equanimity. Indeed, the misery she kept secret from mother and son gave her confidence in a future she would share with them both. "We will give you grandchildren. Have no fear," she blurted out.

Sparetra took responsibility for assuring the wedding costumes would be ready, once the designs were given to the village's craftsmen. But there wasn't much time. And Rachel hadn't even decided whether to accept the wish of her betrothed to dress entirely in the fashion of the Massagetae. A part of her wanted to show that she was different.

Rachel had steered Sparetra into taking on the design of not only her own costume but that of her son. Paralata, Rachel's closest friend among the workshop group, volunteered to help. Rachel was quick to accept. Paralata had shown in the workshop a sure sense of textile design and fabrication. Now they could work together on Rachel's outfit.

Paralata was astonished by Rachel's suggestion that part of her costume express a Sardian style.

"I don't see how you can mix styles," Paralata said. "It wouldn't work. And probably would be misunderstood. If you will allow me, and please don't be offended, your marriage to a Massagetae king is not the place to parade your independence."

Rachel had thought working with Paralata would be fun. Whose wedding is it? she thought. Who's helping whom? But, of course, her friend was right. From the moment she accepted Paralata's advice, their collaboration took flight.


With only a couple of days to spare, the craftsmen came to the workshop to present Sparetra and Rachel the complete wardrobe for the wedding. Led by Paralata, they carefully laid out each of the outfits. Rachel thought their efforts heroic.

When the two women were alone, Sparetra handed Rachel a soft leather pouch.

"I want you to have this. It's been passed down from one generation to another, always on the woman's side. It's very old, beyond memory."

Rachel loosened the draw string and carefully emptied the contents into her hand. Looking down, she saw a single pale white shell strung on a thin leather necklace. More than anything Rachel could

## 16: GREAT ULAGAN VALLEY – 405 B.C.

think of, it resembled the female vulva. "Oh!" she exclaimed. I've never seen a shell like that."

"It's a cowrie shell amulet. Some among our tribe believe it's powerful protection against evil. Others, and I am one of them, believe it assures fertility. Perhaps it does both. In any case, it's yours. I wore it at my marriage. I hope you will too."

The wedding day dawned bright and unseasonably cool, with a wind from the northwest that had started gently at dawn and built through the morning, driving white wisps of cloud across the vast expanse of sky. A day, Rachel might have recognized, had she not been so excited and happy, very much like the day she lost little Iarch.

Paralata arrived at the yurt early. Targitus had already left to meet his mother and help her attend to last minute details.

"You look so intense, or is it just excitement?" Paralata said. "We have plenty of time."

"My mind's in a muddle," Rachel said. "I've been thinking a lot about my family. Wishing they were here. Wishing they could see the wedding. I am sad there's no one from Sardis to share it all with."

Rachel had spread everything she would wear out in front of her.

"You're sharing with me. And with all your new friends. Here, look at this caftan."

Rachel exchanged a knowing smile with her friend. The design they had worked on together had been executed to stunning effect. Delight banished self-pity.

The caftan was short. It was made of squirrel skin, fur inwards. The outside was covered with leather in cut-out patterns suggestive of cock's combs encircling metal rams' heads and branching into lotus flowers. The leather was dyed dark red to contrast with the natural color of squirrel.

"Did we take the leather ornamentation too far?" Rachel asked.

"Compared to what? It's of a piece with your head-dress. Our village has never seen anything like this." Paralata had picked up the head-dress to admire. It began with a loose hood extending to Rachel's shoulders. It was fashioned out of fine leather covered with black colt's fur and decorated with rhombs of cut-out leather covered in gold leaf. Surmounting the hood and extending down its back was a diadem on which they had splurged.

"Wait till they see it!" Paralata said. The diadem consisted of ten little cocks cut from thick leather and gilded. With tails and wings raised and heads turned back, they had an animated, mobile look. Suspended from the diadem were mosaics of colored fur designed to move with every motion of Rachel's head.

Rachel put on the caftan. Paralata helped with the matching apron, which was trimmed with a narrow band of blue-dyed otter fur extending almost to Rachel's feet.

"Now the booties," said Paralata, handing them to Rachel. They were made from soft leather, embellished with leather cut-outs in the same lotus flower motif used in the caftan.

Paralata stepped back to appreciate the totality of Rachel's costume. "It's perfect," she declared.

"There's one more thing." Rachel took from her table the necklace given to her by Sparetra. "Will you tie it for me?" Its simple elegance was a riveting contrast to the intricacies of the rest.

The ceremony began when the sun had reached its apex. From a concealed waiting area, Rachel had watched the audience gather in the center of the village. It numbered more than a thousand from the Great Ulagan valley and far beyond. She could see Sparetra too, facing the crowd from an oversized chair bedecked with flowers of summer. Rachel worried that Sparetra looked more severe than stately in a flowing blue robe with yellow ornamentation. She wore a flat headdress of design matching the robe and held in her left hand the branch of a larch to which flowers of blue and yellow had been tied.

Rachel saw Sparetra look in her direction and then in the direction from which her betrothed would come. She raised her right arm, hand extended, palm out. An Altaian drummer commenced a slow, steady beat, the signal Rachel had been waiting for. Walking lightly in time with the drum and trying her best to look stately, Rachel approached Sparetra and then veered off to take a position to her left. Before turning to face the audience, Rachel cast a radiant smile in Sparetra's direction.

## 16: GREAT ULAGAN VALLEY – 405 B.C.

Moments passed. Again Sparetra raised her right arm and the drummer resumed his slow beat. Soon Targitus appeared from behind a pair of yurts, mounted on a high-spirited bay gelding. Taiga brought up the rear of this entourage, keeping her distance from the hind legs of a horse she was just getting to know.

As custom required, Rachel had not seen Targitus dressed in the costume she had joined with his mother and others in designing. Now, looking him up and down, she found the sight thrilling. His head-dress was a kind of balaclava covering nape and ears. It was made of white felt, decorated with red-dyed leather cut-outs depicting fantastic animals in contorted shapes. Centered on top was a miniature castle and tower made of leather covered in gold-leaf.

His caftan was longer than Rachel's, extending below the waist, its hem resting across his thighs. It was made of white chamois leather with vertical stitching. The border was edged with ermine, dyed blue. Targitus had asked for a deer motif. He got his wish and more besides. At the bottom of the caftan was a deer's head from which a single thick antler extended upward. Branching out from this antler were many sinuous tines, each terminating in a bird's head. Near the shoulders of the caftan the antler narrowed to a band that gracefully reversed direction in a half-circle to descend straight down to the deer's head. Spaced evenly throughout the leather cut-outs were "eyes" of gold leaf. They were Rachel's idea. Golden "eyes" to brighten dark leather. Now, as they winked in the mid-day sun, she knew she had been right.

Rachel's mind was spinning. This splendid man, she mused, whom I am about to marry. How did I get here? How can I slow this ceremony down? It's all happening too fast.

Advancing in time with the drum, Targitus stopped in front of his mother. Dismounting, he extended his left hand to join her right, just as they had rehearsed it. Rising from her chair, Sparetra beckoned to Rachel. She passed her son's hand to Rachel's. The steady beat continued. Sparetra raised a golden bowl tooled with fantastic animals. It was half full of koumiss.

What they did next had only been simulated in rehearsal. Targitus drew a knife and made a cut in his index finger, which he then placed over the bowl, allowing drops of blood to mix with the koumiss, red against white. Rachel took the knife and repeated these steps. She cut more deeply than intended, causing much blood to flow.

It took minutes for the bleeding to subside. All the while Sparetra gently swished the bowl, creating a vibrato of pinks within. Targitus took the bowl, raised it with both hands before Rachel and spoke. "I swear by this gold to keep faith. May this drink become poison, may this gold become anger, if I do not love you until I die." Lowering the bowl, he drank deeply before passing it to Rachel, who repeated the oath and drank what she could. Looking sheepish, she handed the bowl back to Targitus, who glanced inside, then passed it on to his mother. She lifted the bowl in salute to the couple, quaffing the remains.

The drum was silent during the oath-giving. When the bowl had been drained, the drummer resumed, increasing the tempo, a sign to twenty archers, who came forward, aimed their bows at the sun and let fly twenty arrows that quickly disappeared into a blinding radiance. As the married couple embraced, the audience erupted in loud cheers and began to press forward. Attendants were challenged to steer the large throng away from the trio towards the reception area. For several hours, koumiss flowed and a wide variety of meats, cheeses and yogurts, as well as berries of the season, were consumed. Rachel, Targitus and Sparetra exhausted themselves in greeting all who stood in the receiving line. Whether out of respect or curiosity or for other reasons, practically every guest joined the wait to meet the trio and convey good wishes. When it was over, the married couple returned to their yurt for a private celebration, one for which rehearsals had begun long ago, in the Caucasus Range.

# CHAPTER 17

Great Ulagan Valley – 405 B.C.

Rachel resumed work on the carpet. Targitus arrived at the workshop as she was sketching a second border. He came up behind, putting his arms around her waist, looking down over her shoulder at the slate.

"You're just in time. What do you say?"

"Elk, a line of them, grazing."

"Yes?"

Releasing her, he bent over to get a closer look.

"Well, I like the idea of elk. Next to horses, our most important."

"But?" She had caught his frown.

"But they look so relaxed, almost tame."

She had expected this plaint. Expected him to be more vehement.

"What you're used to is what feels right. Altaian artists never depict animals in a peaceful state. They contort the body. I've explored the technique with them. They're looking for energy. Strength. Even fear and violence."

"And they succeed. Why not follow along?" His challenge was friendly but firm, as if his reputation were at stake.

"Your artists have their purposes; I have mine. The carpet's a protected place. For peaceful thoughts. The border motifs should serve that goal. So, I've drawn elk with dignified mien in keeping with horse and rider. I wanted to display their wide-bladed antlers without creating too wide a border. So I lowered their heads. By opening their mouths, I could suggest a slow grazing movement."

By her lights, she had met his challenge. She shot him a questioning look. His frown had already melted away.

"I've only sketched four. There will be six on a side. Can you guess why?"

After a moment's thought, Targitus shook his head.

"I know you're fond of numbers. It's in your culture."

"My father insisted they hold secrets of a universal order.

"I can accept mysticism in numbers easier than a God in charge of earthly matters. Six is talismanic."

Targitus looked confused. "You've got to explain that one," he said.

"Not long after I learned to count, my father told me about the magic of six. It comes from the fact that the sum of its divisors, one, two and three, equals the number itself. A 'perfect' number, he called it."

Rachel's enthusiasm was infectious.

"Twenty-four elk in all. Isn't that the number of squares in the central field?"

Rachel nodded vigorously, excited by her husband's interest.

Seated in front of her loom, Paralata had been listening. Now she came over to the green tablets.

"Targitus, you're good. Here's the next question. Why is Rachel using seven horses and riders on a side?"

Targitus said, "Twenty-eight in all." He searched Paralata's face for a clue. Then Rachel's. Then the ceiling. "What's special about twenty-eight? Or seven?"

"Have you some time? It's a long story. I'll start with the number seven." When she had finished telling of Gilgamesh and the other ancient tales from her dream, she exclaimed, triumphantly, "And as for twenty-eight, it's the next 'perfect' number after six!"

Targitus did the numbers in his head.

## 17: GREAT ULAGAN VALLEY – 405 B.C.

"I had to use it for the widest border. I remember asking my father for the one after twenty-eight. 496, he said. I asked for the next. 'Rachel, he said, you must pay more heed to Yahweh. Only he can tell you.'"

Thus far, she had used celestial imagery for the central field and earthly ones for the two widest borders. She wanted one more motif. As Rachel searched her imagination for the right theme, she was drawn to Sardis. She caught a fleeting sense of nostalgia, which this time did not lead to sorrow.

She had left Sardis of an absolutely free will. Hadn't she? On hearing her tale, Targitus described her departure as an exile. Had he known of her successful demand to the Satrap, this description would have been even more apt. And hadn't the loss of a home been compounded by the loss of a father? She saw her mother in their kitchen, baking the daily loaves of bread. The smell was distinct, as in all baking with yeast, and almost overpowering, because she added anise seeds to the dough. She saw her father, always so serious, speaking to her of Yahweh, recalling the exodus and the miracle of freedom granted by Cyrus the Great, Persian instrument of His will.

She saw the gates of the palace. Then a child of seven, she was asking her father to explain the figures sculpted from marble and placed on the tops of the two pillars marking the entrance. "They're griffins," he said, "fabulous beasts. See, they have the bodies and rear legs of lions. And heads, wings and front legs of eagles." Rachel stared at the griffins. She thought they were frightening. "But has anyone ever seen a griffin?" she asked her father. Benjamin replied, "I don't know. Someone must. In Sardis, they stand for Persia. Domination of earth and sky. Lion, symbol of strength and courage. Eagle, symbol of flight, speed and vision. Here they are guardians of the palace."

Rachel stood up, shaking off her reverie. It would be the griffin. A beast known not only in the art of Sardis but to the Massagetae as well. Rachel had seen the griffin on cheek plates and other horse accoutrements as well as leather bags and personal effects. Then she remembered the wedding caftan made for Targitus. Paralata had drawn a bird's head at the end of each antler tine. She called it "bird of wonder." But now, on reflection, Rachel believed it looked more like the head of a griffin.

As lord of earth and sky, the griffin would link the other motifs, which ranged from the heavenly symbol of cruciform flower and sepal to the earthly ones of elk , horse and rider. She would make five borders surrounding the central field, each defined by a narrow guard stripe. Moving from the inside out, the first would contain winged griffins housed in squares. The second, a wider border, would contain the browsing elk . The third would repeat the cruciform flower and sepal motif of the central field. The fourth, widest of all, would contain the horses and riders. The fifth would repeat the griffins.

The sizing of these motifs took many hours to work out. Progress was slow until her mind turned playful. When the whole carpet was sketched out on the biggest piece of slate, her excitement bubbled over. Dashing out of the workshop, she went in search of Targitus. She found him just emerging from the village meeting hall, where he had heard a report on success in purifying gold. The joy he took in this report was nothing compared to Rachel's gleeful state.

Taking his arm, she guided him toward the workshop.

"I'll go. Willingly. Don't explain. I know you've got something to show me," Tagitus said, as if speaking to a little girl.

"I can't help it. Do you wish I'd act more grown up?" They were almost running.

"Don't even try," he replied, trying to slow her down enough to kiss the back of her neck.

"I've got it. The whole carpet's sketched out. I had to explain the numbers. To you first."

They reached the workshop and went directly to the large slate.

"It's hard to make it out. No questions this time, please." He lifted her hair to find the spot on her neck he had missed on the way in.

"Well, I've fit forty-two griffins in the first border and sixty-six flower and sepal squares in the third. And you know there must be a reason. Forty-two reversed is twenty-four, the number of squares in the central field and the number of elk in the next border. But there's

## 17: GREAT ULAGAN VALLEY – 405 B.C.

more. Forty-two is divisible by six and seven. Six elk on each side of the second border, seven horses and riders on each side of the fourth."

Targitus shared her obvious delight, then feigned concern.

"Impressive, as far as it goes. But what about sixty-six?"

Rachel was grinning impishly. "Add the motifs in the first and second borders. What do you get?"

Now they were both laughing. "Sometimes you're irrepressible," he said.


A routine developed in the workshop. Rachel started the day with instruction for using the five new looms. She then turned to preparations for her own carpet. Here there would be no secrets. She used the planning stage for further instruction as opportunities arose.

In the beginning, with the exception of Paralata, the students didn't take to Rachel. Her intensity and single-mindedness left them behind. Sauroma, who had young children and an impatient disposition, more compatible with felting than weaving, asked Rachel how long it would take to make the carpet, start to finish.

"That's a hard one," Rachel said. "We'll have to spin and dye the wool, then warp the loom and commence tying the knots. I plan on 300 knots per square inch. That's more than we'll want to count before the carpet's done. Good weavers come with patience in their blood stream. Anyone in a hurry should use felt. You all know it takes but a few days, even allowing time to add appliqué. With pile carpets, the design has to be carefully fixed before the weaving starts. There's no easy way to go back. It all takes time. That's the way it is with the creative process."

Paralata broke in. "Rachel, I am sure you don't mean to suggest those who felt lack patience or creativity."

Rachel blushed. "No. Of course not. I was just trying to account for the time this carpet will take." Looking around her, she saw in Sauroma's angry expression what had prompted Paralata's comment. "I apologize for confusing you."

"How many knots a day?" Paralata said.

"Between two and three thousand. I figure the carpet will take from one and a half to two years after the design has been worked out, the thread dyed and spun and the loom prepared for weaving. Just getting to that point will take time. How much depends on how much of the dyeing and spinning you are willing to shoulder. My guess is we'll be ready in four to five months."

The next morning, Rachel had a meeting with Askapaties, a shepherd representing the sheep growers of the village. Targitus had arranged the meeting so that Rachel could explain her needs. It was late in the fall. The time for shearing was less than six months away, and Targitus wanted to be sure Rachel would have enough wool.

Here, Rachel thought, was a teaching opportunity. Before Askapaties arrived, she undertook the necessary calculations. Asking the weavers to silence the looms and gather around, Rachel talked her way through the reckonings, urging the women to check her work and ask questions as they went along.

"Simply put, the amount of wool is the total length of thread needed for warp, weft and knots. The carpet's six feet wide and six feet seven inches long. Let's start with the warp."

"Working from a plan for, say, three hundred knots per square inch," Rachel asked, "how many warp threads would there be?"

No one replied for some time. Then Hylaia, the village's most accomplished artist in wool, said, "There would have to be seventeen or eighteen per inch."

"How did you get that?" Rachel asked.

It's the number of threads across an inch that, if multiplied by itself, would equal 300 or close to it."

"But that assumes only one warp thread for each knot."

Parlata nodded. "Was I wrong?"

"The type of knot I plan to use will take two warps to tie. I'll explain why in a minute. For now, just assume there will be one knot every two warps."

The students understood that implied thirty-four to thirty-six warp threads per inch or more than 2,450 across the six-foot width

## 17: GREAT ULAGAN VALLEY – 405 B.C.

of the carpet. They also knew that each warp end would have to measure six feet, seven inches, the length of the carpet, plus about three extra feet for wastage. The length of the warp threads, then, would be over 23,000 feet.

Rachel observed, "That's about the distance from the workshop to our yurt." The women gasped.

"But," Paralata said, "you told us the warp thread would be plied with two strands. That means we'll need two threads of that length for each warp."

"Good thinking. So, just to warp the loom will take much wool."

"And many sheep," Hestia said. "How much thread can you get from one sheep?"

"I thought your husband raised sheep?"

Hestia nodded, looking embarrassed. "I am sure he wouldn't know either. Remember, we only felt." She used her accent on the word "only" like a sharp knife.

It was Rachel's turn to blush. "Ouch. I am sorry. Again, stupid me. Thread from sheep. Well, it depends on the size of the sheep and the quality of the wool. I am hoping we can spin somewhere in the range of 3,500 to 5,000 feet per sheep.

"Now let's figure the weft. To start, I'll need to explain something about knotting. There are two basic knots: the symmetrical, which involves each knot being wrapped around two adjacent warps, and the asymmetrical, involving a wrap around only one. The symmetrical is wider than it is high. The asymmetrical is more or less square. With the symmetrical, there's a tendency for designs to become horizontally elongated. Circles become ovals, squares become rectangles and so on. The advantage of this knot is its strength. Carpets using it are robust and hard-wearing."

"With all the details you've sketched, I assume you'll be using the asymmetrical," Hylaia observed.

Just then Askapaties arrived, looking dour. Rachel thought he was early. Too engrossed with her students to break off, she asked him to visit the banks of the Bashkaus until she had finished. She missed the distaste in Askapaties' expression as he turned to leave.

"Well, you have a point. Distortion of the animals would be

especially noticeable. But, no, I am going to use the symmetrical. I can solve the distortion problem. And I have a strong preference for that knot, not just because of its strength but because I like its balance. And I like symmetry in design, something I know you've figured out from the overall plan. A weaver is entitled to use the knot she prefers. So, what about distortion? I am going to try two techniques in combination. Something I've never done before. First, I'll use unequal tension on alternate wefts. Doing so allows the warp threads to lie closer together, reducing the width of the knots, making room for more of them. Second, I will shoot four weft threads between each row of knots. This will reduce the number of knots in the warp direction. A ratio of four to one yields an equal number of knots in each direction."

The need for this digression about knots was now clear. Rachel asked them to calculate the wool needed for weft. They came up with about 31,000 feet. Hylaia presented the number and explained how they got there.

"Good," Rachel said. "About one and one-half times the distance from here to my yurt."

"Don't forget to double it," Paralata said.

"Almost done," Rachel said. "I hope our shepherd hasn't fallen in the river. As for knots, you know it's three hundred per square inch, or about 1.6 million knots in all. Each knot will be tied from thread about an inch in length so the total length of knotting thread will be about 133,333 feet. But, as Paralata keeps reminding us, it will be plied with two strands. So, we must double it. To make this concrete, think of a single thread stretching from here to our yurt and back over six times. Now, can anyone tell us how many feet in total, and how many sheep that means we need to shear for the carpet?"

The students came up with a total of about 375,000 feet of unplied thread. Using Rachel's estimates, they came up with from seventy-five to 108 sheep. The magnitude of these numbers was daunting, "Someone fetch the shepherd. I think he'll be surprised."

Surprise didn't do justice to the shepherd's reaction. His face burned with anger as he entered the workshop. He had appeared on schedule only to be sent away. Upon hearing the demand for wool,

## 17: GREAT ULAGAN VALLEY – 405 B.C.

anger mixed with shock. "That's crazy," he said.

Rachel had counted on the royal connections of her workshop to assure priority. It was her nature to assume others would share her enthusiasms. Particularly sheep growers, whose product would be more in demand as weaving at the loom became popular. She was blind to the effect her order would have on the established needs of the village. It was too late when she realized, as had some of the women well before her, that her presumption was seen as the mindless arrogance of a foreigner.

Disaster loomed. Paralata averted it with a question. "I believe you said it was going to take at least two years to complete the carpet. How much wool will you need next spring?"

Rachel replied, "I should have thought of that. Here is Askapaties trying to imagine how to dedicate the fleece of one hundred sheep to our workshop. But that won't be necessary. We only need about one-third of that in the coming season. The rest can wait until the following season. You'll have plenty of time to add to your flock."

If the shepherd was relieved, his stormy face concealed it well. Before he left, Rachel gave him a parting instruction that did nothing to calm him down. "Askapaties, remember that the wool I am ordering must be of the finest grade. I need as much from the shoulders and sides as possible. And good quality wool from the lower back. But, please, no britch stuff from legs or tail."

With unmistakable distaste, Askapaties assured her only that he had understood.


Since Great Ulagan wool had traditionally been used almost entirely for felting, with a small amount set aside for those few who wove for clothing, Rachel feared these growers might not know how to sort wool well enough to assure her the quality she needed. But questioning them would surely give more offense to an already angry group. As her sole source of supply, they must not be taken for granted. She hoped Targitus would have a solution.

That evening, she explained the problem.

Targitus said, "Why not wait until the wool is delivered. Check it over. If it's the right quality, you won't have a problem. If it isn't, you can get the shepherd to exchange it."

"That's dangerous. If I wait until delivery and discover a problem, it will probably be too late to fix it. It could mean the sorting process is defective. That high and low grade wool had been all mixed together. If there's going to be a problem because they don't know how to feel and see the differences, not because they couldn't have learned how but because they never needed to, I had better find out before delivery."

"I see." He had heard from Scalpas that she had already infuriated the growers. Her single-mindedness could easily cause more trouble. "Here's a way to handle it. Arrange a visit to the sheep growers while they still have some of this year's wool on hand. Take your students along. Under the guise of showing your students how wool is sorted, you should be able to get the message across to the growers, and even show them a thing or two, without causing embarrassment."

Rachel's concern was justified. She obtained permission to bring her class of weavers to examine the process. In front of the sheep growers she was able to explain that wool had many grades, of which the top grade was used for the pile of a carpet, the next best for warp, and third best for weft. As she spoke, she could see in the eyes of some of these leather-hard faces a faint hint of surprise, in others perplexity. She showed the women how to examine the clumps of sheared wool visually and by touch and then separate them into graded heaps, the worst being reserved for felting. She explained that skill and practice were required to grade well; that the women couldn't expect to develop the ability except through long training. As she spoke, her back was to the sheep growers. Turning to face them, she said, "I am sure any of you could do this separation in your sleep."

The men looked sullen. For an awkward moment, there was no response. Finally, after some shifting of feet, the chief replied, "We know our business."

Too late again, Rachel saw that she had caused new offense with

## 17: GREAT ULAGAN VALLEY – 405 B.C.

her comment about inferior wool being used for felting. At the workshop she had prepared her students to accept this point. She had not considered how the growers might react.

In the Altai, felt was to shelter and clothing what mother's milk was to an infant's health. One didn't adulterate wool used for felt. She had inadvertently wounded Altaian pride. Only her marriage to Targitus averted disaster. There was no way, now, to make amends. That might come later, as the growers saw what she was creating with their wool. And the demand that would surely follow. She searched for another path.

"In Sardis, I learned to sort; I saw the full range of wool. Your fleece is exceptional. I wish I knew your secret."

Some of the growers stopped frowning. Coming from an expert, her words rang true. A few felt better. The chief replied, "Good pasture and constant care. That's what does it. We love sheep. They're part of our lives, and we are part of theirs. Growing sheep is what we do." Another grower joined in. "Our secret? There is no secret."

Targitus heard from Hestia that Rachel's visit to the sheep-growers was a failure. After she and the class left, the sheep-growers argued fiercely. While some welcomed Rachel's compliments, others saw them as condescending, new insults piled on top of earlier slights and a royal presumption. Filling Rachel's order was going to create problems for established users. Targitus had made his position clear. The debate centered on whether to appeal the matter to the council of elders. Targitus knew of this possibility. Rachel's timetable was at risk. He decided not to tell her.


In the end, the growers decided against an appeal, not out of respect for Targitus but from a sense of futility, and despite the bad taste that Rachel's single-mindedness had left in their mouths.

The following spring, the wool arrived in three batches, graded good, better and best. After a close examination, Rachel was relieved. She thanked them by a visit, carrying sufficient koumiss to unsettle their day's work. More than drink, however, it was her words of extravagant praise that began a thaw in the relationship.

All preparatory work took place in the workshop. Rachel allowed the students to participate at every stage. The wool was washed and then combed to align the wool fibres so that they would lie parallel to one another. The comb was a flat piece of wood with many spikes set vertically. A hank of wool was pulled through these "teeth" repeatedly until alignment of fibers was complete. This was vigorous and time-consuming work. Rachel explained its role in creating strong, lustrous and smooth thread, the kind needed for carpets. There were no combs in the village. They had to make their own.

There were carding implements in the Great Ulagan, each consisting of a pair of flat pieces of wood with handles and small "teeth," which were used together to clean and randomize the direction of wool fibers. The students were familiar with carding, as it was regularly used to prepare wool for felting and for the weaving or knitting of wool intended for apparel. When spun, carded yarn was warmer, trapped more air, felt softer. Characteristics useful for clothing but not for carpets.

At last, they were ready to spin the combed wool. They made their own spindles. The wool would be S-spun into thread and then plied with a Z-twist using two threads. Rachel began the lessons by recounting her childhood love for spinning. Even her successive failures in the contests. And all the little tricks she'd learned along the way. Especially those that seemed contrary to experience. The students were surprised to hear that the solution for yarn spun too thin was to slow down the amount of wool being drafted into the spindle, thereby getting more twist; that the solution for yarn spun too thick was to speed up the draft, thereby reducing the twist.

Rachel insisted that only practice could dispel mistaken intuition. "You must practice," she said repeatedly, until spinning is as natural as breathing." And they did. As a result, the students were able to do most of the spinning of wool for the carpet, with Rachel checking each skein for strength and uniformity of thickness. She was pleased.

## 17: GREAT ULAGAN VALLEY – 405 B.C.

"I hear you've got your class spinning the wool already," Targitus said. They were walking together through the warmth of a late spring day bright with sunshine, headed towards the swimming hole near their yurt. It would be their first plunge of the new season. The water would be frigid. Just the thought produced tiny bumps of anticipation on their skin.

"Will you have them use your favorite twist?"

"We're using top whorl spindles. And I've taught them to spin with their feet. But I didn't want to cross Altaian tradition. You probably don't realize that Altaians spin with the Z-twist. They would have learned it from the Anatolians."

Targitus turned on her, like a dog whose bone was plucked from his mouth. "Why say that? More likely Scythians teaching the Anatolians."

They had reached the river's bank above the deep hole. Rachel quick-stepped behind him and pushed. He hovered awkwardly for an instant over the swift current, then caught his balance and stepped back against Rachel. "You villain," he cried, laughing. Had she really intended to shove him in?

Rachel held him tight. "You'll never know. One thing's for certain. It started with the spinning of hemp, which tends naturally to that direction and came before wool."

The dying of skeins of wool yarn was a difficult and often unpleasant process that extended well into the fall. Finished skeins of wool were tied about the center's walls according to color. When the process was complete, the workshop glowed richly in colors from skein upon skein of wool, hanging at eye level.

Rachel drew from the palette of dyes readily available in the Altai. There was variety enough to give her what she needed. And the Altaians were expert in the use of dyes, which had served to fast-color the felts they made.

One evening, in early fall, Rachel and Targitus rode together to the edge of the Bashkaus and moved downstream past the battle site where the ground leveled out. In time, they came to a lake, surrounded by thick larch forest.

A powerful smell hung about her that evening. Targitus urged a change of clothes for the ride. "It'll be good to get the dyeing process behind us. With each day, the odors you bring home occupy a larger part of our home."

"We're almost through. Endure a few more days. I could tell you where the colors go, if that would make you feel better."

Targitus gave her his most dubious look, without apparent effect. And so they discussed color patterns as their horses trotted along a well used path running downstream beside the Bashkaus. Taiga was out in front, pretending to be the leader.

"I am using three dominant colors," Rachel said, shouting to overcome the gurgle and splash of the Bashkaus. "A soft purplish red, two shades of blue, light with a greenish tone and dark, and a grayish yellow. I also expect to have varying shades of brown.

"It's the red that smells really bad?"

"No, not the red. It comes from an innocent insect, the cochineal, that we drown in vinegar, then dry and powder. The smell comes from the blue. But look over there."

The path they were following had brought them to the west side of a lake. It passed this body of water at a distance of about one hundred yards through a tall larch forest growing to the water's edge. The sun was within a hour of touching the horizon. The riders stopped to face the lake. In the foreground giant trunks of larch stood dark and still, bark deeply etched as if snow and rain had haphazardly eaten into the tree. Shade prevented growth in the under-story and with time had killed the lower branches. "They stand like sentinels," Rachel whispered. The sun's rays shot through the trees much farther up, hitting the lake midway across and infusing the far shore with the warm glow that one only saw at sunset.

"The beauty of this makes time stand still," she continued.

They could see the shadows moving across the lake. Soon it would be dark.

"It's just an illusion," Targitus said. "Let's turn back."

He swung his gelding around, turning her horse as well. "Back to the reality of smells. When will you reveal the purpose of all that

## 17: GREAT ULAGAN VALLEY – 405 B.C.

urine you've been collecting from me?"

As they trotted along the path, side by side, Rachel said, "The blue's indigo. From woad leaves. We grind up the plant and suspend it in a vat filled with urine. Mostly yours. The vat's outside the workshop, but the smell's still bad. It lingers."

Targitus recalled the story Rachel had told him about the robe she wove for Cyrus. "Wouldn't you prefer royal purple if you could get it?

"I don't miss that color. It's beautiful, but, even without the association, I wouldn't use it in the carpet. Too commanding. But, that reminds me, there's an interesting point about indigo. It works like the murex dye in turning the wool its true color only upon removal of the wool from the vat. It takes contact with air for the dye to work. And that makes getting the exact shade of blue you want very difficult, since you can't watch it turn in the vat."

Darkness had settled on the riders. A nearly full moon was due to peak above the eastern horizon, but not before they reached home. The horses were at no serious disadvantage in the dark, having covered the ground many times before. In the path's dips they felt the evening chill, already pushing away the warmth of the day. Above, the loud, trumpeting and shrill cry of a crane pierced the air, to be answered by a muted trill. A pair, Rachel thought. She imagined them flying wing to wing, gray with blackish wing tips, legs and necks outstretched.

"My yellow's subdued, a golden tan. I'll take it from onion skins. Don't worry. It won't smell."

# CHAPTER 18

Great Ulagan Valley – 404-402 B.C.

There was high excitement in the workshop when Rachel warped her loom. Like the end of one journey, the beginning of another. It was late February.

Rachel began to stretch the warp between the loom's crossbeams. Her class gathered around to watch. In all, some 2,300 warp ends would be strung to hold the carpet and the glory of its knotted artistry together. The other part of the foundation, the weft, would be woven in the simple, over and under technique known as "plain weave" to form a fabric, binding the carpet and holding the rows of knots in place.

The weft yarn would be woven one shoot at a time, just as the carpet's surface would take shape one knot at a time. The loom, however, had to be warped all at once, at the start. It was a process demanding great patience.

Too much patience for some in the class. For months, they had toiled to prepare for the tying of the first knot. Rachel had forgotten to warn them that warping took time. As she meticulously stretched the warp ends, she couldn't help feeling restless energy in the room.

## 18: GREAT ULAGAN VALLEY – 404-402 B.C.

Sauroma, in particular, was frustrated by finding no way to speed up the process. They were adults, but they were beginning to show childlike patterns, reminding Rachel of her first days at the palace workshop.

"I know you want to help. You want to see that first knot and then celebrate. So do I. But this is going to take time. If you can't stand it, go outside. Attend to other things, then come back. Or sharpen those shearing knives. I'll be needing them soon."

The warp yarn Rachel was stretching consisted of undyed fibres of gray, white and brown, tightly spun and plied with two threads. The loom had roller beams at top and bottom, allowing Rachel to roll the extra length of warp ends around the upper beam and, as the work progressed, to roll the finished carpet onto the lower beam. By this means, the working area could be kept at hand-level where the knot-tying was most easily accomplished.

The weft would be of the same undyed fibers, but thin and loosely spun. The four shoots of weft between each row of knots would pass across and back, over and under alternate warps, twice. A wooden bobbin, to which the weft thread was attached, would be used to make the passage.

When, at last, the final warp end was stretched, Rachel invited her students to bring balls of knotting yarn in the necessary colors to the loom and hang them above eye level within reach of her hands on a line stretched across the loom. Then, when all was ready, she tied the first knot, cutting it neatly with a well-sharpened shearing knife. The movement of tying the pile yarn to the warps with both hands, pressing the knot down tight and cutting the excess pile with the knife was marvelously fluid and so rapid as to blur before the eye. Rachel held the knife in the palm of her right hand by the middle, fourth and little fingers, the thumb and index fingers remaining free to tie the knot.

There was a cry as Rachel completed the first knot. She had described the tradition of celebrating, and they were more than ready when that long-awaited moment arrived. So, too, the guests. Besides Targitus and his mother, there were family and friends of the students, and a few sheep-growers, whom Rachel had been reminded by Targitus to include.

Koumiss was served. It was afternoon in midwinter. Outside, the sun was bright, the temperature bitter cold. Inside, warmed by fire and the heat of so many celebrants, the air was comfortable. Targitus rose to speak.

"Friends and family. Fill your cups with koumiss now, for I will be asking you to join me in a toast."

The crowd headed to the bowls, set on a table next to the windowless wall.

"Most of you don't know how I persuaded Rachel to come to the Altai. We met in mountains above the Black Sea. She came with us to the weaving center in Scopasis, on the Oarus River, where she planned to remain. I hoped to change her mind. So we spent the winter in that village. As spring approached, I searched for an argument. Rachel's skill at weaving and her artist's eye became famous in Scopasis. I suddenly realized it was right there, in the weaver's workshop. Her weaving skill and her instinct for teaching was a dowry of rare value for our village. And so I pledged that she would find acceptance through this workshop and her desire to teach the art of weaving. Today's celebration speaks eloquently of Rachel's welcome here and much more besides. She is beloved by our village, by all those who know her, and especially by those, her students, who know her best."

Targitus knew that saying something didn't make it true. But he believed that by claiming often enough that the village had accepted Rachel, he could help make it so. In something as subjective as community acceptance, belief and truth were never far apart.

Always on edge at the beginning of a speech, it took Targitus a minute or two to become comfortable. From that point on, he would fall in love with the sound of his own voice, the framing of selected words, the complete sense of command and control. At these moments, he would imagine how others saw him, and admire the craft. He had paused but was far from finished. As he began again, a raucous round of applause shattered the rhythms of his voice. Startled, he stopped in mid-sentence. This crowd was nothing like the village elders, who had been tamed into respect for both the

## 18: GREAT ULAGAN VALLEY – 404-402 B.C.

substance and style of their leader's workmanlike speeches. Applause gave way to cries for Rachel.

Targitus bowed to the collective will. Raising a cup to his beloved, Targitus shouted "To Rachel." All followed his lead.

Standing near the center of the room, surrounded by her students and a handful of friends, Rachel inhaled. Memories of childhood dreams about weaving filled her head. She reveled in the moment. Arms akimbo, face effulgent and wet with tears, she prepared to speak.

"Today marks the end of my beginning as an apprentice, the start of a new life as a weaver. With the tying of that first knot, my dreams ended. Replaced by the reality of this workshop, of a carpet worthy of the Altaian people, and of the future generations who will learn weaving here.

"It's time to be grateful. To Yahweh, God of my people. And to the Altaian gods. To my mother, who bore me, my brother, who gave me the freedom to become Rachel, my father, whose bravery in death saved my life. And to Targitus, whose love, patience and persevering spirit overcame all obstacles, even my own resistance, toughest of all. To him I give the greatest measure of thanks. Finally, a tribute to the spirit whose presence I feel. Not constantly but on the best of days. A spirit that in the past has moved me to create art. I pray it will stay with me. And set down roots in this place, leading all those who work here to discover their own ways to express the truth, the composed energy, of art."

Rachel had not planned these remarks. She hadn't thought of speaking at all. What she said surprised her as much as those around her. The room was silent for several moments. And then, all raised their cups in salute.

As they went home that evening, Rachel refused to descend from the emotional peak she had reached upon tying the first knot. "I want this feeling to linger, at least through the night. Today, I spread the wings you helped me grow. Tonight, I want to indulge myself."

Targitus was not given to indulgence. He was good at taking responsibility, tireless in its discharge. But he rejoiced in the happiness of his mate. He understood her. He wanted to join in her high spirits. He knew better than to speak of it thus, but here was a duty he would gladly take on. Rachel remained elated through dinner. A fire, kept blazing by Targitus, warmed the space around their bedding, beyond which the cold of the Altaian winter asserted itself.

"We need a touch of cold somewhere to appreciate the warmth," Targitus said.

"Come over here and untie my braid."

They were sitting on the bedding, near the fire. Rachel was kneeling, her torso firmly erect, back slightly arched, shoulders squared, head high. Targitus knelt behind and gently removed the yarn tied at the foot of her single, shining black braid, and then unwound the three plaits.

He rose to add logs to the fire. Returning, he saw Rachel toss her hair twice to shake loose the twists. And then he watched as she slowly removed her top garments. Her ivory skin was always a marvel to him, but particularly so tonight, for its lustrous cool color was warmly etched with rose from the flickering light. She was kneeling in the direction of the fire. Targitus observed her figure in profile. Like an actor aware of having her audience's full attention, Rachel very slowly lifted both arms to place her hands on her shoulders. Taking her black tresses in both hands, she moved them from behind her back. With a gentle swish across her shoulders, she ran her fingers over her breasts, spreading her hair to rest where her fingers had been, black on white, conforming to her round curves except for a distinct curl at the ends, where the tie-yarn had held fast her single braid. She turned her head to look straight into his eyes. Targitus saw contentment and quiet desire, spirit and the senses in perfect balance. Rachel extended her arms to feel the chill that lurked just beyond the fire's reach. "Come, now, you've been staring long enough. I want you here, beside me."

Targitus responded to the half-naked woman kneeling nearby. Moving to her side, he tenderly began the discharge of what at first he had welcomed as a duty but now was eager to claim as the satisfaction of mutual desire. Despite his arousal, he was challenged to equal his partner's energy. For Rachel, the excitement of the day had been translated into a personal quest for something that could transcend the pleasures they were now almost too accustomed to give and receive. Targitus did his best. So long did he succeed in delaying his own climax while engaging in a slow steady build-up towards hers, that when it came, she was swept beyond experience, or so she believed, for her vision dimmed during those extended moments on the summit, as if to deepen the feelings inside by darkening outer distractions.


As row upon row of knots was completed, each separated by four shoots of weft, the carpet began to take shape with the first of seven narrow guard stripes composed of thin dark blue borders containing the tri-color motif of repeating rectangles of red bounded first by yellow and then by dark blue. Rachel's unusual memory would prove an essential part of the weaving process. The designs had been rendered on various surfaces, leather and slate, which were now spread out around the loom. They provided Rachel with a guide to the various shapes. She would translate these shapes into knots, memorizing their color, number and sequence. Because the patterns repeated throughout the carpet, the burden on her memory was less than one might imagine.

That didn't mean it was simple. Along each row, Rachel would tie all the knots of one color before proceeding to knots of the next. Thus, within the rectangles, she might tie all the red knots first, then the yellow ones and finally the blue.

This technique made completion of each row swifter. But it also invited errors based on mis-location of knots of a particular color along the row. Once a row of knots was beaten into place between shoots of weft on either side, it became impossible to correct an error that was not caught while the row was being tied. This technique demanded a powerful memory to be able to place each knot of a particular color where it belonged along the row of warp ends.

After completing the outer guard stripe, Rachel began the first border, building the griffin repeats, row by row of traverse knots, from the bottom of their paws up until she reached their heads turned back to face their thrusting wings and curved tails with jaws ajar, tongues extended.

One day, as the body of this fantastic beast took shape, Hylaia asked her if she really knew what a griffin looked like. "You've told us about the symbolism. But, if you've never seen one, how can you be sure?"

Weaving and talking at the same time, she maintained two strands of thought concurrently, keeping them separate and untangled.

Not only could she manage, but the students never saw her make a mistake. As she answered their questions, they watched her slim fingers move deftly, wrapping first one and then the other warp with the pile yarn that stretched from the supply above, cinching it tight, cutting the end of the yarn clean and repeating the process, more than a thousand times in each row.

The soft rhythmic sounds of knots being tied and wefts being beaten offered a musical setting for Rachel's response. "In truth, of course, I don't. Anymore than I know what Yahweh looks like. Believers often think they can spot the works of a supreme being, for example the moon or a flood or war. It's much harder to know how to render God himself so that he will be recognized without appearing trivial. Now, if I wanted to put God in the carpet, what would he look like? I'd be free to make something up, but the risk is no one would get my meaning. For the griffin I am using its familiar shape as imagined by countless artists who preceded me."

"Your griffin doesn't look Altaian," said Paralata. Her face was a smiling challenge. "Are you following a particular design?"

"I think you know I am not. Nor am I going to copy specific renderings in the other motifs. Growing up in Sardis, I saw a great many designs of flora and fauna by Persians and the tribes that preceded them. The eye describes and the mind imprints these images, at least the most compelling of them. They are stored not to be copied, but for influence. I had to compress the beast to get him into the square. The solution was to make his neck rise straight up from his front legs, his head turn to look backwards over his rump and his tail arch over his back.

"As for why my griffin is more frolicking than fearsome, like

## 18: GREAT ULAGAN VALLEY – 404-402 B.C.

those I've seen in the Altai, the truth is simple: I prefer the look of a happy guardian." Rachel thought of mentioning that she had gotten the same argument from Targitus, then decided against it.

It took the Altaians more than a year to convert the knowledge Targitus brought from Sardis into purified gold. As in learning to ride, string a bow and loose an arrow at the gallop, or to spin wool and warp a loom, it is much easier to describe than to do. The first ingots of true quality were produced in late July. Naturally, the refiners thought this a moment to celebrate. They asked Targitus what should be done with the gold. Although he had some ideas of his own, he appeared at the yurt with an ingot one late summer evening and consulted Rachel.

Holding up an ingot for her to see, he exclaimed, "First fruits of our expedition to Sardis."

Rachel stared at him, quizzical. Teased him with silence.

After a few seconds, Targitus said, "Let me rephrase that. One of the venture's rewards."

Laughing, Rachel grabbed his hands to pull him close. She put fingers to his mouth to stop his earnest apology. "Don't be so serious." She kissed him on the nose, fingers still across his mouth lest he blurt out some further nonsense.

He embraced her, off duty at last.

"Now, tell me more about this triumph," she said, breaking away to continue preparing their evening meal.

Reminiscing about Sardis proved unavoidable. They talked well into the evening.

Rachel's idea for using the newly minted gold was to sculpt a large horse and Altaian warrior, bow in hand, and place it in Maytes' tomb.

"Your father's vision made it all possible. He should receive first fruits of that bold idea. The ingots should honor you too. A griffin, perhaps. Guardian of Altaian gold. Leave the rest as ingots. Display them in the village center, reminder of Altaian audacity and skill."

Targitus recalled the perfect form of Argali as she had appeared before Cyrus.

"Do you remember my speaking of Argali? I just had a vision of her in the palace. What a pleasure to watch the Satrap's struggle at self-restraint. He was smitten. I wonder what's become of her?"

Deep in her own thoughts, Rachel could offer no response. Whatever had happened to Argali might have happened to her. There were many possibilities, not all of them good.

"Bringing Argali along was probably the best idea I've ever had. There was luck involved, but we guessed Cyrus' tastes and I picked the right woman."

Rachel's reaction to these musings was a tight squeeze of the hand, a gentle kiss on the forehead and silence. How could she tell him it was her pleading that succeeded without crushing a pride grown deep with time, without engendering questions as to how she succeeded and doubts as to her story?

Rachel was knotting the main border of horses and riders when Targitus arrived at the workshop. It was April. Rachel had taken to wearing her golden spindle as a hair pin. The class had noticed it instantly. In the workshop, Rachel reigned supreme, both as director and mentor. But the atmosphere was open. Recognizing it for what it was, the women wanted an explanation. Casting instinct aside, Rachel lied.

"It's an old family piece, given to me by my father when I left Sardis. I've never used it. In fact, since it's pure gold, I was embarrassed to show it here before Altaian gold became pure."

Targitus had entered unseen by Rachel. Standing behind her, he moved an index finger to his mouth, something he'd done many times in the past. He tip-toed to stand behind her. Putting his large hands on Rachel's shoulders, he gently kneaded her muscles, a routine she instantly recognized. "Doesn't all this knotting give you a sore neck?"

Rachel turned laughing. "You always say that. But aren't my complaints every night, my demands for massage, a clear enough answer? What a nice surprise. We have enough to set a place for you at our table." Looking at her students, she said, "What do you say to

## 18: GREAT ULAGAN VALLEY – 404-402 B.C.

letting this intruder join us?"

"I've brought you something. I thought the best place to give it to you would be here, where you spend most waking hours. Had I planned an elaborate ceremony, you'd have complained. This is perfect."

"What I need most just now is another set of hands and eyes. But look at these legs I am weaving. Can you tell the horses from the men?"

On a deep red background, just above the narrow tri-color guard stripe separating the horse and rider motif from the completed border of griffins, he could make out horse's legs in turquoise above muted yellow hooves. Between the legs he saw what might have been two brightly decorated columns.

"I can make out the horses. If those things in between are riders, you've certainly dressed them in gaudy pants."

"It's my biggest border. The procession is supposed to be dignified yet exuberant, protective yet celebratory. I can't resist embellishing. The pants are a result."

"There will certainly be others," Paralata added with a friendly chuckle that was passed around the group.

Rachel was still sitting on her bench, looking at her work as the others examined the many legs taking shape on the loom. She rose to face Targitus and said, "I am sorry. I've been single-minded. You've brought me a present."

He took from his pouch a small felt package and handed it to Rachel. The felt was made of undyed beige wool and neatly tied with a leather thong. An appliqué in red felt had been cut in the shape of a ewe and sewed with great care in the center of the package. Untying the thong, Rachel removed the felt to reveal an exquisite hair clasp of pure gold. It consisted of a long pin depicting the tree of life. The pin tapered from a thick rounded end to a handle at the thin end. A well tanned leather strap with two holes drilled for the pin to pass through completed the clasp. Tooled on the leather was the image of a ewe, remarkably well defined considering its tiny size.

"This was made from our first ingot," Targitus said. "Its imagery reflects your choice of name. It honors you. Your loss on the mountains above Trapezus brought us good fortune. In some mysterious way, you were important to our getting home safely. In less mysterious ways you are essential to me."

Rachel wished sometimes he would leave imagery alone, to do its task unassisted. "So, you want me to exchange gold of Sardis for Altaian gold. Gladly."

Rachel was thinking of the gold earrings Cyrus had given her, something she had omitted from the Cyrus story. Now she had another reason for making sure Targitus would never know of those earrings.

She pulled the spindle from her hair and placed it on the bench. Then, after a long, admiring look at the handle of the hair clasp, she raised both hands behind her head to lift the braid and pin it in her favorite uplifted position for working at the loom. She felt tingling, followed swiftly by numbness in her right arm down to the fingertips. The gold clasp fell as she brought her arms down to her sides. Targitus, who was standing near, was just quick enough with his foot to break the clasp's fall.

Rachel looked down at the clasp, then up at Targitus. "My vision's blurred," she announced, her voice cracking. She sat on the bench, trembling.

As soon as Rachel was able to compose herself, Targitus took her home, promising to keep the class informed of her condition. The symptoms persisted through afternoon and night. By the following day, after a sound sleep, they were gone. Rachel had never experienced anything like this before. The chief shaman was consulted. He was not the kind tempted by position to pretend. He advised that the symptoms might be worrisome, but it was too soon to say anything definite, that he had no idea what might have caused them, that the speed with which they came and went offered hope of an isolated event.

There was no recurrence through the Altaian spring. Rachel made good progress on the carpet, devoting herself to it with a level of energy, enthusiasm and good cheer that astounded her husband and others in the village who knew of her situation. Paralata was right about the border with horse and rider. On the bottom, Rachel had developed detail upon detail to achieve the diverse textures she wanted. The horses were far more massive than typical Altaian stock. Fit only for gods to mount, Paralata quipped. The procession seemed alive with energy. Rachel gave the horses' heads a muscular bend, as if they were being reined in.

Each steed wore a sweat blanket, covered by another blanket of woven pile, bearing one of three distinct designs and fringed with tassels. One was the tree of life, which she displayed in two versions, one with two trees on either side of the blanket and the other with a single tree in the center. The other designs were a row of squares and an S-shaped figure with rosettes. The central field of each blanket was framed by a stripe containing multicolored squares. Outside the stripe, another row of squares framed the blanket at its perimeter, joined there to the tassels, which flared dramatically like flames, imparting an energetic thrusting motion to each horse. As Rachel had done elsewhere in the carpet, whenever the opportunity presented itself, she used a variety of color in the knots to match her variations in design.

"As I went along," she confessed, "I got carried away. Particularly the chance to show a variety of other designs within a single carpet."


Although winter had ended, there were few signs of spring. Targitus was up before Rachel. He had built a fire, which now cast its warming glow around the yurt. The sun was just above the horizon, its rays illuminating the inside of the felt covering with a false promise of warmth.

Opening her eyes, Rachel discovered she was sightless in her right eye and nearly so in her left. "Targitus, I can't see!" Trying to sit up, she realized her whole right side was numb. Tingling sensations coursed up and down her left side.

Targitus tried to remain calm. Wasn't Rachel too young and healthy to become sick. Could this be the doing of some demon?

Targitus left her just long enough to find someone to summon his mother and the chief shaman. Not knowing whose wisdom on matters of health he trusted more, he sought them both. Rachel's distress mingled physical incapacity with mental shock. It could not be exaggerated. The night before, she was talking vivaciously of her progress. She explained how her students had just completed the yarn from last season's wool. Now it was in balls, spun, plied and dyed, ready for use and ample to complete the project. "The end is in sight," she had said as they pressed together in their favorite position for drifting off.

Sparetra and the chief shaman proved that opposites can repel as well as attract. The shaman wanted to administer medicine and begin incantations to expel the demons that he swore were inhabiting her body. Sparetra demanded to know the contents of the shaman's medicine. He refused. Targitus thought his mother knew the shaman would refuse and was trying to pick a fight.

Sparetra believed she had seen similar cases in the village, before Targitus was born. She recalled the symptoms. She remembered that the person afflicted had recurrences from time to time, but would always recover. Her advice was hot broth and plenty of care. Most important of all, she added, a robust confidence that these problems would pass.

With the experts at an impasse, Targitus realized he couldn't follow the shaman's counsel. To do nothing was really to accept his mother's advice, which is what he wanted to do anyway, at least for a time of testing.

The shaman departed angry. Sparetra stayed. She returned the next day and the one after that. On the fourth day, Rachel stopped slurring her speech. Full vision returned to her left eye and partial vision to the right. The tingling and numbness seemed to subside. Sparetra was thrilled.

After two weeks of care, the symptoms were gone. Rachel returned to her position in front of the loom. Within an hour, she had proved that neither memory nor dexterity had been affected by this strange illness. Progress continued as before.

Spring burst forth in the Altai. Rachel and Targitus were enjoying the lengthening hours of sunlight outside their yurt, where the two streams blended, just below their bathing spot, unused since the fall. With the break in winter's hold on the village, the threat of the

## 18: GREAT ULAGAN VALLEY – 404-402 B.C.

recurring illness dissipated somewhat too, freeing their minds to rejoice in the season's change.

"Have you noticed, Rachel, that the farther north one is, the more sudden the coming of spring. In Sardis, for example, I am sure one eases into it more gradually."

Rachel barely heard him. Consumed with worry, she had, at last, come to the point of talking. "I must tell you something. I've been having trouble for more than three weeks now distinguishing colors. I should have told you sooner, but at first I wasn't sure there was a problem. Then I thought, 'It wouldn't last.' But it did. I didn't want the class to know. I was able to keep weaving because I knew the location of each ball of dyed and undyed yarn. But apparently one of my students put a dark blue ball right next to the red. I couldn't tell them apart, so I wasn't particular about which one I drew knotting yarn from. Before anyone said anything, I had used blue instead of red for the sepals in two of the cruciform motifs on the right border. By the time Hylaia pointed out the error, I was too far along to correct it."

The evening glowed in the setting sun. From where they sat just outside the yurt, one could see a full palette of pastel greens from emergent grasses to willowy bushes along the streams to the gentle needles of giant larches growing in singular splendor here and there on the valley floor. Targitus was afraid to mention the surrounding beauty, lest he embarrass them both. How, he wondered, in the face of nature's exuberance, could Rachel have become so afflicted? He wanted to cry out. To demand how this unfairness came to be. To insist that it go away. Instead, he asked, calmly, "Why didn't someone notice?"

"That's the peculiar thing. They did, but decided either I meant to change colors, in which case they ought not to question it, or it was an error, in which case they were too embarrassed to bring it to my attention. So, they just pretended it hadn't happened. Then, when I did it a second time, Paralata was pushed by others to raise the question. It took me a while to understand what she was saying. What a shock. They showed me the two balls of yarn. I couldn't see the difference. Nor could I tell the sepals were blue, not red. When the students saw how distraught I had become, they insisted the condition was unimportant. They were so cheerful and positive. I will never forget those moments."

Targitus had moved closer to Rachel. He put his arm around her shoulders. He wished he knew how to reinforce what the students had begun.

"What did they say?"

"You know, that sun might as well be blue from what I can see over there, just above the horizon. I am sorry. I can't stop noticing. And, I guess you can tell, I am feeling sorry for myself. The first thing they did was to suggest the idea of alternating blue with red sepals, so the error would be masked. With twenty-four cruciform motifs left to weave, alternating colors would look purposeful. I liked the idea. And, then, they made the obvious point that I didn't need to 'see' the colors to tie the knots, as long as the different yarns were kept in their places, because I had memorized both the place of each color and the color of each motif, and they are all now just repeats from work already completed. Finally, they predicted the color-blindness would pass as all the other symptoms had. After all this, they invited me to take tea with them. You can see why I love them."

Targitus felt his bond to this woman tighten.

"Do you remember the evening we discussed the role of Yahweh in your life? And the afterlife? On the trip from Scopasis. We were at it a long time, and you recited some lines that you had learned in childhood, lines that your father didn't care for but that you were fond of hearing. You said they were important. And would become important to me too. I am going to test my memory."

Rachel was surprised. Targitus had never volunteered to do such a thing before, except once with the Song of Songs. He seemed different. He must have left the stiffness back in the village.

"Here goes," he said.

> "Go thy way, eat thy bread with joy, and drink thy wine with a merry heart; for God now accepteth thy works.
>
> Let thy garments be always white; and let thy head lack no ointment.
>
> Live joyfully with the wife whom thou lovest all the days of the life of thy vanity, which he hath given thee under the sun, all the days of thy vanity: for that is thy portion in this life, and in thy labour

## 18: GREAT ULAGAN VALLEY – 404-402 B.C.

which thou takest under the sun.

Whatsoever thy hand findeth to do, do it with thy might; for there is no work, nor device, nor knowledge, nor wisdom, in the grave, whither thou goest.

I returned, and saw under the sun, that the race is not to the swift, nor the battle to the strong, neither yet bread to the wise, nor yet riches to men of understanding, nor yet favour to men of skill; but time and chance happeneth to them all."

He had a deep and resonant voice. With compelling affect he had captured the rhythms, enhancing their beauty and dramatizing the meaning of the words that flowed easily from his mind.

"Oh, that was done. Beautifully done. What made you think of those lines?"

"I am not sure. I remember their beauty. And I like the lesson about chance. If I accept that, it helps in coming to terms with your strange illness. If your afflictions are not the result of some all-powerful design but just bad luck, it makes things easier to accept. What about you?"

"I don't know that you're right. It's not that I think I am being punished. Just the possibility of a supreme force, balancing one's life between happiness and sorrow. This would throw out pure chance. But the lesson about living life as it's given, fully, immersing oneself, because it's all we get, that idea appeals. But you know that."


Rachel worked with increasing intensity through the weeks of summer and into the fall. Her color-blindness continued. Periodically, she would experience blurred vision, accompanied by slurred speech. She refused to let these symptoms stop her from weaving. Whether they were the cause of some minor mismeasurements would never be known. In this large, complex textile, working from cartoons but using memory and feel rather than mechanically counting knots made it easy to miscalculate the spacing, particularly in the vertical direction. And so, on the right side, near the top of the flower and sepal border, too large a space emerged between the last vertical motif and the one to be woven in the corner. Here, to fill the extra space, Rachel placed a stripe containing small triangles, colored dark blue.

The ever-attentive Hylaia asked whether the triangles had special significance.

"They fit the space," Rachel replied, smiling mischievously.

Miscalculations occurred on the left side as well, near the top of the horse border and again near the top of the outer griffin border. The extra spaces between the last vertical motif and the one to be woven in the corner gave Rachel a chance to add something that had not been part of the original plan. In each space she placed paired eight-petalled rosettes, varying the colors in each pair, so that the ones in the horse border contained alternating red and dark blue petals with a yellow center, while the ones in the griffin border contained alternating yellow and dark blue petals with a red center.

"So these are just space-fillers too," Paralata said, voice skeptical, after Rachel had finished knotting the first pair.

"I do have something in mind. In Sardis, the rosette depicted the center of the universe, creation. I can accept that. But there's a more personal aspect. I am placing them here as symbols of two particular pairs: Targitus' parents and my own. They were our centers."

There was more to the rosettes than that. Rachel wanted a child. They had been trying, but with no success. In the months before marriage, their efforts came from Targitus' pressure, and led to miscarriage. Afterwards, they couldn't even get that far. Putting logic aside, Rachel was investing in the rosettes, willing them to bring this wish to fruition.

Long ago, she had learned of her mother's pragmatic approach to fertility. She recalled loving her mother more than ever upon hearing the story, told to her by the priest's daughter, of how her mother came to sacrifice a goat at Cybele's altar. She had prayed to Yahweh for a sign. Soon after, she had gone outside to hang up laundry on one of those cloudless days for which Sardis was famous. Hearing a shrill plaintive "kree-e-e-e" far above, she looked up in time to spot the hawk before it dove a thousand feet and more, talons extended, to seize a dove flying two hundred feet or so directly above the tree to which she had attached her drying line. The majesty of the hawk could not dispel the violence of the kill or her fear that Yahweh had disapproved. She saw the hawk wheel above her and fly to a large dead tree, where she deposited the dove in a nest containing the hawk's mate and some hungry fledglings.

Rachel's mother now saw another possibility. A kill, yes, but to feed the young. Might this not be a favorable omen conjuring up the image of a nurturing parent? Grasping the affirmative, she took the ambiguous sign to be Yahweh's consent to the sacrifice. Rachel hoped the rosettes would serve her as the hawk had served her mother.

Targitus kept referring to the carpet as their offspring. Rachel refused to abandon hope of creating something more, but kept it to herself.

She completed the carpet in late winter. There were no more mis-measurements. The supply of wool was enough to finish the task, including the selvage. A celebration was planned in the workshop, where the carpet would be displayed. After hanging there for a few weeks, the carpet would go to Sparetra's home to warm the floor for as long as she lived. It would then be returned to Targitus and Rachel.

The students asked Rachel to alert them as she started to tie the last row of knots. They wanted to be there, around her, as she finished. They would enjoy a private toast to their mentor, just as they had done at the outset, when the first knot was tied.

Rachel came to the last row in the afternoon of a day turned dark from its bright beginning. The wind had swung around from west to northeast. Snow was coming. Rachel was elated. And, yet, as she began this final passage across the weft with her proud admirers watching in a semi-circle around the bench, a sense of loss overcame her.

"Friends, I see a big hole in my life and it hurts. Like it or not, want it or not, we can't avoid looking to the future. That's not a bad thing. Some say that anticipating painful events to come is the best way to handle them. But looking ahead sometimes makes it hard to enjoy the present. A moment ago, I was deep in the thrill of having reached this long-awaited place. And, then, my mind broke away to think about a future without this carpet to work on. Triumph turned bittersweet."

Rachel was moving swiftly across the weft, fingers in constant motion as she set the knots in place. At the tying of the last knot, gleeful shouts rang out. Rachel sat quietly in the eye of this celebratory din, arms limp at her sides, hands one over the other at rest in her lap, head bowed. Starting as a shiver low in her back, raw emotion rose to her head and brought a flood of uninvited, not unwelcome, tears.

Once the students noticed her wet face, they too began to cry. "Look at us all," Rachel said, head high as she rose from the bench to embrace them. "We're a sight!" Drinking koumiss, they passed an hour of pleasure in each other's company.

Later, as she rode home through steady snowfall, she thought it ironic that not only were all tears the same, physically, but that their onset felt the same whether they expressed joy or sadness. Or the melancholy state in which she had found herself upon finishing the last knot. She felt a tinge of guilt in having deliberately not invited Targitus to share the excitement.

On the morning of the celebration, Rachel awoke to the symptoms she had experienced before, only worse. Her vision was greatly impaired in both eyes. The right side of her body felt numb. The left had numbness in some areas, tingling in others. She was terrified to discover lack of control over the urinary tract. Only her speech was unaffected.

Rachel tried to make light of her problems. She urged Targitus to go to the workshop. "This illness comes and goes. It shouldn't spoil the event," she asserted.

Targitus did her bidding, leaving friends to maintain the fire and see to Rachel's needs. He had decided to cancel the celebration, promise those assembled a display of the carpet when Rachel had recovered, and bring students and carpet back to the yurt.

It was afternoon by the time they arrived, Targitus leading the way. As he entered, Rachel awoke from a light sleep. She had eaten nothing since dinner the night before. She had no appetite. The presence of her class revived her. With a dramatic flourish, they displayed the carpet for her to see, forgetting that her eyesight was impaired. It didn't matter. Rachel could see every detail of this weaving, its colors and images brighter to her than to anyone else in the darkened room.

"We want to place your carpet on the floor under your bedding, Rachel. And place you in its central field, where the protections you imagined for others will serve you first."

Rachel was carried to a temporary site away from her bedding, the carpet was spread out underneath and she was then moved to lie squarely in the center.

Targitus was watching Rachel closely. Two things were obvious. Her body was much worse than it had been during previous visitations of this mysterious illness. Her spirit, on the other hand, seemed to soar, her mind on edge.

"I am not seeing too well. Where's Targitus?" She spoke softly, with caution, mouthing each word as one might handle an egg in removing it from beneath a hen. "I want to place each of you before me. Inside my head I can see perfectly. Let's go round the room."

Starting with Targitus, who said softly, "Here," the others spoke their names as Rachel locked in to their various locations in the yurt.

"Thank you all, thank you for being here. It's time for me to try to answer the question you put to me many months ago. Targitus, they asked how making a carpet like this could really be worth the time and effort. How quickly one makes felt ground covers, they pointed out. Several in a day. To begin with, this carpet serves human needs. Its function is to impart warmth, something it's doing for me right now. In this sense, it differs not at all from your felts. Agreed?"

The students started to nod. Hestia spoke out, "Agreed."

"But I had other goals. Beyond warming our bodies, I wanted to nourish our spirits. To have the carpet make an artistic statement. I made the design complex in order to challenge us to think hard; I picked motifs that could stir our imaginations. I tried to make the carpet beautiful, to give pleasure.

"As to why, you know one goal was to set a standard for the workshop. The result is here, beneath me. Whether I succeeded will be judged by others.

"But there was another reason for devoting this time and energy. It was very personal. I'll tell you. I was trying to push myself beyond experience. There's at least one here who feared the shamans had bewitched me. I suppose that's a possibility, for I never felt I had a choice."

Rachel's voice had weakened. There followed moments of silence. Then, in a whisper, Paralata said, "And the rewards?"

Rachel frowned. She tried to brush away a wisp of hair from her forehead, a nervous motion of her right hand that she had engaged in from childhood. Her right arm refused to move. Knowing her habit, everyone in the room froze with uncertainty. With effort, Rachel summoned her left arm, which responded slowly, her hand reaching out awkwardly.

"That's a hard one. With the carpet finished, I feel exultant. But, when you're done, there's a hole in your life that needs filling. It's hard to explain. I guess the rewards come mainly in the quest. That's why taking a long time to complete a piece like this is tolerable. It's the perfectly ordinary pleasures, taken day by day, that really count. Not the grand ending."

That night, after the students were gone and Targitus had fed Rachel the tiny portion of food she was able to eat, he cradled her in his arms. He wept. "You must recover, and you're going to. I feel certain. Because of your carpet. You're lying square in the middle of its field, surrounded by its protective borders. Doesn't it feel right that the creator is the first to draw on its powers."

Rachel's mind had been set racing by the arrival of her class. Now, peering ahead into the abyss of uncertainty, she felt afraid. With each recurrence of her illness, new and more terrible symptoms had developed. Where would it end? And when? Asking herself these questions was painful; to share them with Targitus, impossible. Alone and lonely in her thoughts, she searched her soul for some explanation. Could it be she was afraid to give voice to her growing fear? That by speaking the word, it would come to pass? Or, she won-

## 18: GREAT ULAGAN VALLEY – 404-402 B.C.

dered, was she afraid of alarming Targitus, or inviting him to pretend, as he had just done without encouragement? She thought of her parents, wondering how they would have behaved, or counseled her. Of her father, who had no more than a moment, if that, to reflect on death's flight path. Was that a blessing, or was it better to have time to put things in order, and get ready? Get ready for what?, she asked herself. There's no preparation for death, only the pain of anticipation that can suddenly intrude, like thunderheads on a beautiful day. And then, she remembered what her father had often claimed were the memorable words of an aged Jewish philosopher: "Death plucks at my ear, crying, Live! For I am near."

"You expect too much from the carpet. I made it for you and your mother. When it was finished, I felt sad. But now, I am feeling better, less melancholy, more composed. I don't need the carpet's protective powers. But I do like its warmth." Targitus saw that Rachel was smiling for the first time that day.

Holding her in his arms, he knew, and knew she knew, the end might be near. Wanting to speak, he could not bring himself to shatter the fiction. At least not without her invitation. He wondered what she was thinking. How little of the mind's torrent of thought is ever exchanged between even the closest of friends, relatives or lovers. Targitus counted it a good thing too, at least for some of the thoughts that coursed through his mind. But perhaps he and Rachel were especially private people, guarding whole continents of thought from one another.

He imagined himself standing at her burial, before the people of the Great Ulagan, delivering her eulogy. There were things he would say that he had never uttered to Rachel in their time together. Hadn't this been true when he spoke at his father's funeral? He recounted stories from his father's full life that had the villagers in tears. Yet, never had he voiced to his father the praise he proclaimed to the village.

In the days to come, he would carry out the most important speaking engagement of his life: to reveal to her the important things he felt about her, things unsaid yet neatly catalogued in his mind: her constant life-affirming optimism; her skill and creativity pushed to their limits and then beyond; her simple acceptance of him, the good and the bad; and other things about her too mysterious to comprehend.

After Rachel had fallen into a deep sleep, Targitus rose to add logs to the fire. Going outside, he saw that the snow had ceased. A three-quarter moon illuminated white clouds and etched sharp shadows among the tall larches nearby. On a low limb of the closest larch in the moon's path, Targitus saw the distinct outline of a great gray owl. The top of its perfectly round head was bathed in moonlight. Its large yellow eyes could just be discerned, while the concentric circles on its face were so much in shadow that they had to be imagined. Although sightings of this monarch of the coniferous taiga were rare, Targitus knew its markings. As he looked in wonder at the sight, the deeply resonant, unmistakable cry of an owl from far away broke the silence of the night. Moments passed. And then the great bird in front of him answered that call with a similar one of its own: three loud yet muffled hoots, well spaced with nothing in-between.

Returning to the yurt, Targitus gazed at the scene before him. Bedding covered Rachel, asleep on her carpet, a square at the center of the yurt's circle. By the fire's light he could make out the motifs already detailed in his mind: proud griffins, stately horses and riders and peaceful elk surrounding a central field of mystery. Joining Rachel on the carpet, he pressed close to add his warmth to hers.

THE END

## SELECTED BIBLIOGRAPHY

*Spindle and Bow* is a work of imagination. At the same time, it was written within a framework of knowledge about the time, place and people involved in the story and, importantly, about the Pazyryk carpet itself. Throughout, the goal has been to create a tale that in every dimension is entirely plausible.

Albright, W.F., 1957. *From the Stone Age to Christianity: Monotheism and the Historical Process, Second Edition*, Anchor.

Barber, E.J.W., 1991. *Prehistoric Textiles*, Princeton University Press.

Barber, E.J.W., 1994. *Women's Work: The First 20,000 Years*, W.W. Norton & Company.

Barkova, L., 1999. "The Pazyryk – Fifty Years On." *Hali* 107:64-69, 110.

Bickerman, E.J., 1988. *The Jews in the Greek Age*, Harvard University Press.

Böhmer, H. and Thompson, J., 1991. "The Pazyryk Carpet: A Technical Discussion." *Source: Notes in the History of Art* 10.4 (Summer), A Special Issue on the Dating of Pazyryk.

Briant, P., 2002. *From Cyrus to Alexander: A History of the Persian Empire*, trans. Daniels, P.T., Eisenbrauns

Budiansky, S., 1997. *The Nature of Horses: Exploring Equine Evolution, Intelligence, and Behavior*, The Free Press.

Clawson, C.C., 1996. *Mathematical Mysteries: The Beauty and Magic of Numbers*, Plenum Press.

Flint, V.E., Boehme, R.L., Kostin, Y.V., Kuznetsov, A.A., 1984. *Birds of the USSR*, trans. Bourso-Leland, N., Princeton University Press.

Gleason, K.L., 1994. 'Display Garden: The Plants of Lydia' *Appendix 2*,

*Lydian Architectural Terracottas: A Study in Tile Replication, Display and Technique*, Scholars Press.

Hanfmann, G.M.A. and Waldbaum, J.C., 1975. *A Survey of Sardis and the Major Monuments outside the City Walls (Report 1)*, Archaeological Exploration of Sardis in association with British Museum Press.

Hanfmann, G.M.A. and Waldbaum, J.C., 1983. *Sardis from Prehistoric to Roman Times: Results of the Archaeological Exploration of Sardis, 1958-1975*, Harvard University Press.

Haskins, J.F. 1961. *The Fifth Pazyryk Kurgan and the "Animal Style"*, Ph.D. dissertation New York University, on file in NYU Library

Herodotus., 1996 (John Marincola). *The Histories*, trans. De Selincourt, A., Penguin

Mitten, D.G., 1965. *The Ancient Synagogue of Sardis*, The Committee to Preserve the Ancient Synagogue of Sardis On Behalf of the Archaeological Exploration of Sardis.

Pinner, R., 1982. 'The Earliest Carpets',. *Hali* 5.2: 110-115, 118-119.

Ramage, A. and Craddock, P., 2000. *King Croesus' Gold: Excavations at Sardis and the History of Gold Refining (Monograph 11)*, Archaeological Exploration of Sardis in association with British Museum Press.

Rudenko, S.I., 1970, First English Edition (with author's revisions), *Frozen Tombs of Siberia: The Pazyryk Burials of Iron Age Horsemen*, trans. Thompson, N.W., University of California Press

Xenophon, 1962, *The Art of Horsemanship*, trans. Morgan, M.H., J.A. Allen & Company.

Xenophon, 1997, *Oeconomicus*, trans. Todd, O.J., Loeb Classical Library, Harvard University Press.